He's a bad boy ...
and a nanny.

Hard Rock Roots
Real Ugly
Get Bent
Tough Luck
Bad Day
Born Wrong
Hard Rock Root Box Set (1-5)
Dead Serious
Doll Face
Heart Broke
Get Hitched

Tasting Never Series
Tasting Never
Finding Never
Keeping Never
Tasting, Finding, Keeping: The Story of Never (1-3)
Never Can Tell
Never Let Go
Never Did Say

The Bad Nanny Trilogy
Bad Nanny
Good Boyfriend

Triple M Series
Losing Me, Finding You
Loving Me, Trusting You
Needing Me, Wanting You
Craving Me, Desiring You

A Duet
Paint Me Beautiful
Color Me Pretty

Stand-Alone Novels
Fuck Valentine's Day (A Short Story)
Broken Pasts
Crushing Summer
Taboo Unchained
Taming Her Boss
Kicked

Fantasy Novels
The House of Gray and Graves
The Feed
Indigo & Iris
She Lies Twisted
Hell Inc.
A Werewolf Christmas (A Short Story)
DeadBorn
The Seven Wicked: First
The Seven Wicked: Second
The Seven Wicked: Third
The Seven Wicked: Fourth
Chryer's Crest

BOOKS BY VIOLET BLAZE
(MY PEN NAME)

Bad Boys MC Trilogy
Raw and Dirty
Risky and Wild
Savage and Racy

Stand-Alone Novels
Football Dick
Stepbrother Thief
Stepbrother Inked

BAD NANNY TRILOGY BOOK 1

C. M. STUNICH
INTERNATIONAL BESTSELLING AUTHOR

Stunich, CM

Bad Nanny
Copyright © C.M. Stunich 2016

All rights reserved. Printed in the United States of America. No part of this book may be used or reproduced in any manner whatsoever without written permission except in the case of brief quotations embodied in critical articles or reviews. For information address Sarian Royal Indie Publishing, 1863 Pioneer Pkwy. E Ste. 203, Springfield, OR 97477-3907.
www.sarianroyal.com

ISBN-10: 19386235282 (pbk.)
ISBN-13: 978-1-938623-28-8(pbk.)

"Destroyed Aero" Font © Jayvee Enaguas
"Futurist Fixed Width" Font © WSI

The characters and events portrayed in this book are fictitious. Any similarity to real persons, living or dead, businesses, or locales is coincidental and is not intended by the author.

This book is dedicated to chance meetings.

Because you never know when chance is really just fateful circumstance...

CHAPTER 1
ZAYDEN ROTH

"Move for me," I growl, curling my hands around my new lady friend's hips. She's got almost as many tattoos as I do and the kaleidoscope mind-fuck of her arching her back above me is just about enough to send me over the edge.

She squeals and giggles as I flip her over and run my fingers through her hair. It's like cotton candy, all pink and soft and shit. *I fucking love Las Vegas.* Ever since I moved here and got a job as a body piercer, I've had so many opportunities to meet new friends. Friends that smell like body butter, with soft skin, and healthy sexual appetites.

Oh yeah.

This is the real "City That Never Sleeps" and there's no way in hell I would ever leave. I don't think this girl, Kitty, and me have slept in three days. Thank God for holiday weekends, right?

"Oh, Zay," she moans, running her tongue up the side of my face. I grab her wrists in my hands and slam them into the pillow behind her head, nipping at her exposed throat as I thrust hard and fast, slamming our pelvises together with the sweet sound of flesh on flesh. *Oh God yes.* "You are the world's fucking hottest nerd."

I grin big.

"Hey, just because I take breaks to shoot rebel soldiers online with my buddies does not make me a nerd." I put a little extra strength in my next thrust and get rewarded with a guttural groan from Kitty's pretty little lips. If she hadn't walked into the shop to get her tits pierced on Friday, I'd have missed out on all this fun. Lucky me.

"You have a toy collection, Zayden," she says, but I don't respond. If she's able to talk, then I'm not doing my job right.

"What if I asked *you* to be one of my little toys? Because I want to play all night long with your movable parts." Kitty laughs and I groan. Ladies, laughter tightens up all those muscles downstairs. Guys fucking love it. Laugh more during sex, pretty please.

I nibble Kitty's lower lip, tasting cherry lip gloss, and slide my tongue into her mouth. Fuck, do I love women. They always smell so good, feel so soft, taste so sweet. If I had to list my hobbies for a stranger, it'd go like this: fucking, video games, fucking, and listening to pop music. But don't tell anybody about that last one or I'll have to kill you.

I squeeze Kitty's wrists tighter, fuck her harder, and feel myself on the verge of a mind-blowing orgasm when my phone goes off, buzzing across the nightstand like a vibrator gone rogue.

The ringtone is the song *Toxic,* but not the Britney Spears version (even though I secretly dig it). I had to save face, so I put on A Static Lullaby's cover instead.

There's only one person on my contacts list that has that ringtone and he *never* calls.

I pause for a moment, but Kitty wiggles beneath me and I end up dropping my mouth to her freshly pierced nipples. I run my tongue around one and avoid the sore spot, teasing just close enough to make her squirm.

"I'm coming, Zay," she groans as my cock drives deeper and harder. I can feel her tightening around me, getting ready to explode. *Thank God.* I don't think I could hold on much longer.

BAD NANNY

The phone stops ringing and then immediately starts up a second time.

I pause yet again, and Kitty ends up getting her hands free, wrapping her arms around my neck.

"So close," she whispers against my ear. "So close. Don't stop."

So I keep going and then fucking fuck, there goes that damn phone *again.*

"I have to answer it," I say, because my brother, he only calls if there's an emergency. I stay right where I am, wrapped up inside of Kitty, and lean over to take the call.

"What the fuck do you want? This better be good. I'm entertaining company right now."

My brother doesn't hesitate to rip me a new one.

"Do you have any compassion at all, Zayden? What is your goddamn problem? It's not like I ever ask you for anything. You never return my phone calls or texts, never come home for the holidays."

"Okay, and what's wrong with that? It's not as if we're exactly *close*," I say and then sit back in shock when Kitty slaps me across the face with an open hand.

"I *was* close," she snaps at me, shoving me back and climbing off the bed. I watch in stunned frustration as she gathers her jeans and tugs them on. "Enjoy the rest of your Thursday, you dick."

The front door slams closed behind her as I tug off my condom with a growl. Great. Just great. And I didn't even get her number or her last name. What a waste.

"I need your help, Zayden," Rob says, and I catch the strain in his voice right off the bat. Whatever this is, it really *is* serious. I feel a little guilty for being an asshole—to both Rob and Kitty—and climb off the bed to dispose of the condom in the trash can under the window. "It's Mercedes' parents," he continues as I open the top drawer of my dresser and grab some boxers. My hard-on's long gone now, no point in wandering around naked. Feels kind of wrong to have my junk hanging out when I'm talking to my brother, you know what I mean?

"Okay?" I ask, trying to be sympathetic. I mean, Rob might be a jerk, but his wife, Mercedes, is actually pretty awesome. Sometimes when Rob's asleep and she doesn't think she'll get caught, she gets online and joins my raid group. That girl can take on a red dragon zombie boss like nobody's business—impressive, even if it's all part of a computer game.

"They were in an accident," he says, sounding tired and worn-out. Rob works as an insurance salesman, so I can totally see that. If I worked as an insurance salesman, I'd only be at the job long enough to buy a gun and a single bullet.

"Oh, shit, are they alright?" I ask, pausing in the kitchen. It's a disaster of takeout and pizza boxes, and it smells like my cat's litter box. Well, technically, he's not my cat. One of my girlfriends left him here when she moved out, and I kind of like the little bastard. I spy the cat crouched on my stove, completely hairless, a hideous feline monstrosity, and flip it off. Hubert hisses at me and flicks his tail, glaring at me with creepy white-green eyes. The effect is somewhat lessened since he's wearing a black sweater. Hey, this is Vegas and it gets hotter than hairy balls in a pair of briefs. I keep the air conditioner cranked, and Hubert being a hairless cat and all, he gets the chills.

Guess I really am a nerd.

"They're alive, if that's what you're really asking," Rob says, just before a piercing screech crashes through the phone and I jerk it away from my ear like I've been slapped. Either that's a banshee coming to take my soul to the underworld, or it's Rob's daughter, Kinzie. Yes, Kinzie. Weird name. I know, that's what I thought, too.

I am so fucking glad I don't have children.

I work very, very hard to make sure my dick is sheathed at all times. And I always use my own condoms, just to make sure they're fresh and free of holes. Honestly, if I had to choose between having kids and throwing myself off of a bridge, I'd have to think for a while to give you an answer.

"Well, that's good, right?" I ask, shooing the cat off the stove and sliding an old pizza box forward. The slices inside are stiff and tough, like chewy cardboard covered in melted plastic. I shove the end of one in my mouth anyway and turn around, leaning back against the counter. "So what do you need me for?" I ask around a mouthful.

"You know her parents live in South Africa, right?"

"Yeah, and?"

"And that's halfway around the world."

"Okay?"

"Zayden, they're in critical condition. There's a good chance neither of them will make it through the week." I flinch and swallow my bite.

"Man, I'm so sorry to hear that. Give Mercedes my love and tell her I'm praying for them."

"Why don't you tell her yourself?" Rob asks cryptically as I snap my fingers at Hubert who's desperately trying to untangle himself from his sweater.

"Put her on, I guess," I say, wrinkling my brow and finishing up my pizza slice. I scratch my belly with tattooed fingers and wait.

Silence.

"Rob?"

"Zayden, Mercedes and I are flying to Joburg to see them. Tomorrow."

Joburg. Johannesburg. The city that's home to the tallest building in Africa. That much, at least, I know. Everything else here is a mystery to me. I grab a second slice of pizza and then toss it aside. That one has mold on it. Third one looks fine though.

"What the fuck are you getting at? You know I suck at word games, Rob."

"Zayden, I'm asking you to drive up here. You know, to take care of the kids for me."

Holy shit.

"Um, no?" I say, barely managing to keep from dropping my pizza to the floor. Take care of Rob's kids? I've met them *once*. Once. And they were little demons from hell—screeching, wailing, squalling monsters. Oh, and that's not to mention the brand-new freaking baby they just had like last year or whatever. A seven year old girl, four year old twins (who may or may not be human based on their behavior), and an infant.

Oh fuck the fuck out of that.

"Why doesn't Mercedes go, and you can stay with the kids?"

"My wife's parents are on their death beds, Zayden, and all you can think about is yourself? Do you think I'd have called if I had anyone else?"

"That really inspires confidence, bro. Why would you even trust me with watching your kids anyway? I killed two goldfish last week. On accident." I don't mention the fact that it was actually Hubert who murdered Teensy and Woo-woo, two more pets left over from a past girlfriend.

"I work a shit job. I have no money, no family in this world other than you. Mercedes has nobody left other than her parents. Zayden, please. Don't send my wife alone to watch her parents die."

Aw, man.

I stand up straight and pad across the cold slate tile floor to the fridge to grab a soda. My brother's using the sympathy card on me right now, and it's working. I might be kind of a douche sometimes, but I'm really a nice guy underneath. I think? I mean, I try to be anyway.

"The kids don't have passports, Zay. And Mercedes doesn't want to take the baby on such a long flight. Can you imagine trying to care for a six month old in a hotel room? Or how about at the side of a hospital bed?"

"Dude, it's a fourteen hour drive up there and all I have is my ugly ass Geo. The car is older than I am, Rob. I was conceived in the backseat of the damn thing. I can't drive that piece of shit to the grocery store, let alone into California."

I pop the top on my Mountain Dew and down half of it before Rob decides to speak again, his voice low and thick, like he's on the verge of tears. Fucking Christ. In the background, Kinzie screams again, sending a chill down my spine.

BAD NANNY

"You're my last chance, Zay. Please. Please do this. What would Mom and Dad say if they were here?" I roll my eyes and run the fingers of my right hand through the hair on the left side of my scalp. The other side is currently shaved like a military man gone punk. "I'll tell you what they'd say: Family is everything and everything is family. This is as much your problem as it is mine, Zay. We're brothers, and even though you can be an irresponsible prick sometimes, I love you."

"Gah," I stick my tongue out at my own reflection and shake my head. I can't take this lovey family shit. I feel myself just about ready to cave in. My buddy runs the shop I work at, so he'd understand. Besides, I could get the new dude, what's-his-face, to take over my appointments for me. I'd miss out on a lot of nipple piercings, but what choice do I have? I can't tell Rob no and not feel like a piece of human garbage, now can I? "Fine."

Rob sighs in relief as goose bumps break out over my arms.

I'm going to hate this. Every second of it. I know that to be a fact.

"But I want a plane ticket. I can't drive fourteen hours straight, man."

"I can't afford a plane ticket for you. I just spent all of my savings on tickets for Mercedes and me. You'll have to drive. If you leave now and take minimal rest stops, you can be here a few hours before our flight leaves tomorrow."

I start to protest, but the phone is suddenly snatched away from my brother by his wife.

"Thank you, Zay," she sobs, voice thick and sniffly. "Thank you so much. I love you like the little brother I never had, you know that right?"

Great.

I'm a sucker for pretty girls in distress.

I purse my lips so tight that my lip rings stand out like swords on either side of my mouth.

"See ya in fourteen hours then."

CHAPTER 2
BROOKE OVERLAND

Here I am with my hair all mussed up and my kitty cat pajama pants wet from the dew soaked grass. Not exactly the way I had envisioned this night going. Granted, I had known moving back to Eureka wouldn't be pleasant, but I hadn't expected *this*. Mom had led me to believe that she would be here to help me out, teach me to be the parent my sister refuses to be anymore.

So much for keeping my life on track.

I breathe out and my breath fogs white in the cool night air.

"Grace?" I call, searching the massive backyard for my niece. "Honey, it's not a good time for hide and seek." I hear giggling and see a flicker of a white nightgown dart between two trees. My skin ripples with goose bumps. Yikes. Horror movie, much? Nobody in their right mind walks around a mist drenched yard at two in the morning searching for a creepy cackling child.

I suppose I'm not exactly in my right mind then.

Must not be if I was willing to leave UC Berkeley for my hometown, step into someone else's life like this. It's a life I definitely *didn't* want. There's a reason my sister had her first child when she was sixteen, and I'm still a virgin.

"Gracie, baby, it's time for bed. Auntie starts her new job soon and she'd really like to catch up on some sleep *before she*

BAD NANNY

takes her clothes off for strangers." I whisper that last part to myself, doing my best *not* to think about the *adult dancing* job I just landed at the Top Hat Gentlemen's Club. I still have a few days to find something else, *anything* else.

My waist length hair blows around my face in a brunette curtain as I sweep it back and try to slink quietly through the grass toward the back corner of the yard. I think I can see a snippet of Grace's nightgown from here. I'm just about to dart around the tree and grab her when my foot lands in something questionable. One glance down and I see that it's a giant pile of dog crap. Shivers take over me as I cringe and try not to throw up.

Fantastic.

My parents are on vacation in Edinburgh, Scotland, so any chance of help is far out of reach. While they're at the zoo gawking at pandas and whatnot, I'll be here trying to figure out how to juggle my new job *and* my biostatistics classes against a sudden influx of responsibility. How many twenty-two years old inherit *two* children from their awful, selfish, drug addicted sister? What kind of person just up and leaves the country, abandoning their kids *alone* at home? Ingrid didn't even tell anyone. She left a *note* and said good-bye to her girls while they were busy watching Netflix.

Anyway, I'm here now and I'll figure out how to make things work—and I'll excel at it. I always do. *Even if I have to sacrifice some of my dignity and self-respect to do it.*

I light my chin and square my shoulders. I made the *right* choice in moving back here, in accepting a job that pays well, even if it's not exactly my cup of tea. *Even if it sounds like hell.* Ugh. Would my parents have still left the kids with me if they knew I was going to start stripping come tomorrow? Probably not. But they've been saving and planning for this trip for *years*. I can't let Ingrid's choices derail everyone's lives.

Somebody has to pick up my sister's mantle and forge onward.

A cold northwesterly wind whips across the yard and ruffles

the branches of the redwood trees that loom above us like giants, silent spectators to this debacle of debauchery my sister's created.

I'm alone. With a three and a seven year old. Crap.

"Aunt Brooke?" Bella says from the back door, clutching the frame with small hands. Her pale pink nightgown flutters in the icy breeze from the bay.

"Yeah, baby?" I say, getting myself together, running my fingers through my tangled hair. I pick my way back across the wet lawn and pause on the sidewalk at the base of the deck. "What is it?"

"Dodger was crying and crying, so I let him out the front door to go to the bathroom." She shuffles her feet a little. "I keep calling him, but he won't come back."

I see where this is going.

I take a deep breath to calm my nerves.

Grace and Bella have been through a lot already, and it's my job to bring the beauty of stability back into their lives until I can figure out how to get Ingrid to move her ass back here.

Okay. Okay, I can *do* this.

"Why don't you help me find your sister?" I ask as I move up the steps and brush some of Bella's dark hair from her forehead. "And then I'll go look for the dog."

"Um," she begins, squinching up her face. I feel the blood drain from mine. "That's not everything." Oh. Of course it's not. That'd be too easy. "Also, I couldn't sleep so I was playing a game on your phone. I accidentally dropped it in the toilet." There's a long pause here where I start to get nervous. "With some poop."

Poop.

On my first night. And from the seven year old.

I think I'm in serious trouble.

CHAPTER 3
ZAYDEN ROTH

The second I walk in the door, I wonder what the fuck is wrong with me. *What's wrong with being a heartless dick again? Why didn't I leave that phone right where it was, take my time with Kitty's sweet ass?*

Ah.

I miss home already.

"I don't want you to go!" Kinzie screeches, grabbing her mother's purse from the sofa table and throwing it as hard as she can across the room. "I want you to *stay.*" She stomps her feet like she's Godzilla on a rampage through Tokyo, throwing her body onto the couch with another wail that forces me to stuff my fingers in my ears.

"Oh thank God, you're here!" Mercedes says, dragging a suitcase up next to my feet. "We were afraid we were going to have to miss the flight."

My brother breezes past me with barely a nod and disappears behind the minivan. Apparently, I'm driving them to the airport, so I can use their ugly ass car. It's 'safer' than my Geo, and Mercedes has promised me that she's got thirty channels of children's music on her Spotify account. The car's all set up to play that shit on repeat! Woo-fucking-hoo.

"You got most of my instructions over the phone, but I also

left a list." Mercedes points at the sofa table to something that looks more like a dossier than a list. I can feel my shirt sticking to my back with sweat, but I can guarantee it's not the weather. As usual, our sweet little hometown of Eureka, California is sixty-five degrees and cloudy. It's also sixty-five degrees and cloudy the other 364 days of the year, so I'm not surprised. "We can talk more about logistics on the way to the airport."

"Fantastic," I say, setting my bag down near the stairs. Well, I try to anyway. My brother's duplex is so small, that I kind of have to balance the bag on my own foot. "No school today?"

School.

Preschool and 2nd grade.

My two favorite things right now.

"We didn't have time to get them ready."

Mercedes breezes over to a car seat that's sitting on the floor and lifts it up, handing it to me before I can protest. Inside is an alien creature of some sort, some weird ugly wrinkly thing they call a baby. I look down at it—at her—and try to smile.

The kid starts to scream.

"I hate you!" Kinzie screeches, sobbing and thrashing around on the couch. "I hate *him!*"

She points her finger at me and I bare my teeth, sending her into another fit of hysterics.

I can feel my heart pounding in my chest. *I can't do this. I'm terrified. I'm so fucking terrified right now.* I suck it up and take a deep breath.

"I kind of need to get my cat out of the car," I say as Mercedes brushes past me, her wild curls slapping me in the face as she starts up the stairs again. The energy in this house is just … wow. I'm used to slow, lazy days in my condo, the constant gentle hum of the air conditioner, the soft sighs of beautiful women. This right here is frantic and messy, like standing in the middle of a mosh pit at a really intense rock show. I'm already about halfway certain that I'm going to get

BAD NANNY

elbowed in the face—metaphorically or otherwise.

"Make sure you leave the cat downstairs," Mercedes calls out. "The chihuahuas are up here in the bathroom."

Fuck.

"What freaking chihuahuas?" I ask as my brother returns to the front door to grab his wife's suitcase. "You never said anything about chihuahuas. This was a kid sitting thing, not a dog sitting thing. I don't do dogs. Especially not little ones."

"You like cats, right? Chihuahuas are basically cats."

My brother glares at me, his red hair and beard giving him that sort of 'lumberjack' look that companies always put on the labels of syrup and pancakes and whatever. I miss Las Vegas. There are no fucking lumberjacks in Las Vegas. Hell, there aren't even any trees.

"Chihuahuas are not cats, Rob. Chihuahuas are smelly, annoying, ugly, yipping rat creatures. And it kind of freaks me out that you're just saying *chihuahuas* in the plural. How many of them do you have?"

"We have three," Kinzie states proudly, apparently over her temper tantrum in some sort of miraculous mood shift. I'm confused. Ten seconds ago she was shouting that she hated me, and now she's sniffling and smiling and staring at me with squinty eyes. "Can I see your cat?"

"Um, sure."

I don't know what to do with the baby, so I follow my brother outside and try to hand the car seat over. Thankfully, he takes it and starts strapping the kid in.

"Pay attention, so you know how to do this," he barks, and I have to really clench my teeth to keep from screaming. When I said I hadn't slept in days, I meant it. Tack on a fourteen hour drive to the end of that? Not to mention the fact that I was so stressed-out I couldn't even get off before I left. Now I have blue balls, an aching back from the shitty seat in my car, and a pounding headache. I can't have my brother bossing me around right now. I dealt with that for years, and it's not gonna fly.

"I think I can figure out a fucking baby seat," I snap and Kinzie gasps. Rob turns a look on me like I've never seen, nostrils flared and green eyes wide.

"Don't you dare use that language in front of my kids," he snaps, waving his hand dismissively. "And don't just stand there. Do something productive."

I flip him off behind his back and Kinzie gasps again. Holy mother of fucking shit. I'm not going to make it two days here, let alone two freaking weeks. Yeah, two weeks. Two weeks. Why, how, I got roped into this, I can't even remember. It's been a long drive.

Did you know that cats make shitty passengers on long road trips? Hubert yowled and screamed and attacked the bars on the cage. He even pissed on himself, despite the litter box I shoved into the kennel. Now I've got a hairless cat whose sweater is soaked in pee. Today really couldn't get any worse.

And then Mercedes wakes the twins up from their naps, just about at the same time I realize Kinzie has disappeared.

Ten seconds later, a herd of freaking chihuahuas comes yowling and skittering down the stairs.

I wonder what my face looks like in that moment.

If someone were to try and interpret it, I think it'd be: *please fucking end me.*

CHAPTER 4
BROOKE OVERLAND

My crap day starts off much like my crap night ended.

First off, I have no phone. Don't ask *how* I got the waterlogged ruins of it out of the toilet; I don't want to talk about it. Second, I spent an hour looking for that damn dog and I never did find him. But that's okay because the shelter called at the crack of dawn this morning and said they'd picked him up last night. All I have to do is drive twenty minutes out of my way and pay a fine to pick him up.

"Okay," I say as I pull over again and smooth out the directions I printed off the computer. *I know, I know:* nobody uses printed directions anymore. But my phone got fried with poop water last night, so GPS is kind of off the menu. "This shouldn't be too hard. I can figure this out."

I glance up and wrinkle my face. I grew up in this town, but as soon as I graduated high school, I moved as far away as I could, settling in So Cal for school. Since I figured I'd never be back here, I sort of ... obliterated any directional memories of this place.

I am so lost right now, I think as I look up and Bella starts to whine from the backseat.

"I'm gonna be late, *Brooke,*" she says, dropping the word

'auntie' altogether. "I *hate* being late."

"Yeah, I got it, baby," I say as I look around and stare at the quiet roads and the towering trees. *I am so out of my element here.* Somewhere in this dew drenched forest is Bella's school. It's a different one than I went to as a kid, so I have literally no clue where it is. Once I get her successfully dropped off, I get to search for Grace's preschool and *then* I get to go to my first class at Humboldt State.

At this point, I'd settle for any *one* of those things going my way.

"It's not even that hard to get there," Bella says snootily, a dramatic sigh interrupting the snores of her dozing sister. At least one of us is having a good time here. *How much would a full-time babysitter cost?* I wonder. *A nanny? A governess? At this point, I'll take what I can get.* Although I'm sure my new job at the strip club won't cover it. I'll be lucky if I can afford gas, the rent on my sister's house, and food for the kids.

My heart starts to flutter with panic, but I clamp down on it. One thing at a time.

I throw the directions on the passenger seat and pull back onto the road. With a little luck and some snippy directions from Bella, I manage to find the school, dropping her off with a narrow eyed attendant who looks about as pissed as the kid is at me for making her late.

With no time to worry about that, I head off in search of the preschool. That one's a lot easier to find ... but waking Grace up from her nap?

Holy hell.

Grace screams when I gently nudge her awake, flailing around and burying her face in the puffy pink coat I dressed her in. When I try to unhook her from the car seat, the straps start to look like tangled snakes and I can't figure the damn thing out. By the time I manage to get her free, she's in a real mood, red-faced and screaming.

I rush her up to the front door and try to pass her into the arms of the teacher.

Only ... she won't let go.

BAD NANNY

"Come on, Gracie, baby. Auntie Brooke has a finite population sampling class that she's going to be fifteen minutes late to." The kid has no sympathy for me, tearing a button off my shirt as I pry her away from me. The teacher gives me a look, but I don't have time to spend talking to her this morning.

I race back to the car, my white button-up flapping in the center, flashing my pink lacy bra. I'm starting to think things can't get much worse when my heel snaps and I go flying onto the pavement.

Fuck.

That *really* hurt.

I am in *way* over my head here.

CHAPTER 5
ZAYDEN ROTH

They're monsters. *Fucking* monsters. Even the baby.

"Listen, Kinzie," I say as she hauls out and kicks me in the ankle. I grit my teeth, but I'm kind of busy here. I've got a fat chihuahua tucked under one arm and some old, gross toothless one under the other. One of the things my brother neglected to mention to me was that his dogs are ridiculously cat aggressive.

Sweet.

Now I've got Hubert trapped on top of the fridge, the twins in the backyard throwing mud clods at each other, and Kinzie screaming that she wants me to die.

This is gonna be a *fan-fucking-tastic* two weeks.

"Can you *please* take the dogs upstairs and put them back in the bathroom?" I ask as I try to hand her one of the disgusting smelly rat creatures. I miss my life so bad right now it hurts. *The Strip, the hot sun, the sexy tourists, the smell of iodine at the shop.* I make myself take a deep breath.

"They don't *like* being in the bathroom," Kinzie says, crossing her arms over her chest as she glares up at me, brown eyes taking me in like she's not impressed. "Why is your skin all splotchy?" she asks. "And what happened to your *hair*?"

I roll my eyes, moving past her and up the stairs, tripping over toys as I struggle to make it to the bathroom at the top of

BAD NANNY

the steps.

"Get in there, you nasty little rats." I close the door and then run my inked fingers through my hair. If I can just get through this *one* weekend, then I'll have school to look forward to on Monday. That should be sick. How many hours do these monsters go for? I'll have to check Mercedes' dossier, I guess.

"Can I go play with my friends outside? I'm bored."

I turn and find Kinzie hovering on the top step, looking at me like I'm the worst thing that's ever happened to her.

"Um." I scratch the side of my head and try to remember the rules for that shit. Mercedes laid it all on pretty thick on our way to the airport. "Lemme check on that."

She rolls her eyes and stomps into her room, slamming the door loud enough to shake the whole house—and wake the baby from her nap.

Fuckity fuck.

"I'm coming, I'm coming." I move into my brother's room and look down at the weird wrinkly thing in its crib. *Gross.* Okay, so like, how do I pick this thing up? I tilt my head at the kid, using my tongue to play with my lip rings. People—much dumber people—do this kind of thing all the time. I should be able to figure this out. I slip my phone from my pocket and notice a text from Kitty. Huh. I don't remember giving her my number.

I programmed my digits into your phone when you were in the bathroom. You're a fucking asshole, Zayden.

I scroll down to the next message.

I'll be back in town next weekend. Want to meet up?

I feel my lips curl back in a grin and then cringe when the baby lets out a piercing wail. What *is* it with kids and yelling all the time? I feel like I'm gonna go deaf here.

"Okay, Google," I tell my phone. "How do you hold a baby?"

I tap my foot and play with my lip rings while I scroll through some idiotproof pics. Huh. Okay. Looks easy enough; I can do this.

"Alright, kid," I say as I tuck my messy inked fingers under the baby's warm body. "Let's do this thing." I heft the screeching bundle up to my chest and cradle it under my chin, glancing down at the phone screen and breezing through the rest of the instructions. "Stay confident and calm, huh? Well, I got that shit in *spades*."

"You said the S-word," Kinzie chortles from behind me. "You have to put a dollar in the curse jar." I glance down at the little monster with its brown curls in pigtails and its face all scrunched up. Some people might think it's cute, but to me, it looks like a pink-overall-wearing demon.

"Like hell I am," I say as I sneak my phone back into my pocket and make my way toward the stairs. "Listen, kid, but I'm here as *favor* to your mom, alright? I'm not putting money in any curse jar. What are you guys trying for, the ultimate TV family cliché? Lemme guess ... you've got a chore chart and a soccer team, huh?"

"You'll put money in the curse jar or I'll scream and I won't stop."

I turn back at the landing, already trying to puzzle out if this baby in my arms is supposed to drink from a bottle or if I can order in takeout and give it a piece of cut up pizza or something.

"Be my guest, cupcake," I say with a smug smirk. What I've gotta do right now is establish boundaries with these kids, let 'em know who's boss. I'm a twenty-nine year old man, and let's be honest: I've never had any trouble with women before. The kid might be, like, seven or whatever, but I can still charm the heck outta her.

But then I notice the smile curling across her lips and the hair on the back of my neck stands straight up.

"Challenge. Accepted."

By the end of the day, I've already dropped twenty bucks into the jar.

This is gonna be a *long* ass two weeks.

BAD NANNY

By the middle of day two, I am so over all of this. Being trapped in this nine hundred square foot duplex with the pot growing neighbors that live next door is *beyond* the point of torture. How any sane human being—particularly one as smart and cool as Mercedes—could live through this is just ... well, it's a fuckin' mystery, man.

"We don't *like* this song," Kinzie says, speaking for her brothers as they scream and flail against their booster seats in the back of the minivan. I've taken the liberty of removing Mercedes' iPod and replacing it with my own. I'll die before admitting this, but I want the kids to think I'm cool, so I put on some metal-rock-screaming-loud-whatever music instead of my usual pop tracks. The band that's on right now, *Indecency* or whatever they're called, has some really angry dude yelling about pain and heartache.

"Don't care," I say as I follow what few memories I have left of this place and head towards Sequoia Park. It's next to the zoo and a duck pond and all that other kid shit. I figure I can let the little bastards run around here, burn some energy, and then go home and spend a hot, sweaty night sexting with Kitty. There is, like, *no* privacy with this many kids around. I have no idea when I'm gonna find a private moment to, you know, spank it if I don't get them to fall asleep in their *own* beds. "I'm the grown-up, and I don't want to listen to the *Barney* soundtrack."

"Ugh. You are *so* old," Kinzie spits, and I swear to Christ, she sounds like she's sixteen, not seven. "Nobody watches *Barney* anymore. *I* like *Monster High*."

"Great. Well, too bad. This is what we're listening to. Get over it."

I breathe a sigh of relief when I see the swing sets and the redwood trees come into view. I cannot wait to get some space to myself. Do babies play at parks? Do I hold it? Leave it in its stroller?

At least I can spend a few hours away from those damn chihuahuas.

"Alright, guys," I say, trying to be cheerful as I switch off the screaming man on the stereo. At least *his* yelling sounds melodic. The twins are like, well, like devils or something. I try to pretend that they don't kind of look like I did at that age. "*You* are going to go play on the slide or whatever, and Uncle Zay is going to play on his phone for a little while. Won't this be fun?"

I let myself out and then start trying to unload brats.

As soon as I set them on the ground, they explode like fireworks, running and screeching and mixing into the other running/screeching monsters in the wood chips. As soon as I get a good hundred feet from them, I'll be cool.

"Okay, Sadie. It's just you and me, I guess." I get the stroller out and spend a good fifteen minutes trying to figure out how to wrestle it into position. "Are you fucking shitting me? It ain't goddamn rocket science." I rake my fingers through my hair and glance up to find, like, a dozen moms staring at me. Half of them look like they want me to grab them around the waist and toss them in the back of the mini for a quick fuck; the other half look like they want to call the cops on me.

I flash one of my signature Zay grins and a boy scout salute ... *eeeeeeven* though I've never actually been in the scouts. Well, okay, I was for like one day but I got kicked out for beating up some snot-nosed brat that called me a weirdo.

Standing up, I examine the strange wheeled device before me and then lift the baby's seat out of the car, hooking it into place on top and standing back to admire my handiwork.

Yeah. See that? See it? *I got this.*

"Fuck yeah," I say and several of the moms scoff at me. I ignore them and park myself at one of the picnic tables under the trees, whipping out my phone for a little sexy texting with miss pink haired Kitty cakes.

BAD NANNY

Thirteen days left. Thirteen days and Hubert and I will be back in Vegas.

I've never wanted anything more in my life.

Until I met Brooke Overland.

Incoming: a serious fucking wrench in my life plans. ETA: twenty minutes until my life goes *boom.*

CHAPTER 6
BROOKE OVERLAND

Thank God today is Saturday. No class for me or the girls, time to keep searching for an alternative to my upcoming job at the strip club.

Just the thought of it gives me chills and I clamp my arms over my chest.

"Are you okay, Aunt Brooke?" Bella asks as I pick up my purse and sling it over my shoulder. I do my best to smile down at my niece, but inside, I'm screaming.

Strip? I'm going to strip?

I never thought I'd find myself at such a point in my life where I'd even consider it. This body ... it's *my* body and my choice and ... I really don't want to do this. But Eureka is an economically depressed area, and these girls need me. There's rent to pay and food to buy, and my parents are on a fixed income; my dad is sick. They can't help us, and I can't bear to rip the girls away from their friends and their school to move to a foreign city.

Deep breath.

I *have* to do this. For them.

"I'm fine, honey," I say as I reach down and ruffle the dark chocolate color of her hair. We're practically twins, Bella and me. She has the same dusty brown eyes, pointed chin and arched brows as I do. We both take after my grandmother while Ingrid and Grace take after my mom: blond hair, blue eyes, round face and plump cheeks. "Are you ready to head to the park?"

She nods enthusiastically, eyes shining, face bright. That makes it a little easier, that expression. Especially after last night. She tried to hide it from me, but I heard her crying in her room, tears soaking into her pillow. It took me hours to get her to sleep. *Fucking Ingrid.*

I hate my older sister a little bit right now.

"Grace!" I call out and the little girl appears at the top of the stairs, the dog following directly behind her. I think we all need an activity to take our mind off things, distract us a little. I know I sure as hell do.

Soon, you'll be taking your clothes off for strangers.

The thought makes me sick, so I banish it with a big breath, leading the girls out to my Subaru and loading them up. They're easy enough to get into the car. But Dodger? The dog is a Chinese crested, a nasty little hairless rat. I am *so* not into little dogs, but what am I going to do? The girls treat this thing like it's their brother. *Although it could probably win an ugly dog contest no problem.*

"Alright, Dodger," I say as I bend down and try to coax the hideous little gray and white creature into my arms. "Let's go, buddy." The dog ignores me, trotting over to a tree and lifting its leg.

My jaw clenches tight.

Oh, hell no.

There is no way I'm letting a stupid dog get the better of me. Not today.

I sprint over as the dog lifts his leg on another tree and grab him around the waist, lifting him into the air before he can bite me—something he's already done twice since I got into town last week. The little fucker.

I toss the dog into the car and climb into the front seat, starting up some rock music and hoping the girls won't complain. I know Ingrid was always a *huge* country music fan.

Me, I like a little screaming in my songs.

"Time for some *Amatory Riot*," I say as I scroll through my playlists and find the one dedicated to my favorite band. I smile at the girls as I pull down the sun visor and check my makeup, my hair. As soon as I pull out of the driveway, the song picks up into a raging feminine roar and I head bang my way straight over to the park.

When the girls get out of car, they both pretend not to know me.

"Have fun, ladies!" I call out with a grin as I grab the dog and set him on the ground, closing the car door with a bump of my hip.

I don't make it ten steps into that park before I see the most beautiful creature known to man.

Holy panty-wetters.

I think I've just spotted the God of Tattoos and Piercings.

And *I* am an ardent worshipper.

I find myself freezing ankle-deep in wood chips as children stream around me like I'm a rock in a river, water parting around my shocked and panting heart.

Who ... the fuck is that? And why is he in Eureka, California? Nobody hot lives here.

The man is sitting on a park bench under the trees, one leg propped up, his elbow resting against it as he texts with a furious thumb—a furious *tattooed* thumb. Half of his head is shaved short and dark, the other half is standing up in a Mohawk. Tattoos peek out from under his tight red T-shirt, staining his neck and arms with vibrant color. I raise an eyebrow at the shirt. It's straight-up nerdy: it has a graphic of the original Nintendo and says *Classically Trained,* but ... the muscles underneath are taut and sculpted and strong.

BAD NANNY

What a beautiful dichotomy, I think as I bite my lower lip and then grunt as a kid slams into my knees and knocks me into the wood chips.

"Sorry!" she screams, but doesn't stop, sprinting away in a fluttering wave of pigtails as I blink away the shock and try to drag myself to my feet.

"Holy sweet baby Jesus. You okay there?" A tattooed hand appears in my vision. When I reach up to take it, the skin is smooth and dry and warm. My breath rushes out in a burst as Tattoo God pulls me to my feet with little effort, his phone still clutched in his opposite hand. When he smiles at me, I see butterflies. No, like literal butterflies etched into the skin of his throat, right above the neck of his tee. "Sorry about that," he tells me with a loose, easy shrug. "You wanna sit down or something?"

I nod, but I'm having trouble finding the right words to say to this guy and his gorgeous lips, a piercing dancing on either side, winking in the sun. He's got one in his brow, too, and one in his nose.

Basically, he's hot as hell.

"You hurt?" he asks me, gaze traveling up and down my body appreciatively. When he gets back to my face, he smiles this easy, goofy smile that belies the harsh look of his tattoos and his hair, like he's a bad boy on the outside but a super nice guy underneath.

The last thing you need right now is a man. You need to focus on the girls, and on your master's degree, and your new life in Eureka.

I take a deep breath and run my fingers through my hair, dislodging a few wood chips in the process.

"I'm okay," I say as I take a seat next to God Guy and try not to stare too hard at his tight jeans, the belt with the skulls on it, the fact that he's not wearing shoes ... there are tattoos on the tops of his feet, too. "The name's Brooke Overland, by the way."

I hold out my hand and he takes it, gripping hard, his palm brushing against mine and making my heart thunder in my throat. If I was in a different place in my life, I'd seriously consider asking this guy out. Well. I look down at his hand don't see a ring, but he *is* at the park with a kid.

A gurgling sound draws my attention to a stroller and a *baby*. Holy crap. Okay, well, clearly this guy's not married but he's obviously taken. Why wouldn't he be? Men this hot don't stay on the market forever and let's be honest, outside of a ridiculous romance novel, where can they be found anyway? In rock bands? Please.

"Zayden Roth," he says as he looks me up and down again, still smiling that easy smile of his. "Sorry about Kinzie. She's kind of an asshole." I raise my brows. Never heard a guy call his kid an asshole before, but hey, she … kind of is an asshole. That really did hurt. I rub at my knee and the torn spot on my nude tights. I'm not even sure why I'm wearing them; I never wear tights. Maybe it's because I felt this crazy urge to put on tons of layers today? Like that would protect me from taking them all off later.

I almost start hyperventilating and manage to pull it together at the last second.

"That's okay. I'm sure it was an accident."

Zayden rolls his gorgeous green eyes, the color pale but striking. Like sea glass.

"I wouldn't necessarily say that. She's kicked and punched me so many times today that I'm seriously considering calling a therapist or something. The kid has issues."

He snaps his fingers at me and grins a little wider, piercings bright in the sun. I notice his ears are ringed in silver hoops, from bottom to top. *I wonder what else is hiding under those clothes?* I force myself to take a long, deep breath.

"Which ones are yours?" he asks as he scans the playground and lifts up a hand covered in ink, the knuckles labelled with the word *EASY*. I wonder what the other says? I crane my neck to try and sneak a peak when he notices and grins big, curling his hands into fists and putting them together for my viewing pleasure.

LIVE EASY.

BAD NANNY

I smile.

"I'm here with ..." I start to say *my sister's kids* but I don't want to get into the whole torrid story with a sexy stranger. What does it matter? It's not like I'll see the guy ever again anyway. "The beautiful Bella." I point out my dark haired look-alike. "And gorgeous Grace."

"Nice alliteration," the guy purrs as he winks at me and I feel my skin heating up from the inside. "I like a girl who can *alliterate*." Zayden leans back, sunlight skipping between the redwood branches above our heads, speckling his skin with sunlight.

"I can rhyme, too. Oh, and list palindromes."

Zayden grins.

"Sexy. You're a real smarty-pants, huh?"

"I try," I say, straightening the boring brown skirt I decided to wear today. Again, not my usual style, but I think I'm overcompensating for the whole strip club thing. I feel my face fall, but I can't help the rush of emotion. *I don't want to do this. I'm scared. I shouldn't have to do this.*

When I glance up, I notice that Zayden's studying me carefully, watching my face like he can sense the emotional turmoil inside of me.

I look away and study the original play set from when I was a kid, a structure of wood and metal that's older than I am. It sits in the center of the park under a copse of old-growth trees. The redwoods are so big they distort the proportions, making it look like the playground's in miniature.

"Something on your mind?" Zayden asks, his voice deepening a little with the change in mood. "I hear I'm a killer listener." When I look back at him, he's grinning at me again. "Feel like spilling your guts to a stranger?"

"Thanks for the offer, but the thing that's bothering me, there's nothing I can do about it. I'd really just rather forget about it while I can."

"Fair enough," he says as he leans back, elbows on the top of the table. "I feel you."

I smile, but the expression does nothing to shake the awful

feeling settling over my shoulders. I have a handful of days left to find another job, something where the hours won't conflict with my school schedule. As of right now, it looks like I'll officially be taking my clothes off for money.

"I like your tats," I say, gesturing with my chin as I examine a colorful sugar skull on his upper arm. It's mixed in with a strange variety of other things: a bundle of lollipops, a tree with leafless branches, a woman with angel wings, a pinup. This Zayden guy must be an interesting character.

"Thanks," he says, holding his arms out, so I can get a better look. "I started collecting them when I was eighteen. Think I might be a tad addicted." Without any prompting, Zayden lifts his shirt up and flashes me his midsection.

Holy ... shit.

Color spills across his chest, peeks up from his waistband. The ink above and below his abs only emphasizes how tight they are, how flat and sexy and touchable ... I blink several times to clear my head. I can't really look at him without getting light-headed. I glance away and pretend not to be interested. *Were his ... were his nipples pierced?!*

"Nice ink," I say, hoping I sound cool. I mean, not that I care because this guy's a complete stranger with at least two kids, one of whom's a baby. *I bet this man makes a lot of babies.* The last thing I need to be doing is sitting here and hitting on him like this. *I do not need to be making any babies.* Or trying to lose my virginity with some Tattooed God Guy.

"What about you? Got any tats?" I shake my head as I look back at him. I'm sure his story's a hell of a lot more interesting than mine.

"Nope. Not a single one. I've always been scared of getting poked." I flush as Zayden grins at me, forcing myself to smile like I meant that double entendre. *If he only knew how true that was ...* "Does it really hurt as much as everyone says it does?"

"Naw," he says, reaching up to scratch at the back of his head. "Personally, I like getting poked." A wink that's clearly meant in a flirtatious sort of way. "Got any piercings?"

BAD NANNY

I shake my head and smile.

"Same problem. The whole ... you know, poking thing."

"Gotcha," he says as he looks me over again, clearly checking me out. Basically, I'm in complete shock. I'm wearing torn nude tights, a brown chiffon skirt, and a white tee that's a little too small for me. On my feet are a pair of suede boots with scuffed toes. Essentially, I'm a hot mess. "So, how come your," a pause to look down at my hand, checking for a ring I think, "boyfriend isn't here with you today?"

I raise my eyebrows as my heart starts to pound. Holy crap. This guy really *is* hitting on me.

"I don't currently have a boyfriend," I say, trying not to think about *that* particular screw up. Three years with the wrong guy, a guy who was *supposed* to be perfect. And the reason I'm still carrying my V-card. He said he wanted to wait until marriage, that his faith was important to him. Yet, he was sleeping with my friend on the side. Yeah. Great. "I'm not looking for one either," I add, even though I *really* like the idea of this guy liking me.

"Well," Mr. Tattoo says, handing his phone out to me. "I've got plans to bring the kids over here tomorrow, too. If you're gonna be around, we could always hang out. No strings attached. Personally, I'm not a fan of the tangled little fuckers either."

I smile and—almost reluctantly—accept the phone from his hand. *I am so stopping by the store and using the last of my money on a new one after this.* I plug in my number and hand it back, knowing as I do though that I'm probably making a mistake here. I've got two kids and a dog to worry about, a degree, a ... job. A job that I hopefully won't have to go to. If I look hard enough, maybe I could find a gas station or convenience store gig, something overnight that doesn't involve ... *that*.

"Maybe I could bring bread for the ducks?" I say, even though I don't expect anything to come of this.

Zayden flashes another grin at me as Bella and Grace wave me over from the direction of the slide.

"Come watch!" Bella yells as they dart up the steps.

"Sounds like a plan," he tells me as I stand up and wave good-bye.

I really don't expect to see Mr. Tattooed and Handsome ever again.

And I especially don't expect that I'll be asking him to be the girls' nanny.

Funny how life works out sometimes, isn't it?

CHAPTER 7
ZAYDEN ROTH

If I'm gonna be in town, I might as well have a little fun. The young looking mom with the kids was fucking ballin', baby. She had no idea how hot she was in that little white tee, her flat bare belly showing above the waistband of that ugly skirt. I mean, not that I mind a chick that knows how hot she is, but Brooke was so clueless it was kind of funny.

I grin and spin my phone in my hand, getting ready to shoot her a text message. I've also got sexy little Kitty waiting for our video chat session tonight. *Maybe these two weeks don't have to be god-fucking-awful, right?*

I park my butt on the couch just in time to hear a crackle from the baby monitor. *Shit.* Don't I, like, ever get a break here? I mean this is *nonstop.* How does Mercedes ever find time for games? Seriously. Does the woman not sleep?

"I'm coming, I'm coming." I clomp up the steps two at a time, setting my phone down next to the baby's crib and hefting Sadie into my arms. She screams and throws her fuzzy brown head back, wailing like a goddamn banshee. A fist pounds on the wall from next door and I hear a grumbling shout. *Motherfucker.* What the hell am I gonna do about a goddamn baby? I mean, it's not like I enjoy kids or anything, but seriously? What is that asswad's problem?

I scowl as I carry the kid downstairs and manage to juggle getting a bottle under the hot water, all the while trying to pretend that it's not Mercedes' breast milk that's inside the clear plastic.

"It's cow tit juice instead, right?" I coo at Sadie as I bounce her and try to get her to relax. It doesn't work, no matter how I move or what I purr at her in babbled baby talk. Damn it. I balance the baby against one shoulder and squirt some milk onto my skin to check the temperature. Yeah, I actually *read* Mercedes' dossier. This guy knows what he's doing.

Sort of.

When I sit down and try to feed the little chick, she won't take the nipple in her mouth, screaming and howling around it. When I check her diaper, I find it ... full of crap. Jesus. So *that's* what the smell was. Personally, I thought it was the fucking chihuahuas. They go every which where it seems. I keep stepping on tiny poops.

I am in literal hell.

I change Sadie's diaper and she finally calms down, falling asleep on my shoulder before I deposit her upstairs. By the time I do, I find my phone's all blown up from Kitty and her texts and calls.

Not around, I guess. Well, screw you. I've got other options.

I mouth the word *shiiiiiiiiiit* and then fall onto my back on my brother's bed, bangin' out a quick response.

Tomorrow night? Sorry, babe. The baby was crying.

Hopefully that'll win me some sympathy points, right? I'm about to put the phone away when I think of that girl, Brooke. What the hell? I'll send her a text, too. She doesn't want a boyfriend right now; the last thing I want is a girlfriend.

This could be beneficial for both of us.

Zay Roth here, from the park. Want to hit that together tomorrow? We'll be there at two if you're down.

I drop my phone next to me and take a deep breath, trying to let out all the tension in my muscles. I'm starting to get there, to feel my pulse slowing, my eyelids getting heavy ... when a phone call comes in from my brother.

Wakes me. And the baby.

Thanks *Toxic*.

I swear, I am changing that goddamn ringtone.

I'm woken up at five in the morning by the twins bouncing on the bed and shouting at each other, the neighbor banging away on the wall between the duplexes. I groan and roll over, putting a pillow over my head and trying to dive back into the dream of me and Hubert, back at our apartment, sun streaming through the picture window in my living room, the air conditioning cooling my naked skin as I pump away at a beautiful girl in my bed.

It takes me a few seconds to realize that I'm fantasizing about Brooke Overland, the chick from the park. In my dream, her body's as soft and supple as it looked at the park, her hair smelling like peaches, her mouth hot and wild on my tattooed cock, tongue playing with the piercing in my balls.

I smirk as I drag my phone under my pillow next with me and check my texts. There's a single emoji from Pink Haired Kitty and a time that I'm assuming is for our, uh, *session*. The other is from Brooke, confirming that she'll be at the park. I try not to get too excited, but damn. Two dry weeks in Eureka is two too many. Having a friend with benefits around would be a huge relief.

"Alright, you little fuckers, get off the bed." The boys gasp as I sit up and toss the pillow onto the floor. "Get your butts in that bathtub. I'm not meeting a girl with smelly kids hanging off my legs."

The twins scream and leap from the bed, falling over each other in an attempt to escape first. I grin and chase after them, scaring them down the stairs before I head back in and grab the baby. Things are lookin' up. Mercedes' parents are stable, and it looks like they're gonna make it; Kitty's forgiven me for last night; and I've got a date with Brooke Overland.

Hard to see this day getting much better than that.

By the time our park visit rolls around, *Iiiiiiii'm* about ready to blow my head off.

"You're gross and weird. Our neighbor, Shiela, said you're going to the H-place because you have tattoos on your body and God doesn't like tattoos."

I almost slam my face into the steering wheel at the next light.

"The H-place? What the ... who the frick is Shiela?" I'm think it's time for a neighbor to get punched right in the eye for that shit. My brother and sister-in-law aren't religious; it's not up for some *neighbor* to start telling the kids that kind of crap. "No. Nobody goes to hell for having tattoos. That's the dumbest thing I've ever heard. Forget she ever told you that."

Kinzie makes a dramatic sound from the center row and I glare at her in the mirror, grabbing a Taylor Swift playlist from iTunes and cranking it up enough that I don't have to listen to the twins scrabbling at each other in the backseat.

I thought today was gonna be great, but ... it can't get any worse, right? The baby puked milk up all over me, the dogs chewed a small hole in the upstairs bathroom door, and that pot growing neighbor next door is such a fucking dick that I'm about one incident away from marching over to his place and telling him like it is.

Park day with that hottie, Brooke Overland. That's what I need.

"This is boring. Why are we going to the park *again*?"

BAD NANNY

I ignore my niece and decide that I don't care if the kids think I'm cool or not, I'm singing pop music all the way home. Clearly the little bastards don't much like me anyway. Hope they *do* like P!nk, Elle King, and Selena Gomez ... cause *that* is what we're listening to for the next two weeks.

I pull into a space, my eyes already scanning the park for little Miss Overland.

I spot her at the bench we were sitting on yesterday, her phone in her hand, long dark hair blowing in the breeze. When she looks up, it fans across her face, turning my cock to diamond. Damn. Wow. She has big round eyes, curvy lips, and a long graceful neck. I know, I know, weird thing to check out on a chick, a neck. But when your lips are pressed up against the pulse in a girl's throat, a hot neck makes a big difference.

Just sayin'.

"Let's go, snots," I say as I do the whole unloading ritual. This time when I get the stroller out, it unfolds perfectly. Hah. See, not all that hard. Don't know why guys are always bitching about this stuff. When you've got Google in your hand, what can't you do?

I run my fingers through my hair and slide my tongue across my lower lip. Oh yes. Brooke looks amazing sitting over there in some kind of loose black dress, the neckline plunging to reveal a curvy set of breasts. I'd do just about anything to get my face down there to worship those.

"Be cute and get me laid, okay?" I tell the baby as a mother whips her face around and glares at me with narrowed eyes. "She doesn't talk yet," I whisper with a wink as I move past her and find myself standing in front of my new friend.

God, I love making new friends. *Especially* lady friends.

I smile as Brooke glances up, her pale brown eyes shadowed in liner. Based on yesterday and today, it looks like her style is all over the place. She looked like a a sexy hipster before and now she looks like a pseudo goth chick.

Either way, totally cool with me.

"I remembered the bread," she says as I slide onto the

bench next to her, resting a foot against the baby's stroller. "For the ducks, I mean."

"Killer," I say as I study her curvy figure under the soft black jersey of that dress. I want to get my hands all the hell over that. "It's been, like, eleven years since I've been down to the duck pond. You'll have to remind me how to get there."

"It's been about five for me," she says with a soft smile, one that turns the slightly harder angles of her face to gentle lines. I watch her tuck some silken hair behind an ear and wish I could tangle it around my fingers. "I just moved back."

I make a face.

"Aw, bummer." I snap my fingers when she raises her brows at me. "I mean, unless you like living here. It's kind of ... in the middle of fucking nowhere." The girl leans her head back, the perfectly smooth angle of her throat even more enticing when she laughs.

"That's true. But I didn't exactly have a choice about moving back."

"Damn. I'm here on a temporary basis and then it's," I point a pair of fingers in the direction of the zoo, "back to Vegas."

"Vegas, huh?"

"Yup."

"How'd you decide to move there?"

I let my mouth curve up at both corners, right into a nice easy smile. Brooke follows the movement, her eyes drawn to my face as she struggles to catch her breath. Yup. Got this one in the bag. She wants me; I want her. What's there to lose?

"Vegas never sleeps. There's always something—or somebody—new to do." I wink at her and her smile fades a little. Hmm. Interesting. Okay. Different tactic. "So you grew up here? I don't remember seeing you around when I was in high school?"

"When did you graduate?" she asks as she looks up at me, fresh-faced and sexy. I could capture that chin in my fingers, pull her in for a kiss. We could ... hell, I dunno, load the kids up on sugar and soda and watch 'em crash. Then maybe I could take her upstairs to my brother's bedroom ...

BAD NANNY

"Eleven years ago," I say with a loose shrug. Brooke raises her brows and nods her head.

"Five years ago," she says and then it's *my* turn to raise my eyebrows. I glance over my shoulder at that brunette kid that looks just like her. Whoa. She must follow my train of thought because she shakes her head and lifts up her hands, a plastic ring with a candy jewel gleaming from her ring finger. Makes me grin. "They're not my girls. I mean, they are now, but ... they're my sister's kids."

"Ah," I say as I realize Brooke and I are in the same boat. "Hey, I know all about taking care of other people's brats." Even better. No kids. Even less chance of any sort of ... I don't, complications or whatever. "So where's your sister at?" I realize as soon as I say it that there's a chance her sister could be dead, and I could be stirring up awful memories.

"She ... left the country to be with her boyfriend." There's a long pause before she looks up at me. In the background, a bunch of kids dart into the forest with foam swords and full suits of plastic armor. Heh. "They're both addicts. It's not a good situation. My sister was an awful mother, but the girls miss her like crazy."

"No dad?" I ask and Brooke shakes her head again, that long hair of hers fluttering defiantly in the breeze, no matter how hard she tries to stop it. It hits all the way down to her ass. *It'd be perfect to pull ...*

"She doesn't know who the girls' dads are." Brooke rolls her eyes and sighs, glancing over at the blond kid. "Or if she does, she won't tell anybody about them."

"So that leaves you to shoulder all the responsibility? That's rough for a twenty ... three year old?" I guess.

"Close. Twenty-two. I was seventeen when I graduated."

"Ah, so you really *are* a smarty-pants, huh?" Brooke smiles and shrugs her shoulders, but I can tell she's proud of herself. I lean in close and let my mouth get enticingly close to Brooke's ear, enjoying the way her body shivers and her hands curl into fists. "So, Smarty-Pants, tell me, what else do you do?"

"Do?" she asks, jerking back from me like a frightened rabbit, all jumpy and twitchy all of a sudden. "Like, as in a job?" I nod and she bites her lip, glancing away toward the forest to her right. It's a protected swath of redwood trees and trails, one of which leads to a hundred year old stone fireplace and a duck pond. The others ... well, I've always been kind of a lazy gamer asshole. It's not like I've hiked a single one of them. "I have an interview for this evening. I know it's ... weird to have an interview in the evening, but I guess the manager wants to make sure I can actually show up? I don't know."

"Where at?"

Brooke's cheeks flame as I lean back and watch her with my curiosity—and a few other things—piqued.

"That gas station down on Broadway, the twenty-four hour one."

"Aw, a Smarty-Pants like you?" I ask and she sighs, digging her nail into the wood of the table.

"I'm getting a master's degree in biostatistics, but I've got a whole year left and the few grants and loans I get won't cover everything the kids and I need." Brooke closes her eyes for a moment, a heaviness pulling at her shoulders. "I ... have a job lined up, but I'd really like to get this one instead. It makes half what the other does, but ..." She pauses and shakes her head to clear the thought. "Forget it." She slaps her palms on the table. "You ready to walk down to the pond?"

I shrug my shoulders and lift my fingers to my lips, whistling for my brother's brood. The twins *shockingly* decide to show up, but Kinzie ... she looks over at me and then turns away to talk to some other girls near the slide.

Oh fuck that.

"One second." I get up and jog my way over to her, sending the other girls scattering from the base of the redwood tree stump where the slide is located. When my niece looks up at me, it's with a certain level of distaste on her features. I wonder briefly if she's this big a brat all the time, or if it's just me that brings it out of her. "Come on. We're doing an activity, just like you asked. Let's go."

"I'm happy playing here. I don't want to go meet your new *girlfriend*."

"Aaaaand earlier, you told me you hated the park and didn't want to come at all. Now, I'm telling you we're leaving. Let's skedaddle."

"No."

I blink down at her in her blue sundress, white tights, and sneakers. Her outfit choice, not mine.

"What do you mean, *no*?" I ask as Kinzie glares up at me, brown pigtails ruffling in the breeze.

"I mean I'm not going with you. You're not my dad. I don't have to listen to you."

I stare down at her for a minute and then reach out and tuck her under my arm, dragging her away from the slide while she screams. Parents turn to look, but I'm not hurting the kid. I'm just letting her throw a fit in my arms.

When I get back to Brooke, it's starting to sound like Kinzie's about to have a seizure or something. My new friend looks up at me with a grimace on her face as I try to smile my way through this.

"Maybe we should reschedule?" she asks, and I feel my jaw clench. Great. But I take a breath and nod, trying to talk over my niece's violent screeches. Even when I put her down, she doesn't stop, throwing herself into the grass as I fight the urge to toss her over my knee and spank her. Apparently, Mercedes doesn't believe in spankings. Maybe that's what got the kid to this point in the first place?

"Sure. Um, same time tomorrow?"

"You mean, after school tomorrow?" she asks and I snap my fingers. That's right. School. Blessed, blessed school. Of course, I'll still have the baby, but maybe I'll be able to take a bathroom break in peace. And when I say bathroom break, I mean jerk off session. Maybe with a certain brunette in mind to perk me up a little?

"Sounds good. Good luck at your interview, okay?" Brooke nods and smiles as she moves away and I'm left with a

weeping pile of child that I have no fucking clue what to do with.
    Fan-flippin'-tastic.

CHAPTER 8
BROOKE OVERLAND

The interview doesn't go well, not even with the blessing of that Tattooed God of a man that I can't get out of my mind. And for some reason, he seems determined to hang out with me. Three days into the week, I'm sitting at the park with him again, talking about something stupid and pointless and fun. It's a good way to get my mind off the fact that ... tonight I have to start my new job.

The job I really didn't want. But what I can do?

Panic rises in my throat, but I choke it back, trying to focus on what Zayden's saying. He's surprisingly good at saying a lot without telling me a damn thing. I honestly don't even know any of his kids' names—or if they even are actually his kids. I mean, they must be, right? He's with them everyday.

"I am not a nerd," he's telling me, but I don't think he actually believes that. Zayden folds his hands behind his head, his dark hair spiked up and pretty in the sunlight. He's a handsome guy, but he's got this silly, goofy attitude to go along with his cursing and his tattoos that makes me smile. I think I actually kind of like him. In a loose, normal, acquaintance sort of way that is. "Playing video games does not make somebody a nerd."

"Playing video games, collecting action figures, wearing shirts with—" I wave my finger at the black *Monster High* tee he's wearing "—that on it, makes you a nerd."

Zayden pinches the fabric of his outfit with two fingers.

"*This* is not mine. My shirt was wicked cool, but it got baby puke on it, so I improvised. This belongs to my brother."

"I see," I say, biting my lip and then pausing as I feel a buzzing against my thigh. I reach into the bag and pull out my new (really shitty but still expensive) phone, glancing at the caller ID.

It's Nelly, an old friend of mine from high school. It's not like we're besties or anything, but it's been five years since I moved away from here. I don't exactly know anybody anymore, and I can't exactly leave the girls alone while I work tonight. She watched them for me yesterday evening and did a good job, so I figure I can trust her with an overnight.

Overnight. Overnight without my clothes on, with men I've never met seeing me naked while no man I've ever actually liked has seen me naked.

My hands start to shake, but I clamp down on the pain, squeezing my fist around the phone. If Zay notices, he doesn't say anything.

"Sorry," I tell Zayden as I stand up. "I have to take this." He gives me a sexy little wave with his tattooed hand and picks up his own phone. "Hey, Nelly! How's it going? Are you all ready for your sleepover tonight?" I make my voice sound as cheerful as I can, trying to keep things positive. Letting myself lament the circumstances will only make me miserable. *Although I feel like I already am; I feel like my soul's falling apart.* Does that make me pathetic?

"Hi, Brooke," she says, her voice dropping with an awkward sort of regret. "I am so sorry, but I ... am not sure I can take the girls tonight."

I move forward into the grass, blinking at the bright sunshine as I come out of the shadows.

"What do you mean? I ... I'm starting my new job tonight. I don't have anybody to watch the girls until my parents get

BAD NANNY

back into town."

"I know, sweetie, but my boyfriend came home a night early from his business trip, and he wants to take me out."

"Then ... then cancel. I know I'm asking a huge favor here, but I already paid you fifty dollars to do this."

"And like I said, I'm sorry. Abraham wants to take me out, okay? I really wanted to help, but I can't exactly tell him no, now can I?"

"Um, *yes*, you can. You said you'd help me out and now I have," a glance at the time on my phone, "like five hours to find backup. We set this up yesterday, Nelly. Who else am I going to get to watch the kids now?"

"There's nothing I can do, Brooke," she says in that nasally little voice of hers I've always hated.

"Then I want my fifty bucks back, you hear me? Nelly? Nelly?" I look at the phone screen and see that the bitch has hung up on me. *Oh hell no.* I dial her back, but there's no answer; I get voicemail. "Listen up, you crabby little cunt," I start and then jump when I feel a hand on my leg.

"Aunt Brooke?" It's Bella, staring at me with big brown eyes. "What's a crabby little cunt?"

Oops.

"It's a ... type of endangered sea crustacean." I drop down to one knee in the grass and take her shoulders in my hands. "Look, let's ... people don't like to talk about them because they're almost extinct, okay? Let's never repeat those words again." Bella nods, but she doesn't entirely look like she believes me. Instead of commenting on it though, she drops a daisy chain into my hair and then skips away to rejoin her sister.

"Nice save," Zayden says as I rise to my feet, glancing over my shoulder to watch him slow clapping at me with his gorgeous hands. *I want to suck his fingers into my mouth and see what they taste like.*

Uh.

Forget I just said that.

"Your babysitter quit on you?" he asks as I move back over

to the bench and plop down on it, curling my fingers around the splintered wood.

"Actually, yeah." I look over at him, lounging on the picnic table like it's a recliner or something, like the man doesn't have a care in the world. It makes me want to know him, to hoist all of my cares onto somebody else's shoulders. But no. I'm stronger than that. I can *do* this. "Who do you use for your kids? Maybe I could borrow them for a night?"

Zayden laughs, this easy, open sound that makes my skin tingle.

"Oh, these aren't my kids," he says, finally admitting it and gesturing at the baby with his thumb. "I'm just the nanny. I might not look the part, but I come dirt cheap."

My heart flutters—but not from his shockingly good looks this time. I spin in my seat and lean forward, reaching up to take Tattoo God by his strong, sexy shoulders.

Oh, that feels nice.

"Oh my God. I ... listen. I gave my last fifty in cash to that bitch, and I don't exactly have the time or money to scour around for a babysitter." I glance over at the happily sleeping baby. Leaving the girls with a stranger is ... but if this guy's a nanny, then somebody must trust him, right? Besides, if I've learned anything over the years, it's that the people who aren't trustworthy often try to look it. If this guy was up to something, why would he advertise himself with all these tats and piercings? I mean, he's been nothing but normal and cool thus far. "Do you have references? I mean, I could check those real quick and we could work out a payment plan."

"Um, Brooke," Zayden starts, but I'm desperate here. If I don't go to work tonight, then I have no job. No money. No rent. No food.

"I'll get paid in two weeks—decent money, too. Oh, and tips. What's your going rate?"

"I, uh," he starts as two twin boys appear and launch themselves into his lap. He wrangles them under the bugling biceps in his arms and holds one on either side while they scream and giggle. I follow him up, rising to my feet and

BAD NANNY

clasping my hands together in front of me.

"Please, Zayden. Please, please, please. I need help. I ..." Tears sting my eyes without my meaning them, too. I just feel so overwhelmed right now, like I can't breathe, like I'm suffocating beneath the weight of my new responsibilities. *A twenty-two year old virgin stripper with two kids and an ugly hairless dog.* What the hell happened to my life? "My sister got on a plane and left the country to live with her boyfriend. She left her kids behind and I'm all they've got and my parents are out of town and tonight I have to start a horrible new job ..." I'm babbling and crying at the same time right now, but I can't help it. It all just comes tumbling out.

Zayden bites his lower lip and deposits the twins on the grass in a giggling heap as he looks me over.

"Please," I whisper, my voice breathy, hair sticking to my wet cheeks as I sniffle and look up at him. "I don't have anybody else to ask." I pause and take a deep breath. "Unless you think I should try Craigslist?"

Zayden arches a pierced brow and puts his hands on his hips, cursing under his breath.

"Fuck," he says and that's it. "Just fuck."

I smile and then throw my arms around the neck of a perfect stranger.

I have no idea why I do that; fuck doesn't exactly mean *yes*.

CHAPTER 9
ZAYDEN ROTH

I am such a huge fucking sucker for pretty girls in distress.

That shit is gonna *kill* me one day. I can barely handle the *four* brats that I have now. Take on two more? I must be going insane. Like, literally insane. Hello straitjacket, sign my bitch ass up, so I can start my journey on the crazy train.

My fingers rake through my hair as I pace back and forth and check the time on my phone.

Seven fifty six.

It's just about time to head over to that chick's house. Like, I wouldn't even go, but if she's naïve enough to just give me her address and invite me over to watch her kids, then I'm worried about her. What if she really does get on Craigslist and call up some weirdo? I ... fuck. I couldn't live with myself.

Why the fuck did I make that nanny joke? And why didn't I correct her? References? I don't have any references. My brother's exact words were: *Do you think I'd have called if I had anyone else?* That does not inspire much confidence in anyone.

A text comes in as I'm pacing. It's from Kitty again—and it's a picture of her pierced tits.

Looking forward to tonight, it says and I swear, I can feel my cock crying tears of frustration.

BAD NANNY

Sorry, babe. Babysitting isn't going well. You want to reschedule for tomorrow night?

But then, that probably won't happen either. That girl, Brooke or whatever her name is, kind of implied that she needed me, like, *all* week. And I kind of didn't correct her because holy shit, what a hottie. I mean, wow. She might not be as colorful as Kitty with the Pink Hair, but that body ... I squeeze my crotch and groan.

"What are you doing?" I jump and stifle a scream as I spin to find Kinzie glaring at me. Is there seriously no such thing as privacy? I'm in the *bathroom* AND I've locked the goddamn door.

"Did you pick the lock?" I ask and she grins at me, tossing a hair clip thing in the sink. "With a barrette?"

"That's a bobby pin, stupid," she tells me. "Mom taught me how because the twins always lock themselves in and refuse to come out."

"Great," I say caustically, raking my fingers through the hair on the left side of my head. "Weren't you napping or something? Can I please have a minute here?"

"I'm up now, and I'm hungry. Can we have burgers?"

"Yeah, sure, whatever. Get your shoes on. We've gotta go."

"It's almost *eight o'clock,*" she says, and I narrow my eyes. "It's bedtime. And you haven't even fed us dinner yet. Frozen blueberries aren't dinner."

"Listen up, you," I tell her as I lean over and give her a look. "You have a serious attitude, okay. I'm trying my best here. Cut me some slack, yeah?" Kinzie gives me a look ... and then hauls out and kicks me in the shin. I grit my teeth, but I don't have time to play games right now. No, I'll save those for later. Because you know what? No spankings doesn't mean no time-outs, does it? And it doesn't mean I can't unplug the TV and take away her video games, right? Although that does sound unnecessarily cruel ...

Anyhow, it's time to whoop some metaphorical ass here.

I gather the kids up and get them all in the car while the baby and the twins squirm and scream and cry about being woken up. Of course, by the time I get to Brooke's they're all asleep and I have to start the *entire* process all over again.

The house is ... kind of shitty, but it's definitely an upgrade over the duplex with the Bible-thumper on one side and the pot dealer on the other. I mean, Jesus, a trailer would be an upgrade over that place.

"Let's go," I say and notice that Kinzie's flat-out refusing to leave the car. Fine then. I lock her in, confident that the child safety locks will keep her there, and head to the front door, knocking twice before it swings open and Brooke's standing there with two lines of dark mascara tears running down her cheeks.

Holy ... shit.

My knight in shining armor meter starts pinging.

"Yo, Brooke, what's wrong, doll?" She shakes her head and sniffles, running her arm under her nose as she steps back to let us in. I carry the baby into a shabby little living room with a single couch, a love seat and a coffee table. Other than the TV and the rug, that's pretty much it. Not a lot of art or decorations or even toys. But at least there's space. And there's not a baby-hating asshole on the other side of the wall. *I am going to murder that man, I swear to Christ.* "I have to go back out and grab Satan's spawn. You gonna be alright for a second?"

"I'm seriously fine," Brooke says, but her voice is a goopy sob and her makeup's a mess. Her very, very thick stage makeup that looks nothing like what she's been wearing to the park these last few days. *Where the hell is she working tonight?*

A second before I drag myself away—cannot stand to see a pretty girl cry like that—Kinzie appears at the front door and slams it behind her, sitting down hard on the couch and folding her arms cross her chest.

Well, shit. At least she didn't run off.

"I've got to go finish getting ready," Brooke says as her girls appear on the steps and the brunette one, Bella I think it is, gets her first look at Kinzie. The two of them haven't exactly been playing together at the park. In fact, based on the looks they've been tossing each other's way ... I think there's a good chance that they're rivals.

Great. Nothing I love more than seven-year-old-girl drama.

"Ugh, this is gonna suck," Kinzie spits, kicking the coffee table.

"Hey," I snap, but I'm slightly distracted by Brooke as she moves up the stairs, sniffling and shaking like she's about to have a panic attack. Jesus.

"Boys," I dig my phone from my pocket and pass it into their grasping hands. "Play *Angry Birds* or poop game or something, that one where it bounces and giggles and shit."

"Curse jar," Kinzie mutters as I lock the chain on the front door—would not put it past my niece to take off—and grab the baby, moving up the staircase to search for Brooke.

I find her in the bathroom attached to the master bedroom, a curler in her hand, her long silky hair twisting around the curled metal end as her hands continue to shake.

Sadie goes on the floor, still strapped into the car seat (because I learned from Google that it's like, totally unsafe to leave a baby *un*strapped in one). Some blessing from an ancient god keeps her asleep as I lean my forearm against the door frame and watch Brooke getting ready inside.

"What's the matter? And don't tell me nothing because I don't buy that shit." Brooke glances at me in the mirror, but she doesn't stop curling her hair. Downstairs, I hear a TV turn on. A quick tiptoe down the hallway and a glance at the living room shows the twins mesmerized by my phone and the three girls settled in various parts of the living room to watch some weird ass cartoon with glittering purple ponies. *Ooookay.*

I head back to Brooke and cross my arms over my chest.

"Well?"

"It doesn't matter," she says as she sniffles one last time and squares her shoulders, feet spread apart in a warrior's pose. "Telling you won't change anything."

"You won't know that until you actually conjure the words to speak, huh?" Brooke whirls around, still clutching the iron and glaring at me with those vibrant eyes of hers. The color might be pale, but the intensity is … just wow.

"Let me have some pride, okay? If I tell you then everyone will know. I don't *want* everyone to know." Her eyes water again, but she glances away before the tears can fall. When she pulls the curling iron away from her face, a bouncy brown curl drops onto her forehead.

"It can't be all that bad, right?" I ask and then wish I hadn't said it as her breath catches hard in her throat and she tosses the curler into the sink, leaning forward to put her hands on the counter. I step into the room, putting a hand on her lower back and rubbing in circles. It feels good to touch her, like my hand's on fire, the palm licking flames against the small band of exposed flesh between her pants and shirt.

"I'm stripping," she whispers and it takes me a second to register that. "Is that what you wanted to hear? Tonight, I'm taking my clothes off for fucking strangers, and I hate it. I hate it. I feel sick to my stomach." She leans even farther forward, putting her forehead against the white linoleum surface. "This is my body. Mine. I don't want to do this. I don't want to take money for this."

"Then don't," I snap, getting pissy and defensive. This is so fucked. So, so, so fucked. A cute little naïve girl like this? She … this isn't right. I feel protective and righteously pissed on her behalf. "Take some more time. Find another job. Hey, listen, it's not like I need the money, okay? You can just not pay me."

Brooke lifts her head and looks at me in the mirror, curls tumbling around her face. Some loose strands of hair brush my hand from where they rest on her back.

"That's nice of you, Zay, really. But I need food. And I need rent. And my sister hasn't bought Bella shoes in like three years. All of hers have holes in the toes. I need gas to get to the university, and I need money for electricity. I don't *have* another choice. Eureka isn't exactly a bustling metropolis. There aren't a lot of options for me here. Look, I know we don't know each other and this is kind of the last thing you want to be dealing with."

BAD NANNY

"Not a big deal," I say even though it kind of is, but hell, it's not really *her* that I'm pissed at. I'm not exactly sure *who* I'm supposed to be mad at, so I curl my hands into fists and lean into the door frame again as Brooke starts to fix her makeup. "I can understand why you don't want to do this."

"It's worse than you think," she says and I raise an eyebrow as she accidentally smears liner across her cheek and curses, grabbing a wad of toilet paper and trying to dab it off. "Have you ever heard of a virgin stripper before? Only in stupid romance novels. And this isn't a stupid romance novel."

No, it's a damn good romance novel, I think and then wonder where *that* weird ass thought came from. Anyway ...

"What do you mean *virgin*?" I ask as Brooke smears red across her mouth. "Like virgin as in never stripped before or ..."

"Virgin as in never been poked." She said it, not me. Both of my brows go up now as I hook my fingers behind my head and suck in a deep breath. Holy hell. A twenty-two year old virgin. I mean, those aren't unheard of, right? My buddy at the shop has a brother who's twenty-five and still a virgin, some hopeless romantic kid that wants *the one.* Is that who this girl is? Holy fucknuts. "So now a bunch of weird, gross guys are going to see me naked when I haven't even gotten to decide who I *want* to show myself naked to."

She starts to shake again and I see why this is such a seriously big deal for her.

Ouch. I can't even imagine. Yikes.

"There ... I don't want men with money to be the first people to see me naked."

There's a long, awkward pause there where I realize that *I'm* the only man in the room currently. But no, no. After what I've just learned, this girl is an absolute no. Never gonna happen. A virgin stripper with two inherited kids? Fuck that shit.

"Listen, Brooke," I start as she turns to me and looks at me with those big fucking Bambi eyes. Jesus, they're like marbles or something. She sweeps her long, dark hair over her shoulder and then reaches down to the top button on her shirt.

"Please," she whispers, and I have no idea how I'm supposed to tell her no. Especially because my body is one hundred percent on board with this plan. Brooke's shaking fingers start to pull buttons apart as I take a step back and she follows me into the room. I'm not sure what the hell I'm supposed to be doing with her at this point, but I settle for scooting Sadie over and sitting on the bed. The baby's still asleep, but I tilt her seat away from the action anyway. "Just look at me," she says and my entire body flushes hot and warm, my cock rising to the occasion with gusto. My fingers curl into the blankets as I force myself to hold still and watch.

Brooke pulls her purple plaid top off and tosses it aside, leaving her breasts trapped in mint green fabric with little pink roses. I kind of want to bite them all off, but I make myself stay sitting because, hell, I'm not a fucking predator. I'm not gonna pray on some chick who's about to have a panic attack. When she starts undoing her pants though, a groan builds in my throat and I wish with a wild fervor that we were both in Vegas, strangers undressing in my apartment—alone—without six kids in the house.

Kids.

Those kids could come up here at any minute and yet ... I don't hear anyone on the stairs, so I make myself sit stone still, watching, my eyes eating up the sight as Brooke pushes her jeans to the floor and steps out of them, her undies a baggy pair of black cotton granny panties that'd be hilarious under any other circumstances.

"You were going to strip in those?" I ask, but it's not as funny of a joke as I'd meant it to be. When Brooke moves closer, putting a knee on one side of me and then straddling my lap—and the hard bulge of my erect cock—I'm powerless to resist. She's a beautiful girl and I'm turned-on as hell and here she is, offering herself to me. Who am I to say no?

Brooke wraps her arms around my neck and kisses me, her tongue hot and slick, sliding into my mouth and flicking across my teeth. Hmm. Not bad for a virgin.

BAD NANNY

I put my hands on her hips and kiss her back, showing her how to move her tongue, let me in to take control. And that's what she wants right now, I can tell. She wants someone else to take control of the situation, stop her from doing this. I can't exactly make that call, now can I? But I can give her this. If she wants to take this away from those men, this first look at her naked body, then I'll take it for her.

My hands smooth up to Brooke's waist before I lift her away from my lap and stand up.

"Take it all off," I say as I strip my shirt and she takes a small step back, pausing for a split second before tossing her bra and stepping out of those hideous panties. Her breasts are full but not huge, perky and taut with hard pink nipples and a rosy flush. I want them in my goddamn hands *now*.

I step forward and breathe in Brooke's sweet scent. God, I love how women smell. Like fruit and flowers and vanilla. A sweep of my hands through her long hair makes the scent stronger, reminds me of cucumbers and watermelon. *Yum.*

"Lay down," I whisper as I move back and let her crawl onto the bed, her bare ass perky and plump as she turns and then lays back, letting me get a good, long look at her, at the shaved line of her pussy, the whiteness of her thighs. When I crawl onto the bed, it dips under my weight, squeaking softly as I line my body up with Brooke's and kiss her mouth hard, let her touch and caress my back and chest and belly. Her hands are everywhere, like she's desperate for me, her hips lifting up off the bed, grinding into me as I clench my hands in the sheets and struggle to keep this above the belt.

I said I'd *look* at her, not … fuck her.

Christ.

What the hell am I doing?

Brooke's arms circle my neck, trapping our mouths together as she arches her breasts into my chest, encourages me to press her into the mattress with my weight. In the back of my mind, I know we *really* shouldn't be doing this or anything with the *realm* of this.

But I can't stop.

Naw, maybe I *don't* stop?

When she drops her hands to my jeans and tears the button open, I let her, let her stick her hand in there and touch me, sliding her palm down my shaft with a gasp tearing from her throat.

"We should probably wait," I grind out because, shit, I guess I'm fucking crazy as hell. Must be nuts to say no to a girl as pretty as this—especially with her hand pumping furiously on my cock. It's amateur as fuck, but also kind of sexy.

My mouth drops to her collarbone, licking up along that graceful neck of hers, teeth nibbling the sensitive skin of her throat as she moans and digs the nails of her right hand into my bicep. Her left is still working me with a frantic, wild rhythm, begging me for something that I'm not sure she even really wants.

"No."

I reach down and take her wrist, pulling her hand out of my pants.

When I sit up and scoot to the edge of the bed, she shoots up and presses her back into the headboard, breath coming harsh and quick, her breasts rising and falling with the motion. I glance back at her, but I can only look for a second.

It's too much. It's all just too much.

"I looked at you," I tell her as I stand up and button my pants, grabbing my shirt and slipping it over my head. "I looked at you, Brooke." My hand curls around the handle of the sleeping baby's seat, and I move out of the room and down the stairs to find the kids still enraptured in their show.

"You sure look stupid right now," Kinzie says as I pause and glance into a small mirror at the bottom of the stairs. My hair is mussy and my pupils are huge, like I'm high or something. Nothing I can do about that, I guess. "Can we eat now? It's late and I'm *hungry*."

"Yeah, yeah, I'll get right on that, your majesty." I move into the kitchen and find that the fridge has been stocked with plenty of food. Well, hell. Somebody's thinking way ahead of me, that's for sure. I start to pull stuff out when I hear the front

BAD NANNY

door slam and pause, heading back into the living room and looking out the window just in time to see Brooke's car pull out of the driveway.

I wonder if I'll regret letting her leave like that.

CHAPTER 10
BROOKE OVERLAND

I have no idea what came over me upstairs with Zayden. Like, literally none. I feel like I went crazy there for a minute, like I was sure that anybody would be better than the customers at the club. But ... then after I left, I just felt cheap and weird, and I didn't know what to do.

So I pulled over on the side of the road and I just sat there in my ugly panties and my top with the buttons all screwed up, and I put my face in my hands and cried. For an hour. An hour that made me late to my new job.

When I got there, my new boss screamed at me and then fired me right on the spot.

So apparently I was freaking out for nothing. I'm not going to be a stripper.

But what I *am* going to be is homeless and hungry and praying that my nieces don't get dragged into foster care, or maybe that when my parents come home, they'll be able to take them—even though my dad has early onset Alzheimer's.

Because it doesn't look like I'm going to be able to handle this.

I stay out for most of the night, as long as I would've worked, just sitting in the parking lot with the cheap, cheesy glow of the club's lights bathing my car in neon pink and blue.

BAD NANNY

I don't do anything but sit there and watch men go into the club, laughing and joking and hanging on one another. When they come out, they look like they're even more drunk than they were before.

After a while, I admit defeat and head home, unlocking the door and letting myself into the living room to find Zay asleep on my sister's couch. The baby's with him, sleeping quietly on his chest, her tiny body wrapped in strong, tattooed arms.

I suck in a deep breath and wrap my own arms around myself. I don't see any of the other kids, but I guess that they're parceled out upstairs. Without saying anything, I slip my heels off and move inside, plopping down on the small couch and turning on my side.

The cushions smell like dog piss. In fact, as I'm *thinking* that, I see Dodger run up to the coffee table and lift his leg.

Great.

I can't wait to start cleaning this place up for the inevitable move. Can't stay in a house if you can't pay the rent.

I stare across the moonlit room at Zay with the baby on his chest and try not to smile. I don't want to smile, not after the shitty day I've had. But I can't help it. What is it about tattooed guys and babies that make girls crazy? Is it that juxtaposition of hard and soft? I have no clue. Clearly, I'm no good at psychoanalyzing myself or else I would've known I was incapable of making a sacrifice for my family.

I'm such a selfish bitch.

I close my eyes and breathe deep, almost falling asleep before I hear a rustle from across the living room. It's Zayden, laying the baby gently in the folding crib he brought over. She fusses, but he coos at her, singing some soft song under his breath. I think it's ... *Africa* by Toto? What the hell? But anyway, it's cute as hell when she settles with a little smack of her lips and falls back asleep.

"How was work?" he asks, voice guarded against the weird virgin-stripper girl that tried to jump his bones this afternoon. No *wonder* he thinks I'm nuts. I *feel* nuts right now. And I can't believe I did what I did earlier.

"I got fired," I whisper, lips brushing against the gross pilling gray fabric of the couch. Zay makes a sound under his breath and comes over to sit next to me, crossing his legs as he settles on the floor between the couch and the coffee table.

"Before or after?" he asks, his voice weird and tinny.

"Before," I admit and there's a long pause before he sighs.

"I mean, that's kind of good, right?"

"If you like cold houses with no food and cars with no gas. If you like kissing your master's degree good-bye because you can't find a job that'll work around those hours. If you like having to move your sister's kids into a new city, a new town, just so you can have some hope of actually landing some work with a bachelor's in statistics."

Zay smiles a little, his silver lip piercings catching the wan moonlight.

"When you put it like that," he starts, but then he just shakes his head a little, reaching up to run his fingers through the thick hair on the left side of his head. I can still feel a tingle in my fingertips from when I touched it. "Do you know what I think?" he asks and I shake my head, cheek rubbing against the dog pee cushion.

Zay reaches out and pokes me in the center of my forehead with a tattooed finger.

"I think you got off lucky. Don't do something if it's going to break you like that. You've got a right to your own body, you know?"

"What else am I supposed to do?" I ask, trying not to cry again. The last thing this poor guy needs is to see me cry. Haven't I done that enough already? I mean, seriously. We *really* don't know each other at all. Honestly, if I was being straight with myself, I should wonder how I ever thought to leave him with the kids. Or how I'm totally cool with laying in a dark living room next to him.

He could be crazy. He could be a murderer. He could be ... all sorts of things.

I should kick him out of my sister's house.

"I have no clue," he says with a loose, exaggerated shrug,

lifting up his palms for emphasis. "I've always been pretty shitty when it comes to adulting."

"Adulting?"

"Yup. Adulting. The act of being a boring, tightwad with no personality and nothing to do but bitch."

"That's adulting?" I ask with a raised brow. "I thought adulting was when you, you know, paid bills and took care of the kids and did what you had to do to survive?"

"Naw. Stop being so practical, Smarty-pants. Seriously. For somebody with a degree in math, you sure seem a little dumb."

I smile, but it's a crooked, loose smile. It fades as soon as I see the dog pissing on the bricks of the fireplace. *I should've left that fucking rat at the shelter.*

"I'm sorry about your money," I whisper, realizing that we've never actually agreed on a price. The thought gives me chills. "I'll get it to you as soon as I can."

Zay sits there for a long while looking at me.

"Look, like I said, I don't exactly need the money right now, okay?" There's another long pause as he leans back against the coffee table. "All I'm doing for the next week and a half is watching these monsters." Zayden jerks his head toward the stairs. "I mean, what are two more?"

I sit up suddenly and glance away, hair falling over my face. I sweep it back over my shoulder with a quick motion.

"What are you talking about?" I ask as I glance his way and try to take him in. He's still a Tattooed God, but ... he looks a little human right now. "You'll be our nanny for free?"

"Why not? You can spend all day pounding the pavement, looking for another job or something."

"Why would you do that?" I ask as I stare in his beautiful, pierced face. When he smiles, it's almost magical.

"Because ... why the hell not?"

CHAPTER 11
ZAYDEN ROTH

No more pretty girls.

Seriously. No more pretty girls *ever*.

Brooke takes her kids to school the next morning, and I manage to wrangle my monsters into their appropriate pens, but after that ... I get back to my brother's place and flop down on the bed. The enormity of what I promised in the quiet dark last night is seriously pinching my nipples.

I just agreed to be a ... a fucking nanny? I mean, who the fuck has a fucking nanny in this day and age? I mean, might as well have a larder and a chambermaid, too, huh?

So now, I get a mere *four* hours of alone time a day before I have to start picking up kids like pinballs, bouncing from one school to another in this weird awkward stretch of time between one and three. Why do they all have different times?! Why can't all the damn kids go to school at the same damn time? Maybe that's what nannies are for because I don't know how any normal human motherfucker gets around to all these places without Hermione's time-turner from *Harry Potter*.

The baby starts to fuss a few moments later and the pot dealer neighbor starts his wall banging.

I lay there for all of two minutes before I throw myself out of bed and jam the monitor in my pocket, taking the stairs three at a time before I jump down to the main floor and explode out the back door.

I have just about fucking *had it* with this son of a bitch.

I head into the backyard, climb up onto the small cement area where Mercedes grows an organic fucking garden, and gaze over the fence. There's a big ass rottie back here, and the dog growls at me, but what's he gonna do from there?

I reach down and grab the wooden handle of Mercedes' clippers. They have about a four foot reach, and she says she uses them to cut blackberry clusters off the thorny vines that peek above her fence.

I use them to reach into the neighbor's yard and snip his weed plants off at their bases. It takes me about two minutes, and then it's done.

"Eat shit, you cocksucker."

I drop back into the yard and head inside. Twenty minutes later when that son of a bitch finds his prized crop, there ain't none of it left.

His scream is enough to lull me into a soft, melodic sleep.

Six kids. One car. Nightmare from hell.

Kinzie and Bella are screaming and fighting over one of those dead dolls with the weird eyes and the freaky body proportions while the twins kick and yell and argue over possession of my phone. I have a blinding headache, and I kind of want to ... die right now. My cat's stuffed in a kennel in the front seat, and the horrifyingly putrid little chihuahuas are trapped in the back, yipping and growling and fighting with each other. Suddenly, there are like, three of them. I thought there were only two? Did they multiply? I can't remember how many goddamn chihuahuas I'm supposed to have.

I drive the whole kit and fucking caboodle over to Brooke's house and pull into the driveway, my heart constricting at the empty swath of pavement where her ugly ass Subaru was sitting this morning.

I'm really on my own here. Really, seriously, truly alone with six children and four dogs and a hairless cat named Hubert.

My life is so over.

"Alright, guys, let's do this shit with military precision, shall we?" Nobody's listening to me, so I just start unloading demons from the seats and making sure they get in the front door. Once I think I've got everyone, I start counting and realize I've lost that hideous hairless gray dog thing. You'd think Hubert's hairlessness would endear me to that rat, but all it does is make me realize how much I despise little dogs.

Seriously.

Get a cat. Get a large dog.

What's with this in-between shit?

A quick search of the vehicle and I find the creature eating a dirty diaper under one of the seats.

Don't cringe away from that. Reread it. I had to *live* it, okay? And it's fucking gross.

As I'm dragging the rat-thing in by its harness, I find my phone on the cement outside the front door. When I pick it up, I see the screen is cracked.

My mouth twitches.

"Who did it?" I ask as the rat-thing attaches itself to my leg and starts to death shake my pants, growling and snarling and … is it hissing at me? No, that's Hubert. Who's out of his kennel. Shit. I shake the dog off and try to ease forward toward my cat. "Come on, Hub. Don't do this to me, man." The cat takes off up the stairs, the chihuahuas on his ass like white on rice.

Great.

"Best day of my goddamn life," I grumble as I hunt down the herd of wild dogs and corral them in an upstairs bathroom. I feel bad for the things, but what am I supposed to do with them? They're not *my* dogs, and these aren't *my* kids. The only thing here that's mine is the damn cat, and he wasn't even mine to begin with.

Vegas, Vegas, Vegas, I think as I tromp back down the stairs and into the kitchen to make snacks or whatever. It takes me a while to come up with something, and I start slapping together PB&Js for the whole lot of them. That's what our parents fed us. My brother and I had stupid peanut butter and jelly sandwiches for lunch at least five times a week. All kids like 'em, right?

"I have a *gluten* allergy," Kinzie barks as I toss the plate of sandwiches on the coffee table and let the kids go at it like animals.

"You have a … what?" I ask as I shove bread and jelly and peanuts into my mouth.

"A gluten allergy, stupid." I narrow my eyes at Kinzie and then point with the whole of my sandwich.

"Okay, that's it. Last warning, kid. Next time, it's a time-out." She scoffs at me, but I'm not playing around here. Seriously. My niece has slapped and kicked and punched and spit at me. I'm finished with the attitude.

"I don't *like* time-outs," she says, picking up one of the sandwiches and tossing it onto the floor for the gray rat-dog thing. I watch as it gobbles it up and then set my own food down on the table.

"Well, you've just earned yourself one. Get up. Let's go. You're going to sit in this downstairs bathroom for …" I brainstorm time periods and decide that since she's seven, we'll go with that. "Seven minutes. Get in here and I'll start timing you."

Kinzie makes about … zero moves to get up and listen to my directions. In fact, she looks right at me, hauls back her head … and spits.

The projectile lands harmlessly on the floor between us, but I've had just about enough of that shit. I move around the couch, lean down and haul my niece over my shoulder while she screams and flails and kicks. I'm not hurting her, but she acts like I'm in the process of beating her to a bloody pulp, wailing and punching and … *fuck,* did she just *bite* me?

I sit Kinzie down on the closed lid of the toilet with its fuzzy pink cover and kneel down in front of her.

"I'm done with the attitude, okay? I've been nothing but nice to you. Until you have a change in attitude, you're sitting here until I say otherwise, got it?" Kinzie kicks and yells, but I'm not here to argue. I get up and leave the room only to have her burst out of it fifteen seconds later. With an eye roll, I follow her up the stairs and into the master bedroom where Brooke and I almost fucked yesterday. Part of me wishes I'd just gone through with it, let myself see what that soft, curvy body of hers would feel like wrapped around mine. The other parts knows I made the right decision.

Last night, Brooke Overland was angry and desperate and hurting.

Today, she ... well, it was hard to say exactly *what* she was, but it wasn't all that much better.

Clearly, the girl has issues. I'm not saying she's not hot and that I wouldn't mind spending the rest of my time here tangled up in her sheets, but ... it ain't gonna happen.

Brooke is too fragile, too sensitive; she's clearly got issues up the wazoo.

Kinzie dives underneath the bed and I follow after her, carefully wrapping an arm around her waist as she screams at me, and dragging her out from under the bed.

This time, when I put her back on that fuzzy toilet seat cover, she sits there for a good two minute before she makes another run for it.

This is gonna be a seriously long goddamn day.

When Brooke gets back to her sister's place later that night, her long brunette hair is tangled and her lips are pulled down into a permanent frown. The makeup she put on so carefully this morning is gone, replaced with black smudges around the eyes, purple circles underneath them, and a dab of red along the side of her chin that I think used to be her lipstick.

"Rough day at the office?" I joke when she lets herself in and pauses, blinking several times at me like she'd forgotten I was even here. It is awkward as *hell* in that living room, but I stand my ground, Sadie tucked up against my shoulder as I rub my hand in a circle on her upper back. I'm already starting to get the hang of this baby thing. Honestly, I think she's *easier* than the older ones. At least she doesn't walk, talk, or otherwise move around. No broken cell phones, no spitting, no kicking me in the shin. All this one does is eat, poop, and sleep. Those three things, I can handle.

"Thanks for staying so late," she says, lifting her chin up in that proud way she's got. I wonder where she learned that from? "I meant to get back before dark, but I ended up stopping back by the strip club and talking to the owner."

Deep breath from her as I raise an eyebrow.

"He says he'll give me another chance. I need to be back there tomorrow at nine sharp. Is there any way you could stay the night again?" She flicks some loose hair back over her shoulders and challenges me with a look that I can't interpret.

"Usually when a chick asks me to stay the night, she has other things in mind." I smile when I say it, but Brooke doesn't smile back. I wonder what's been going through her head all day, about what happened between us. Maybe that's what's bothering her? "Look, about yesterday ..."

"I'd rather not talk about yesterday," she says, and I nod.

"Okay, then. Well, to be honest with you, your place is a hell of a lot better than where I've been staying. It's bigger, quieter." *There's no Bible-thumpers or pot dealers living next door.* "If you don't mind, maybe I'll just go back and grab the rest of my stuff? Camp out here for the next week and a half?"

"The parents won't mind. I mean, the parents of ..." She gestures at Sadie, and I realize that I haven't exactly explained the whole situation to her. "Your ... charges?"

"My charges?" I laugh and the sound echoes in the nearly empty house. Whatever Brooke's sister was doing before she left, it certainly didn't have much to do with interior decorating. "No, the parents won't mind. They're in South Africa until the end of next week."

Brooke raises an eyebrow at me. It's got the perfect shape, you know, like the curve of the Gateway Arch, this deep rounded design that makes me want to grab my kit from the car and pierce it. Brooke would look great with a few careful pieces of metal. I like to think of them as accent pieces for the human body, chrome detailing for an already a beautiful sports car. And Brooke, Brooke is a fucking *killer* sports car.

"What are they doing in South Africa?" she asks as she steps inside and kicks her shoes off by the door, setting her purse on the back of the couch. Before I get a chance to answer, Hubert's exploding from underneath it with a yowl, launching himself up the fabric and arching his back in Brooke's direction.

As soon as she sees him, she lets out a startled scream and I realize I've forgotten to introduce the two of them.

Oops.

"What the hell is this thing?" Brooke asks as Hubert yawns and stretches his ugly little peachy paws out, clawing the crap out of the back of the couch. When he's done, he arches his back again and tries to rub his wrinkly hairless body along Brooke. "Is this a ... is this a *cat*?"

"Uh, yeah. He's mine ... well, long story. An ex of mine left him at my place and we've kind of grown close." I set Sadie down in her crib and move over to pat Hubert on the head. He hisses at me and tries to scratch me, but hey, we're cool.

"Why is he ... wearing a sweater?" Brooke reaches out a tentative hand to stroke Hubert's head as I catch my breath and tell my cock to stop dreaming about her frantic, wild touch. She's so ... inexperienced and amateur and ... God. I want that hand wrapped around my shaft, gripping hard, palm sweating with nervousness as she tries to figure out my body. If Brooke Overland wants to learn what it's like to be with a man, I'd be more than happy to teach her.

BAD NANNY

No.

No, I would fucking not.

Didn't I *just* go over all the reasons this girl is bad news? Like, ouch. Clearly, if she's waited this long, she's looking for something "special". I specialize more in the once in a lifetime variety of loving, if you know what I mean.

Best I just text Kitty Pink Hair a picture of my pierced cock and wait for a response.

If I need a friend with benefits, I can go hit the bars or something.

This here ... this is gonna be straight-up platonic.

"He ain't got no hair." I wink at Brooke and she raises her brows at me, her perfectly arched and begging to be poked brows. I grin again.

"You live in *Vegas*. As in desert. As in hot."

"Yeah, but nobody actually hangs out outside. It's all about the A/C, baby. Hub's gets the chills, don't ya, Hubs?"

"*Hyoobs?*" Brooke asks as she pets the cat and then takes a very calculated step away from me. Damn. Not used to that. Usually girls are trying to find their way *closer* to little old me. "That sounds like *boobs* or *pubes*."

"Aw, see, look at you rhyming again over there, Smarty-Pants." That gets me an almost smile as I scratch Hubert's bum and he turns and bites me. Dickhead. "His full name's Hubert. Not my fault. I didn't name the little bastard."

"It's kind of an ugly name, but then ... he's kind of an ugly cat." I raise my brows at her, but it looks like she's trying to hold back a smile.

"Well, you have kind of an ugly dog," I answer back, wiggling my brows.

"Yeah, well, he would not have been my first choice either." That cute little half-smile widens, turning Brooke's young face into something spectacular. I almost whistle. Wow. Wow, wow, wow. I don't usually go for girls like this, the emotionally damaged but ridiculously sexy fresh-faced kind. I like the take-no-crap tattooed, pierced, bitchy sort. But Brooke ... she's fucking hot.

There's this long moment where we're just staring at each other. I'm checking her out, loving the way her hip's cocked to one side, her hand resting there with this little pop of attitude. I feel like she's scopin' me out, too, like her eyes are undressing me with a slow burning heat.

Brooke bites her lower lip and causes me to run my tongue across mine.

"Um. I'm home now, so ..." Awkward pause. "You can go now."

I blink a few times as I feel a frown start to take over my face. Huh? What?

"Are you ... kicking me out?" I ask and Brooke shrugs, grabbing her purse and heading for the stairs. I follow her with my eyes, mouth gaping as she starts up the steps and glances over her shoulder at me.

"See you again tomorrow? You can bring your stuff over then."

"Um. Yeah. You got it."

I pick up my hairless cat, my monsters, and my chihuahuas. And I leave.

Feeling ten times as intrigued by the girl I shouldn't let myself have than I did before.

Nicely played, Brooke Overland. Nicely played.

CHAPTER 12
BROOKE OVERLAND

I kick Tattoo God out of my house and then watch as his minivan pulls out of the driveway.

Gah.

That man is, like, way too attractive for his own good. And he knows it. And he knows I know it. *And I had him shirtless on top of me last night, his body pressing me into my sister's mattress.* Yuck. Super yuck. But also ... not. I mean, I *wanted* him. If he'd kept going, slipped on a condom, put his thick, hard cock inside of me ...

I shiver and shake my head, turning away from the window and heading down the hall to check on Bella and Grace. They're sitting on Bella's floor, playing with a pair of dolls, a giant monster truck, and ... a copy of *War and Peace?* Not sure what that's about.

"How was your day today?" I ask, trying not to let the deluge of emotions I'm feeling into my voice. Not that anyone cares, but *my* day was not a good day. My class ran late and caused me to then be late to an interview. Next, my phone died and I forgot the new charger, so I had to use a crappy printout from the school library to try to get to my next one. In the end, I wound up getting lost and showing up five minutes late to that, too.

Oh, and I stopped over at that endangered sea crustacean's house and got my fifty bucks back.

Bitch.

Going back to the strip club was one of the hardest things I've ever done in my life, but I sucked it up and I went. I did it. I got my job back.

"Fine," Bella answers. Grace ignores me and uses the old book as a stage for her doll.

"Was ... how was Zayden?" A shrug as Bella grabs Grace's doll from her hand.

"No. Not like that," she snaps, turning the doll's lopsided dance into a complicated hip-hop routine of moving parts. I raise a brow, but I well remember the joys of having an older sister.

"He was nice? Polite? Did he feed you? Nothing ... weird happened, right?"

"Kinzie got *four* time-outs, but she deserved them because she's a bully and she spits."

"Um, okay." I retreat from the room when it's clear there's nothing remarkable to talk about. Good. That's what I need from a nanny. Plain, boring, normal. No incidents to speak of whatsoever. *Except for the fact that I almost had him run my V-card and make a hefty transaction.* I shiver when I remember the crazy way I grabbed at his dick, like I was trying to spot shine it or something.

I am such a weirdo.

Flipping my long hair over a shoulder, I head downstairs and pause on the landing, the faint sound of music coming from the kitchen. I find an iPod that's distinctly *not* mine sitting on the table, pop music trickling softly from the speakers.

When I pick it up, I find a god-awful playlist with *Britney Spears* on it. Who listens to Britney Spears anymore anyway? My mouth twitches as I flick my thumb down the playlist and find several other atrocities against mankind: Beyonce, Bruno Mars, Miley Cyrus. *Ewww.*

"Aw, cool beans! You got my iPod."

A tattooed hand shoots over my shoulder and snatches the

MP3 player from my hand as I whirl and find myself chest to chest with Zayden.

"What the ... you can't just come in like that!" I say, my heart beating in my throat as I realize I can feel the warmth of his body from here. He even smells good, like blackberries and cinnamon. I swallow hard as he looks down at me with a confused pucker to his mouth.

"Huh?"

"You ... left, and then you came back. That means you have to knock." I ease myself along the length of the table and slip away from him. Being that close to him makes me remember yesterday, and I think that's a memory best left forgotten. "Seriously."

"Ooookay," he says as he taps his iPod against the shaved side of his head, green eyes focused on my face with a perplexed expression. "Will do, Mistress."

"Mistress?"

"Isn't that what nannies call the lady of the house? Close enough, right?"

He pokes me in the forehead with a tattooed finger.

"Got the kids in the car. Gotta run, Smarty-Pants." Zayden gives me a stupid boy scout salute and turns on his heel, lifting his iPod up over his shoulder in a wave.

I wait until he leaves out the front door for the second time before I reach up and touch a hand to my cheek. Holy crap. I really *am* blushing.

Better be careful with this guy. He doesn't just smell like fruit and home ... he smells like trouble.

And I am so allergic to that.

The next morning goes a lot smoother. I get the girls to school on time and manage to make it to class with minutes to spare, sliding into a seat before the professor even gets to the room.

Of course, week two and I'm pretty sure this course is going to kick my ass, but it feels good to be here. I'm twenty-two; *this* is where I'm supposed to be.

I work *really* hard not to think about tonight.

Or about Zayden Roth.

For some reason, my mind is desperate to conjure up images of his rock-hard body, his colorful kaleidoscope of tattoos, all those weird goofy mannerisms of his.

After class, I head home with metal music thrashing around my shitty old car, tapping my hands on the steering wheel in time to the drums, wishing I was back in Berkeley on my way to a party or a club or something.

Well, I *will* be on my way to a club tonight. Only this time, it's gonna be me who's the entertainment.

My mouth purses tight and I swallow hard, pulling into my driveway to find ... Zayden waiting for me. *What the hell is it with this guy?*

I climb out of the car and find him dancing to Lady Gaga with the baby giggling on his shoulder. The minivan door is wide open and the music is blasting into the yard as he swings his hips to "Bad Romance" and sings the lyrics. I expect him to stop when he sees me, but he doesn't. In fact, it doesn't even look like he's embarrassed.

If I were him, I sure as hell would be.

I cross my arms over my chest as he bounces the baby in a gentle rhythm and turns in a circle, foot tapping to the music as I glance over my shoulder. But nope. There are no neighbors around right now; they're probably all at work or something.

One eyebrow raises up as I study Zayden in his red Dr. Martens and his black skinny jeans, his hands this vibrant splash of color against the baby's peach onesie. Fuck, I hate this song, but ... the whole scene is kind of ... cute?

"What are you doing here?" I ask when the song ends and Zayden smiles over at me, oozing confidence and don't-give-a-shit swagger. He literally looks like he could not care one crap less about what anyone thinks of him. *How did this guy ever get hired as a nanny?* But then I see the gentle but firm way he cradles the little girl against his chest, the kindness of his eyes buried behind all those piercings and tattoos.

I guess it's not *such* a far stretch. I mean, *I* hired him. Only ... I'm not paying him any money.

"I don't need you until nine or so," I say, but he gestures with his chin at the car and the duffel bags in the back. I hear a hiss from somewhere inside and assume he's got his cat with him again.

"Cops busted a neighbor at one of the other duplexes for drugs. There are police everywhere; it's fucking chaos over there. Figured I'd stop by early if you don't mind? If it's too much trouble, we can camp out here."

"You think I'd leave a baby outside on the driveway? Come on." I move up the single step and unlock the front door, stepping aside to give Zay plenty of room to squeeze inside. "Was it the neighbor in your building?"

"Nope. Not the pot growing asswad directly next door, but the Bible-thumper on the other side. Looks like she was cookin' up meth with her gospel." Zayden chuckles as he pulls the blanket off his shoulder and tosses it on the floor, setting the baby down and stepping back with his hands on his hips.

We both watch as she attempts a shaky crawl, her floral headband bright against the dull colors of the living room.

"I've got a baby hack figured out. See, I let her do this for a while and then she just," Zayden slaps his palms together, "conks the hell out. Works like a charm every time." He looks up at me suddenly and then snaps his fingers. "Hey, let me grab the dogs and I'll be right back. Watch her for me for a sec?"

I nod as Zay disappears outside and returns with three yipping dogs. He almost trips and drops the cat carrier in his hand as they tangle their leashes around his legs. Dodger appears immediately, standing guard in the kitchen doorway, teeth bared and hackles raised. I ignore him. Nobody in their right mind would find that thing threatening.

Zayden drags the dogs across the floor and then lets them all outside—Dodger included.

"Fuck, you're so lucky you have a yard. The duplex has a tiny square of cement that pretends to be a porch. The dogs crap all over that and then run into the five by five space where there used to be grass and go there, too." He shivers as I raise a brow again. I want to ask who has money for a nanny that doesn't have money for sod or a better house, but then I realize that I'm in pretty much the same position.

Maybe Zayden does a lot of charity work? If so, where does he get money to live?

I narrow my eyes on him and wonder for the millionth time if I'm getting roped into a scam or something here. He just stares at me, bends down, and then releases his hairless sweater wearing cat.

Hmm.

Okay, so there's no way in hell a guy with a sweater wearing cat could be up to anything devious. It's just too … nerdy. But then I remember that I dated a guy for *three* years and couldn't figure out that he was cheating on me, abstaining from sex because I was going to be his perfect wife one day.

I sigh.

"My shifts are from nine to two every day this week. I know it's a pain in the butt, but if you could just, I don't know, stay and then go home on the weekend, that'd be great. I'll start up again Tuesday of next week."

Zayden sits down and tries to put the cat on his lap, but it thrashes around in its black sweater and takes off like a shot up the stairs. He watches it go and then shrugs like his shoulders are made of water, nice and loose and easy and flowing.

"You alright, Brooke?" he asks me instead and I pinch my lips, staring at his face for a long moment before responding.

"I'm okay," I say, but then that's how I felt when I freaked out originally. Okay. Fine. Decent. Managing it. Until I wasn't. Until I was panicking and tearing my clothes off my body like they were poisoned, throwing myself at some strange guy I met at the park. I look up at Zayden, at his modelesque face, the silver points of his lip rings, the butterfly tattoos on his throat. "Actually, I'm flipping the fuck out."

BAD NANNY

He smiles at me and nods his head like that's the answer he was waiting for. Next to me, the baby struggles across the blanket, working her way towards Zayden with a shaky sort of intensity, like she's as fascinated by him as I am.

"Tell me about it." He crosses his arms over his chest and looks at me with those sea glass green eyes of his. The muscles in his arms bunch with the motion and I find my gaze tracing them greedily, finding new designs in his tattoos each time I look. There's a woman bleeding from the eyes, her hands locked in prayer ... right next to a smiley face emoji. Interesting. I wonder what his stories for all these things are.

I dig my fingers into the dirty beige carpet beneath my hands and take a breath.

"I think men that go to strip clubs are pathetic."

A nod from Zayden.

"Have you ever been to a strip club before?" I ask.

Slight smile.

"Yup."

"So then ... I think you're pathetic."

I sit up straight and lift my chin. Zayden just keeps nodding at me.

"More than likely, yeah."

"I feel like ... I don't want to give monetary value to my body." I put my hands together over my chest, my loose red peasant top ruffling with the motion. "To me, it ... there is no amount of money that's worth *me*. I am priceless. I am ... my value is more than just dollars."

"Exactly." Zayden snaps his fingers and then leans forward, putting his palms against the floor, his face getting *way* too close to mine for comfort. My heart starts to pound and sweat trickles down my spine. "So don't think of it that way then. Stripping is a job, that's it. It doesn't define you, just like, say, working as a soulless insurance salesmen doesn't. You can either suck it up and bang it out, or you can't. Don't torture yourself, Smarty-Pants."

"I don't exactly have a choice, Zayden."

"That's a goddamn lie," he says, dropping to his belly on

the carpet and turning his face towards the baby. She giggles and reaches out a chubby hand to slap at his face. He sticks his tongue out and she smiles a goofy smile. "There's always a choice. Sometimes it's between a few shitty things—like pretty much every presidential election ever—but that doesn't we can't make up our own minds about it anyway. From what I figure, sometimes the "bad" choice is really the harder choice."

"I have fifty bucks. Literally. Exactly fifty, and only because I drove over to Nelly's house and threatened to beat up her boyfriend."

Zayden pauses, pushing himself up onto his elbows and looking up at me.

His smile's almost as goofy as the baby's.

"You go girl. Tougher than you look, huh?"

"What's that supposed to mean?" I scoot away from Zayden and drop to my tummy, so that our faces are at the same level. I tell myself I'm doing it for the baby, but really I just want to look this guy in the face. "How do I look?"

Zayden pauses and stares right at me, tilting his head to the side. I notice that today, there are stars shaved into the short side of his hair. They weren't there yesterday. *Did he do that himself?* Huh.

"Soft," he says and then lifts his palms up in surrender, elbows pressed into the carpet. "Not in a bad way. You just look ... I don't know, young? But maybe like you're trying too hard not to be."

I pinch my brows together as Sadie moves in between us and starts heading for the small table against the wall. Zayden scoots back and picks her up, depositing her on the opposite side of the blanket and letting her have at it again.

"Trying too hard?" I ask, doing my best not to be offended. I asked his opinion, and now I'm getting it. I can't complain if I don't like the results. "I just want to do the right thing."

"No such thing," Zayden says as he puts his hands on his hips and watches Sadie in her peach and white outfit, the lavender flower headband wobbling as she starts her journey from the beginning. "The right thing, I mean. It's a myth. All

BAD NANNY

we can do is try to walk our own path and not screw up anybody else's. That's life, man."

"According to Zayden Roth," I say as I stand up and check the time on my phone. I have a little while before I have to get Grace, so I may as well use it to get my head together. Maybe I'll put on some music and lock myself in the upstairs bedroom? Let the sweet trill of rock music wash all my pain away. "I'm not sure how valid your opinion is, based on the music you listen to."

He swings a look my way and then winks at me.

"And what do you listen to? Rap? Country? Where's your pedestal, Smarty-Pants?"

"Rock. Metal. Punk."

"Ooooh, angry music. Gotcha."

"Well, I think the music you listen to is shallow, technically uncomplicated, and so drenched in mainstream bullshit that any message the words could've delivered is basically null and void."

"Shots fired," Zayden says, slicking two fingers across the shaved side of his head. "But oh, I guess that was a miss, Smarty-Pants." He winks at me again and I feel an unwanted warmth rush through me. Whoa. I know I'm in trouble when I start wondering what those two fingers would feel like slipping inside of me.

Yikes.

"I'm going to take a shower," I say, grabbing my purse and heading up the stairs.

"Godspeed, Brooke Overland," Zay says as he flops back down in front of the baby, lifting her up and getting her into a sitting position. Then he takes her arms in his tattooed fingers and lowers her back to the floor, helping her sit up and then putting her down again. He makes weird sounds as he does it and she giggles like crazy, like this is the best game ever.

I watch him for a few seconds and then retreat into the bathroom—and lock the door behind me.

It's not Zayden that I'm scared of though, it's me and what I might do if I get my hands on him again.

CHAPTER 13
ZAYDEN ROTH

As predicted, Sadie conks out about fifteen minutes after Brooke heads upstairs.

I get her situated in the portable crib I brought over with me, making sure she's situated on her back before I pop the baby monitor on the table next to her and head over to the couch to sit down for a minute.

Whew.

Talk about a tough job. I've decided never to make fun of Mercedes again when she flops down into her computer chair and moans through the mic about how tired she is. Learned my lesson here, folks. Taking care of kids is fucking hard; I'd much rather pierce tits for a living.

I check my phone and find a duck face selfie from Kitty on the Strip, her fingers raised in a peace sign, her top low-cut and enticing as hell. She's cropped the damn thing, so I can't see anything but a tantalizing line of cleavage disappearing into the frame.

I stare at her for a minute and sigh. Now's not exactly the best time to start up a sexting session, is it? I tap my red Doc on the floor and then get up, slipping the baby monitor into my back pocket and heading up the stairs to find Brooke.

"Hey," I say as I knock on the door and wait for a response.

BAD NANNY

"You want me to pick up all the kids?" Bella and Kinzie go to the same school, so there's not really much point in us both going all the way out there. "Brooke?"

I tap my knuckles against the wood and then reach down for the knob.

It's unlocked.

I slip inside and find the room empty; the sound of the shower is audible through the bathroom door, so I sit down to wait, crossing my legs at the ankle and leaning back into the bed. Hard to believe that I had her naked underneath me the day before yesterday—and that I turned it all down.

I dick around on my phone for a few minutes, waiting for the water of the shower to die away, for the click of the lock. When Brooke emerges, I sit up and find her in nothing but a towel, her long dark hair hanging down her back, cheeks flushed from the warmth in the bathroom.

"You want me to pick up all the kids?" I ask and she jumps, screaming and whirling, the towel flying to the floor with the motion as she slams her body into the dresser behind her.

The sight is fucking swag as hell. Brooke's body is a dream, this curvy slice of perfection, her chest heaving with surprise, eyes wide, dark hair hanging over her breasts like some kind of wild woman. Oh yeah. I'd sure like to show her *my* wild side.

Wait. No. Nope. Didn't I, like, already decide this girl was off-limits?

"What the ... FUCK?!" she yells as she dives down and retrieves the towel, tucking it up against her breasts. The motion hides all the good stuff, but I can still see an intriguing amount of flesh on either side, including the perfectly round shape of her hip. "Are you *insane*? Don't you have any sense of propriety? Get the hell out of here!"

"Propriety? Big word there, Smarty. I have no idea what it means." I stand up and brush my shirt off while Brooke turns and hefts up a small wooden box, flashing me the ripe shape of her ass. When she turns back, she pulls back her arm and launches the box my direction.

I duck, and the thing hits the wall, opening with a spray of pennies across the floor.

"Out. Now. Leave." She points her arm at the door, panting hard and staring at me with that intense gaze of hers. I shrug my shoulders, not sure what the big deal is here, and start out, pausing next to her to smile.

"It's not like I even saw any of the good stuff." I make an X across my chest as she watches me and then turn back towards the door, stepping into the hallway and cringing when the wood slams closed behind me. Damn. Guess I made a mistake right there?

Whoops.

I start down the hallway when Brooke opens the door in a loose tank and shorts, her nipples hard beneath the thin layer of black fabric.

"Just because I'm stripping tonight doesn't give you the right to peep at me naked, okay?"

"Of course it doesn't," I say as I glance over my shoulder and wrinkle my nose. "I just didn't expect you to come charging out of there with your towel flapping. It's my bad, sorry."

She watches me for a minute and then sweeps her fingers through the tousled wet hair on top of her head. With a deep breath, Brooke moves down the hallway with softly padding steps as I turn to look at her. She pauses in front of me for a moment and then lifts her arms up and puts them around my neck, lifting her mouth to mine and sliding her tongue between my lips.

I have, like, literally no idea what's happening.

But I also suck at turning down pretty girls.

"You do this a lot, right?" Brooke asks as she pulls back a fraction. I cock a pierced brow.

"Huh?" I know I should push her away, demand an explanation or something, but ... I only have so much self-control. "What do you mean?"

"Casual sex. You do this a lot, don't you? So you should be good at it."

"Uh, this is kind of my thing. I don't mean to brag or anything, but ... I'm hella boss at sex."

"Good."

Brooke pushes her lips against mine, searing heat into my mouth as we stumble back and I push her into the wall, dropping my palms to the boring beige walls on either side of her head. Wet hair tickles my face as we slant our mouths together, tongues slick and hot, chasing the ember of heat in my blood into a fucking bonfire.

Oh, hell yes.

This is wrong on *so* many levels, but she came onto me. I'm pretty much helpless to resist.

Brooke's nails dig into my skin and I feel the sharp bite of pain morph into pleasure, channeling a line straight down into my cock. I got diamond in my jeans, baby. Holy Christ.

I push my body harder into Brooke's and she groans, opening up to me, letting me slip a leg between her thighs. Without any prompting, I feel her grind her body against the leg of my jeans, pressing hard as she rocks her hips in a frantic rhythm.

In the back of my mind, I wonder where the hell this came from, but I don't really give two craps. I haven't had sex in a week, haven't even gotten the chance to touch myself. My balls are tight and they hurt, and fuck, this girl is smokin' hot.

"Bedroom?" I mouth against her lips. There's no way I'm taking some chick's virginity up against a wall like this. No way. That's too messed up. If I'm going to run with this, I'm going to do a good job at it.

"Mmm," Brooke moans, gasping as I pull my leg away and cup her heat with my hand, feeling a dampness in the crotch of her shorts that has nothing to do with the shower she just took.

"You absolutely positive you want to do this?" I ask and she nods, letting me cup the side of her face with my hand. "This isn't just a moment of panic that you'll regret in the morning?"

"I think if I don't do this, I'll regret it in the morning." Brooke takes a deep breath and sweeps long hair back over her shoulders. "Listen, I was with this one guy for three years. He said that … well, he wanted us to save our virginities for our wedding night."

I cock a brow at that one. Huh. I saved my virginity for my best friend's older sister, waited until I was fifteen years old. Pretty proud of myself for that one.

"Anyway, my point is, I've been holding off on this for all the *right* reasons." A pause as she looks down the hallway and then back at my face. If she's thinking what I'm thinking, then she knows we have just about an hour before we have to start picking up kiddies.

A tight timeline to ease someone out of their virginity, but I'll manage.

"So why not do this for the wrong ones? Please. I know you don't know me, but that doesn't even really matter, does it?" Brooke makes eye contact with me and holds my gaze. I can see her, but it's like everything is hazy, like there's a film over my vision that's obscured by lust. I want her so bad, I can barely breathe. "Please."

Come on. Those big brown Bambi eyes, those hot swollen lips (both sets), the way her chest is rising and falling with a strained need.

I just can't say no to any of that.

"Come on." I reach down and take Brooke's wrist, pulling her into the bedroom and popping the baby monitor out of my pocket, setting it on a dresser so I'll be able to hear if Sadie wakes up. *God, I hope not.*

I kick off my shoes and peel my socks away, tossing them aside while Brooke watches and crosses her arms over her belly. When I stand back up, I drag her onto the bed next to me and lay so that we're facing each other.

One of my hands reaches out and takes her gently by the back of the neck, encouraging her to move in closer, press our bodies together. When our mouths meet this time, it's like there's an uptick in the fervor, a frantic swelling of need. I tell myself that's because I've been tromping through the Sahara Desert of sex here, but who the hell knows.

My hand drops to Brooke's hip, fingers dipping under her

shorts to find that natural handle that all chicks have, that curve of the pelvis bone that feels like it was made to be grabbed. Brooke groans when I squeeze her there, tugging her even closer. I let her drape a leg over mine, putting my thigh up against the hot heat of her pussy again. This time, I encourage her to move against me, guiding her with my hand, pushing my leg up tight so she has enough resistance to get off.

Her chest pushes into mine, nipples taut and perky, scraping me through the fabric of my shirt. *Time for that shit to go. Buh-bye.* I break our mouths apart for a split second to strip down my upper half. Brooke follows suit without any prompting, exposing the full ripeness of her breasts to me.

I can't help it; I am a boob connoisseur, baby.

My hands cup each one of the full mounds, thumbs teasing the pink nipples into a red rosy blush, tightening them up to fine points as she moans and lets her head fall back. I don't think I've ever been with a girl whose hair is this long. It's exciting, the way it drapes down her back, curls against the pillows in a chocolate swirl.

My lips quirk into a smile as I slide a hand around to Brooke's back and pull her close, dropping my mouth to her breasts and tasting the sweet warmth of her skin. She smells like soap and fruit, and her body is unbelievably soft. God, yes. I seriously don't understand why all women aren't gay. Why would anyone in their right mind want to be with a guy? I mean, eww. Chicks are *so* much hotter.

I kiss my way up between her breasts, making my way to Brooke's throat and tasting her pulse with my tongue. It's beating so frantically, it's a wonder she's not passing out from the rush.

When my right hand sneaks down her belly and dips into her shorts, Brooke tenses a little. I make sure to kiss her, drag her mind back to her lips while I slide my middle finger between the scalding warmth of her folds.

She makes a small noise against my mouth, scooting closer, her body leaning against mine.

I grin against Brooke's mouth as I slick my finger up to her clit and circle around it while she gasps in these hiccupy little breaths that I've never seen from a chick before. It's beyond fucking cute.

"Oh, I like that," I say as I lean into her, pushing her gently back into the pillows as I position myself above her and gasp when she grabs onto my nipple rings and pulls. "Look at you, Smarty-Pants."

I pause for a moment as Brooke explores my chest with her hands, rubbing her palms over the silver piercings as I run my tongue along my lower lip.

"Be as rough as you want with 'em," I say as I drop my mouth to her ear and bite gently on the lobe. "Do whatever you want." Brooke takes my words to heart, yanking hard on my nipple rings as I grunt and shove a single finger into her.

There's a ragged burst of breath as her hands grip my biceps and she thrusts her hips up against me.

"You are so fucking tight," I whisper as I work that single finger in and out, teasing Brooke's slickness as I struggle to breathe against the tightness in my balls and cock. I haven't even put it in the girl yet and I feel like I'm ready to burst. "And your clit's swollen as hell. What were you up to in that shower of yours?"

I'm just talking dirty for fun, but I guess Brooke's one step ahead of me.

"I was touching myself," she whispers and I groan, dropping my forehead down and adjusting my hand, so I can get a second finger inside of her. She accepts it easily enough, but her breath flickers and flutters as she digs her nails into the tattoos on my upper arms.

My thumb slicks up to her clit and I give her the signature Zayden Roth treatment, guaranteed to make any woman come in record time. My fingers press tight against the upper walls of her pussy, teasing that special warm spot right at the opening. They call it the G-spot, but personally, I like to call it the *Z-spot*. It sounds lame, I know, but if you were in Brooke's place, you wouldn't think so.

With shaking hands, Brooke slides her fingers down my

belly and struggles with my belt, working my pants open so she can get her hand back to the spot it was in two days ago. This time, her touch is a little less frantic, but just as unsure.

"Grip harder," I whisper against her ear and she groans, biting her lip as I push my fingers in to the knuckle. I close my eyes as she works my shaft, breathing in the sweet smell of her hair, tasting the soft flutter of her pulse until the tightening down below matches up.

That's when I know she's ready for me.

I withdraw my hand slowly and cup her bare pussy tight before I draw back and stand up, shoving my jeans to the floor and then bending down to fish the condom out of my back pocket. Yeah, I'm a dickhead; I always keep one with me for emergencies. Never know when the ballsy blues are gonna strike, right?

"This is so fucking crazy," Brooke mumbles as she shoves her shorts down and tosses them aside, sitting up and curling her legs to the side. Her long hair drapes down and pools in her lap. "You do this thing all the time? Sleep with strangers?"

I shrug my shoulders as I stand up and let her get a good, long look at me.

"They're only strangers until you sleep with them," I joke with a wiggle of my brows. "And then you're just *lovers*." I lean forward and put my hands on the side of the bed. "You ready for me to be your lover, baby?"

"Is your ... are your *balls* pierced?" I stand back up and let Brooke have a good, long look. I've got quite the collection down there: tattoos all around my hips, my inner thighs, my cock, my balls. I've got a Prince Albert—a silver ring through the head—and a frenum piercing which goes through the tissue on the underside of my shaft. Can't be a body piercer without displaying my craft, right? "Oh my God." Brooke points out the two silver metal pieces on my cock. "My favorite drummer ever has one of those. Or maybe both. Can't remember which."

She looks up at me and then bites the inside of her cheek.

"Am I going to feel those? Will they hurt?"

"Oh, you'll feel 'em, babe, but in a good way." I grin and flash the condom in my fingers. "Ready for this?" I ask and Brooke nods, her mouth slightly parted, eyes flickering with desire. She watches me as I climb onto the bed on my knees, tearing open the condom and slicking the lubed up latex down my shaft.

Brooke puts her hands on my chest and opens her legs for me, letting me kneel between her perfect, white thighs.

Oh, yeah. This is gonna be great.

Brooke and I make eye contact as I slide my tongue along my lower lip and then kiss her, enjoying the warm feel of her hands on my chest as we relax back into the pillows, warm sunshine leaking through the peach colored curtains above the bed.

My right hand cups Brooke's left breast, kneading the flesh as she makes more of those crazy sexy small sounds against my mouth, breath coming frantic and wild as I tease her folds with my cock, giving her a taste of what's to come. She spreads her knees wide for me, putting her palms on either one of my cheeks. For whatever reason, that particular move makes me crazy horny.

I can't wait anymore; I think we both need this.

The head of my cock pushes up against the tight heat of Brooke's body as she sucks in a massive breath, and I thrust my hips forward, filling her up with a wild groan. *Whoa, baby.* I feel like I'm getting the tightest, warmest, best goddamn hug around my cock.

"Holy sweet baby Jesus," I whisper as she gasps and squeezes my face between her hands. "Aw, Brooke." I lay there for a moment to let her get settled, get used to the feel of my body inside of hers. This is so my favorite part of sex, watching a woman's face as she takes me in, gets off on the hard pressure of my cock. This is my reason for living right here, to give chicks pleasure like this. "No pain?"

"I said I was a virgin, not that I didn't masturbate," she whispers, still carrying some of that attitude hiding behind her fresh-face. "I have dildos bigger than you."

BAD NANNY

"Bullshit." I thrust my hips and her cheeks flush warm, head tilting back and pelvis rising to meet mine. I thought I was going to have to move slow, but I guess maybe she's alright. Not that she isn't tight, but clearly, there's nothing stopping me from giving this my all. I move back, pulling myself almost completely out of her and watching as her mouth pinches tight, hips straining to take me in.

Brooke yanks my nipple rings as punishment and I hiss under my breath, thrusting my shaft deep and hard, bumping our bodies together. She puts her soft mouth up to the side of my face and kisses my jaw, her breath like honey and fucking clovers and shit.

I'm in goddamn heaven right now.

Our mouths meet again, Brooke's straying to the side to snag one of my lip piercings in her teeth, taking the tiny piece of metal and swirling her tongue around it. When her fingers slide up my neck and start playing with my hair, I am so done for.

My body moves of its own accord, the long length of Brooke's rubbing against me every which where, teasing every nerve in my body with her soft, round curves, drawing me into her orbit. Did I say I hated Eureka? Fuck that. I was lying. I *love* it here.

Maybe being this chick's pro bono nanny won't be so bad?

Brooke's fingers trace the stars I shaved into the right side of my head, her other hand tangling in my hair as she encourages me to pay special attention to her neck, nibbling my way along the smooth flesh and breathing in her fruity scent. I still have no idea how or why we ended up in here doing this, but I'm pretty fucking grateful for it.

The soft creak of the bed, the little nook where our bodies fit together in the dip of the mattress, the sunshine on my back. It's sweaty and warm and weirdly intimate (not usually my thing), but I don't let that freak me out. I embrace it, dropping a hand to Brooke's ass and encouraging her to lift one of her legs up to give me deeper access.

When she gasps and flutters around me, I *know* there's not a dildo in the world that can match my movements. Hot, long strokes, diving deep and drawing all the way out. That's my style, at least until I feel Brooke's heartbeat start to pick up. That's when I drop our pelvises back together and grind up and forward, making sure her clit is moving along with me.

Brooke's voice raises up in a lilting whimper, her hips frantically churning to meet mine, her nails digging into my skin. She's too far gone to kiss me now, her lips parted and her head tilted back into the mound of pillows. When I'm afraid she's going to outlast me, I reach down and slip two fingers in with my cock, stretching her just enough that she loses it, thrashes, comes hard all around me, squeezing me so tight that I don't have to work to finish myself. I just slow and relax into her, coming hard and lowering my body against hers as we both try to breathe past the pleasure and the swirl of happy hormones clogging our brains.

It's always in this moment that I feel like I can really see everything clearly, when the world is crisp and sharp and unclouded.

I look down at Brooke and I'm not sure exactly what it is I'm seeing right now.

Who ... who is this chick I just nailed into the mattress? A twenty-two year old virgin with two kids? What am I *doing*? This isn't a woman I picked up at the shop, some girl who's clearly on vacation with her friends that wants a *what happens in Vegas* story.

No.

This is something else completely.

I grab the base of the condom and roll off of Brooke, laying there with my arm across my forehead, my eyes focused on the ceiling above the bed. The sex was awesome, and wow, Brooke feels good. But ... didn't I tell myself no on this one?

I glance over at her, looking for any sign of tears or disappointment or frustration. Instead, she's also looking at the ceiling, her chest rising and falling with rapid breaths.

"Thanks," she says, turning her head to look at me with a small smile. "That was great."

I smile back and feel a small amount of relief wash over me.

"Good. Wouldn't want to disappointment you on your first time."

Brooke stares at me for a moment, her lips twitching.

"So ... can you get out now?"

I blink at her several times before raising both brows. Is this chick kicking me out *again*?

"Time for you to pick up the kids," she says, sitting up and sliding off the bed.

I watch her disappear into the bathroom, that perfect ass flashing as she moves, before I groan and reach down to pull the condom off my dick.

Right. Kids.

So much for my after sex glow.

CHAPTER 14
BROOKE OVERLAND

Whoa.

I wait until I hear the sound of an engine before sneaking out of the room and into the hallway. I slide along the wall like some kind of hero in an action flick, peeking past the curtains until Zayden pulls the minivan out of the driveway.

My entire body is on fire right now, tingling from my toes to the crown of my head. The sensations running through me are hard to explain, like the pleasure I get from masturbating ... but different. I feel alive, vibrant, like I can do fucking anything right now.

In the back of my mind, I know all I'm feeling are residual shots of oxytocin from the orgasm, but I don't care. I feel too good to care. *I just let some guy I met four days ago take my V-card on a shopping spree.*

Remaining balance ... zero.

I put my fingers up to my temples and press hard, breathing out as I shuffle back to my sister's—now my—room. When I came upstairs to shower, I couldn't stop thinking about Zayden or the way he played with that baby like it was his own. I think some girly hormones are at fault here because ... he's just so goddamn cute with that kid. Maybe it's some basic biological instinct telling me that he'd make a good dad or something?

BAD NANNY

I ignore those feelings and try to let myself just enjoy this moment. I got what I wanted, didn't I? Going to the club and stripping tonight ... I'm still not excited about it, but I feel better. Zayden saw me first; Zayden slept with me first. He might be a stranger, but he's a nice guy and at least I get to know that *I* made the choice to sleep with him.

Oh. And did I mention it was great? Beyond great.

It was exactly what I was hoping it would be, all this time. Makes me not feel so bad about waiting it out like this. Suddenly I wish I was back in Berkeley and Zay was some guy from one of my classes. Maybe we could date for a while or something? I could hit a party with my roommate and tell her all about my encounter with Zay's perfect inked flesh.

But instead, I have to do my hair and paint my face and get ready for tonight.

This time, I'm not going to be late. I'm going to show up on time, and I'm going to do what I have to do to make money. I'm not going to take crap from anybody, I'm not going to get fired, and I sure as hell am not going to let anybody touch me.

It's going to be okay. Everything is.

Because I'm going to make sure it turns out that way.

My night at the strip club is weird. That's the only way to describe it. Or maybe I feel weird because of what happened with Zayden and me. It's like there's this secret surprise waiting inside of me that I want to tell everyone about except that there's no one around that cares or wants to listen. I shoot some texts to my friends back in Berkeley, but it's just not the same without being there in person.

The manager of the club tells me to do exactly what I did during the audition. According to my friends, some places in So Cal were willing to hire girls on the spot based on looks alone, but I had to actually *try out* for a job here at the Top Hat.

It's the only club in town and most of the girls look like they've actually taken dance lessons before. At least it's clean inside, and the bouncers look big and brutal.

The crowd is pretty much nonexistent, and some of the other dancers complain, but I feel myself breathe a sigh of relief, dressing up in my black teddy, matching thong, and the towering heels I bought for a Halloween party once. Oddly enough, my roommate back in Berkeley thought it would be super awesome to take pole dancing classes, so in a freak turn of luck, I know exactly what I'm doing.

Afterwards, I don't feel as bad as I thought I would. I mean, it's not great and it's definitely not my dream job, but at least bullshit and harassment aren't tolerated by the bouncers or the management. I can tell customers to fuck off if they get too rowdy and not worry about being fired. Honestly, in another job, it might be worse having to deal with subtle misogynistic crap all the time.

I think I can do this—at least until I get my degree. Then I'll be able to get a job as a biostatistician and make a cool hundred grand a year to start. I might have to move the girls at that point, but at least things should be more stable then.

As I'm driving home after, I let the radio play and listen to some stupid pop songs instead of my usual hardcore stuff. I have no idea why, probably because of Zayden or something, but I'm definitely not in a place to psychoanalyze that right now.

I pull into the driveway next to his minivan and take a deep breath.

Please don't let this be weird, I think as I climb out and make my way to the front door. I let myself in with my key, finding the baby asleep in the portable crib, baby monitor sitting nearby. I don't see Zayden at first, but then I notice that the back door is cracked and move over to peek outside.

He's sitting on the tire swing that's strung up in the back, hunched over the glowing screen of his phone. As soon as he hears my heels on the damp wood of the deck, he glances up and gives a little wave, hopping off and jogging across the yard.

"Well." Zayden claps his hands together in a prayer position and puts the tips of his fingers against his lips, eyes wide as he looks up at me. "How was it?"

I pause and swing my keys in a circle on my finger, trying to figure out how to put my night into words ... and then direct those words at the guy standing in front of me. I never thought *I* would be in the position of having slept with the nanny. Isn't that spot usually reserved for old guys smack dab in the center of a midlife crisis?

"It didn't break me the way I thought it would," I say as Zayden drops his hands and comes up the steps. The guy has a serious personal space issue, getting way too close for comfort. When he pauses in front of me, I realize he's got either blood or ketchup splattered across his shirt. I hope it's the latter, but knowing how kids are, it could go either way. "Everyone okay?" I ask as I point at the stain and Zay glances down, wrinkling his nose. The silver ring through his nostril winks at me in the moonlight.

"Define *okay*. I think Kinzie's going to be the fucking death of me. But this ... to be straight-up honest with you, I haven't got a goddamn clue what it is." Zayden lifts his shirt up, sniffs it, then shrugs his broad shoulders loosely, twisting the fabric up to glance at his bare chest underneath. The sight of all that skin brings back thought obliterating memories. "Ah, okay. Cat scratch." I notice a dark red gash between Zay's pecs. "Well that explains the hell outta that, huh?"

"The kids were okay for you?" I ask, hoping to God that he'll drop his shirt back into place. The whole sex thing is awkward enough as it is without him flashing me like that.

"Your kids?" he asks as he finally folds his white t-shirt over the wound and raises his pierced eyebrow. "Your two are, like, fucking seraphic compared to those other ones." Zayden pauses and nibbles his lip for a moment. "Except for the baby. I like the baby."

"Good, good." I stop swinging my keys and clutch them in the heat of my palm, remembering suddenly how good

Zayden's nipples felt when I was teasing them with my fingers. *Damn.* My body feels addicted to his, like I could go another round or two or seven.

"So," he says gesturing as he moves over to the back door and leans against it to open it for me. "Tell me about your big night. I want all the deets."

"Deets?" I raise my brows but slip past Zayden into the kitchen. The most logical, rational part of me wants to tell him to go home again, but that's not fair to the kids. He's doing me a huge favor here and he shouldn't have to wake up a six month old, two four year olds, and a seven year old just because I'm having trouble controlling my hormones.

"Yup. Deets. The down and dirty. The skinny. I want it all." Zayden gestures at me with his tattooed fingers in a *come on* gesture, the word *EASY* flashing upside down at me from his knuckles. I watch him as he turns and opens the fridge, grabbing a plate of premade peanut butter and jelly sandwiches. He plops them down on the table between us as I stare, not entirely sure what's happening right now. "Milk?" he asks as he lifts up a jug. I nod slowly and pull out a seat as Zay brings two glasses over and sets them down, yanking out a chair and spinning it around so he can lean forward and cross his arms over the back.

Zay stares at me from his pale green eyes for a long, quiet moment before reaching forward and peeling the plastic wrap off the plate. He grabs a sandwich with the crust cut off and hands it to me. I take it gingerly and look down, wondering when the last time I had a PB&J was.

"There weren't that many people in the club," I say as I realize there's light music trickling into the room. It's some Avril Lavigne song that makes me wrinkle my nose. "The other girls were complaining the whole time, but honestly, it was a huge relief."

"They teach you to dance or did you just shake your shit?" Zay asks with a smile that clearly says his words are a joke. I take a tentative bite of my sandwich and chew it carefully. Perfect jelly to peanut butter ratio. Nice.

BAD NANNY

"Believe it or not, when I lived in So Cal, my friends thought it'd be hot to take pole dancing classes." I shrug my shoulders. "Guess it's coming in handy."

"Oooh. Well, I'd pay to see that." He winks at me and grabs a sandwich, shoving half of it in his mouth before he starts chewing. One more bite and that sucker's gone completely. I nibble at mine as he drains the entire glass of milk in one go. "So ... it went well then?"

"It went okay. I would never want my nieces to have to go through anything like this, but yeah. It was fine. I can do this —for a little while anyway." I keep chewing on my sandwich as Zay taps his fingers in time to the shitty pop music that's playing. I guess we're not going to mention the sex which is good because I have no idea how to bring it up or if I even *should* bring it up. "Why are you being so nice to me?" I ask, not because I'm trying to be rude. I just don't get it. This guy, he doesn't owe me anything at all.

Zay tilts his head at me and then runs the fingers of his right hand over the shaved side of his head.

"Why wouldn't I be? You want me to act like a dick?"

"No, I was just curious." Zayden shrugs and then laces his fingers together behind his head.

"I know girls say they like assholes and all that, but really, ya get more flies with honey, Miss Overland." Another wicked slow smile and a wink. "I've never had any trouble getting women by being friendly, you know? But since we had sex this afternoon, I can be a prick if you want."

I throw the last corner of my sandwich at him, but all it does is make him laugh. I figure it takes a lot to faze this guy.

"Can I see your work attire?" he asks me, eyes twinkling, leaning forward and peering at my tank and jeans with a burning expression that makes me squirm. "I mean, if I'm spending the night and you're spending the night and you did just let me take your virginity ..."

"Are you ... serious?" I ask, but I can't help the warm flush that takes over my body. I feel my thighs suddenly clenching tight and my breath fluttering with excitement. My turn to lean forward over the table. "You want to sleep together ... again?"

"I don't even snore." Zayden sits up and lifts two fingers in some kind of weird salute. "Swear to God. You can ask any of my ex-girlfriends."

I stare at him across the table, and I have no clue what to say. This guy's in town for, what, another week or so? And he's my nanny. My *unpaid* nanny. But he really is hot and I'm eager to try all sorts of other things in the bedroom ...

Before I can answer, the baby starts fussing and Zay gets up from the table, patting me on the head as he passes.

"Be right back," he says as I lean forward and try to sneak a peek at him through the pass-through window into the dining area. I catch sight of Zay's dark head bending down and standing up with Sadie clutched to his chest. He moves away for a moment and I hear some rustling before he appears in the kitchen and flicks on the tap, a bottle clutched in his hand. "Guess somebody's into an early morning snack today."

I stand up, my chair sliding across the kitchen floor as my heart pounds in my chest.

I want to have sex with Zayden again, but I'm not sure I can handle it right now.

"I'm completely worn-out," I say as I take a few backwards steps towards the dining room/living room area. Zayden turns and watches me as I slink away, raising his brows at me. "You'll take the kids to school in the morning?"

"Nanny Zay to the rescue," he says with a smile. I don't wait around to see what else he has to say, retreating into my new bedroom and closing the door ... but not locking it.

I kind of hope he barges in again, like he did earlier.

He doesn't. But that doesn't keep me from dreaming about it.

CHAPTER 15
ZAYDEN ROTH

This Brooke girl is tricksy, tricksy, tricksy. *Like a fox.*

I smile as I wrestle a screaming twin into his car seat. Even this many days in, I can't tell which one is which. Mercedes and Rob decided to name the boys *Michael* and *Ike*. Like they somehow missed the joke, right? Mike and Ike. Like the candies, those little colored chewy things? You know what I'm talking about.

"Listen up, candy cakes," I tell Mike (or Ike), "we all have to grow up someday. Boy, this is *your* day." The kid just screams as Kinzie and Bella whine and stick their fingers in their ears. The little blond one, Grace, is already asleep. "Sorry, bud, but you're going to preschool today if it kills me. Uncle Zay needs a fucking break."

"Curse jar," Kinzie screams over her brother's shouts as I move back and bump right into Brooke. If I said the collision of our bodies didn't make me hard as a rock, that'd be the biggest fucking lie I ever did tell.

"Off to class?" I ask and Brooke nods, a pair of black glasses on her face that I've not seen before. I push them up her nose as she bats my hand away. "You wear glasses?"

"Contacts normally, but my eyes are too tired today. That,

and I have a quiz. I have to be able to focus completely on this."

"Well, if it helps, you look all studious and shit. Very sexy." I gesture at her wrinkled black button-up and slacks, at the long beige coat she's wearing. Brooke gives me a weird look and slides by, heading to her car as I watch. Hmm. My usual tactics don't seem to work very well on this chick.

I wave good-bye as she pulls down the driveway, wondering if she really just used me yesterday or if I might be able to convince her to give sex with me another go.

You're making a serious mistake here, bro, I tell myself, but I brush the thought off immediately. Nah. Nah. I know what I'm doing. Like I haven't been in this situation a million times before. I have more ex-girlfriends than I do fingers and toes. Not a biggie. Either Brooke wants to play the friends with benefits game with me, or she doesn't.

"Can we please *gooo*," Kinzie whines from inside the van.

I roll my eyes and climb in, starting up some Hailee Steinfeld as we back down the driveway to start the arduous journey to preschool ... and then kindergarten ... and then elementary school. And then home to feed the baby and read books made out of cardboard.

Ah, what sweet hell is this?

"Are you out of your fucking mind?" Rob screams at me as I pull the cell away from my ear and feel myself frowning. "*You* are not a goddamn *nanny*, Zay. What the hell do you think you're doing with this girl?"

"Um, first of all, I'm doing her a *favor* here. Second, I didn't tell you all of this, so you could scream at me. You know, Kinzie's the worst one of them all. She kicks and spits and *bites* me. What the hell is up with that?"

"Listen, Zayden," Rob starts as I flop down on Brooke's

couch and accidentally sit on a chihuahua. The weirdest part of all is that it doesn't seem to mind. I lift my butt up and push it away from the center couch cushion. "Kinzie has hyperactive blah blah blah blah blah." Of course, Rob doesn't really say all those blahs, but who the hell cares *what* he's actually talking about. Not this guy right here.

"Personally, I think she needs a spanking with a wooden spoon, kind of like the ones Mom used to give us as kids."

"You lay one finger on my daughter, Zay, and I swear to God, I'll—"

"Look, before you finish that sentence," I start as I lean forward and put my elbows on my knees. "You'd best consider that I left my house, my life, my job, and dragged my and my hairless cat's butts all the way up here for *you*. I'm not gonna spank the kid myself, but I sure as hell am giving her time-outs."

"Time-outs don't work with Kinzie," Rob states firmly. I can imagine his red beard wagging, bushy brows drawing together as he slams his fist into the palm of his hand for emphasis. "We've tried that, Zayden. Don't you think we know our own daughter?"

I don't answer that question. First off, because I'm pretty sure it's rhetorical and second, because I think the answer is *no*. Sometimes people get too close to a situation to see what's really going on. I figure that must be the case with Kinzie because that kid is *insane*.

"You do know you named your sons after a really gross box of candy, right?"

"Huh? Zay, what the fuck are you talking about?"

"Ah, and now I know why the curse jar was already half filled when I got here. Nice one, bro."

"Listen, Zayden. You need to tell that girl you don't know shit about children and get the hell out of there. Using somebody's kids, their desperation, to get laid is despicable. I thought even *you* were above a stunt like that."

I feel my jaw clench tight. Rob doesn't get it, not at all. Never has.

"I'm not doing this to get laid—" although it makes for a nice aside to the whole situation "—so clearly you're missing the point. Did you hear me? This girl doesn't have anybody else."

"This isn't your problem, Zayden. Take the kids home. We'll be back in a week and a half, and then you can go home to Las Vegas and wait another three years to visit with your family."

"You know what? Fuck you, Rob. How's that sound?"

I hang up the phone before he can answer, rising to my feet and running my fingers through the hair on the left side of my head. My brother is a serious goddamn asshole. Wow. And he wonders why I never visit. Ain't a mystery to anyone but him.

My new favorite person in the world is this baby. She smiles at me and laughs, but she doesn't complain unless she's hungry or has a dirty diaper. Seriously huge improvement over everyone else in my life. That chick Kitty got pissed at me for skipping out on our last session and sent me a text of her flipping me off. Oh well. There's always another pretty little tattooed chick walking into the shop, leaning over the glass counter and flashing me her tits.

I pick Sadie up out of her crib with a yawn—on my part—and sit us both down on the couch, a stack of books at my side. If I'm going to be here, I might as well hang out with the kid, right? Maybe one day she'll actually like me—unlike her older sister. Wouldn't hurt to have some family that cared whether I lived or died.

The first book I grab is splashed with color and bits of fuzzy fabric that Sadie latches onto with fervor, eating the corners of the book as much as she looks at it. Good for her. At least one of us is having a good time right now.

Somewhere deep down, I know that I'm waiting for Brooke to show back up, sweep in here in that non-style style of hers, look at me like I'm both the biggest mistake of her life—and the most intriguing. It's an interesting dichotomy, that's for sure.

"What do you think of Uncle Zay's new lady friend?" I ask

BAD NANNY

Sadie as she slaps her hands on the book and laughs. I lean back and nod. "Yep. That's how I feel, too. Now all I gotta do is convince her that I'm not the enemy, you know? I think a week spent in each other's arms would do us both a lot of good, don't you?"

Sadie babbles something back at me as the sound of a rattling car engine pulls into the driveway.

Yes, ma'am. Here we go.

I lean back casually and wait for Brooke to unlock the door.

"Hey, how was class?" I ask as I glance over my shoulder and watch her step inside ... with a guy on her heels. Huh. Who the hell is this dude?

"Fine, thanks." Brooke closes the door and comes over to stand at the end of the coffee table, pushing her glasses up her nose. I notice then that she's got a sprinkling of glittery pink eyeshadow on her lids. It's kind of random ... and a little bit sexy. "Zayden, this is Dan, my study partner for survival analysis." *Um, no clue what that is.* I smile anyway and nod. "We'll be in the kitchen working on a project." I lift a hand in a loose half-wave and the guy smiles at me, pushing some dark hair off his forehead. I hate him instantly. "Zay's our nanny," Brooke adds, making my mouth twitch as she turns and her camel colored coat wafts out behind her.

"Nice to meet ya," Dan drawls, shrugging his shoulders, his rain spotted leather coat rustling as he turns and follows after Brooke. There's a moment of silence and then some giggling from the kitchen that makes my skin prickle with nerves. It's not like Brooke and I are anything to each other—obviously we're strangers—but I'm not all that keen on watching other guys hit on girls I like. Just bugs the hell out of me.

"You hungry, doll?" I ask Sadie and she makes a sound that I'd like to think means *hell, yes, Uncle Zay, get your ass in that kitchen and see what's up with this dude.* I grin. "You got it, babe."

I get up and move into the ugly linoleum kitchen with its builder-grade cabinets, noticing as I do that Brooke's eyes flick up to watch me. I give her my best award-winning smile and kick the fridge open.

"You okay with applesauce, chickee?" I ask as I reach in and grab a jar with my right hand, the open book tat on my skin fluttering with the motion. "And look at that, unsweetened and organic. Pretty posh." I heel the door shut behind me and sit Sadie in the high chair I brought over. I pretend not to be interested in what Brooke and Dude are doing, but I'm totally watching.

"Did you get the reading done last night?" Dude asks as he flips through some pages in a thick textbook and glances over at her from under his eyelashes. He's totally checking her out, but she's not paying attention, opening a laptop up next to her own textbook and logging in with a quick flicker of her fingers across the keys.

"I did it after my other class yesterday," she says and then bends down to dig something out of her bag, coming back up with a notebook. "I also got that study sheet filled out, but I didn't have time for the extra credit. Did you want to work on that first?"

"Yeah, sure." Dude What's-His-Face shrugs out of his jacket and flashes a really ugly tribal tattoo on his right arm. Puh-lease. He stretches his arms above his head like those weak ass triceps of his mean anything. I narrow my eyes at him as I fish one of those rubber baby spoon things from my back pocket and spin it around in my fingers, dragging a chair from the table and flopping down on it. "Your baby?" Dude asks Brooke as he shuffles around in his own bag.

"Me? Oh. No." She waves her hand in my direction. "Zayden has other kids he watches. He's ... kind of staying here for the week to help me out." When she looks at me, she smiles and the expression is genuine as fuck. Screw Rob, that dickhead. This is totally worth it, my good deed of the year or whatever. Lord knows I'm kind of a selfish fuck. Maybe I owe the universe this?

"Ah, cool, cool." Dude looks back at me and I meet his dark gaze. Silent man communications are sent. He's digging Brooke; I'm telling him to eat shit. I let my smile simmer wide ic and hot and when Brooke isn't looking, I flip the guy off. He gapes at me as I turn back to Sadie and lift up a spoonful of applesauce.

Brooke can do whatever she wants with this douche when I head back to Vegas, but this week … this chick is so mine.

CHAPTER 16
BROOKE OVERLAND

"Don't think I didn't see what you were doing in there," I say as I close the door behind Dan and lean against it, watching Zayden as he pauses in the middle of the living room, wearing a t-shirt that says *I Would Pierce the Fuck Outta You.* I don't quite get it, but okay. "Trying to scare that guy off. You're not very subtle, you know."

He lifts up his hands, palms out, and flashes me the tattoos that start at his wrists and go all the way down to his elbows and beyond.

"Nah. Subtle isn't exactly my cup of tea, Miss Overland. I didn't like that guy. Did you see his ink? It was some fake tribal shit he probably got off of the internet." I raise my brows and stand up, pausing near the back of the couch to pet Hubert. *God, this is an ugly cat.* But, at the same time … it's a little bit cute. Not at all like Dodger. I pause and listen to the chorus of yaps coming from the backyard. Hopefully we don't get any noise complaints. That'd really get me to the end of my rope.

"He's just a study partner. I met the guy like three days ago."

Zayden shrugs his sexy shoulders at me.

"So?" He grins at me. "You also met *me* three days ago." I purse my lips at him and give the hairless cat a scratch near the base of his tail. His sweater today is red with a black guitar on the back. It's the dumbest thing I've ever seen in my life.

"Five. And I don't exactly make a habit of sleeping around. Virgin, remember."

"Um, not a virgin anymore," Zay says with a massive grin that I pretend I don't find at all charming. The thing is, he's super charming. Crazy charismatic. It scares me a little to be honest. I almost wish he was more of a dick. "Anyway, that guy has ulterior motives. Big time. I can smell it."

"Like you don't?" I ask with a laugh as Zay moves around the couch and gets up close and personal with me. I'm not even sure he realizes he does that, gets up in other people's personal space like that.

"I never tried to pretend I didn't. See, that's the difference between that guy and me. I'm telling you exactly what it is that I want."

"Which is?"

"Well, of course, it's *you,* Smarty-Pants."

I take a step back, but Zay follows me in, pausing for a moment as the baby gurgles and then sighs softly in sleep. My heart is pumping furiously, my body tingling as I feel the warmth rolling off of him. I can still remember the way it draped across me, that heat, that hard hot body. I suck in a breath.

"I thought you said this was a casual, no strings attached sort of a deal?" Zay grins and brushes some hair away from my face with his tattooed hand.

"It is. Look, this is a perfect arrangement, don't you think? You can experiment with me, get all those virgin mistakes out of the way early on, and then in a week and a half, I'll be gone. Boom. Back to Vegas, baby. No worries at all, no awkwardness, no crossing paths."

I narrow my eyes at him, but inside, I'm going completely crazy. I can feel butterflies and tingles and this weird sort of buzzing that I've never felt before. I guess I'm having some kind of ... sexual awakening or something. I feel hot and squirmy with need. I'm aware it's all basic human chemistry and hormones and pheromones and all of that ... but damn.

"You're offering to ... teach me or something?"

Zay snaps his fingers and leans in close, the piercings on his face winking at me in the weak sunshine.

"Yeah, sure, why not? What do you have to lose?"

I look up at him, at this stranger that I let into my sister's house, that I let take care of her kids ... that I let take me to bed. *Why do I feel like I can trust this guy?* I'm not stupid. I'm completely and utterly aware that I don't know this man at all, but God, I want to say yes. I want to stop being the Brooke that does everything right all the time, but that no one notices.

My sister, Ingrid, was always one step ahead of me. If I got an A in chemistry then she got an A+ in AP chem; if I got an after-school job, she had two; if I made the team, she was the captain. But now, here I am, trying to pick up the pieces of her mess. I feel like a background, a side character, a pawn on a chessboard.

And I'm sick of it.

I can do something for myself, can't I? Even if it's stupid and it makes no sense and it's probably a really bad idea.

"Penny for your thoughts?" Zay asks, snapping me out of my reverie. I blink up at him and then sweep some of my stupidly long hair over my shoulders; I should cut it all off. Make a fresh start.

"I'm trying to logistically convince myself to sleep with you again."

"Oh. Any arguments I can offer to help make that happen?" He snaps his fingers at me again and then takes a step back, reaching down and tucking his inked fingers under his shirt. "Nah, don't say anything, Smarty-Pants, I got ya." Zay tears his shirt off and flashes me his perfect midsection, a landscape of muscular hills and valleys, a sea of color and piercings that draws my eye and refuses to let go of my gaze.

I'm about to step forward and run my hands down all of that delicious perfection when a knock sounds at the bay window to my right and I jump, glancing over to find an older woman glaring at us through the glass.

BAD NANNY

Shit.

It's my great aunt, the one that decided she was *currently unable* to help my parents out with Bella and Grace, the reason that I'm here. My dad's too sick to deal with little kids right now, and if my parents didn't have me here, they wouldn't have been able to go to Scotland. My aunt suggested they call it off, but what happens if my dad ends up never getting to go? This is literally the first—and probably the last—time he's ever left the country. He deserves this.

"Crap. Put your shirt on," I whisper as I scurry to the door and Zay groans, leaning down to grab his discarded tee as I unhook the chain and crack the door. I don't owe this woman anything, but I'm afraid if she thinks I'm up to no good over here that she'll call my parents and bitch. I really don't want anything to interfere with their trip. "Hey, Monica."

I make myself smile even though the two of us have never really gotten along. Monica's always liked Ingrid more than me. She used to laugh and call me the ugly sister; I never found that to be very funny.

"Brooke," she says, sweeping some black-going-gray hair over her shoulder, eyes flicking up past my shoulder to Zayden. "Am I interrupting something?" I wave my hand dismissively although I sort of want to scream. *Yeah, you kind of are.*

"Something I can help you with?"

"Aren't you going to invite me in?" she asks as I bite back a sigh and step aside, watching as my aunt's eyes narrow on the sparsely decorated house. I want to scream that *none* of this is my fault, but I know she won't listen to me. The frustrating thing about her disapproval is that she knows Ingrid's whole story. How my sister graduated with an accounting degree, got a decent job at the bank, how she took a hefty portion of my parent's retirement savings to buy a house, promising to pay them back.

How she got addicted and lost the house to foreclosure.

How my mom went to pick the girls up from school and found they'd never gone, came over here and discovered my sister's note.

She knows all of that and yet, here she is, judging me.

Monica squeezes her red coat tighter around herself and pauses next to Zayden. They look weirdly opposite, one of them old and conservative and closed off, and the other young and wild and outgoing.

"Zayden Roth," he says, extending the hand with the book on it, taking my aunt's and shaking it firmly. He grins nice and wide. "I'm Brooke's nan—"

"Boyfriend," I insert because God, if Monica finds out about the nanny thing or the stripping thing or just, well, any of it then she'll definitely call my mom up and demand she fly home. I don't want to deal with the drama. "From Berkeley. He's up visiting," I say because, again, I don't want to be judged for picking up a guy two weeks after arriving in town. Although that's really none of her business anyway.

Monica looks at Zayden like she recognizes his picture from some FBI most wanted list.

"Oh." That's it. No *nice to meet you* or *hi, I'm Brooke's aunt, Monica*, just ... oh. When her eyes swing over to the folding crib on the other side of the room, her dark brows soar. "I just came over to see if you needed any help with the girls —" several days *after* my parents leave town when she knows I've been struggling to find a job "—but I don't see them anywhere? Are they upstairs?"

"They're at school," I say, trying not to sound frustrated as she makes her way over to the sleeping baby. "That's Zayden's —" My mind scrambles for a way to describe his relationship to the baby. His charge? His steward? I don't know what nannies call the kids they watch.

"That's my niece," he says, sliding his hands into his front pockets in a way that draws my attention, sticks it to him like glue. The way he moves is so ... fluid, like nothing really matters, like any problem can be solved with a wink and a smile. I'm envious, even though I don't think an attitude like that really works in life. Not for long anyway and not successfully. "Brooke isn't the only one who got strapped with babysitting duties."

BAD NANNY

"Oh?" Monica asks, pausing and curling her long fake nails over the side of the crib. She always gets these crazy long acrylics that used to scare me as a child. When I was ten, I was always refused to open Christmas gifts from her because I was convinced she was going to wrap up a spinning wheel for me to prick my finger on. "Your sister doesn't mind you taking her baby out of town? A child this young?" I try not to roll my eyes, but I think I do anyway. Who the hell does this woman think she is?

"Brother, actually. And no. He's in South Africa with his wife. Her parents were in a pretty horrific car accident." Monica stands up and lets go of the crib, moving away and reaching up to play with the gold cross around her neck. I've always hated this, but I definitely look more like her than I do my own mother. Like Bella, Monica also takes after our grandmother.

Zay and I exchange a quick look, and I try to tell him with my eyes that I appreciate his coming up with a quick story. A weirdly specific story though ... unless of course it's true? I've never asked where the kids came from or how he got involved with them.

Holy crap.

And I was just going to sleep with this man again? Am I losing my mind?

"I didn't know they had cars in Africa," Monica says and I feel my brows shoot up. She waves her hand in the air. "I thought it was all lions and zebras and safari grass."

"Um. Nope. There's, like, several million people that live in Joburg alone." Zayden smiles as he says this, but his pierced brow is quirked up.

"When do you pick the girls up? I was hoping to take them to get their nails done."

See what I mean? Grace is four. You don't take four year olds to get their nails done.

"I don't think that's going to happen today, Aunt Monica," I say, trying to be as nice as possible so I can get rid of the woman. "Maybe if you give me a call sometime later this week, we could work something out?" She nods, but I can tell she's not ready to leave yet. *God, I hate busybodies.*

"Have you found a job yet?" she asks, but it's not like she really cares. If she did, she would've stepped up sooner to help out. It's not like I don't notice her designer purse and coat, her expensive haircut, the bracelets she's wearing.

My mouth twitches as Zayden's cat comes creeping down the stairs and pauses with his bald face around the corner. After a moment, he hisses and disappears back the way he came. At least the cat has the right idea.

"Still looking," I lie as I pass a look Zayden's way. It's highly doubtful he'd be stupid enough to blow my cover, but you never know with people. He just smiles at me with that sexy mouth of his, lacing his fingers behind his neck. The move makes his shirt ride up a little in the front, flashes me a tight belly with just a trickle of hair and a ring through his belly button. I never thought that kind of thing would look good on a guy, but he manages to pull it off.

I take a deep breath and drag my eyes away, doing my best not to think about how I'd like my mouth down there, kissing across the flat bridge of skin above his waistband, curling my fingers around the denim and pushing it down.

"Well, Zay and I were just on our way out, so ..."

"Isn't the baby sleeping?" Monica asks, gesturing back at the crib with a hand, her pale brown eyes taking in the room as she sneaks over to the bathroom and peeks in, takes a long lingering look at the kitchen, pauses at the sliding glass door to the back and stares out at the pack of chihuahuas/hairless rats that are cowering under the awning. There's a doghouse out there with a pile of freshly washed towels in it, but apparently they'd all rather sit here and stare at us.

Before I can come up with an answer for that, Zay's leaning into the crib and hefting Sadie up and onto his shoulder, rubbing her back with his colorful hand. I hate the way my heart jumps and shudders when I watch him holding her like that. Eww. No. I'm too young to be thinking about how sexy a guy looks with a baby on his shoulder.

BAD NANNY

"She'll fall right back asleep in the car," Zay says as he smiles at Monica. "Sorry you stopped by just to see us on our way out. But if you want to spend time with the kids, maybe you can watch the whole brood for us on Saturday? Brooke and I were planning on a date before the sitter cancelled. What do you say? Six kids, think you can handle that?"

"Six?" Monica asks, blinking mascara laden lashes at him. "There are six?"

"My four. Her two. If I can handle it, I bet you'd have no problem." He winks at her and bumps my aunt with his shoulder. Her shocked expression is so worth it. "Let's say you meet us here around seven?"

"Well, I don't know—"

"Perfect." Zay leans in and kisses her on the cheek, and Monica takes a shocked step back. "Thanks Aunt Monica. Can I call you Aunt? Brooke and I are so damn close, we'll probably be getting hitched before you know it. Come on, we'll see you out."

He moves towards the door and opens it, waiting for the two of us to follow him. I'm not sure what he's up to, but I give him a look. Zayden remains unfazed as I lock the door behind us and walk Monica out to her fancy black sedan. She climbs in, but doesn't seem to be going anywhere.

"We better get in the van," Zay whispers, tickling my ear with his breath. I can smell him when he's this close, like fruit and spices, like a warm house on a cold day. My skin jumps and prickles, all the places I want him to touch flashing neon in my mind.

I don't intend to actually go anywhere with him, but I climb in the car anyway and wait as he straps the baby in. Monica's still not gone when Zay gets into the driver's seat and starts up the engine.

"Where are we going?" I ask as he backs us out of the driveway and waves at my aunt. I watch over my shoulder as we pull away and see that she's on her phone. Admittedly, that kind of freaks me the hell out. She could be calling my mom. What time is it in Scotland right now? I have no fucking clue.

"You don't think she'll actually show up and watch all the kids, do you?"

Zay shrugs.

"Why not? It was worth a shot. Besides, if she does show up, think of all the fun we'll have together. It'll be a big sacrifice on my part, but I'm always willing to let you try a little exhibitionism with me, see if it's your thing."

"Uh-huh." I cross my arms over my chest and turn to look at him, glancing around the van at the scattered toys, at the stickers spread across the backs of the seats. "Whose van is this?"

"My sister-in-law's," he says as he pulls up to the intersection and turns right.

"So," I pause and think for a second. "That story you told my aunt, it was true? The kids are all related to you?"

"Yup. All four of them." Zay doesn't look at me as he follows some predetermined route he's got in mind. I blink at him a few times. "Don't ask why anyone would want to breed so many monsters so close together. I haven't the slightest fucking clue."

"How long have you been their nanny for?" I ask, because he did say he was going back to Vegas soon, didn't he?

"About, uh, seven days?" he says, like it's a question even he doesn't know the answer to.

"And ... you were a nanny back in Vegas then?" There's a long pause where Zayden reaches down to scratch at his belly, eyes focused wholly on the road. Before he answers, he reaches over to the radio and turns up some stupid chart-topping pop song.

"Not exactly," he says with a slight crinkle of his eyebrow. It makes his piercing dance and sparkle in the sun, but I'm not paying attention to that. Nope. Not looking at the full, ripe shape of his lips, the way his tattoos emphasize the muscular lines of his throat.

"If you weren't a nanny back in Vegas, then what did you do?" Zay lifts up a finger and points at his nose ring.

"Body piercer Zayden Roth at your disposal," he says,

BAD NANNY

flashing me a giant smile as I feel my heartbeat pick up speed. This time, though, it's from irritation.

"Body piercer?" I ask, thinking that particular title suits him a hell of a lot better than *nanny*. Then again, he seems so good with the kids. It was one of the reasons I took a leap of faith in the first place. "Zayden, a body piercer is *not* the same thing as a nanny. Why did you tell me you were one? To try and win my trust?" I feel like getting pissed now, shoving up the sleeves of my black button-up as I turn in my seat and put my legs in the space between us.

"What? No. No. Hell, I was just fucking around with you, but as soon as I said the word nanny, you jumped ship on me and got all cute and doe eyed."

"Doe eyed? I do *not* get doe eyed. And how are you acting like this is my fault? If you weren't really a nanny, you should've told me that in the first place." I sit back and lean against the window, trying not to hyperventilate. It hits me suddenly, looking at this guy, that I *just* lost my virginity to him. And I don't even know who he is. Like, at all. "Why ... why would you lie about that?"

"It was a *joke*," Zayden emphasizes as he takes us past the park and turns left toward town. "My brother called and *begged* my ass to come up here and take care of his kids."

"So, you have other experience caring for children then? Babysitting friends' kids? Taking care of younger siblings? Oh my God, do you have your *own* kids?"

"Um, no, no, no, and definitely not. I'm sort of playing it by ear here. It's not nearly as hard as everyone makes it look." Zayden lifts up his phone; it's covered in some brightly colored skin with a Japanese anime girl on the back of it. I pinch my lips tight. "When you've got a smartphone, what can't you do? I ask and it tells. Easy as pie."

"I think children are a little more nuanced than Google can get across, Zayden." I'd wonder if that was his real name if I hadn't actually asked to see his driver's license when I first 'hired' him. "You let *me* believe you were qualified to handle this. I've been leaving you with six children. Six. I've been *trusting* you with my nieces."

"Duh, yeah. And you know what? That's one of the reasons I decided to do this in the first place. You picked me up at a park, Brooke. For all you know, I could be some sort of crazy person. If you were willing to hire me on the spot, I didn't know what else you'd do. Not all guys are as easygoing as I am."

"Is that why you took my virginity then?" I snap, feeling my skin get itchy and hot with irritation. "Because I might make a stupid, naïve decision and give it to the wrong person?" I pause and wrinkle my forehead. "Is this a *boy band* playlist or something?"

"Like you don't enjoy old school *Backstreet Boys* or **NSYNC*."

"I'm almost a decade younger than you. I didn't listen to either of them."

"Weeeell, then maybe that's your problem?"

"My problem is that I don't listen to boy bands?"

"Your problem is that you're too judgmental, but also not judgmental enough."

I scoff at him and turn the stereo off with the palm of my hand.

"You don't know me at all, Zayden Roth."

"I'm intuitive," he says, pointing at his temple with the finger that has the letter *E* tattooed on it. He pretends to pull a trigger and makes a *boom* sound. I've never met anyone in my life with such over the top gestures. I'm not sure what to even make of them. "I can sense your pain. You're damaged but also sweet, like you still want to believe the world has some good in it. That's why I decided to help you out. The last thing I'd want to see is someone like you get hurt. This planet's shitty enough as it is without watching another person get swept under the rug of shit."

"I can take care of myself," I snap as I sit up straight. "I don't need you looking out for me. And I sure as hell don't need a *body piercer*—" at least his shirt makes some semblance of sense now "—pretending he knows how to take care of my

BAD NANNY

girls. Take me home and get your stuff. Go back to wherever it is you came from."

Zayden laughs and shakes his head, running his hand across the shaved side of his head.

"Please. Relax and let's go get some ice cream."

"Ice cream?" I ask incredulously. "We're on our way to get *ice cream*. What ... what are you thinking? You just admitted you lied to me about being a nanny. You had *sex* with me."

"You seem really focused on the sex thing, Brooke. Relax. It's totally natural what happened between us."

"Ew. Dear God, please don't talk like that, okay? That was ... wow. What a horrible mistake. And I was going to do it again," I mumble under my breath. Zayden leans theatrically towards me and then punches the stereo back on.

"Wait, wait ... what was that, Smarty-Pants? See, I knew it. You want to fuck me again."

"Take me home," I say, turning the music off again. "I'm not going to get ice cream with some guy who lied to me. I've had just about all I can take with liars in my life." Zay sits up, but he doesn't make any effort to turn the car around, instead taking us in the direction of Old Town. It's a cute area if you're a tourist, but after one walk around to look at all the local hipster shops, you're pretty much done. Maybe there's an ice cream place there now, but I wouldn't know since I haven't had a chance to head down there since I got back. "Zay."

"I'm not just some guy anymore," he says as he taps his hand in time to some awful song that says *girl* and *baby* every three seconds. "I'm your friend, and as your friend, I'm telling you that you need ice cream like, *stat.*"

"Are you buying then? Because I don't have any money. What little I scrounged up in tips last night is already allocated for bills."

"Whoa. Are you adulting all over me right now? Sure. I'll buy you some ice cream, but I want you to listen to what I'm saying. Relax. Let me help you out, okay? Where are you gonna find a replacement nanny before work tonight?" I glance at the clock and get a kind of nervous flutter in my tummy. Last night wasn't so bad, I guess, but what if there are more people there tonight? How am I going to handle an entire crowd?

Like you did last night, when you thought of Zayden's hands on your body.

I hate to admit it, but ... it made things bearable.

I cross my arms over my chest and lean back in the seat with my eyes closed. This is sort of the last thing I needed right now ... and sort of the exact thing I needed at the same time. It's weird, I know, but ... I open my eyes and them slide over to Zayden as ... he starts mouthing the words to "Lucky" by Britney Spears?

Um.

My mouth breaks into a smile and he raises his eyebrows, pointing over at me.

"See? This is why I like pop music." When he starts snapping his fingers and biting his lower lip, I draw the line.

"Jesus, okay. I get it. Please stop." Zayden laughs, ruffling up the side of his head that still has hair. I resist the urge to reach out and trace one of the stars he's shaved onto his scalp. *He's just a little bit cute though, right?* I refuse to admit that I like him—even a little. "You're really doing all this to help me out? Just because you're a nice guy?"

"I've got a white knight disorder," he says as he glances over at me with those gorgeous eyes of his. They're the same color as the lichen that clings to the sides of the trees in my sister's backyard. Pale, but pretty, mysterious. Ugh. "That's why I have so many exes. I know they're bad news, but I want to help 'em out, you know?"

"And that has nothing to do with sex?"

"Well, that's just a consolation prize." He gives me a look that's a lot less *cute* than the last one. It makes me squirm, the way his eyes rake over my body. "If it was just sex I wanted, I can get that, too. But I always end up getting tangled in these," he gestures with his right hand and I find myself mesmerized by his tattoos, "fucked up relationships."

"Do you think that speaks more to *your* character than to

BAD NANNY

your million exes? Maybe there's something wrong with you and not them?"

"Ooooh." Zayden taps his right shoulder with his left hand and makes a sizzling sound. "Ouch. Burn, much? You could be right, I guess." He looks over at me and his face gets that … *look* again, like he's about to drive his hips into mine. I squirm and wiggle in my seat, squeezing my thighs tight against the sudden pulse between them. "So tell me, what's my problem then?"

"How should I know? We"—I gesture between the two of us—"are not in a relationship."

"Sure we are. Any connection with another person is a relationship. It's *how* you define that relationship that matters. Me and you, we're friends now."

"We are not friends. We are strangers. *Strangers.* And you are a non-nanny that's watching my kids for free and eating all my organic applesauce. Are you sure this isn't a scam? Are you trying to pull one over on me?"

"I stuck twenty bucks in your purse when you weren't looking, to cover the cost of the food we've been eating. Now shut up and get some ice cream with me. When you need to, you don't think hard enough. When you don't, you think too much."

Zayden pulls up to the curb outside one of the Old Town shops. The streets are made of red bricks, and the city has managed to maintain the original horse hitching posts and streetlights from way back when. The whole area is made up of Victorian shops with fine architectural details and bright colors. In all the flower beds and at the bases of all the trees are crushed up white oyster shells.

Welcome to Eureka, California, USA. Population 30,000. Nightlife: none. Seafood: plenty. Gods: one covered in tattoos and piercings. Clues: none because I have no idea what to do about him.

With a sigh, I shove open my door and climb out, waiting while Zayden unhooks Sadie from her car seat and puts her in a fold out stroller. When she's successfully strapped in, he looks up at me and smiles, nodding his chin across the street at a place called Seaside Coffee and Ice Cream. Must be new because it definitely wasn't here when I was in high school.

"What's your favorite flavor?" Zay asks as he checks both ways and starts us across the street. "Personally, I'm a rainbow sherbet kind of a guy, but ..." He leans over and breathes hot against my ear. "If I'm licking a scoop off the body of a beautiful woman, I'll take just about any flavor."

I pull away from him and toss a look his direction.

"I'm still not sure what I'm doing with you. Even if it started off as a joke, you still lied to me. And besides, I never said I wanted an ongoing fuck buddy scenario with you." Zay pushes the stroller, looking ridiculously sexy in his black boots, grungy jeans and tight t-shirt, very edgy and cool. With the white and blue stroller and the soft skinned baby inside of it, he's ten times more attractive. I notice other women staring enviously at me as we make our way down the brick sidewalk towards the front of the shop.

It smells *heavenly* when we step inside, like espresso and vanilla, the soothing sounds of brewing coffee and the clack of laptop keys making for a pleasant atmosphere. The walls on either side and in front of us are made entirely of brick, looming up two stories into old wooden rafters. I guess if I have to live in this town, I could find a worse place to hang out and do homework.

"Whatcha want?" Zay asks, pausing in front of the glass ice cream case and planting his wicked sexy hands on his hips. Looking at him now, it's like the sex is a dream, like it never even happened. But then my hip bone tingles and I remember the hot brush of his fingers, the warm press of his body, the sudden knowledge that I was sharing my space with somebody else, that he was *inside* of me.

I shiver.

"Something with coffee in it. I have a feeling this is gonna be a long night."

Zay grins and salutes me, stepping up to the counter to order while I wait with the baby.

BAD NANNY

She stares up at me with dark brown eyes, her head fuzzy with hair, her skin the color of a good mocha. She blows a raspberry at me and I smile, reaching down to squeeze the pink and white sock on her foot.

"Hard to believe my lumberjack dickhead of a brother made this, huh?" Zay asks, pausing next to me to point at the baby with an ice cream cone. He hands mine over to me and I notice he's taken the liberty of ordering a waffle cone with chocolate and sprinkles on it for me. I kind of love him for that. "I give my sister-in-law all the credit. Mercedes never misses a raid, and she *annihilates* on first person shooters. You should see her in action; it's impressive."

Zay pushes the stroller over to a pair of seats near the front so we can look out the window while we eat. I notice he watches me lick my ice cream before starting in on his. And then when he does, he makes such a sensual face that I laugh.

"Trying too hard?" he asks as he looks at me with half-lidded eyes and then runs his tongue along his lower lip. "You don't seem to like that. Should I scale back a little?"

"I'm not sleeping with you," I say and he smirks at me. The expression on his face sort of makes me want to slap him.

"Not sleeping with you *again*. Don't forget the *again* part. I'm a part of your life narrative now, Smarty-Pants."

"Why do you keep calling me that? If anyone's the smarty-pants in the family, it'd be my sister Ingrid. She was always outdoing me on everything." Zay scoffs and his face gets dark for a split second.

"Doesn't look like she's outdoing you now, leaving her twenty-two year old sister to watch her kids. What a bitch." The overprotective part of me wants to tell Zay not to talk about my sister like that, but the other part of me is happy to have someone on my side for once. I know my parents are disappointed in Ingrid, but I don't feel like they care *enough*. What she did, leaving like that, losing her house, starting the drugs, it's practically unforgivable and yet my parents talk about her like she's on an extended vacation.

"Fuck her," I say and Zay raises his eyebrows. I take a

nice, long lick of my ice cream and close my eyes against the sweet cream taste, the bitter notes of coffee pinging around on the back of my tongue. In the background, soft jazz music plays. It's not my usual thing, but it's pretty, relaxing. I could use a little bit of relaxing right now. I'm only on day two of my new job and I'm already wondering how I'm going to get everything done. *How I'm going to do this without Zay.* Because it's been *one* day and I can't figure out how to juggle it, who I'm going to get to watch the kids, clean the house, take care of the dog. I wish for a second there that he really was a nanny so I could hire him permanently. "I can't believe you're a *body piercer.* Do you actually make money off of that?"

"On the Strip? Are you kidding me? There's a constant stream of new customers fresh off of gambling." Zay takes an erotic lick of sherbet, swirling his tongue around the rim of his cone and making my heart palpate. I hate how much I wish that was *me* under his hot mouth instead. "But, I sort of suck at managing my money. I still have the same crap car I packed all my shit into and moved to Vegas with, no savings or retirement money set aside. I do have a pretty kick ass condo though."

I pause and set my cone into the little metal stand on the table, cleverly designed for this exact purpose, and reach down to unbutton my shirt. Zay watches me, his pupils clearly dilating in those sea glass green eyes of his. I shrug it off onto the back of my chair, leaving me in nothing but a tight white tank. I act like I don't notice him checking me out, gaze landing on the pale curves of my breasts, the tantalizing bit of white lace from my bra that's peeking out above the neckline.

"You flew up here as a favor to your brother then, like you said? Or was that a lie, too?" I try to smile a little when I say it although I'm still pretty pissed off. I *really* hate being lied to, even if it's just a joke. The man that I dated for three years, he was the ultimate liar, hiding behind a cloak of superiority and religion. I'll never date a man like that again.

"Nope. Cross my heart and hope to bleed, baby." I pucker my lips at that and take a tentative lick of my ice cream. "But I didn't fly. My dick brother made me drive. Neither one of us

BAD NANNY

had the money for a plane ticket. I blew all of mine on a collector's edition computer game and a crazy three day weekend with some pink haired chick named Kitty. We drank and ate ourselves to death. Oh, and fucked. There was plenty of that, too."

"I really don't want to hear about you sleeping with other girls, but thanks for offering up the info." Zayden laughs at me and his ice cream splats to the table, topples right off his cone and lands in a rainbow splotch.

"Oops," he says and I wrinkle my nose as he scoops it up in his hand and plops it right back on top of the cone. "Three second rule."

"That's disgusting," I say, but I'm laughing because this guy is like a caricature of a human being, and I can't help myself. He's so ... weird. But kind of cool, too. Like, he looks like every stereotypical bad boy ever, but he's sort of ... nice? I always wondered how all those dickhead bad boys in books and movies got laid. Who wants to sleep with some piece of shit, like that big time rock star everyone's obsessed with right now. What's his name? Turner Campbell, from that band *Indecency*. Nobody in their right *mind* would *actually* date someone like that. But I get it now. Like Zay said, more flies with honey. He's got the look, and he's friendly and open. Can't beat that I suppose.

"It's only gross if you think about it," he says as he whips his tongue through the sherbet and smiles at me. He smiles a lot. I like that. I could use more smiles in my life. *Until he flies back to Vegas at the end of next week. Stop letting him charm your pants off and remember that.*

Right.

Las Vegas.

"If you're for real, and you're actually helping me out because you have a—what did you call it—white knight complex? If that's what's really happening then ... thank you." I make myself sit up straight and take a deep breath. "Seriously. I would've been screwed without you."

"No problem, Smarty-Pants. No thanks necessary.

Remember, you don't owe people shit, okay?"

"Sure." I lick my ice cream and listen to the jazz music simmering around me. I want to stay in here forever. The last thing I want to do tonight is head over to the Top Hat and take my clothes off. Long term, this could kill me. But I won't let it. I'm going to stay strong because I have to be. "So you'll be here for a little while? I mean, just so I can figure out who to get to watch the kids."

"Sure thing. You've got me for eight more days, Brooke Overland."

Eight days.

I didn't think that was nearly long enough to lose my heart.

Frankly, it was about six days too many.

CHAPTER 17
ZAYDEN ROTH

Busted, baby.

I guess I feel relieved that Brooke knows I'm not actually a nanny, but at this point the chances of getting her to relax and fall into bed with me again are pretty slim. Oh well. I peel some chewing gum out of what little hair this ugly gray and white dog has around its neck and give Kinzie a look on her perch atop the fuzzy pink toilet seat.

"Dude, you are so in much freaking trouble right now."

"You're going to the H-place for licking other grown-up's privates in the shower. God doesn't approve of that. That's what Shiela told me."

"Um, what? That's weirdly specific." I stand up and wad the gum up between my fingers. Fuckin' gross, man. "Where did you hear that?"

"I *saw* mom and dad doing that in the shower when they thought I was sleeping. I picked the lock and everything."

I try not to be really disturbed by that, but shit. I'm creeped the hell out.

"Okay, stop picking locks on the bathroom door *unless* an adult asks for your help getting the twins out. People deserve privacy in the bathroom, Kinzie." She kicks the wall hard and I grab my cell, clutching it tight in the hand that's not covered in gum and holding it out like a weapon. "I'm restarting the time-out clock. Every time you kick or hit or scream or spit, I restart it. How many minutes you trying for here, sweetheart? A world record?"

Kinzie turns away from me as I head into the kitchen to extract the gum from my hand. It's like, seriously stuck. Takes some hardcore scraping to get that off. I've noticed that with everything the kids spit out, like it's all glued to whatever it lands on. Even the baby has that special ability. How that's bloody possible is beyond me.

I grab a dish towel and head back into the kitchen, taking in the four kids that are seated around the TV, eyes glued to the flickering screen like it's made of pixie dust. It's definitely easier to park them in front of it and let the boob tube do the babysitting for me, but I feel kind of bad about it. Maybe I should, like, try to do an activity with them or something?

"Hey Google," I start, lifting my phone up to my lips. "How do you make cookies?"

"Cookies!" Bella says, her head whipping away from the TV and over to me. She pushes herself off the couch and bounces over to stand in front of me, her long dark hair and pale brown eyes making her look like a miniature Brooke. Staring at her like that makes me a little curious about what it would be like to have kids with somebody, make my own mini me. Or maybe I'm specifically fantasizing about what it would be like to make mini Brookes. *Oh yeah.* I haven't forgotten the feel of her body beneath me, writhing and moaning, those small noises in her throat, those frantic breaths like the beating of a bird's wing.

Hmm.

Maybe I do sort of give a crap if she fucks me again. Because *I* really want to fuck her. I need to make this happen.

"I'm on my way out," Brooke says, appearing at the bottom of the stairs in a long black trench coat à la an old western movie or something. I smile at her total lack of style—and then start getting real, real curious about what's under that thing. "Do you need anything before I go?" she asks, her pale eyes like hazelnuts. *Good enough to eat.* I smile. I think I actually kind of miss the big thick black hipster glasses.

"We're making cookies!" Bella says, drawing those candy twins my way. Mike and Ike bounce and scream and hang off my pant legs.

Brooke raises an eyebrow at me. *God I want to pierce her so bad.* I grin and try not to let myself get caught up in the pun.

"Do you actually know how to bake?" I lift my phone and wiggle it at her.

"I got Google, like I said. How hard can it be?"

"Oookay," she says, making me ten times as sure that I've gotta do this. I have to prove this chick wrong. "I better get going."

"One second," I say, peeling a twin off my leg and depositing him on the couch. I seriously have no idea which one of my nephews is Mike and which one's Ike. "Go watch TV for, like, five more minutes while I get everything set up."

The kids scurry away like ants as I gesture for Brooke to follow me outside for a minute, scooting heaps of chihuahuas away with my foot as I step onto the deck.

"What's up?" Brooke asks as I move over to the right side of the deck, out of view of the children. Before she can get all logistical up in that crazy head of hers, I grab her jacket by the front and gently push her back into the wall, drawing a sharp gasp from those pretty lips. Her makeup's perfect, but I figure better for me than for those assholes at the club.

I lean in and kiss her hard, slipping my tongue into her mouth on the tail end of another gasp. The way her breath rushes around my mouth makes it hard to concentrate as my hands drop and undo a few of the top buttons on the coat. My fingers slip inside and find a lacy teddy and a slim waist, a warm and willing softness that leans into me with little prompting.

Oh yeah.

This chick still wants me. With her pressed up against me like this, I feel like I'll do anything to get her. Just *one* more night would be fucking killer.

Brooke groans against my lips, her hands dropping to the waistband of my jeans and curling around it, nails scraping my skin as she tugs me closer.

"Cha-cha-ching, Smarty-Pants," I whisper as I pull back an inch. "If you want, I can be naked and waiting for you when you get home."

She doesn't answer me as rain starts to fall, pattering against the wood and the grass and the majestic trees dancing above our heads. If there weren't a million kids in the house, I would lift her up and fuck her right here, right against the green siding of this shitty house. *I'd make a million miniature Brookes with her right now if she wanted.*

Uh. Where the fuck did *that* thought come from?

Ew. No. No way. No kids. Not for me. Sorry. I don't care how cute the girl is.

I take a sudden step back, pretending it's because I can hear screaming from inside. In reality, I've just freaked myself the hell out.

Brooke looks up at me with those giant doe eyes that she says she doesn't have, breath panting, her hot pink lipstick smeared across her chin. She clutches her jacket tight in front of her and then starts frantically buttoning it up.

I know I should keep laying it on, encourage her to experiment with me. After all, one night of sex in her whole life? At age twenty-two? She has *got* to have some built up frustration brewing in that sexy body of hers.

But I can't. Honestly, I think I just scared the crap out of myself. Damn. A few days with these kids and my bio clock is a-tick-tick-tickin'.

Brooke doesn't say anything, just squeezes her hands into fists, fingers digging into the shimmery fabric of her trench as she closes her eyes and sucks in several deep breaths. When she opens them again, she takes a step forward and then smooths her hands over the slick texture of her hair, fixing her bouncy ponytail before she wets her lips to speak.

"I ... I'll think about it."

BAD NANNY

She shoulders past me and disappears into the sliding doors as I let out a deep breathe, my anxiety slipping away with it.

And then I grin. Nice and big.

Bingo, baby.

Making chocolate chip cookies is *soooo* much fucking harder than I thought it would be. We're like halfway done with the damn things and I've already put thirty dollars into the curse jar (and then secretly taken about fifteen of it back when Kinzie's not looking).

"Jesus fucking Christ," I curse when I pull the first batch from the oven and find them solidified into small black discs of charcoal. "The recipe said eight to ten minutes until done, not until fossilized. My God."

"Um," Bella says as she disappears for a moment and comes back with a stepping stool, pushing the oven door closed and then standing on it. "My grandma said our oven cooks hot. I think you need to turn it down." She presses the button and adjusts the temperature by about ten degrees. I'm loath to admit it, but the little monster actually kind of looks cute in her apron. If you tell anyone, I will seriously leap out of this book and kill you, buuuuuuut ... I'm also wearing an apron. It's pink, sure. And it has ... I think they're mice or rats or bunnies or something. Anyway, they're all smiling giddily and they are also *all* wearing aprons.

Fan-fucking-tastic.

"Do you think we should make the next batch *monster* chocolate chip cookies?" I ask as I rummage around in the cabinet for some food coloring. I know that shit supposedly gives kids ADD or something, but I ate heaps of it and I turned out fine, didn't I?

I grab the box and drip several splotches of blue and red into the dough as the kids stare up at me with awed expressions. They're like, seriously so fucking gullible. It's the absolute best part about them.

"This is monster blood," I tell them and Kinzie scrunches up her face.

"Um, no it's *not*. I saw that *Goosebumps* episode and it was *green*." I pause and lean down, putting my hands on my thighs as I look Kinzie right in the face.

"There are different *breeds* of monsters, just like there are dogs." I stand up and point at the ugly row of rat-dogs sitting at my feet, begging for scraps of cookie. "See. Brooke's dog is gross and hairless, and your dogs are gross and hairy." I pause. "Well, except for the old one. He's just nasty and partially hairless and all around weird. But anyway, different monsters have different colors of blood. Ask anyone."

I stick my tongue out at her and pick up the spoon to stir the dough.

"My turn!" Grace says, fighting off the evil twins for a spot clinging to my leg. "I want to do it!" I drop the spoon and lift her up, spinning her in a quick circle while she screams with laughter.

"You go for it, chickie," I say as I deposit her on the counter and let her slap at the dough with the spoon. "Uncle Zay's going to put on some music."

"Is it the same as what we listened to on the way home from school?" Bella kicks her foot and looks shyly up at me from beneath a fall of brunette hair. Aww. So much fucking cuter than my own niece. Why is the one that's blood related to me such a brat? "Because I liked the *pretty* song."

I think for a split second and then snap my fingers.

"What you want is "Sit Still, Look Pretty" by Daya." I start the song on my iPod and crank up the volume on the attached speakers. "Actually, the moral of that song is *not* to sit still and look pretty, just so you know."

Bella and Kinzie both stare at me with circles for eyes. It's almost possible to forget they're devils sent specifically from hell to torment me. Almost.

I hear a crash from behind me and turn to find the cookie

dough bowl on the floor, the glass shattered into pieces, dogs gobbling up purple goo from the white linoleum.

Huh.

What was I saying about forgetting? *You* just forget I ever said that.

Hate kids. Yup. I hate 'em.

Several hours later, I wake with a start, Sadie lying across my chest as I yawn and struggle into a sitting position, clutching the baby to my chest as I breathe deep and watch Brooke slipping inside the house.

She locks the door behind her as I rise to my feet and tiptoe the baby over to the crib.

Shit. Crap. Fuck a duck.

I was supposed to be waiting all naked and sweaty and hard in Brooke's bed. Instead, my hair is plastered to my head with purple cookie dough and I have baby drool all over my neck. I lay Sadie in the crib as carefully as I can, praying to the God of Love and Sex that she'll stay asleep for me.

Cha-cha-ching. Somebody's listening to me.

I look up, across the shadowy living room to where Brooke's standing in her coat, watching me with eyes cloaked in darkness. It's impossible to figure out what she's thinking from over here.

I move around the crib, pausing less than a foot from Brooke. She rests her hand on the rounded end of the newel post for a moment, eyes still shadowed and hard to read. Her fingers tap out an easy rhythm as I wait, my body already thrumming with anticipation. My cock refuses to forget how tight and hot her pussy was, how her body writhed against me with pleasure.

I take a step forward and gently put my hand on Brooke's

shoulder like I did before, turning her to face me. When she doesn't move away or protest, I reach down and start to undo the buttons on her jacket. Again, nothing from her, but don't think I miss that frantic flutter in her throat. Her pulse is racing and when I push the jacket back and off her shoulders, I can see her chest rising and falling with quick breaths.

The lace teddy underneath is like a wet dream come to life, see through in all the right places, tantalizing opaque in others. A faint floral pattern traces over Brooke's full, ripe breasts, all the way down to the lacy little skirt that rims the bottom, carefully accenting a pair of ruffled boyshorts.

When I drop my hands down to cup her firm cheeks in my hand, she moans and lets herself fall into me. A weird, hot, wild jealousy spikes through me as I press my mouth to her neck and kiss hard, sucking harder, nibbling *hard.*

Brooke moves her breasts against my chest as she wiggles in my grip, tilts her head away from me and encourages me to mark her. *Oh yes.* There's something about this girl that's mind-fucking the hell out of me, but I can't seem to put my finger on it. Maybe it's watching all these kids, screwing with my hormones and making me wish I had some of my own? Or maybe it's those giant round eyes of Brooke's, gazing up at me when I pull back, and looking at me with something akin to desperation.

See. Told you. Seriously damaged.

Eh, but I kind of like her anyway. She's a cool chick.

And I am hot as *fuck* for her.

My hands drop to Brooke's waist, guiding her back against the wall so she has something to brace herself against when I slant my mouth to hers, tongue slicking and sliding into her groaning lips. Brooke lets me have whatever I want and grasps onto my shirt, begging for more. I've always heard virgins were crazy horny, but I've never really had the pleasure of hanging around any. The girls that come into my shop, the ones I usually pick up, they're tatted and pierced and experienced and sexy as hell, but they are *definitely* not virgins.

Oddly enough, Brooke's the one that popped *my* virgin

BAD NANNY

cherry. Hah.

I cup the sides of Brooke's throat, hold that beautiful neck in my inked up hands and tilt her chin up with my thumbs. Neither one of us speaks, and it's hot as hell. Her breath feathers against my mouth as I hover mine inches from her face, just feeling the warm, frantic breaths that escape her lips. When her hands drop to my jeans and start to undo my belt, I wait there with a sinful smirk slashing across my lips as she lets my cock spring free from my jeans and wraps her hand around it.

Brooke tries to kiss me, but I hold her still, both hands on her throat, thumbs gently running over her lower lip and down her chin. She makes that frantic little sound that drove me crazy last time and I press my forehead against hers, closing my eyes as I let the pleasure of her hand wash through me.

"I can't," Brooke whispers, but I keep my hold on her, firm but gentle.

"Sure you can," I whisper back as she strains for my lips and I let her brush against them, just enough to make her pulse jump beneath my hands. Her tongue slicks across my lower lip, but I don't let it go any further, pushing my hips forward so that my cock's trapped between us. Brooke grapples clumsily to get the job done, but hell if I don't like it, if I don't push my pelvis into her touch.

I keep us there, trapped against the wall until I feel the orgasm creeping up on me. Only then do I let our lips crash together. Brooke groans so loud that the sound echoes around the stairwell. I pray to that same god that kept Sadie asleep that none of the other monsters will wake up.

My hands squeeze gently against the sides of Brooke's face, my thumbs dipping between our lips. She alternates between kissing and sucking on them, playing with my tongue. The white hot electric shiver that explodes through my body is goddamn deafening. I feel like I can't see or think or even exist without Brooke's hands all over me.

I slide my cheek against hers and breathe out hard into her hair, coming all over the front of that perfect little teddy. When

I finally release her throat, she looks completely stunned, standing there and gaping up at me with her chest rising and falling in short, staccato bursts.

"You're ... not done, right?" I laugh and jerk her against me, not caring that we're getting all messy. If you're afraid to get messy during sex, you won't have any fun.

"Gimme ten minutes," I whisper against her ear, reaching down to take her right leg. I slide my fingers up under her thigh and lift it, putting her foot against the step of the bottom landing. I make sure my fingers are clean and dry before I slip them inside her ruffled boyshorts and tease the dripping wetness of her opening. "Holy fuck, Smarty-Pants. Not bad for a virgin."

Brooke bites her lip and closes her eyes, leaning her head against the wall as I dip inside that molten slickness and groan at the sensation of her clamping down on my fingers. I don't have to work very hard to slip a second and then a third in there. She wants me so bad her hips are bucking against my hand while hers are tangling in the front of my shirt, pulling our bodies tight.

I get my fingers nice and sweet and wet, working some of that liquid heat up to her clit before I drop my thumb down, flicking against the hardened nub with a soft touch until I find her spot. Every girl is different; Miss Brooke likes that spot just to the right and above her clit played with. I put a little more pressure into the touch, getting that wild flutter of muscles that I was looking for.

And just like that, I'm ready again. Told ya I had skills.

I slip my fingers reluctantly from Brooke's heat and dig into my back pocket for a condom, slipping it carefully down my shaft and making sure I don't get any cum on the outside.

"Alright, Smarty-Pants." I reach up and pull that long hair over her shoulder, working that band out and tossing it aside so I have a nice long fall of chocolate to wrap around my hand. "I think you're gonna like this." I yank her head gently to mine and kiss her hard before I let go, using my left hand to push her right thigh open a little wider. With the wall and the step and

BAD NANNY

the heels, we've got literally the perfect position for this.

I hook my right hand under Brooke's left thigh and lift up, opening her wide as she gasps and throws her arms around my neck for support. Some careful maneuvering with my left hand and I find her opening with my cock, pushing in deep and slamming her ass against the wall.

The sound she makes ... oh *God,* the sound. I'll remember that sound for the rest of my life.

I brace my left hand on the wall behind Brooke's head and dig the fingers of my right into her ass, pulling her pelvis into mine and drinking in the expression on her face. Blissful abandon. That's what it is, what's coloring her features with a hot pink flush, parting her full lips, drawing beads of sweat down the sides of her face.

I use hard, powerful thrusts, but I make them slow and languorous, thrilling in the pleasure of her clamping down tight, trying to keep me inside with the strength of her muscles. I can see everything from here: the ripe swells of her breasts, the peekaboo lace, the faint glimmer of my seed on the front of her sexy teddy.

"I'm the only guy that's ever seen this face?"

Brooke nods as I burrow into the crook of her shoulder, loving the way she claws at my neck as I press her into the wall. Good thing I've spent a lot of time working out my arms because they're already burning like hell. But it's a good feeling, a wild feeling. Sweat drips down my body, trails over my spine, slicks across my belly. I'm not letting go of her until we both come.

"Good. I like it that way." I shove hard and Brooke whimpers, the slick warmth between us making me wish I could take this damn condom off. At least I've got the ruffled texture of her panties rubbing against my shaft with each thrust, the thin piece of fabric doing literally nothing to keep me away from Brooke's core. "I like that you're still wearing your panties for me. You can strip down at that club, but that doesn't mean shit. You being naked doesn't mean a goddamn thing."

Uh-oh. I'm getting ... aggressive. Some of that possessive

male urge I usually shake off creeping down my shoulders and into my arms, my fingers curling tight into Brooke's soft flesh as I slam against her with a vigor I can't quite explain.

I breathe in deep and pull her scent into my lungs, this delicious concoction of fruit and soap and sweat, the faint tease of cigarettes from the club. I hope she can smell me, too, taste the heat of my desire on the back of her tongue with each inhale. And I hope she can feel my piercings, too, feel the warm metal through the condom, brushing down her ridged walls and drumming beats of pleasure into her body.

I play Brooke Overland like an instrument, use my body to strip her of any control, bring her all the way down, crashing into my arms with tears prickling the corners of her eyes as her head drops back and she gasps, cries, shudders in my arms.

Brooke struggles a little against the pleasure, fights the orgasm and tries to push me off, but I won't let go, jerking her tight against me as her legs collapse and the entire weight of her body falls into me, her pussy locking down hard and yanking a small growl from my throat.

I nuzzle hard into Brooke's shoulder and fuck her against the wall until I feel that bright burst of color in my brain, that annihilation of all my thoughts and worries and rules and bullshit. In that split second of clarity I get with each orgasm, I see Brooke in all her wild female glory. I feel like an animal that's just found his mate, seen her standing across a field and just *known.*

But holy *shit,* that is so goddamn stupid! What the *fuck* am I thinking?

I come hard, my body sheathed inside of Brooke, fingers grasping tight enough to bruise. The wash of relief afterward comes with a weird sort of panic as I pull back and finally allow my aching arms to release her weight.

Brooke can't stand up, her back to the wall, sliding to the floor with her right leg still propped up on the step. It leaves her in this wildly sexy position with her thighs spread, her own liquid heat glistening from either leg, breath panting and lips open, head back.

BAD NANNY

I stumble a few steps away, overwhelmed with a thousand strange emotions I don't understand, my heart pounding frantically as Brooke wraps her arms around herself and closes her eyes, fighting for each breath.

I can't stop staring, my brain a strange tumbled mess as I snap the condom off and jerk my pants back into place. I've had ... well, let's just say a *lot* of sex. But this is ... this is ... and there's nothing all that special about it, not really. No special positions or toys or weird shit, but—

I'm not doing this right now, letting myself get into my own head.

I move back over to Brooke and kneel down next to her, fighting that violent urge to get the fuck out of there. I'm not like some of my friends, freaking the fuck out because some chick spends the night and wants to stay for breakfast. So what? Big deal. Be an adult. Take her to dinner or something and don't be an ass.

This ... I've never been so scared in all my life and I've known this girl for a matter of *days*. She's as much a stranger as any of those women that come into my shop and yet ... she feels like somebody I *should* know.

"Hey." I sweep some of that crazy long hair of hers back from her face with inked up fingers. "You alright there, Smarty-Pants?"

She makes a sort of strangled half-sob/half-laugh sound that makes me smile.

"That's what I've been missing out on all these years? I'm a goddamn idiot."

I chuckle as I sit down cross legged in front of her and take her hands in my lap, rubbing her knuckles with my thumbs.

"Naw. Nobody's as good as old Zay is." I wink at her when she glances up at me from beneath a fall of chocolate hair, her mascara running in two dark lines like it did that first day. I lift a hand up and scrub one of the lines away with my thumb.

"Don't call yourself old," she sniffles and then laughs. "It's creepy."

My smile gets a little warmer and that panic flares again, but I push it down. What's the big deal? So I like this girl *slightly* more than usual. Oh well. Come hell or high water, when my brother gets back into town, I am done. Outtie. Back to Vegas and bye-bye Brooke.

"Come on. I'll take you upstairs." I stand up and help her to her feet. When she stumbles in her heels and falls into my arms, I feel this warmth ride over me, this contentment, like *this* girl is supposed to be something more than usual. More than a mistake or a quick fuck or a friend.

But that's dumb. And I don't believe in fate and feelings and bullshit.

Eight days and this is done. *Permanently.*

CHAPTER 18
BROOKE OVERLAND

I'm so exhausted from work and from ... Zayden, that I forget that the kids have school. Around noon, I wake up in a panic and flip over in search of my phone.

Only to find Zayden's bare back instead.

He's laying next to me with no shirt, no pants, just a pair of black briefs, his legs tangled around a pillow, one arm above his head and the other thrown out across the rumpled surface of the bed. Like this, he looks innocent and peaceful.

Last night, he was anything but.

I wrap my arms around my body and suck in several deep breaths, realizing as I do that I'm wearing *his* shirt, the one that says *I'd Pierce the Fuck Outta You.* There's a questionable stain on the front of it that I pick at with my nail, my cheeks flushing with red heat. When I'd walked into that door a few short hours ago, I'd been determined I was going to tell the bastard no. But then he walked towards me in that dark living room, and I just wanted somebody to be on my side, to stand with me, look at me, hold me.

Ugh.

That was so stupid, but ... kind of wonderful, too.

I blink away the sudden influx of memories. The kids.

Shit.
    School.
    School!
    I shake Zayden's shoulder and he groans.
    "The kids have class," I tell him as I climb out of bed and grab two handfuls of sheet, jerking them away from him. The motion's enough to jar him out of sleep for a second. He looks up at me and blinks slowly a couple of times before his mouth curves into a smile that makes me go weak in the knees.
    Oh.
    Or maybe I'm *already* weak in the knees. I feel sore and sated between my thighs, but the muscles feel stretched, tight, unused to *that* particular sort of stretch. I clutch the rumpled white sheets to my chest and squeeze my legs together tight.
    "Zayden."
    He sits up and rubs at the shaved side of his head.
    "What's up?" he mumbles as he looks up at me in the early morning sunshine, blinking away the fog in his brain. As soon as his eyes clear, I catch this weird glimpse flickering across his pale green irises. It looks a little something like fear, but he blinks once more and it's gone. "What's the emergency?"
    "The kids have school," I say as I search around for my phone. "*I* have school."
    "Hey, Smarty-Pants. Relax yourself, chickie."
    I raise my brows as I glance over my shoulder at him, realizing as his gaze drops that my ass is bare beneath the fabric of this t-shirt. Crap. I spin and tuck the sheets tighter around my body.
    "I already took the kids to school," he tells me as he tosses a pair of thumbs-up in my direction. "For the next seven days, you have got yourself the best damn nanny this side of the Mason-Dixon line, baby."
    I blow out a long breath and my hair flutters uselessly in front of my face. I keep searching for my phone and then pause as Zayden holds up his. I tiptoe forward to squint at the screen when I realize I've slept in my contacts on accident. Damn. I groan and rub at my eyes, realizing that the sticky, dry

BAD NANNY

feeling is from more than just lack of sleep.

"If I don't hurry, I'll be late," I say as I struggle into the bathroom with the wad of sheets trailing behind me. "There's no way I'm going to be late on my second week. It's not happening." I let the white tangle of cloth fall to the floor and strip the shirt over my head before I realize that Zayden's followed me into the bathroom.

Before I can say a word about it, he's stepping up behind me, his hands coming around to cup both my breasts in firm, colorful grips. The sight of that ... of his tattooed fingers curled around me like that, really *does* make my knees go weak. I almost collapse, but Zayden catches me, holding me up with an arm around the waist.

The feeling of his tight arm muscles pressed into my side makes me remember last night, how he held me up as I crumbled, using his strength to finish us both off before he let go. I make a little sound in my throat when he slides his thumbs across my nipples and purrs in my ear.

"You are so fucking hot," he murmurs against the side of my throat, giving me flashes of recent memory, of his hands gripping me in place, of his breath feathering against my neck as he came with his body locked inside of mine.

I start to pant, feeling wetness bloom between my thighs. The reaction is so sudden it makes me gasp. I reach up to pull Zayden's hands away and end up curling mine around his and squeezing instead.

"Do you want to hang out after class with me?" he whispers, each movement of his mouth a lesson in exquisite torture. "I'll make it worth your while."

"I ..." I want to tell him no because this was supposed to be a onetime thing. This was supposed to be an experiment, a way to capture a little something special to take to the job with me. Instead, it's ... addicting as hell. "Sure." The word pops out of my mouth before I can stop it and Zayden groans, pushing me forward so that I'm leaning over the counter in the bathroom, my hair hanging in the sink in a dark swirling pool.

"How soon do you have to leave for class?" he asks me as I

swallow a few times in a struggle to find my voice. I can't believe how bad I want this right now. I lift my head up and catch sight of Zay's face in the mirror, his tongue sliding across his lower lip, playing with his silver lip piercings. "Do you have ten minutes to spare?"

"I ... no. No." I push back into him and he groans as my ass rubs against the hard bulge in his briefs. It's tempting to keep going, to writhe and wiggle and arch my back. Um. Okay. This is definitely not happening to me right now. I refuse to give into an urge I don't even fully understand. "I'm sorry, but ... we'll talk after I get out of class."

I push past him, but I can't stop thinking about last night, about his hands on my throat and his cum on my fingers and—I just can't shake any of it.

"You have more self-control than I do," he says as he leans in the door frame of the bathroom and I glance back at him, finding nothing less than godly about his appearance, even with sleepy half-lidded eyes and mussy hair. Definitely the God of Tattoos and Piercings. And I am definitely one of his most loyal followers.

I snag an extra contacts lens case from the dresser and grab a pair of glasses, snatching up clothes on my way out of the room. I'd really love to shower before I leave, but I can't see that happening without something *else* happening.

My steps slow as I near the bottom of the stairs and eye the spot where Zay held me last night. My heart starts to pound and I almost drop the pile of clothes in my hands. It feels almost impossible that that actually happened, that that was *me* with my back to the wall and my tongue in Zay's mouth.

When I hear him following after me, I retreat into the downstairs bathroom and slam the door, locking it up tight and taking my contacts out with a shaking finger. I'm almost positive I'm imagining it, but it feels like I *look* different today. I know I *feel* different, but I can't quite figure out why that is. Maybe it's because my life's become unrecognizable in the last week?

Just last month, before Ingrid ever left, I was getting over my breakup with Anthony, hitting bars with my friends, making appearances at campus parties. I was planning the next year of my life out to the smallest detail, making sure everything was on track for graduation and the beautiful future I'd envisioned for myself.

Now, I'm hiding in the downstairs bathroom of my sister's place, trying to figure out why I can't breathe when Zay's around, why I'm letting myself go around a complete stranger, how I'm going to manage these kids in the long run.

I lean to the side and let my body rest against the wall. Because of Zay, I'd almost forgotten my night at the club. But how could I? It was *ten times* busier than the night before, and the crowd was rowdy and awful.

I hated every second of it. *Second* being the key word. That was only my *second* night working, and I feel like I want to pull my hair out. All those eyes on me, the grinding thump of the music, my sweaty hands gripping the pole.

A knock at the door makes me jump, snaps me out of last night's memories.

I put my clothes on as quick as I can and open the bathroom door to find Zayden waiting for me, still wearing his briefs and nothing else. He doesn't even seem to care that the bay window looks in right on his nearly naked form.

"You want a PB&J for breakfast? I'm gettin' real good at making those."

"A PB&J?" I ask, blinking at him as I try to figure out the most strategic way to squeeze past him into the living. Only there is no strategic way because he's a big dude and he takes up the whole space. "Yeah, sure," I say, just to get him to move away, pad into the kitchen with an exaggerated yawn, arms stretched over his head, the muscles in his sleek back lengthening into a painting worthy image of perfection. Oddly enough, there isn't a single tattoo on that long, lean stretch of muscle. Other than the sprinkle of color at the top that connects his shoulders and trails up the back of his neck, this is all blank canvas.

I feel my breath catch again and have to close my eyes for a long moment. Never in my life have I been this jumpy about a guy before and it's a little concerning if I'm being honest with myself. In my mind, I tell myself I'm acting this way because I lost my virginity to the guy. Everyone always acts like people develop immediate feelings for the partner that was involved during their first time. Maybe it's true?

I walk up to the doorway between the living room and kitchen, folding my arms in front of myself as I watch Zay slap together another sandwich for me. He even wraps the bottom half up in a paper towel so it's portable.

"Here ya go." He passes it over to me and lets his fingers linger against the pulse point in my wrist. "Have fun at school, okay? And tell Dan the Douche to fuck off if he tries to hit on you."

"Um." I slap the sandwich against my palm. "And why would I do that? What if I like the guy?" I kind of don't, but that's not really the point.

Zay flashes a grin over his shoulder.

"Cool beans. Like the guy. Do whatever you want with him ... *after* I go back to Vegas. Until then, Smarty-Pants, I'm totally laying my claim on you."

The campus at HSU is lush. I'd be hard-pressed to admit it, but it's definitely prettier than Berkeley, less competitive, too. It's not like I have a problem with competitiveness. Trust me, I can keep up. I didn't graduate high school early to then fall behind, but ... an academic world without that cutthroat background buzz is nice, peaceful. Even though Humboldt State is a hell of a lot less prestigious than UCB, I think I might be able to adapt. Maybe even come to like it here?

I pass under trees dripping with dew, past jurassic ferns that have probably grown here since the beginning of time, and head out to my Subaru, pausing when a hand clamps down on my door and a girl appears, leaning into my personal space like Zayden does.

"Hi there," she says, smiling prettily at me. And wow. She *is* pretty—tall and thin with tattoos on both arms and electric blue hair that mimics the small bit of clear sky I can see above her head. "You're Brooke, right?"

"Yeah?" I answer her like it's a question, mostly because I'm already worrying about what's going to happen between Zayden and me when I get home, and partly because I'm a little confused as to how she knows my name.

"Tinley," she offers as introduction, pointing to herself with a finger tattooed in hearts. "You're Dan's study partner?"

I blink stupidly a few times and lift my hands to my hair, pulling it all away from my back so I can lean against the car's seat without it yanking my scalp off.

"Sure." Now that she's mentioned Dan, I'm thinking about Zayden's words. *My claim on you.* Claim? What claim? That's just stupid guy talk, and I hate it. I won't listen to it. "Why?"

"Because he's my ex, and I just wanted you to know that he sleeps with anybody he can get his hands on." A pause as the girl steps back in her tight black jeans and tank top. "*Anybody.* Basically, he's a slut."

I raise my eyebrows.

"Right. Okay. I wasn't planning on sleeping with the guy, but thanks for the heads-up."

"No problem," she says as she takes another step back and watches as I climb into the car and shut the door. I turn on some metal music and let the angry sounds wash over me. Something about all that chaos keeps me calm in a way Zayden's pop music never could.

I push my glasses up my nose and buckle myself in, pulling out of the space and noticing as I do that the blue-haired girl is watching me and smiling. Huh. Doubt I'll ever see her again, but still, that was weird, wasn't it? Totally weird.

I head home and pull into the driveway next to Zay's minivan, straightening out the boring gray tank I wore to class, wishing I'd taken the time to put on makeup before I'd left.

"Not that it really matters," I mutter under my breath, running my fingers through my hair before I climb out and head inside, opening the door to blaring Eminem/Rihanna as I move into the kitchen and cross my arms over my chest. Zayden's rapping to the baby in her high chair as she bounces and laughs at him.

When he sees me, he winks and starts singing Rihanna's portion of the song, completely unashamed of how stupid he looks.

I seriously cannot fight that smile.

"Sing it with me, Smarty-Pants," he says as he spins in a theatrical circle on the soles of his knee-high Converse. They're black and white, covered in straps studded with bits of metal. They look ... devastatingly sexy with his black skinny jeans and his red tank. When he puts his hands together in a prayer position and gestures at me with them, I feel a warm heat between my thighs. "Come on, baby. Let's do this thing."

He reaches out as Eminem spins his melodic rap, taking my hand and spinning *me* in a circle this time, wrapping his arm around my waist and turning me around the kitchen as Sadie giggles and screams in joy, bouncing in her seat.

When Rihanna starts singing again, Zay puts his lips against my ear and whispers the lyrics with his warm breath tickling my throat. I swear, I can still feel his hands there, pressing gently against the sides of my neck and face. Chills skitter through me as the song peters off and I take a step back, thighs bumping into the small round table that sits in the center of the kitchen.

When a silly pop song starts pinging in the room, I curl my fingers around the wood and watch Zayden as he whisks a bowl of cereal from the counter and puts it in front of Sadie, still doing a stupid little jig that's really not all that stupid in that outfit with those tattoos.

Hmm.

His hair is spiked up on the one side, the stars freshly shaved back into place. With the slight layer of stubble around

BAD NANNY

his soft mouth, the piercings on his lips and nose, his eyebrow … I'm deep in lust before I can stop myself from feeling that way.

"Look at that," he says as Sadie picks up the puffy bits of cereal with clumsy hands and shoves them in her mouth. "She's got this all figured out."

"Glad to see you're enjoying yourself," I say as I force myself to stand up straight and shove some hair back from my face. "For somebody's who's barely taken care of a child in his life, you're kind of good at it."

Those white teeth flash at me in a grin.

"Right? Maybe I should quit piercing and become a full-time nanny? How do you like them apples? Because they taste *nice* and juicy to me." Zay slaps his hands together and even though I have no clue what he's talking about, I smile anyway. But then he looks over at me, *really* looks at me and I start thinking about the feel of his hands gripping my ass, the spicy scent of sweat, the heat of his breath against my skin as he came. "You know what else looks nice and juicy right now?"

"That better not be a reference to me," I say as Zay smiles and I point at the baby. "There's a kid in here."

"So?" Zay looks down at Sadie. "Don't you think Brooke looks smoking hot today?" Sadie gurgles and pats the cereal in her high chair tray. Zayden looks back up at me. "She agrees, so if she agrees and I agree, then it's pretty much an unarguable point."

"I haven't forgotten about that whole *claim* line you laid on me this morning. In fact, the more I think about, the more it annoys me. Has anyone ever told you that? That you're annoying?"

"All of the fucking time."

Zay pulls a kitchen chair out and gestures for me to sit in it.

"The kids are starting to bitch about the sandwiches, so I've decided to try my hand at cooking tonight. First time since I took home ec in high school, so this should be interesting."

"You took home ec?" I repeat as I reluctantly sit in the chair and watch as Zayden opens the fridge. There's more food in there than there was this morning. Looks like somebody went shopping. "Why?"

"To hit on girls, of course," Zay says as he starts tossing ingredients onto the counter. "Classic move that every teenage guy knows." I watch as he lays out a tray of chicken breasts and a stick of butter, moving over to the cabinet for some instant rice, three cans of soup and some salt and pepper that I know I didn't buy. "Alright, here goes nothing." He whips his phone out of his back pocket and slicks his thumb across the screen.

"What are you making?" I ask, unable to keep sitting there and staring at his ass. It looks far too sexy in those tight pants of his, the straps of his shoes twisting up to his knees. I know this sounds weird, but how often do you see guys dress up like this? With a studded belt and some bracelets on one arm, silver piercings lining his ears, hair all clean and styled into place. When I get close to Zay, I get that blackberry/cinnamon smell again and it calms my racing pulse.

"Some kind of casserole thing. The recipe says it's easy as fuck. Basically, I mix all this crap together and toss it into the oven. Bam. Done." Zay pauses as I come up beside him and looks down at me, his eyes smiling along with his mouth. His expressions just take over him completely, from head to toe. It's kind of refreshing, the way he doesn't hold back like that. My parents and my sister were always trying to hide their emotions, chug along as if everything were A-OK. I don't want to be like them. "Want to help?"

"Sure," I say, even though I probably know less about cooking than Zayden does. I didn't even take home ec in school; it was all STEM classes all the time. Zayden hands me a stick of butter and a knife.

"It says *pats*," he tells me with an easy shrug. "I have no idea what that means, but I guess we spread the butter out across the top of the casserole. It's a make it work moment." He snaps his fingers above his head and then grabs a knife, spinning it around his fingers in a way that makes me raise my brows. "Time to tackle this chicken."

BAD NANNY

Zay slaps a breast onto the plastic pink cutting board I once remember my sister using and then starts to slice into it with careful motions. He's so animated, I wonder what he'd be like if he were angry? Would that emotion take over his whole body the way his joy does? Would his eyes burn and his hands clench into fists?

I look back at the butter and start cutting thin squares off the end until it's half-gone.

"How much?" I ask as Zay glances over at me and smiles, his body grooving to a Kelly Clarkson song that I hate. I smile again.

"Looks about right. You want to start mixing shit together?" I nod and dig into a drawer for a can opener, examining the three soups in front of me. Cream of chicken, celery and mushroom. Hmm. I start opening them one at a time. "That claim thing I said this morning?"

I feel myself stiffen up, but I don't stop what I'm doing.

"Yeah?" I feel Zay's muscular arm bump against mine and wonder how such a simple move could feel so good. "What about it?"

"I'm not so sure why I even said it," he admits as he drops chicken into the clear glass casserole dish sitting in front of me. At Zay's direction, I add the soup in after it and stir it all around with a plastic spoon. "I think I'm just getting all *male* around you, you know what I mean?"

I wrinkle my face up as I tug Zay's phone from his back pocket and check the recipe. Two cups of instant rice. Got it. I put the phone back just so I can have an excuse to touch his ass through the jeans. *It's so firm!* I breathe in deep.

"I'm not sure what that means, no. Keep explaining maybe?" I glance over at him and find him smiling weirdly, not as happy, more like he's creeped out by something. Is that something me? I hope not. If so, I can't figure out what I've done. He dumps the rest of the chicken into the dish and then stops to wash his hands.

"You know, getting all excited because I'm your first and all that." Zay turns and dries his hands off before grabbing one of the empty cans, leaning his hip against the counter and swiping his finger around the inside of the metal. I wrinkle my nose again as he slides the finger into his mouth and sucks on it. Not because of the gesture though, that's actually hot. It's his words that are making me wrinkle my nose up.

"Seriously? Zayden, no offense or anything, but my decision to have sex had pretty much nothing to do with *you*. So don't get all excited or anything."

"I'm not," he says with pouty lips, dipping his finger back into the can again. The motion makes his red tank ride up and flashes me tantalizing hints of skin. I want to put my mouth on it and kiss my way down, see what it'd be like to take his cock into my mouth.

My eyes snap back up to Zayden's face.

"All I'm saying is that I like you. We have a pretty hot connection, don't you think?"

"This might sound like a dumb question," I say as I spread the chicken-soup-rice mixture around the pan. "But isn't it always like this? The sex and the … all of this." I point between us, trying to encompass the obsessive attraction I'm feeling. I'm not stupid, just inexperienced. Honestly, my ex, Anthony, and I never had anything like this heat I've got with Zay. I figured it was just because we hadn't had sex yet.

Zay smiles softly at me and shrugs his shoulders loosely, shakes his head a little. It's a conflicting answer to my question.

"Not really," he says as tosses his can into the sink and turns the water on, rinsing it and tossing it into the recycling bin near the back door. Zayden grabs one of the other cans, fills it up about halfway and then adds it to the casserole dish, sliding his fingers over my hand and taking the spoon away.

"Not really?" I ask as he spins it around and then drops the spoon in the sink, taking my pats of butter and spreading them out across the top of the casserole like a crust. "I'm even more confused than I was when I left this morning."

Zayden finishes with the butter, wipes his hands on a dish towel and pulls the oven open. He pops the food into it and heels the door shut, pausing to look at me with his hands on his hips.

"It's not usually this ... intense," he says, eyes sliding over to Sadie. It feels more like he's talking to himself than he is to me at this point. Maybe it's not me that has the problem? "We haven't *done* anything all that different and honestly, you're kind of amateurish."

I purse my mouth as he chews his lower lip and nods his head like he's trying to convince himself of something. I cross my arms over my chest again and tip my head down, trying to give him a fierce look over the tops of my glasses.

"Excuse me? Are you *trying* to insult me? You're telling me I'm bad at sex? Well, screw you. How is that my fault? You knew what you were getting into."

"No, no," Zayden says, moving over to Sadie and lifting her up from the chair. When he tucks her under his chin and starts to rub her back, I feel like melting into a little puddle on the floor. "That's not what I'm saying. You're *not* bad, and that's the point. You have no clue what you're doing and yet ... last night was the best sex I've ever had in my life. I can't figure it out."

I feel my entire face heat up, shoving my glasses back into place and heaving out a big breath.

"What does that mean then? I don't get it."

"Neither do I," Zay says as he hugs his niece to his chest and gives me the weird half-smile version of his grin again. "All I want to do is fuck you though. Like, seriously, it's all I can think about."

"And that's unusual?" I ask, even though my throat is tight and I cannot *believe* I'm actually having a conversation about this. Zayden's grin ratchets up a notch.

"Yeah, a little. I mean, I love sex. It's my first and third favorite past time, but usually I like to take breaks to play games or listen to music or whatever." Zayden pauses and his grin fades a little, his eyelids dropping until they're half-shuttered and shadowed with intensity. "Brooke, when it's with you, I don't want any breaks."

He turns away before I can come up with a response to that. Holy crap.

I follow Zayden into the living room and watch him plop down on the couch with the baby. He sits her in his lap and picks up a colorful cardboard book.

"That's it?" I ask as I blink at him and he glances up at me.

"Hmm?"

"You're going to deliver a line like *that* and then just … walk away?" I move into the living room and watch as his eyes take me in slowly, pausing on my breasts, the curve of my hips, my calves in the brown suede boots I stole from my sister's closet.

"Um?" Zay pauses and looks up at the ceiling as Sadie giggles and laughs, grabbing his tattooed arm and putting her mouth on it. She's dressed up cute again, with a headband decorated in hearts and a pink frilly dress. It's clear that Zay's taking his babysitting duties seriously. I appreciate the fact that he's actually trying. "That's all I had to say. Just that. Why? What's up?"

I gape at him and move into the living room, sitting down next to him so I can keep the book open for the baby. My thigh and Zay's line up; our arms line up. It feels *really* good actually.

"Well, I think that's a lot to throw at someone all of a sudden." I reach out and turn the page slowly, trying to keep my attention on the splashy illustrations and not on the fine hairs of Zayden's arm brushing against mine. "If you feel all those things, then … what does that mean?"

"Mean?" he asks as he takes a deep breath. "Nothing. I just thought you should know that this is a little bit different than usual. That's all. I guess what I'm trying to say is, if you sleep with Dan the Douche, it won't be nearly as good."

I scoff and then start laughing, unable to hold back the sound as I crumple over. The funniest part is, I don't think that's even supposed to be a joke. When I sit up, I have to shove my glasses back up my face again. I'm sitting on my hair which is annoying but normal. I just don't want to move to get it out, not from this spot in this moment.

"Seriously? Don't worry about Dan. His ex stalked me to my car today to warn me off of him." I pause and look up at the popcorn ceiling. I hate it. I have urges to get on a chair and scrape it all off. If this were my house instead of a rental, I'd do it in a second. "Or maybe she was telling *me* off of him. Not sure exactly which. My point is, how can you say all these things? Tell me I'm different from all the other girls you've ..." I glance Zayden's way. "Slept with, and then try to act like that doesn't mean anything."

"No, you're right: it means something," he corrects himself as I turn the page for Sadie again. "It does. But what I'm trying to say is, it doesn't *change* anything. Between us, I mean." Zayden glances over at me and smiles. "I think we should enjoy our week together, that's it. That's all I'm trying to say."

"Right." I'm so confused right now, but I think he is, too, so whatever. That's okay. That's *his* problem, not mine. I stand up from the couch and head to the back door to let the dogs in, cringing at the muddy footprints they splatter across the floor in their wake. An instant letter, I hear a hiss and a yowl and watch as Hubert tears out from under the couch with three chihuahuas on his heels.

Oops.

Zay gets up and hands me Sadie.

"One sec, 'kay?" he says and then he turns and swings around the newel post, heading up the stairs as I look down at Dodger and use my foot to stop him from lifting his leg on the edge of the baby's crib. The stupid little rat can't seem to stop marking his territory, even though none of this stuff really belongs to him. He *wants* it to be his, but he doesn't want to have to take any responsibility for it.

Zayden's the same way, I think. That's what all his posturing in front of Dan was about, why he said he was laying his claim on me. He wants to piss on me and mark me as his, but he doesn't want the responsibility that comes along with it.

Zay might be good with his nieces and nephews, with mine,

but he's exactly what I thought he'd be: the perfect one-night stand.

Oh well. If he thinks that's news to me, he's wrong. I didn't sleep with a stranger expecting to be romanced.

Zayden Roth can watch my kids for me for free, save me some money, give me some time.

And you know what? I'll let him touch me because I want it, not because he does. I'll use him exactly the way he's using me, and then I'll be done.

It'll be a nice ending for both of us when he goes back to Las Vegas.

CHAPTER 19
ZAYDEN ROTH

I am like, so screwing up this Brooke thing.

I know it; she knows it.

What the hell are you doing, Zay? I wonder as I corral the little brown and tan dogs in the upstairs bathroom and close the door. Ugh. What did I just say to that chick? *It means something, but it doesn't change anything.* Like I was one of the other assholes from the shop, protesting too much about how this thing between us is actually not a thing at all.

Why am I so determined to tell Brooke off—at the same time I want to *get* her off?

I muss up my hair with my fingers and lean my head back. I'm definitely losing it. Maybe it's the climate? It's so goddamn moist up here that I feel like I'm sucking in saltwater with every inhale. I miss the desert and the dry warmth and the bright lights of the Strip.

I pull my phone from my pocket and check for messages from my friends. The owner of the shop I work at—a placed called *Needle in My Eye Body Piercing*—texted me a picture of some girl's clitoral hood piercing. I stare at it and then scroll down.

The ladies miss u dude. Come back soon!

I smile and pocket the phone, shoving away all of that

weirdness from downstairs. I shake it off and take a deep breath, pausing to fix my hair in Brooke's bathroom before I go back down and find her sitting with Sadie on the couch.

Mmm.

Yikes.

I pause there with my hand on the newel post and fight back the urge to put the baby to bed and drag Brooke upstairs, screw her bareback into the mattress. Wouldn't it be cute to see her pregnant? To have a baby to play with the way I play with Sadie? One that was actually *mine*?

Um.

No, it wouldn't.

Whoa, Zay. Put the brakes on there. I'm twenty-nine years old, so I guess it's right about that time where I'd start thinking of making babies, but hell, what am I doing? I don't know Brooke. And I don't live here. And she already comes with *two* inherited kids of her own. Besides, she's twenty-two and trying to get her master's degree. If I'm going to fixate on someone like this, I should find somebody closer to my own age.

Deep breath.

I move into the room and pause, sitting down on the arm of the big couch.

"Want to go somewhere? We can pick up the kids while we're out?" *Because if I don't get the fuck out of here, I'm going to throw you over the back of this couch and screw the hell out of you.* I smile, so Brooke can't see what I'm thinking about. "We could ... go get some coffee at that place on the water, what's it called?"

"Um, the Waterfront?" Brooke says with a little sarcastic lilt. I grin at her and snap my fingers.

"Exactly. We can even get some fish and chips or something." I grab my wallet from its place on the coffee table and flash the black leather at Brooke. "I'm whippin' out the credit card. My treat, okay?"

"What about the casserole?" she asks and I shrug.

"Fuck the casserole." I bounce off the couch and into the

BAD NANNY

kitchen, opening the oven and using a mitt to pull the glass out. Surprisingly, the damn thing actually smells good. "I'll hide it from Hubert and we can finish cooking it later."

The glass is barely warm, so I cover it with foil and shove it in the fridge. I feel like I need to get out of here for a second, try to find some space to breathe.

"You game?" I ask as I come back around the corner and cross my arms over my chest. When Brooke looks up at me, I wiggle my brows and toss her a wink that I don't really feel. Fuck. I am so not myself right now. Want to know why I tattooed the words *LIVE EASY* onto my knuckles? Because that's how I like to do my thing, nice and easy and uncomplicated. Life's just more fun that way, you know?

All of this? This is complicated as *hell*.

"Sure. Why not. I'm not too proud to turn down free food." Brooke hoists Sadie up in her arms and stands. When I see her lean in and kiss the baby on the pudgy cheek, I feel a little thrill shoot through me and know that I best keep the bio clock hormones on serious lockdown here.

The Waterfront Café is off the beaten path, across two bridges that span a marshy preserve that's full of brackish seawater, clumps of grass as tall as I am, and flocks of white herons.

"My dad used to tell me stories about these bridges," I say to Brooke as we pass over the first one. "That when he was a kid, when they were first built, there were no rails on either side. Just an empty swath of road suspended over the water. One little swerve and bam. Done for."

"They let people drive on it like that?" Brooke asks, like she doesn't believe me. I shrug my shoulders.

"Guess so."

"Where does your dad live now?" Brooke asks and my smile gets real tight.

"My parents are both dead." I don't elaborate because hell, I'm already having trouble with this chick. The last thing I need to do is start sharing personal details. I never do anyway, with the girls I fuck. I like to keep things light and fluffy and fun. Nothin' fluffy and fun about dead parents.

Brooke doesn't say anything, turning her head to stare out the window as we hit a small patch of land between the two bridges. For a few minutes, there's nothing but the sound of pop music in the background.

"My dad has early onset Alzheimer's," Brooke blurts, turning back to look at me. I keep my eyes on the road as I start over the second bridge, but I can feel her gaze like a laser beam through the side of my head. *Boom.* Explosion.

I suck in a breath.

"I don't know how I'm going to say good-bye to him. Did you get to say good-bye to your parents?"

"Um." *Shit.* Shit, shit, shit. Brooke's got those doe eyes on again, big and watery and brown and sexy as hell. I want to cup her face in my hand and pull our mouths together. *Ahh.* I am, like, so seriously screwed it's not even funny. "I didn't actually. It sounds fake as hell, but they actually died in a boating accident when I was ... twenty-two." *Same age as Brooke is now.* "On Lake Tahoe."

"I can't even imagine," Brooke says, reaching over and taking my hand. Crap. Did not expect that. I was hoping for an *I'm so sorry to hear that* at most. This is ... a lot harder to process. I wish her hands weren't so soft, her fingertips so hot. I wish she didn't smell good, like flowers and soap. I need to go home and get mind-fucked by some crazy chick with tattoos on her face. That's what I need to do. Yep.

Brooke lets go of my hand and I feel like I can breathe again. It's bugging me though, how jumpy I'm getting. Like, hello Zayden, you've never gotten this way before. You always make fun of Jude for freaking the fuck out over every girl he sleeps with. If he even catches a glimpse of them again after, he starts panicking that he's going to be stalked or something. I've always thought he was a douche.

BAD NANNY

Now *I'm* the douche. Me. I'm acting like the weirdo.

And yet, all I can do right now is hope that Brooke will let me fuck her again when she gets off of work. How messed up is that? But every time I look at her—*every time*—I see that image of her on the floor, her back pressed to the wall, one foot propped on the step, the other leg open wide. I can see her panting chest, her moist lips, the glitter of liquid on her inner thighs.

"The doctor says the average life expectancy from the onset of symptoms is about eight years. It's been just a few months since he was diagnosed, but that means by the time I'm thirty," a pause, "by the time I'm your age, he'll be gone."

Brooke takes a deep breath and threads her fingers through her hair. I see now. It makes sense why she's watching the kids, why her parents haven't stepped in. The whole thing makes her sister, Ingrid, seem like even more of a douche-y bitch.

"Anyway, sorry. My fault. I shouldn't have brought that up," she says.

"Naw, that was totally me. Hey, relax a little. You made it to the end of the week. Yay." I pretend to wave a little flag and Brooke smiles. I can see the expression from the corner of my eye. I like the way her lips curve up, giving her this sexy porn star look in the mouth while her big, black glasses look dorky as hell. "One more night of work and you'll be off for a few days. Hey, what do you want to do on Saturday?"

"Saturday?" Brooke echoes, like she's completely lost.

"You know, your aunt's babysitting and all that. You want to hit that art festival in Old Town or something?"

"Arts Alive?" Brooke asks and then starts gathering her hair into a ponytail. It takes her some serious effort because it's all caught up under her ass. *I'd sure like to be caught under this chick's ass.* "I don't even know if Monica really will show up. She hasn't contacted me since."

"If she does, you want to go? I could show you some of my favorite haunts down there." I pause and let a smile tease my lips. "Some of the best places to fuck without getting caught."

Brooke's mouth drops open as I take a left towards the restaurant, pulling into the parking lot without hearing a response from those pretty lips of hers.

When I park the car and turn to look at her, she's finally closed her mouth and is staring at me like I'm insane.

"Who says I even *want* to hang out with you on Saturday? I might make other plans."

"With who? The endangered sea crustacean chick? Dan the Douche? His ex? Come on. I'm the only friend you've got in town right now."

"I just moved here," Brooke says defensively, but I just shrug my shoulders loosely. Straight-up, I don't know why I'm hounding her anyway, asking her out on a date. I mean, it's not like I'm generally opposed to taking girls out, but never one I've felt this magnetic sort of a connection with. This could be the end of me right here. "Sure, why not? I always loved Arts Alive. It's one of the few things I ever liked about this place."

"Amen, sister," I say, reaching out and giving her a tap on the shoulder. Brooke smiles and I toss her a wink, climbing out of the car and heading around to the sliding door to grab Sadie. I carry her inside with the car seat and then get her set up in a wooden high chair.

"Do you think she'll be okay in there while we eat?"

"Bam." I produce a bag of that Gerber puff cereal crap from Sadie's diaper bag. I Googled *how to go to a restaurant with my baby* and got all sorts of sweet tips. "Lookie there. Zay plans ahead, Smarty-Pants."

"Nice move. I'm still figuring all the kid hacks out. My mom gave me a sort of crash course last week, but it didn't even begin to cover everything." Brooke pauses and flattens her menu out on the table. "Bella's been crying at night." A pause. "Well, not since you started staying over, but before that. And Grace ... has she snuck into the yard to play hide and seek yet?"

"Oh yeah. Twice while you were at work the other night. It's so creepy, total horror movie-esque."

Brooke laughs.

BAD NANNY

"Yeah, exactly. I actually get *scared* to go out there and look for her, like I'm afraid the next time I see her she'll look like the zombie girl from the first episode of *The Walking Dead*."

"Ah, I knew it. You like horror stuff? Zombies?"

"Definitely. The darker the better. What about you? I figured since you liked pop music ..."

I wave my hand and Sadie giggles. I think she digs all the colors on my arm. I read that babies her age dig movement and bright things. Guess I'm a lot of both, huh?

"I love horror shit. Especially in video game form. You play?"

"I was a huge *World of Warcraft* girl back in high school." I lean over and give her a high five. Brooke accepts it with a laugh and smiles. "I haven't had much time to play games since I graduated though. Biostatistics is kind of a tough field. I worked my ass off to get into that masters program at Berkeley." She looks down at the table for a moment and her eyes flutter with emotion. I feel my own mouth tighten and start getting pissed on her behalf. So not cool. A girl like this, with everything in the world to live for and here she is, cleaning up somebody else's mess.

If I ever see her sister, Ingrid, I might just up and deck her in the face.

"You'll make it," I say, pretending to shoot a basketball. "Slam dunk. I can just tell."

"Thanks," Brooke says with a small laugh, leaning back against the cracked green leather of the booth. I still think she has no idea what she looks like, how her arched brows give her this permanently curious expression, like frames for the bright intelligence of her eyes. Long lashes, full lips, that long dark hair that I haven't had a chance to fully play with yet ... Yep. Total package.

I drum my fingers against the tabletop.

"What do you think you'll do with the kids while you're working? After I leave, I mean."

Brooke shakes her head, giant ponytail flopping.

"No clue. I guess if Monica really does come through tomorrow ... and then maybe I can make it until my parents get back from Scotland. My dad isn't going to be able to do much, and I'd hate to put that extra burden on my mom, but if the girls are asleep most of the time, maybe she can handle it?"

"When do they get back?"

"About two and a half weeks from now." I raise my eyebrows, but I get it. Brooke's dad is sick; this could be her parents' last chance to get away together. "If my mom can't do it, I guess I'll hire a sitter."

"Not off of Craigslist though, right?" I ask as I point at her with a tattooed finger. The letter *E* stands up sharply between us. Brooke gives me a sexy little smile and puts her hands on the table, leaning forward enough that I can see straight down her shirt to the lacy gray bra she's wearing. *Damn.* I feel my cock respond instantaneously, rising up to meet my tight pants with a vigor even I wasn't sure he was capable of. *Oooouch.* Guess we're both Brooke Overland fans.

I drop my hand to my lap and try to clamp down on the rush of need—literally. I press hard and take a deep breath, pretending that I'm just unfolding my napkin in my lap.

"You didn't *really* offer to help me because you were worried about me, did you? I mean, you *wanted* to fuck me, didn't you?"

I feel my mouth turning up in a grin.

"Listen up there, Smarty-Pants, *I'm* not the one that froze up like a deer in the headlights in the middle of those child infested wood chips. Don't think I didn't notice you gazing at me like that. If anyone was gunning to fuck anyone, it was *you* lookin' at me."

"Okay, fine," Brooke says, leaning even closer, her hair trailing over her shoulder onto the tabletop. "But when I asked you to be the nanny, you were just thinking about getting in my pants."

"Nope." I lean in towards her, matching her stance. "I was legit worried about you. Little naïve there, Brooke Overland, especially for such a Smarty-Pants."

BAD NANNY

She grins at me and I like the expression so much that I lean forward just a little bit more and press our mouths together, my tongue sliding in and capturing her before she can pull away from me. There's a moment of hesitation on her part, but then she starts kissing me back and I smile.

"Stop it," she moans when she drops back into her seat. "Don't smile while we're doing that."

"Why not?" I ask as I prop my elbow on the table and drop my head into my hand. "It's fun. Don't you like to kiss people? You might be never-been-fucked, but don't tell me you're never-been-kissed, too?"

"I kissed people," she says as the waitress stops by to take our order and Brooke flushes at her bemused smile. Clearly, she saw the tongue tangle that was happening over here.

We both skip the coffee and head straight for the good stuff, getting fresh fish and chips and a couple of sodas. Nice. I like a girl that can eat. Weirds me out when you people order salads and shit. What the hell is that all about?

"Who?" I ask when the waitress leaves. Brooke raises an eyebrow and I just seriously want to pierce the fuck out of it. Hey, I mean, it *is* my art. I know it's kind of a weird art form to have, but what can I say? I like the human body. I like to enhance it the best way I know how: with needles and metal. Brooke ... she's so pretty, all I really want to grab is that perfect eyebrow. Wonder if she'd let me if I asked? Or do biostatisticians not get pierced?

"Who what?" Brooke asks as she smiles over at Sadie. The kid's currently occupied with dropping her head back and making a small O with her mouth as she stares at the ceiling. Damn. I think I actually *like* babies. Kinzie ... you know, I'm working on learning to like her.

"Who did you kiss?" Brooke makes a face at me and tilts her head to the side, hair swinging.

"Why do you care?" I shrug my shoulders as she sighs and looks up at the ceiling like Sadie.

"Just curious. Were you one of those goody-goodies that only kisses like, one guy during high school?" Brooke drops her gaze back to mine and narrows her eyes.

"I kissed Ingrid's boyfriend once. Well, more than kissed. We almost screwed, but then she came home and caught us. Maybe I owe her all of this to make up for that?"

I laugh and Brooke smiles again. I like the expression. I want her to keep talking just so I can see that right there, that press of her lips, the little dimples she gets in her cheeks.

"Look at you, you bad girl," I say, giving her a goofy side smile. "Cheating with your sister's boyfriend. So much hotter than screwing the nanny."

Brooke laughs again and wads up her napkin, tossing it at me as I chuckle.

"When you put it like that, it sounds creepy as hell. You're the old guy here you know. *Seven* years older. If anyone's the creeper, it should be you."

I slap a hand to my chest.

"Hey, I was *complimenting* your choice to screw the nanny. And then you go and insult me? So not cool, Brooke Overland."

She pokes me with her foot under the table and I give her a slow, lazy wink. I feel ... I don't know what I feel right now, but it's not a normal feeling. It's ... weird and warm and fuzzy. I think I'm getting ... like, butterflies or something? Do dudes get butterflies? What the fuck?

I sit up and feel my half-lidded contentment sliding away from my face. Brooke notices and gets stiff, sitting up suddenly in her seat.

"What's wrong?" she asks, a note of panic in her voice. Aww, man. Now I'm *scaring* the poor girl. It doesn't get anymore awkward than this.

"I just ... I need a second." I gently scoot Sadie away from the table and make a quick rush toward the men's room, barricading myself into the kitschy blue and white bathroom. A fake fish stares at me from the wall as I try to catch my breath, turning and looking at myself in the mirror. I *look* like the same guy, but I feel *weird.*

I think I'm getting my first real crush.

BAD NANNY

I curl my hands around the sides of the porcelain sink, the bright colors of my tattoos looking almost garish in the fluorescent lighting. When I glance up, my face looks downright friggin' morbid. *Jesus, Zay, get a goddamn grip.* I flick my lip piercing with my tongue and stare myself down.

I'm a twenty-nine year old body piercer/nanny who's currently obsessed with a girl that's all wrong for him, that likes angry music, that studies something he can't pronounce, with two inherited kids, that's *way* too young for him.

But that he really likes. That he wants to ... like, claim or something? Pee on? Act like some wild buck on a nature documentary, start fighting off other dudes with his horns.

Fucking fucknuts.

That's what it is.

Brooke Overland, I don't know the girl for shit, but ... I've got a crush on her. A big one.

That's going to be a problem.

CHAPTER 20
BROOKE OVERLAND

Zayden is definitely an ... *interesting* person.

After he comes back from the bathroom, he acts normal, but I can see that something's bothering him. Makes me want to figure it out, try to unravel his mysteries. But ... I don't have time for that. We eat our food and I notice he leaves the waitress a pretty generous tip. My dad once told me you can get a good idea of a person's character by how they treat waitstaff at a restaurant.

That makes me smile a little.

We start picking up the kids, pinging between schools until the whole brood's collected in the back and Kinzie and Bella are fighting over a *Monster High* doll. This particular one looks like a centaur, with a purple horse body and a ponytail high on top of her human head. I have no idea what the appeal is, but they're both screeching at the tops of their lungs over it.

"Yo," Zayden says loudly as we pull into the driveway. He stops the car and turns around in his seat, giving the girls a look with raised brows. "Whose toy is it anyway?"

"It's *mine*," Bella says as she yanks the doll away from Kinzie. The other girl lets out a bloodcurdling scream that chills me straight to my core. Suddenly, I feel a burst of panic in my chest. *This* is going to be my life? For the next ...

fourteen years? What if I stay here and put years of my life into raising these girls and then Ingrid shows back up? Worse: what if she comes and goes as she pleases, flitting in and out and making things even harder.

I feel sick all of a sudden.

I rip my seatbelt off and shove the door of the van open, practically tumbling out onto the pavement. I figure Zayden got to have his own personal freak-out at the restaurant, so it's my turn now. I move quickly away from the screaming and fighting and let myself in the back gate, kicking it closed behind me and then jogging my way over to the tire swing.

With a quick exhale, I flop onto the wet black rubber and grab hold of the chains, kicking off of the ground and then letting my head fall back, hair trailing behind me as the swing starts to sway.

Looking up, all I can see are the thick branches of the trees, heavy with green needles even in winter. I can hear the faint sound of the front door opening and closing and then ... nothing. No kids, no club music, no lectures. Just quiet.

I breathe in and out slowly, letting the massive tire hold my weight as I lay back and let go of the chains. The swaying motion continues, the branch above me creaking and shedding droplets of dew.

I let myself get so zoned out that I don't hear Zayden's footsteps until he's right beside me, sitting down in the grass behind my head. I let myself drop a little further back, so I can stare at him upside down.

"You okay?" he asks me, holding the baby monitor in his lap. I can hear the faint murmur of a TV through it. Sadie must be in her crib in the living room.

"I'm alright," I say as the swaying starts to slow. Zayden lifts up his foot and uses the white sole of his Converse to push against the rubber; I start to swing again. "I just ... that fighting is enough to make anybody lose their shit. And then I thought about how *this* is my life now. I'm not here on vacation like you are; this is *it*. Ingrid's been gone for about a month now, and my mom tried, but she can't handle the girls and my dad's health problems all by herself." I sigh and close my eyes. "When Ingrid does call, she doesn't even want to talk to her own daughters; she has no plans to come back anytime soon."

I squeeze my eyes shut tight. I hate this house, but I like the yard at least. It's peaceful back here. But then, that's kind of the problem. This whole *town* is peaceful and laid-back and easygoing. I don't want that. I want exciting and new and fresh. Once I get my degree, I suppose I can move. But then I'll be taking the girls away from dad in his last few years ...

I put the heels of my hands over my closed eyes and I want to scream. But then, I don't want Zayden to hear it. Any of it. It's not like this is his problem.

"Is any of this ..." he sounds slightly tentative which is weird. I haven't seen the guy be anything in the realm of tentative since I met him last week. "About me perchance?"

I almost smile.

"Perchance? Do people still use that word?"

"Fuck yeah they do," he says and I hear a rustle of sound as he gets up. I keep my eyes closed and then feel a warmth fluttering against my lips. "Do you have a crush on me, Brooke Overland?"

"Why would I?" I ask, but when Zay spoke, I could feel his words against my mouth. The sensation almost makes me want to tell him yes. "Do *you* have a crush on *me*?"

No response. But then he's pressing his lips to mine and sliding his tongue deep, tasting me as I lay on my back on the tire swing, eyes closed, the sharp breath of winter in my lungs. The air smells fresh and wild back here, a far cry from the cloistered confines of that houses. *Maybe I could save up enough money and the girls and I could move?* But I can't spend too much time thinking about that because Zayden is sliding his fingers through my hair, supporting my head in his hand and bringing my mouth tighter against his.

It's a different feeling to kiss upside down. I feel Zay's tongue teasing along the length of mine, gliding across the top in a way that's just not possible the other way around. It almost makes me laugh.

"Do you have a crush on me *now*?" he jokes when he pulls back. I open my eyes and stare at his sexy chin and the faint dusting of stubble there.

"I'm starting to feel better, if that's what you're asking." Zay sits back as I turn around and lay across the swing on my stomach. "Your kiss definitely has the power to distract." He gives me a crooked smile and stands up, reaching down to tug gently on my ponytail. Makes me wonder what'd be like if he had a firm grip on it while he fucked me from behind …

I almost gasp right there. I've—obviously—never had sex in that position and most of the girls I've met have said it's their favorite … I bet Zayden would let me try it out with him if I asked.

"Will you be naked and waiting when I get home tonight?" I ask as he starts to move away. That gives him pause though and he stops while I study his knee-high Converse with all the black straps and the metal studs. The guy's got style. Weird style maybe, but definitely a look. I feel like I'm a different person everyday of the week sometimes.

"You got it, babe," he says and then disappears up the steps of the deck and into the house.

I wait until I hear the sliding glass door closed before I let out a burst of wild laughter.

Bella, Grace, and Kinzie are all obsessed with my getting ready process tonight, and it's kind of scaring me. They keep asking questions about where I'm going and what I'm doing. The absolute *last* thing I'm telling any of these kids is the truth.

"I already told you: I'm going to work. What does it matter where?" I slick my hair back into a perfect ponytail. My hair is *way* too long when it's down to dance properly, at least for me. Some of the other girls there make pole dancing look like an art form.

"You always ask about my day at school," Bella says with a crossed arms pose that reminds me of myself. It's kind of cute. I notice Grace putting one of my bras on over her shirt in the reflection of the mirror.

"Good point. But I'm an adult. Nothing we do is interesting."

"Why are you putting on so much makeup to go to work? My dad never wears makeup to work," Kinzie states which is actually also a very valid point. I lean into the mirror to check my makeup, happy to be wearing my contacts again. If I'm going to come home and ... well, do whatever with Zayden, then I'd rather not have to deal with my clunky glasses. Besides, if I break them, I am seriously SOL.

"I'm going to ... a fancy club. To serve tables."

"Serve tables?" Kinzie asks, taking her hair out of the pigtails Zay put them in and trying to imitate my ponytail. It'll be years before she gets here, but I smile anyway. "Like a waitress?"

"Exactly." I stick a tiny diamond stud in each lobe and then look at my face. After staring at Zayden all day, I feel plain. I touch the sides of my neck, wondering what it'd look like covered in tattoos. "I'll be waitressing."

I let my gaze stray away from my face to the girls and notice Grace digging through the dirty clothes pile in the corner. The last thing I want her to do is find any of my *work* clothes—particularly the outfit Zayden and I screwed in.

"Okay." I clap my hands and move into the room, grabbing my niece under the arms and lifting her up. "That's about enough of that, don't you think?"

I've got my trench coat on again, and even though I feel stupid in it, it keeps everything hidden as I shuffle out of the room and into the hallway. Most of the girls at the club come dressed in jeans and t-shirts and change in the back, but I feel like I need to do it here, in this safe space first. I need to dress up and let my anxiety cool a little before I leave; it's the only way.

"I bet that casserole is just about done," I say as I heft

BAD NANNY

Grace onto my hip and move down the stairs. Dodger does his utmost to intercept me at the halfway point and trip me, thereby killing both me *and* my niece when he knocks us down the stairs, but Zay's somehow just there, catching me as I start to pitch forward with a gray and white dog lodged between the toe and heel of my shoe. "Thanks," I say as he takes Grace from me and carries her the rest of the way.

"No problem. You sure you don't want a slice of delicious chicken-rice-soupy goodness?"

"When you put it like that, how could any girl say no?" I smile when he winks at me, feeling good. Not great, but good. I'm just going to have to live in the moment, I guess. I can't think about how I'll probably be working this job for another year plus ... or how my sister might flit in and out of her girls' lives like it's nothing. Hell, or maybe it's worse if she *never* comes back at all. I can't decide at this point. "I'll be back around two," I say with a little wave, turning and reaching for the doorknob, almost wishing that Zay would call me into the backyard again for a kiss.

He doesn't though, waving with an oven mitt from the kitchen as I smile and head outside, watching him for as long as I can before it closes with a soft snick.

At least I have something to look forward to. In just a few hours, I'll be letting myself in this door to find him waiting for me.

My heart thrums and palpates with excitement and I start to wonder if Zay's right, if I really *do* have a crush on him.

Guess it doesn't matter much either way, does it?

After my first Friday night at the club, I can see why the manager gave me Saturday off. I feel overwhelmed as hell by the whole scene. It's *definitely* not my thing, not at all. The first time I got up on stage, with My Darkest Days' song, "Porn

Star Dancing" playing in the background, I froze up like a deer caught in the headlights. My heart started to pound and my pulse was flickering so quickly I thought I might pass out.

I unlock the front door slowly, tentatively, and find Sadie asleep on her back in the crib. Zayden's not in the living room which might mean ... he really is waiting for me upstairs. I squeeze inside and close the door as quietly as I can, tiptoeing up the steps and pushing into my bedroom with an anxious swirl twisting around in my tummy.

Oh my. Fucking. God.

Zayden's lying on his back, completely nude with nothing but a thin crumple of sheet covering his cock. He's leaning against the headboard with one arm tossed over his head and the other resting loosely on the rumpled surface of the bed.

When he sees me standing there, he smiles slow and sultry, letting the expression build into a crescendo across his shadowed face.

"Is this what you ordered, Smarty-Pants? Because I aim to please."

I stand there in my black trench, the lacy lingerie underneath itching to be seen by this man and this man alone.

"A tattooed nanny?" I ask, my voice huskier than I'd meant it to be. "Why the hell would anyone want one of those?"

"Ah, see, you've forgotten the best feature of all." Zayden takes the crumpled white sheet in his inked fingers and slides it aside, revealing the pierced glory of his hardened shaft. "One hot and *ready* tattooed nanny. See, I try to offer my clients a full set of services: cooking, cleaning, childcare ... and some hair pulling and a hot fuck from behind. What do you say, Brooke Overland? Are you in?"

My breath rushes out in a whoosh and I reach down to untie the trench coat, letting it fall to the floor in a heap of black fabric. Underneath, I've got on a pink lacy bra, matching panties, and a garter belt to hold up my white thigh highs.

Zayden's eyes are impossible to see in the darkness, but his smile is wicked sharp.

I move across the room and climb onto the bed, letting him

pull me into his lap.

"You're the best nanny ever," I groan as his lips find my throat and kiss their way down to my collarbone. I can feel his grin against my skin.

"I know. I make the best PB&Js ... and I fuck like a goddamn world champ."

Zayden grabs hold of my ass and yanks me closer, settling the hot warmth between my thighs right over the velvety length of his shaft. When I wiggle my hips a little, he groans and encourages me to move against him, teasing his erection with the lacy texture of my panties.

"How did you know I wanted it from behind?" I whisper as he curls my hair around his fist and uses it to gently shift the position of my head. His grip is firm, but not cruel. I find myself melting into it with a soft sigh.

"I had no idea," he whispers against my ear before biting down gently. "It's just what *I* wanted."

I let out a little scream of surprise as he flips us over and drops his mouth to my belly, kissing his way across the top of the garter belt and then snagging the clasp with his teeth. A little tug and it comes undone. The sight of him down there, with his mouth all over that pink lace, piercings winking at me in the near perfect darkness of the room, makes my lower stomach clench tight with anticipation. I want him to stretch me open, fill me up from behind, keep that gentle pressure on my hair.

It'll so suck when he goes back to Vegas.

I banish that thought from my mind by concentrating on Zayden's mouth yanking the second clasp open. He then slides his hands underneath me and undoes the back two clasps with an expert level of skill.

"No school tomorrow," he says as he grabs hold of my panties and starts to yank them down my hips, revealing the clean, smooth expanse of my belly and my pussy, a gentle curve that leads to the delicate folds below. Zayden keeps his eyes on me as he untangles the panties from my legs and tosses them to the floor. "No work. I hope you're ready for a wild night on the town."

"I don't think it's *possible* to have a wild night on the town in Eureka."

Zayden's grin gets a little wider as he tosses my underwear aside.

"Really? Then you've never been out with me." Zay lifts up a finger and twirls it in an easy circle. "Turn over and put your ass in the air. I'll give you a little extra love after, but I can't wait. I've come three times waiting for you to come home."

I gulp in a deep breath and feel my pulse thundering. I want to protest that I'm not ready, that I need more foreplay, but … I don't care. I can't wait either. I need this.

I sit up and turn over, getting onto my hands and knees and gasping as Zay leans over and tucks two pillows under my hips.

"Trust me: you'll be grateful for those later." He sits up, the heat of his body moving away as I pant and try not to feel exposed. But how can I not in this position? I'm so … *open*. I take a few, calming breaths as Zay rustles around for a moment before positioning himself between my knees and putting his hands on my hips. He grips tight and draws a desperate sound from my throat.

"Relax, Brooke. It won't hurt if you relax." I bite my lower lip and drop my head, closing my eyes as Zayden positions himself at my opening and pauses there for a moment, nudging into my folds with a slow, deliberate motion.

When he bucks his hips into mine, filling me with his warmth, I almost scream. There's this uncomfortable tightness for a moment, and I tense up. But then I feel his hand on my lower back, rubbing and soothing, the hot heat of his palm comforting against my skin.

"Relax your muscles, babe. You're way too goddamn tight." I pant heavily, doing my best to relax, feeling a natural urge to tilt my hips up and back. As soon as I do, I feel myself relax, the pressure easing considerably. "There ya go. That's it, Smarty-Pants. Just like that."

Zayden slides out slowly as I curl my fingers into the sheets and brace for the impact of his pelvis against my ass. From this position, I can feel the ring in his balls against my pussy. Each time he slams into me, it teases my body, twists my fervor up another notch until I'm gasping, struggling for each breath. I lean forward, putting my elbows against the bed and letting the pillows prop up my hips.

Oh.

Zay really *does* know what he's doing.

My cheek drops to the bed and I bite down on the edge of a pillow to hold back a scream. So many sensations are running through me that when Zayden grabs a hold of my ponytail and jerks my head back, I really do cry out. I know I could wake one of the kids, but I can't stop the sounds. I'm not in control of my body right now. I feel possessed, consumed by Zayden and the perfect rhythm of his cock inside of me.

I push back against the bed for some resistance and he groans, pulling my hair harder as I arch my back and tilt my chin up, giving up and letting him do whatever he wants. It feels good to let someone else be in control for once. I have so much to deal with, I don't want to worry about this. I tell him with my body that he can do whatever he wants, fuck me however he wants. I don't care; I want it all.

"Goddamn it, Brooke," Zayden groans as he pumps into me. "God-fucking-damn it."

I feel his hand move to the clasp on my bra, loosing the hooks and letting my breasts free to swing with each movement of his body. When I adjust my hips, I feel the metal in the head of his cock through the condom. It's this hard pressure against the velvet thickness of his shaft, and it makes me crazy. My own body starts to move, pushing my hips back so we meet with the sweet sound of flesh on flesh.

Our noises feel extra loud in the quiet dark of the room, but I like the erotic symphony we're creating, like a song written for just the two of us.

"Zayden," I whisper as he pushes against me, his body jewelry making my clit tingle and throb. I can feel that explosion of stars behind my eyes, that hot fire raging through me. He rides me all the way down into it, until I'm gripping the bed and biting my lip to keep from screaming.

Zay releases his grip on my hair as I collapse forward, drawing away from him with a groan. I feel like I can barely move, but he's clearly not done with me, dragging the pillows out from under my body and tossing them to the floor.

He turns me over with a steady grip on my hip.

"I can't," I whisper as Zayden slides his sweaty body over mine. I wrap my arms around his neck and press my face against the shaved side of his head as he kisses my throat. That smell of him is so comforting, I feel like I'll never be able to get it out of my head, the way it wraps around me and holds me tight like that. "I can't go anymore."

"Trust me: the second orgasm's always better than the first. Relax. I'll do all the work, baby."

Zayden cups my face in his hands and kisses me, his bodyweight heavy but just as comforting as his scent. On instinct, I spread my knees open and adjust myself so that we're cupped together at the hips. This time when he enters me, there's no pain, just the slick slide of his shaft into my swollen body. The sensations are so different this time, each stroke tender and deep.

"I've got such a huge crush on you, Brooke," he whispers into my ear. I reach back and curl my fingers into the pillow under my head. I can't listen to things like that, not while we're doing this. I've got no experience in this department and it's totally screwing with my brain. I'm feeling things for Zayden that no person in their right mind should feel, not this quickly. I know it's because of my inexperience, but God … telling me he has a *crush* on me doesn't help at all.

"Fuck me harder," I say because I want to flip the switch on this meeting, strip away any false sense of tenderness or caring, make it dirty and hot and crazy. "Do it hard and don't stop."

Zayden nuzzles the side of my head, buries his face in my hair and makes an *mmm* sound that has me bucking my hips up to meet his. When he lifts up and braces one hand next to my head, the other gripping my hip tight, I close my eyes against

BAD NANNY

the sight of his face above me.

With rough, angry thrusts, he gives me exactly what I was asking for, driving into me with a fierceness that leaves no room for thoughts, that obliterates any worries or fears or questions in my mind, yanking a second orgasm literally screaming from my throat.

I'm so busy thrashing and trembling under him that I almost miss his orgasm, the last few wild bucks of his hips as he comes with a deep guttural male sound that I don't think I'll forget for the rest of my life, no matter how many lovers I have.

When he collapses on top of me with a chuckle, I find that I'm still gasping and panting for breath. My chest is rising and falling with rapid inhales and frantic exhales.

"Mmm," Zayden says as he rolls off and removes the condom. I try not to look at him. The sight of all that naked, tattooed flesh just makes me feel hot and ready again. Dear God. "Gimme ten and we'll go for round two."

"Round two?" I echo as I roll away from him and curl my knees up. "How many times do you think we're going to do this?"

"As many as we can," he says, his voice strangely grave. I glance over my shoulder and find him ruffling up his dark brown hair. "We've got six days left, so ... like at least thirty times, don't you think?"

I laugh as I turn fully towards him and he smiles over his shoulder at me.

"I can't leave you without a full roster of experiences to draw from, you know? Like, you totally haven't sucked my cock yet, and I haven't gone down on you, and then there's anal to worry about ..."

"Whoa, whoa, whoa." I hold up a hand as Zayden grins and gives me one of his signature winks. "Anal? You're getting way ahead of yourself there, Nanny Roth."

"Nanny Roth?" he asks as he gets up and disposes of the condom in the bathroom trash. When Zay comes back, he lays behind me and pulls my body into a tight spoon. *Oh. That feels nice. Really nice. Too nice, maybe.* The urge to snuggle back into him is strong, but we don't have that kind of relationship, do we? "I like that. Call me nanny while I'm fucking you, okay?"

"Absolutely not." Zayden grins against my ear and leans his warm, sweaty body into mine, kissing my cheek with his stubbled face. I wrinkle my nose against the brush of his hair against my skin, but I actually do kind of like it. "So, you really do have a crush on me, huh? Even when I'm so bad at sex?"

"I didn't say bad. I said *amateurish*. Totally different thing. But you know what? Tonight you really took it like a champ. I have to say, excellent hip movements. Good doggy style form. Total pro moves."

"Yeah, sure," I say as he sighs against my skin and goose bumps break out all over. "Nice lines. Do those work on every girl?"

"What do you think?" he whispers against me, reaching down to lift my chin up, tucking my head under his. "Is it working on you?"

I smile and open my mouth to answer him when the doorknob jiggles and I hear Bella's voice outside the hollow core door.

"Aunt Brooke, I heard somebody screaming, and I'm really scared. I can't sleep."

I look back at Zayden and he gives me a sad half-smile, standing up and grabbing a pair of black sweats from the floor. I watch his tight ass as he drags them over his hips and tosses me a baggy t-shirt and my kitty cat pajama pants.

I kick my legs over the edge of the bed and tug them on quickly, waiting on the edge of the mattress as he opens the door and Bella throws her arms around his waist.

"Did you hear that?" she whispers ominously. "It was a *banshee*. I learned about them from YouTube. They come in the night and scream when you're going to die. Am I going to die, Uncle Zayden?"

I smile when she calls him uncle, this stupid sloppy smile that I wipe quickly off my face lest Zay sees it. Ugh. I don't want him to think I'm going to go all crazy virgin on him and start professing my undying love. Even if he is adorable with my niece. And good in bed. And silly and funny and sexy and brimming with personality.

Um.

I stand up quickly and brush my hands down the front of the shirt. It's one of Zay's and it says *Too Kewl For School.* Heh.

"It wasn't a banshee," Zayden says with all due seriousness. "Aunt Brooke just stubbed her toe." He lifts up his fingers and gives her a salute. "Scout's honor, Bella, I swear it. I actually activated an anti-banshee spell around the perimeter of the house. We're all safe here."

I smile another dumb lumpy smile as Zay glances over his shoulder. He *totally* sees that one and I feel the blood drain from my face. Great.

He turns back to Bella and reaches down to ruffle her dark hair.

"Even if it was Brooke, I can't sleep now. I'm too awake." Zayden nods for a moment and then snaps his fingers.

"I got it. You want to go downstairs and bake some midnight cookies? Midnight cookies actually taste better than regular boring old day cookies. You game?"

Bella's face lights up and she claps her hands together, nodding her head vigorously and giving Zayden this adorable grin with her teeth showing and her eyes squinched shut.

"I'll go get the sugar and flour out!" She disappears down the hall before I can say anything.

Zay looks back at me and holds out a tattooed hand.

"You want in on this?" I nod and move over to take it, gasping a little when he pulls me into his arms and ... hugs me? Zay squeezes me tight and breathes against my neck, letting go only when he hears the sound of a door opening.

It's Kinzie.

"You down for midnight cookies, squirt?" he asks as she blinks at him and rubs sleep from her eyes. Her smile, when it does come, is slightly less cynical than usual.

"You're not going to ruin them this time, are you?" she asks and Zay laughs, holding out a hand for her to take. I watch them start down the steps together, voices low and gentle in the early morning dark.

And then I feel something deep stir inside my tummy.

I don't know it at the time, but it's the beginning of my love for Zayden.

How cliché is that? The master of the house falling in love with the nanny?

I really am a crazy person.

CHAPTER 21
ZAYDEN ROTH

When I wake up in the morning, I am so totally confused. First of all, I'm wondering why there's hot air blasting me in the face. My first thought is that the A/C is broken. I try to roll over and shake my date awake—because let's be honest, I *always* have a lady friend over—when I realize my arm is trapped behind *another* body.

Hmm.

I'm not saying I've never had two chicks in my bed before, but I feel like it's something I would've remembered. Then I notice a *third* warm body across my lap and finally blink myself awake.

I'm sitting on Brooke's shitty inherited couch with my feet propped up on the coffee table. The heating vent in the ceiling is spouting hot air like a politician, and the three bodies around me finally make sense. I've got Kinzie curled up on my left side, Bella on my right, and Brooke with her head nestled *riiiiiiight* up against the warm bulge in my sweats.

My morning erection solidifies into stone as I carefully try to extract myself from the pile of people around me, cringing as a hiss explodes in my ear and a claw lashes me across the neck.

"Goddamn it, Hubert you little cocksucker," I snap as the

useless cat grumbles and moves away from his position curled against the back of my neck. As the three ladies moan and snore in their half-sleep, I ease myself up and away from them. It's totally great to have Brooke's hot breath against my dick, but *not* with the fucking kids on either side of me. That's just goddamn gross.

I tiptoe over to the downstairs bathroom and release the chihuahuas, tripping and stumbling over the panting, hopping little bodies as I struggle over to the back door. As soon as I let them out, Dodger comes ripping down the stairs and explodes out into the yard behind them.

"Useless rats," I snort as I yawn and scratch at my belly with tired fingers. When I check the bathroom out, I find that the little shits have crapped and pissed all over everything. Great. Perfect way to start the morning.

"Zayden?" Brooke says as she sits up and leaves the two seven year olds sprawled out across the sofa. "What time is it?"

I check the clock and find that it's kind of freakishly early.

"Um, ungodly?" I joke as I peek in the crib and find Sadie wide awake and sitting up all by herself. She has a pink stuffed bear that I grabbed for her at the store, the end of one of its legs shoved into her tiny mouth. I smile and wink at her, reaching in to pinch her cheek as she laughs. "You want some breakfast?"

Brooke shrugs her shoulders, wrapping her arms around herself and looking so fucking ridiculously sexy in my t-shirt that I kind of want to toss her over the kitchen table and screw her right now. Damn. If only we were alone ...

I pick up one of the blue sugar cookies we made last night with food coloring and shove it into my mouth.

"I can make pancakes. I think. At least, I once had this ex-girlfriend who was obsessed with them. I used to cook them for her in little heart shapes." I use both of my pointer fingers to draw a heart in the air as Brooke wrinkles her nose at me. Stupidly, I can't stop thinking about how cute *that* is, too. Like, I'm completely and utterly obsessed with this girl. I wasn't

BAD NANNY

even this crazy interested in anyone in *high school.* And that's what I'm acting like right now, like I'm in fucking high school or something.

"Don't talk about your ex-girlfriends," she says and lifts her palms up. "I'm not trying to get weird or anything, I just ... I don't want to talk about them right now, okay?" A strange shadow of emotion flickers across her face and is gone. I try to interpret it, but I'm no good at this stuff, so I just shrug my shoulders and open the cabinet.

I pull out the box of pancake mix and read the instructions carefully. Huh. Easy peasy. I got this shit.

"You want them in heart shapes?" I ask as I waggle my eyebrows and grin at her. Brooke pulls out a chair and sits in it, crossing her legs in a pair of pink cat pj's that kind of make me want to kiss her face off. "Or if that bugs you, I can do ... smiley faces? There's bacon in the fridge. We can go classic breakfast cliché and do fried eggs, too, if you want."

"Do hearts," Brooke says firmly and then after a long pause, "and fuck your ex-girlfriend."

I throw my head back and laugh, putting my hands together and touching my fingers to my lips.

"Yeah, yeah, I like that. Let's reclaim the heart pancakes from that bitch." I grab a rag and wipe off Sadie's high chair before heading to her crib to grab her. "And she *was* a bitch, that much I can assure you. I felt bad for her because after we slept together, she cried and told me her whole life story, like how she was homeless and everything."

I snag Sadie's diaper bag with my foot and toss a blanket onto the living room carpet to change her.

"Your white knight disorder again?" Brooke asks from her spot in the kitchen. She sounds bemused, and I wonder what her face looks like, cleaning Sadie up as quick as I can and hefting her against my chest.

"Yup. Exactly. That shit gets me into such serious trouble. The chick ended up stealing like, a thousand in cash from the safe in my closet and bailing after two months." I park my niece in her chair while I get some music started and make up a bottle. My song pick for the morning is "Queen of Hearts" by *We The Kings*. Oh, I so totally dig this tune. "To be honest, I never even really liked her that much."

"You date girls you don't like?" Brooke asks as I let warm water run over the bottle and start prepping the pancake batter, jamming to my groove as I move. "I think there's a few psychological issues hiding in there somewhere."

I snort and grab a cup and a half of water to toss into the mixing bowl, whisking out the lumps as I bump and grind my hips and Brooke laughs at me. When I look back at her, she slaps a hand across her mouth and shakes her head at me. I just give her a wink and keep movin'.

"For sure. No doubt there. I think I have commitment issues. Like, if I date girls I hate, then I don't have to worry about falling for them, you know?"

"Wow. I mean, you're actually *aware* of that?"

"Hell yeah. Have been for years. What about you? Do you think dating a guy for three years that won't sleep with you *or* marry you means anything?"

"You think *I* have psychological problems?"

I shrug my shoulders as I check the bottle's temperature. Perfect.

"You want to feed this kid for me?" I ask with pouty lips. I know I'm supposed to be the nanny here, but I also sort of want to see Brooke hold the baby. She nods and reaches her arms out for Sadie, propping her up against her chest as I watch, feeling all possessive and shit. Like, maybe this girl's supposed to be my woman or something?

Buuuuut, I just did say I have commitment issues, didn't I? I was not fucking kidding about that shit.

I go back to the pancakes and stir the batter with vigor as the song repeats itself. I like to put my songs on loops sometimes, listen to the same damn thing a hundred times in a row. Who doesn't, right?

"I guess I was scared," Brooke admits as I get out a pan and rub some butter around the bottom. Pancakes always taste better when they're soaked in butter, right? "My sister got pregnant really young and then went through a long string of semi-serious boyfriends. None of them turned out to be who she thought they were. Maybe by dating Anthony, I felt like I was safe from all of that. *He* was safe. Everyone always said what a good guy he was, how nice he was, how dedicated he was to his faith ..."

"Oh, that is so not sexy," I laugh as I get out the bacon and eggs from the fridge. "Dedicated to his faith? Gross. Don't you want a guy that's dedicated to you instead?" I glance over my shoulder and find Brooke's cheeks turning a funny pink color. "A guy that can nail you to the mattress?"

"Um, children present," she says, but she knows they're asleep and that Sadie can't understand a damn thing we're saying. I grin at that.

"Good guy. Nice. Dedicated. Yuck. No wonder you fell into bed with me."

"What's that supposed to mean?" she asks as I start a second pan up for the bacon.

"I'm, like, the complete opposite of that guy, don't you think?"

"Not really. You might not be religious, but you *are* kind of a nice guy. I mean, you *look* all badass and tough, but you're kind of sweet, Zayden." I turn around and wrinkle my nose at her.

"Ouch. Sweet and nice?" I put my tattooed knuckles together. "You just haven't seen me get up the need to kick anybody's ass yet. I totally can." I flex for Brooke and she laughs, sunlight streaming through the glass of the sliding doors and turning her hair into a glittering sea of bronze. Damn. Damn, damn, damn.

I make myself turn away from her, pulling my phone out to Google how long bacon needs to cook for. There's a text from that pink haired chick, and a few from my buddies at home. A couple Facebook messages from a girl I hooked up with last month. I stare at it all, the proof of my life back home and I feel this weird emptiness yawning open inside of me.

Fuck.

I jam the phone back in my pocket and refocus on breakfast. I can't think about anything but this moment. I just have to live *this*. I've got an exhibitionist date booked with Brooke for tonight and a week of guaranteed fabulous sex waiting for me. At the end of the week, we'll see how I feel.

I bet I'll be gunning to get the hell out of here.

Surprise, surprise.

That bitch, Monica, really *does* show up like I asked. I think Brooke's in complete shock, her mouth hanging open as she pushes the door wide and lets her great aunt in. The woman gives me a look that's worth a thousand words, most of them synonymous for *dickhead* or *serial killer.* I don't think she can decide exactly *how* much she hates me. S'okay. I'm used to it. People love to judge me based on my appearance. I got this.

"Yo, Monica," I say as I pry one of the twins off of my leg and use my foot to stop the ugly hairless dog from humping the ugly not-hairless one. The kids keep asking me what they're doing, and I had no clue how to answer. When Brooke suggested they were "dogging" and that it was some sort of game, I went with it. "No dogging, Dodger." I grin when I say it and enjoy the way Monica's face pales. "We're callin' the whole humping thing a euphemism." I clap the woman on the shoulder and she gasps, putting a hand to her chest as I wink and twirls my nephew around my waist like a swing dancer. He screams in joy as I deposit him back on his feet. "You'll get the hang of it pretty quick."

"I'm not—" Monica starts, but I ignore her. She's one of those selfish, judgmental assholes that I hate. Who cares what she has to say? Not me. All I want right now is for her to watch these rugrats so I can go screw their aunt into the side of a brick building during the arts fair.

BAD NANNY

"Alright everyone, listen up." I clap my hands together and lean down, ignoring Monica as she clutches her red coat in front of herself and frowns. Her lipstick's this weird dark brown color that looks like dog crap. Huh. "This is Brooke's Aunt Monica, okay? You guys can call her whatever you want, but you need to behave. You got that? Anyone that steps out of line has to help me clean chihuahua poop out of the backyard."

"Can we call her poop face?" Kinzie asks and sends all the kids into a giggling fit. I roll my eyes as I stand up straight and glance over at Brooke again. To be honest with y'all, it's hard for me to pull my gaze away for even an instant. The kid cleans up good, that's for sure. Her makeup is clean and fresh, not heavy like it is when she's on her way to the club. That long chocolate mane is straight and shiny and gleaming, and her outfit is ballin', baby. Smart chick. She choose a short black skirt and a flouncy pink top, paired it with a pair of old brown boots and called it done. It's the weirdest thing I've ever seen in my life and I'm totally digging it.

"No more poop or fart jokes, okay? I'm starting to wonder if you need to see a therapist or something." I ruffle Kinzie's curls and pass over a couple twenties to Monica. "Order 'em pizza or something, okay? Oh, and I left instructions for the baby on the counter. You've taken care of babies before, right?"

"I have two kids," Monica says, blinking at the chaos in the living room like she's never seen this much activity in once place before. Sort of looks like she might be close to having a heart attack. Hopefully she can just hold off until we get back. She does and I'll buy her casket myself.

"Ready, Brooke?" I ask as I head to the front door and open it for her, waving good-bye to the kids before I step outside into the cool darkness of a Eureka evening.

"She ... actually showed up. The most selfish woman on the entire planet," Brooke mumbles as we head over to the van and I dance a few steps ahead to open her door. She raises a brow at me but climbs in anyway, getting control of my iPod before I do. Within seconds, we're listening to some crazy loud screeching song about pain and death. Ech. Eww. I so hate rock and metal music. Buuuut, I so love to see Brooke's face as the music washes over her and she smiles. "I haven't been to Arts Alive since I was seventeen."

"'bout the same here. Since I was eighteen. It's totally hippie chic from what I remember. Lots of live music, art, people smoking pot." I grin as I back out of the driveway and head towards Old Town with some tortured soul screeching out of the van's speakers. "I don't know if you can tell, but, like, I am flipping excited as fuck."

"We're not *really* going to have sex there, right?" Brooke asks, but not like she wants me to agree with her.

"Listen up, Smarty-Pants, I don't joke about sex in public places, okay? This shit's a serious art form and you, my dear, are about to get an introduction by a master."

Brooke leans against the window and studies with me her pale brown eyes, sweeping long hair away from her face.

"What's the weirdest place you've ever done it?" she asks, and I have to chew my bottom lip and think really hard for a minute. I snap my fingers as it comes to me.

"One time, I fucked this chick at a *hotel*."

"Um ..." Brooke starts, but I'm not done.

"No, like I was there for this comic convention thing—"

"Nerd," Brooke whispers under her breath as I reach out and push her shoulder playfully.

"—and there was this romance readers convention happening in the other ballroom."

"You screwed a romance reader?" Brooke asks with an incredulous expression. "In a hotel. I'm still not seeing the big deal here."

"Because you're not letting me finish the story. I didn't screw a reader; I screwed an author. Right in the back of the room, behind some banners of half-naked guys *during* the book signing. Like, with people everywhere and all that. Most of the attendees thought I was a *cover* model."

"You're a weird person, you know that?" she says, but she sounds like she's half-laughing and half ... jealous? Is Brooke jealous? I can't tell if I want her to be or not. "You know, we forgot to tell my aunt that you have a weird hairless cat wearing a pink glittery sweater."

"Hey, that sweater is *not* pink. It's a pale *red.*"

"Which, by definition, *is* pink," Brooke shoots back as the song changes to yet another brain pummeling metal song. "She might seriously have an aneurism and die if she sees him."

"Oh, come on. Hubs isn't *that* scary lookin', is he?" I glance over at Brooke as we pause at a red light. Now that I think about it, the cat actually lets her touch him which is a good sign; Hubs kind of hated that pink haired girl, Kitty. Kind of ironic, huh, considering the name and all?

"He's cute in his own gross, weird sort of way," Brooke admits as we accelerate through several different layers of suburbia. That's kind of all this town is: neighborhoods on top of neighborhoods on top of neighborhoods. There's no real *city center* so to speak. The area we're heading to, Old Town, is right on the bay, just a few blocks of local shops and a fountain with some pigeons. Not all that exciting, although the vibe is kind of hot. Very artsy and eclectic. "Which ex was this one from? The homeless one?"

"Nah. Hubs is from the klepto."

"The klepto, huh? You have a very colorful history, Mr. Roth."

"It's *Nanny* Roth, remember?" I ask, dropping my voice a notch.

Brooke ignores me, turning her music up and then jamming to an admittedly sick guitar solo with her fingers. I tap my hands along with the music and we get into this double groove which is awesome. I love a girl that can let go and have fun, especially one with as much shit going on in their lives as Brooke's got.

When we hit the buzz of Old Town, I snag a spot near the brewery and hop around to Brooke's side of the car to let her out, wrapping her arm through mine as we walk down brick paved sidewalks towards the sounds of live jazz. The murmur of the crowd softens the sound as we head over to Main Street and find ourselves in a laid-back crowd of locals and artists, booths with postcards and prints and paintings everywhere. The old fashioned streetlights are strung up with Edison bulbs and everything just has this amazing glow to it.

"Whoa. Such a different vibe than Vegas," I say as I pause and watch the crowd stream by. There's no glitz and glamour here, just a modest street fair lit up by the people involved in it, peddling handmade goods from booths, the local shops that usually close at dusk displaying their wares on the streets, doors flung wide. It smells like weed and the breeze off the bay, and it is fan-tab-ulous.

"Homesick?" Brooke asks as the big band jazz croons its sweet melody into the crowd. I look down at her in her flouncy pink peasant top, a bit of black lace bra showing, those white legs of hers sculpted and sexy as they taper into the too-big-for-her brown boots she's wearing.

"Fuck no." I drag Brooke into the crowd, weaving us through the mass until we get to the beer garden set up in front of the stage. I order us a pair of pints and lead Brooke over to one of the tall tables in the center. People are drinking and dancing, swaying with the music. Laughter sweetens the air as Brooke and I clink glasses and down some nasty ass tasting local ale. But hell, I'm already enjoying myself and we just got here. Now imagine how that finale between me and Brooke is gonna feel ...

"Want to dance?" she asks, surprising me as she finishes her beer and holds out a hand. I raise my brows and reach out to take it, letting her lead me into the fray. She guides my hands exactly where she wants them, placing one on either of her hips as she wraps her arms around my neck. The warm feel of her body against mine is so goddamn intoxicating. And I love-love-love the fact that I'm out with her in public, all these people seeing us dancing together. I want to lay my claim on her in front of all of them.

Um. What? Jesus Christ, Zayden.

I put a huge red stop sign on all of that shit and focus on the way Brooke's breasts squish against my chest. Her hands feel

BAD NANNY

like brands on the back of my neck, burning hot prints into my skin as we swirl and rock in an inexpert little waltz, doing our best to match the music.

She smiles at me the whole time, her hair swinging with the motions, her mouth painted with this silly peach-pink color that makes her look several years younger than her fresh-face really needs. But wow. Those lips are full and they curve in the most sinuous sort of way. Her lashes are long and dark and the eyes they frame are brimming with intelligence. She is, like, so much smarter than I am it's not even funny.

When the song ends, Brooke pulls away laughing and does this stupid little jig that I can only credit the alcohol with.

"Are you a lightweight?" I ask as I lean my elbow against the tall surface of the table and watch her finish off the rest of *my* beer.

"Not really," she tells me as she slams the empty glass down on the table. "I just feel like this might be my last night to go out for a while. With the new job and class and the girls, it's only going to get harder, especially without you around." She pauses and flicks her gaze up to me, blushing a little before she turns away. "You know, because I'll have to find a babysitter." A pause before she looks back and smiles at me. "And a new lover." Brooke leans across the table toward me and I let her put her mouth against my ear. "Because ... I think I'm starting to get addicted to having sex."

"Whoa, whoa, baby. Listen to you, you dirty bitch." I wink at her and she laughs, taking my hand and leading me out to the street. We parade up and down Main, checking out the booths and disappearing into crowded shops filled with black and white photos, dragon statues, glass bongs, and all sorts of ocean inspired art.

Brooke buys herself a stupid white wool cap with a pink flower and a snags a few colorful pinwheels for the kids from a local artist, jamming them into a knitted brown and orange bag she buys from yet another vendor.

"I know I shouldn't be spending anything," she says, but I wave her excuses away before they come.

"No. Stop that. Look, you're twenty-two, Brooke. Relax, have some fun and don't worry about justifying any of it." I look down at her in that weird hat and think she looks so damn cute that I shove a fifty into her purse when she isn't looking to pay for it. I kind of owe her because I am drinking in her quirky look like it's lemonade, baby. Sweet and sour all at the same time.

I buy Brooke and me some burritos at one of the food carts and we walk along the boardwalk together, the soft whisper of water against the shore mixing with the music and the chatter. For a small town get-together, it's totally bomb.

"What's it like, living in Las Vegas? I can imagine what it'd be like to visit, but to live there? Is it just craziness all the time?" I laugh and chew my bite of burrito, doing a little twirl to the chortling of the saxophone as Brooke chuckles and clutches her foil wrapped food in both hands.

"It's always a hoot and a holler, you know? Our shop is right," I slick my hand through the air, "on the Strip, so there are tourists galore parading in and out at all hours. We're open twenty-four seven, too. So much weird shit happens at night."

"Do you pierce … everything?" Brooke asks, glancing sidelong at me as we pass under puddles of light from the street lamps, couples gathered on benches, cuddling up or necking like teenagers. "Like …" She waves one of her hands in the area of her crotch. "Vaginas and stuff."

I laugh again and shake my head, kicking my red and black knee-high Converse against the pavement as I hop up on a bench and take a look out at the bay. Damn. One of the few things I missed about this place was the view of the water. I mean there's water in Vegas, in all the fountains and faux waterfalls and fake ass lakes, but that's just it—it's artificial as hell. In the middle of a goddamn desert and there's just … all of this crap everywhere that doesn't belong there. It's never bothered me before, but to be honest, it's kind of bugging me right now.

"Yep. I pierce pussies, sure. Cocks. Lots and lots of nipples. I mean *hordes* of fucking nipples. Belly buttons, lips, noses, brows, ears, whatever." I look down at Brooke and smile. "In fact, since I first met you, I've been checking out your eyebrows." I point at my own face and tuck my fingers into my back pockets. "You have gorgeous brows, you know that?"

Brooke reaches up and smooths her thumb over one.

"I've never really thought about it, no. Why?"

"Because I want to pierce you so goddamn badly." Brooke's cheeks fill with fire as she glances away, out at the darkness of the water. There are a few boats out there, lights shimmering in the navy blue night sky.

"You want to pierce my ... eyebrow?" she asks as she turns back to me and finishes off the last bite of her burrito, tossing the crumpled foil into a nearby trash can.

"If biostatisticians are allowed to have pierced brows, then sure. I want. So badly."

"Do you have the stuff for that? I mean, doesn't it take special needles and disinfectant and all that?"

"I've got everything I need in my car." I slap my hands together. "I could do it easy. Real quick. We could stop by my brother's place after this and do it." I grin down at her. "You game for that, Smarty-Pants?"

Brooke climbs up to stand on the bench next to me, turning and staring out at the water for a moment.

"Why the hell not?" she asks and I pump my fist. When she looks back at me, I'm grinning big at her. "You are *actually* a body piercer though, right? This isn't like the nanny gig, is it? Because I really don't want an infected piercing next to my eye."

"I am legit as fuck. And good, too." I point at my cock. "Who do you think pierced your new best friend, Brooke Overland? Hmm? That was me." I point at my belly button, my nipples. "I pretty much pierced all of my own shit. And trust me, I've got some *very* satisfied customers back at home, girls who can vouch for my *piercing* abilities all night long. Let's just say, I'm *really* good at sticking long hard things inside of people."

"That is so gross," Brooke moans, jumping down off the bench. The way she moves, I can almost imagine what it'd be like to see her dance. I feel sort of guilty for even thinking about it considering how upset she was about the whole ordeal, but ... damn. I *really* want to stop in at that club before I leave town and see her in action. I wonder if she'd be cool with that? "Please don't ever say that again."

"Your wish is my command, mistress. Nanny Roth is so at your service." I hop down next to her and grab her hand. "Now, come with me and I'll show you my special place. Considering it's still there, of course. I haven't been back to this spot since I was eighteen."

I pull Brooke down the boardwalk, past the empty lots that never got developed the way they were promised. Used to bug me. Now I kind of don't care because it makes this place seem more real, less commercial. Screw fancy condos and big box shops. Whatever. Keep Eureka weird, okay?

Brooke follows me back toward Main Street and behind the fountain, to the little alcove that houses the doors to several shops. Since these particular places are off the beaten path, they've closed at their normal hours, leaving a darkened space that's just about perfect for what I've got in mind.

"Exactly as I remember it," I tell Brooke as I drag her into the shadows and tug her against me. I lean in and whisper against her ear. "If you're quiet, nobody will know we're in here."

The music and the crowd are still clearly audible, and if we lean out of the alcove just a bit, the people standing at the top of the brick incline where the fountain sits pop into view. It's a good, easy, safe spot for a little dirty fun.

This close, I can hear Brooke's heart pounding against my chest, her breathing picking up in what's either excitement or fear, I'm not sure.

"What do I do?" she asks and I roll my eyes to the ceiling in silent thanks to the gods. *Yes.*

"Follow my lead," I whisper as I push Brooke back a step and give her a little wink. "The key to public sex is keeping it quick, easy, and clean." I reach down and undo the top button on my jeans, using my foot to kick over the thick welcome mat from in front of the chocolate shop.

Brooke looks down at it and then back up at me.

"Oh, no," she says, taking a step back. "I can't do that. Not for the first time. Not *here*."

"Why not? I promise it's kind of fun."

"How would you know?" Brooke asks, reaching up to adjust her silly hat. It looks even more ridiculous with that porn star mouth of hers. She leans in toward me. "Like *you've* ever sucked a cock before."

"No, but I eat pussy for breakfast."

"Oh my God," Brooke groans as she spins in a circle and comes back around to stare at me with her hazelnut brown eyes. They remind me of that pumpkin pie spice mix my mom used to put into everything during November and December, that yummy orange-brown powder that smelt like home and warmth and holidays. "Please don't ever say *that* again either."

"I thought it'd be hot for your first time to be here, but ..." I button up my pants and lift my hands palms out. "You don't want to suck me off? Okay. Lean against that door right there and drop your panties. This sort of violates the *clean* part of the public sex rules, but I'm okay with that. I will rock your excitement all over my face, Smarty-Pants."

"I'm not doing that either," Brooke whispers as I cross my arms over my chest and smile at her, slow and easy, letting her see in my face that she's not getting out of this one. She's nervous, but her chest is rising and falling in rapid pants and her eyes are shimmering with desire. Plus, she won't stop licking her lower lip and fisting her fingers into the fabric of her skirt.

"Okay." I shrug my shoulders and lace my fingers behind my neck. "Let's go get another beer or something then."

"But ..." Brooke starts as she gives me a quick once-over, taking in the green t-shirt with the video game characters splashed all over it. I don't normally wear this thing outside my own apartment, but I feel safe with Brooke, like *maybe* I could accept that I'm one tenth nerd. Or maybe one twentieth. Anyway, I feel like maybe I could learn to embrace that. "I thought you were going to, you know." She gestures her hand at one of the closed and locked doors in the alcove.

"Fuck you? Yeah, I *was* going to. But you don't seem all that into it. I don't want to pressure you into anything you don't want to do."

Brooke narrows her eyes on me.

"I see what you're doing and I don't like it."

I stay there smiling, my arms still crossed over my chest as Brooke sighs and drops her stupid yarn bag to the ground.

"Okay," she says as she takes several deep breaths and rubs at her white and pink hat. "Let's do this."

I raise an eyebrow as she steps over to me and looks me in the face, reaching down and tearing open the button on my jeans. I damn near cream my pants at the determined expression she's wearing, the fierceness she's using to tackle something as simple as sucking me off.

Kind of makes me like her a little bit more.

Brooke drops to her knees on the welcome mat as I lean back against the door to the shop and suck in a massive breath, enjoying the slow slide of her fingers as she parts the denim and finds out that hey, I'm not wearing any fucking underwear.

"Rule number four," I whisper as her hand wraps around the base of my cock and I groan. "Always come prepared." Brooke pauses for a moment, mouth twitching in a slight smile and then leans forward to run her tongue up the side of my shaft.

I seriously almost blow it right there—pun so totally intended. The way she moves, the way she touches me, the stupid ugly hat on her head, all of it makes me fucking crazy. I want to grab the back of her head and thrust my hips against her mouth, come on the back of her tongue and watch her swallow me down that gorgeous throat of hers.

Instead, I relax into the doorway, leaning my bodyweight back against the glass as I reach down and tug that hat off of Brooke's hair, tossing it aside and curling my fingers in the silky chocolate strands, twining them around my fingers as I tug her closer, encourage her to part her lips and take me into her warmth.

"Oh hell to the fuck yes," I groan as the music swells and the crowd cheers, a horde of people flowing in a mass just outside of our little bubble. Makes it so much hotter. I almost want to be caught, want somebody to stumble into our nook and see this girl with her mouth wrapped around the head of my cock. I want them to look at us and feel fucking jealous as shit that they're not me, that they can't have her the way I can. "That's it, Brooke, right there."

She slips her tongue to the sensitive underside of my shaft, flicking it up against the metal of my frenum piercing until I can't take it anymore, pushing me in deeper, just a few inches more but *damn*. The warmth of her wrapped around me like that is intoxicating, especially paired with the cool air from the bay swirling against the rest of my exposed skin.

Brooke slides back and takes a breath, exhaling against my moistened skin. I glance down at her and she looks up at me.

"Am I doing this right?" she asks and I groan, shoving the heels of my hands against my eyes.

"Are you *trying* to make me blow my load like, right this fucking second? Don't talk like that." Brooke huffs out and the flutter of warmth makes me moan and buck my hips.

"Does it hurt if I touch your piercings?" she asks as I drop a hand back to her hair, teasing and twining it around my fingers.

"Nope. Go for it, Smarty-Pants." Brooke grabs hold of the base of my cock and leans in, slipping her tongue through the silver ring of my Prince Albert, giving it an experimental yank before she grabs it with her teeth and pulls harder. I clamp down on the sounds building in my throat, trying to keep quiet. Did I mention that was rule five? Fuck. I'm starting not to give a shit anymore. Besides, the music is loud and the crowd is louder ... a guttural groan escapes my lips when Brooke tugs on the piercing in my balls. It's just a plain silver ring at the midline, but holy *shit*. When a pretty girl's got her fingers all over it? Heaven, baby. Pure heaven.

My head drops back against the glass of the door as I knead my fingers into Brooke's scalp, riding the high of the moment, savoring the feel of her mouth, her hands. She doesn't feel so amateurish right now. Or maybe that's just the part of me that's crushing hard that's talking? When it comes to Brooke, that little piece of me doesn't quite see straight.

"Hey, hey," I say, reaching down and taking her chin, tilting her face away from me, my cock sliding from her lips. "That's perfect, baby." I help Brooke to her feet, her face flushed, her mouth moist with saliva. I lean forward and kiss her mouth hard, tasting myself on her tongue, loving every fucking second of this. "Now, turn around and show me your ass," I whisper, snagging a condom from my pocket as I watch Brooke turn and bend over, putting her palms against the glass of the door opposite the one I'm standing in.

I step forward, gliding the lubed condom over my shaft as I slide my fingers up Brooke's thighs and find ... that she's not wearing any goddamn panties either.

"Are you fucking serious?" I whisper, my brows shooting up in surprise. The look she tosses over her shoulder is playful and sexy as fuck.

"You think you're the only one that prepared for this?"

Holy shit. So totally crushing right now.

I grab hold of Brooke's hips and she moans, tilting her pelvis back so that the warmth of her ass and pussy is pressed against me. I guide myself to her opening, teasing it with my fingers and finding her already slick and ready.

"Hell yes, baby," I whisper, pushing into her tight heat, feeling her ridges slide down me, engulf me, fucking consume me. And I want to be consumed by this woman. Who wouldn't? My eyes eat up the sight of her arching her back, her long dark hair streaming over her shoulder and getting caught in the drafty breeze that sneaks through our alcove.

Outside our safe little space, people clap and cheer as a blues band takes over the stage and the singer's sexy croon takes over the cool evening air. It's a different backdrop, that's for sure, turning Brooke's and my sordid little affair into

BAD NANNY

something more sensual.

My fingers knead her flesh, dig into the soft pale skin over her hips. I take hold of that natural handle, that perfect curve of hip bone that feels like it was designed for me to grab onto. In this position, I can push all the way in, every single inch. I can feel her moistness spreading across our combined flesh, can feel the contractions taking over as she succumbs to the pleasure, her breath fogging against the glass in front of her face.

I feel a satisfied smile drag across my mouth as I let my head tilt back and move my hips hard, loving the resistance she's giving me, the firm stance of her legs, the press of her palms into the glass. I give her everything I've got, fucking hard and fast, my balls teasing her pussy, my piercing playing with her clit.

I don't expect her to come so quick, to push back into me and collapse, my hands on her body the only things that keep her from hitting the ground knees first. I follow Brooke to the pavement and encourage her to stay on all fours, knees to the pavement, hands splayed open wide as her head hangs down. And then I fuck her harder, as fast and frenzied as I can. I let go completely and I don't worry about a goddamn thing except for this.

When I come, I feel her react to the sounds I'm making, the way I'm squeezing her body and pumping those last few, furious thrusts. She bucks her hips back into mine, easing her body down my shaft as I finish hard and quick.

"Fuck," Brooke mumbles as she pulls away from me and curls against the door with her knees up, one hand resting on her calf as she gives me an almost-glare and I grin, tearing the condom off and rising to my feet. I toss it into the trash can just outside the alcove and then cross my arms over my chest.

"Don't tell me you didn't like that," I say as I move back into the shadows and reach my hand down for Brooke. She's shaking when she lifts her palm up and places it gently, tentatively inside of mine. The brush of our fingers sends a warm thrill through me as I tug Brooke to her feet and into the circle of my arms.

"I'm shaking," she admits, but I just smile.

"I know."

"Can we go pierce my eyebrow now?"

I tilt my head back with a laugh and then drop my chin, pressing a kiss to Brooke's forehead.

That gentle, easy touch … it makes us *both* shiver.

CHAPTER 22
BROOKE OVERLAND

I seriously cannot believe I just did it in the middle of Old Town. Like, anybody could've seen us. And I so totally didn't give a shit.

I wrap my arms around myself and pretend like I'm not wet and uncomfortable downstairs. Too embarrassing to talk about that with Zayden. While he's driving, I send off some secret texts to my girlfriends back in Berkeley, telling them to call me or better yet—come visit my ass like *yesterday.*

"You didn't tell me your brother lived over here," I say as we pull into a slightly shadier area of town, down a street populated entirely with copies of the same duplex in different colors.

"Yeah, well, my poor bro works his butt off as an insurance salesman and he and his wife *really* wanted to own their own place ..." Zay trails off a little as we pause in front of a green and white duplex with a really beautiful right side decorated in flowers and outdoor statuary ... and the other side, well, not so beautiful. "They bought this place with the life insurance money our parents left us." Zay eyes the ugly side of the duplex with his pierced brow cocked up in disgust. "And then they rented out one half to this doucher over here." He points his thumb in that direction as we pull into the driveway behind a beat up old Geo Metro. "They've tried to evict the fucker, but he always threatens to sue 'em or squat or whatever the fuck."

Zay parks the car and we climb out, slamming the doors closed behind us.

Not ten seconds later, some guy with a beard and a *shotgun* comes out the front door of the ugly duplex and points the muzzle at Zayden.

"You fucked with my crop, you piece of shit," he says as I put my palms up and take a small step back. Zayden just tucks his hands into his back pockets and stares the guy down.

"What are you gonna do about it, you baby hating motherfucker? The law says you can have *six* plants. Not, like, thirty. And not to sell. Go eat a dick and stop banging on the wall. The next time you do it, it won't be your weed that I snip off." Zay makes a cutting motion with his fingers as the man cocks his shotgun and takes a step forward, his hands shaking with rage.

Uh-oh.

What the hell did you do, Zayden?

"Shoot me. In the front yard. With several witnesses. How do you think that shit'll go down?"

I don't exactly think antagonizing a guy with a gun pointed at your chest is the best idea in the world, but … it's kind of hot to see Zayden standing up for himself. I dig my phone out of my back pocket and start up a live video feed, just in case.

"This guy's threatening to shoot us. I hope it's just a joke," I say as I point the camera at the bearded guy in the *Go Fuck Yourself* t-shirt. "I'm trying to decide if I should call the cops or not. What do you think, Zay?"

"Naw. I think this asshole's going to go back inside and start looking for alternative housing. I don't think you've got much room to threaten my brother anymore. If you don't want us to show this video to the police, then you won't wait for him to evict you. Get the fuck out of my face." Zay shoves the shotgun to the side and turns around without waiting for a response.

BAD NANNY

I keep the phone up as I take a few steps back and then follow Zay around the corner and down the short walkway to the front door. Shotgun Man never takes his focus off of Zayden, but before we can even get the front door unlocked, I feel the house shake with a slammed door from the opposite side.

"What did you do?" I whisper and Zayden shrugs, avoiding a really small, very badly burned paper bag on the porch. Really? People still burn shit bags as a prank? I guess Shotgun Man really was pissed.

"Every time Sadie cried, the asshole slammed his fist against the wall. I got sick of it, so I took my sister-in-law's clippers and cut down his crop. Every last plant. I have no clue what exactly that means for him because I don't smoke the shit, but"—Zayden shrugs as he unlocks the door and smiles at me—"it sure seemed to piss him off."

"Depends on the strain. Might just decrease the yield; might change the high, make it less potent, more short-lived," I say and then shrug back at him when he raises his eyebrows. "You didn't learn anything growing up around here? This is Pot Capital, USA." Zayden grins at me and shoves the door open, holding his hand out to welcome me in.

"Well, look at you. So full of fun facts." He reaches out and pokes me in the shoulder playfully. Too bad all that small touch does is reignite the wetness between my legs. I suck in a harsh breath. "Feel free to check the place out. I'll be right back. Gotta grab something from my piece of shit car."

Zayden disappears as I look around at the tiny foyer and the walls covered in family photos. There's a set of stairs to my right and a small pathway to the living room on my left.

I move inside and scope the room out. It's small, but the wall is painted with a rich eggplant and the furniture, while small, is perfectly sized and carefully arranged to give the place the maximum amount of space. Somebody's hung a shelf behind the sofa and covered it in chihuahua statues. Makes me smile.

I spot a picture of Zayden and a redhead that must be his

brother. He called him a lumberjack when he was talking about him, and I see that the description is dead on—right down to the flannel shirt he's wearing. Next to that, in a silly black and white frame with grinning pink skulls on it, there's a picture of two little boys that match up to the men next to them.

I pick up the frame in my hands and feel a warm smile chasing across my lips.

Zayden is *so* goddamn cute in this shot, wearing a little Mohawk and grinning big. He looks like he's maybe eight or nine in the picture, his hand wrapped around a plastic hammer while his brother clutches a yellow foam lightning bolt. They have the same mouth, same chin. Despite the difference in hair color, it's easy to tell they're related. No wonder I thought Zayden's nieces and nephews looked like they were his.

I have a weird idea that it'd be kind of fun to make babies with him. Someday, of course. Not now. Way, way, way later. I'm kind of thinking my first baby will be at thirty-five. And don't give me all the silly medical facts; science and medicine evolve everyday.

"I totally kicked his ass that day," Zay says as I jump and almost drop the picture, setting it quickly back on the side table and shoving hair over my shoulder in a wave. *Was I just fantasizing about making future babies with this guy? Like that would ever happen.* Zayden's made it pretty clear that he's not interested in having a relationship; I think I've made the same clear. And I meant it. I did.

Don't get all virgin cliché and start falling for this guy, Brooke.

"Kicked his ass?" I ask as Zayden moves over to a closer door I hadn't noticed before and opens it to reveal a bathroom. "Were you guys sparring or something?"

"Rob was playing as the god Zeus, and I was supposed to be Thor. He kept getting pissed at me because I was saying *Shor* instead, and we ended up getting into a real fight." Zay waves me into the bathroom and lays a towel down on the toilet, gesturing for me to take a seat. "He gave me my first black eye, and I knocked two of his teeth out."

BAD NANNY

"Yikes," I say as I sit, but I'm smiling anyway. I like hearing Zay's stories, getting to know him better. And why shouldn't I? All his girlfriends probably heard this story and he claims to not even have liked them. So he dates people he hates. Totally weird. I find that it bothers me more than it should, like why were they worth dating and I'm not even at that level?

I blink those thoughts away and sweep my fingers through my hair, suddenly nervous about the whole idea of getting pierced. *Although you already let Zayden pierce you in the most intimate way possible, so why not?*

"Were your parents pissed?"

"Oh hell yeah," Zay says as he opens a silver kit filled with medical supplies. "They made me and Rob work, like, forever doing obscure chores to pay for that dental work. Have you ever had to sweep the street in front of the house? The actual road for an entire block. Who does that?"

I laugh as Zayden comes over to stand in front of me, reaching up to take my chin in his hands. I can see in his eyes that he's in total work mode right now, but the touch of his hands makes me remember the other night—not to mention our exhibition experiment. *Oh God.*

I feel my eyes flutter closed and Zayden exhales sharply.

"Stop that," he says, but he sounds goofy and playful, like he doesn't much care if I tear his pants open and start sucking his cock again. And I kind of want to. I ... actually really liked it. "I've been fantasizing about this since the day I met you. Now hold still."

Zayden looks at me for a few seconds and then grabs some black gloves out of his kit, snapping them onto his fingers in a way that's oddly erotic. I want to feel that latex on my body—and not just inside of it.

Fuck. Who thinks about condoms like that? I'm being totally weird.

Zayden grabs a white antiseptic wipe and then comes to stare at me again.

"Right or left?" he asks, and I pause. I have to really think about that for a minute.

"Do you have a preference?" I ask. "I mean, it's your art."

"And it's your body," he says, but almost like he wishes it were his, too. "Let's do the left. Then me and you can be piercing buddies." He waggles his own pierced brow and I smile.

Zayden lifts the wipe up and cleans a spot on my left brow with the cool feeling of alcohol, pulling back and tossing the little square into the can between the toilet and the sink. Once he's done that, he stares at me for another few seconds, like he's really taking this seriously. I like that about him. He's a goofy guy, someone that likes to have fun, but he takes the things that matter and he actually applies himself. Whether it's being a nanny or a body piercer ... or introducing a girl to her first sexual experience, I can tell he really gives it all he's got.

"Sixteen gauge," Zayden mumbles to himself, heading back to the kit. "You can change the jewelry in about six months, but for now, we're going with medical grade stainless steel." I nod and watch as he opens up a package with a silver bar inside it and lays it on top of its package on the counter. Next he opens up a new needle and a package with a little wooden toothpick thing inside of it. It has a purple dye on the end and I can't figure out what it's for until Zay comes back and puts the jewelry to my face, using the dye to mark an entry and exit point.

"Alright, Smarty-Pants," he says as he stands up and steps into the doorway of the bathroom, using his hand to indicate the mirror. "Check it out and tell me what you think. And don't be shy, baby, tell me if you don't like it."

I stand up and tuck some hair behind my ear, my eyes straying to Zayden in his sexy black gloves. I love the way they cut across his tattoos, emphasize the brightness with all of that latex as contrast. He notices my gaze lingering and wiggles the fingers of his right hand.

"You like these, I take it? Some people have a fetish for 'em."

"What about you?" I ask, deflecting the question as I lean in

BAD NANNY

and examine the proposed placement for my piercing. It looks perfect, balanced at just the right spot on my eyebrow, which is basically what I expected. I can't imagine Zayden failing at something he's obviously so passionate about. "Do you have that fetish?"

"A little bit," he purrs, leaning in and breathing against my ear. To keep things sterile, he makes sure his gloves are nowhere near me. It's kind of sexy, knowing he couldn't touch me even if he wanted to. "I'd like to touch you all over with these, slide 'em into the pink perfection of your pussy."

"Look at you and your alliteration," I joke with a hot flush, retreating away to sit on the lid of the toilet again. "So clever."

"Not near as clever as you," he says as he tosses the toothpick thing and picks up a pair of what look like tongs. "You with your bachelor's in statistics and all. I barely graduated high school."

"And yet I'm still working as a stripper," I say, and I hate how bitter that sounds. I don't want to be that person, lamenting all of the awful things in their life. Yeah, sometimes life sucks, but it's just like the shadows in a painting: there are always highlights to offset all that darkness. "At least when I get my master's, I should be able to get my dream job."

"Which is?" Zayden asks as he positions himself in front of me, his tongue sticking out slightly to the side as he concentrates on what he's doing. He massages my brow with his thumb and forefinger for a few seconds and then uses the tongs to pinch my skin so that it's sticking out.

"I want to work for the CDC," I say and he makes an impressed sound in the back of his sexy throat. I study his tattoos, realizing that I've never taken note of the words under his right ear. In a fine black script, the phrase *In Head and Heart* is written out. I wonder what it means? "I don't really care where, but I'd like to analyze data on diseases that pose a risk to public health."

"Sounds hella fancy," he says as he smiles at me and I feel my heart flutter. Being this close to him is like a drug, like each breath we share in this small room brings us closer, drags me inexorably into this man's arms. Not good. I want to look away, but I can't because he's bringing a needle up to my face and pressing it against my skin. "And important, too. Instead of being a useless waste of life like yours truly, it sounds like you're going places, Brooke Overland. Now suck in a deep breath."

I pull air into my lungs and then start to panic. Wow. This is *actually* happening, isn't it?

Before I can get myself together enough to protest, Zayden's telling me, "breathe out."

I do, and then the pain of the needle is slicing through me, hot and sharp and sudden. It happens too quick for me to cry out, and then Zayden's standing up and grabbing the jewelry from its spot on the counter.

"See? Not so bad," he coos and I feel myself smiling again. That voice must work on all his clients; it's definitely working on me.

"You're right. It wasn't bad at all. Maybe I should get my clit pierced next?" Zayden laughs as he pushes the silver metal bar through my skin and then tosses the needle into the trash, slipping a metal ball onto the opposite end. One more wipe with an antiseptic square and it's done.

"Clit piercings are actually pretty rare. What you're probably thinking of is a clitoral hood piercing." He smiles as I stand up and pose in front of the mirror, leaning in close to examine my new piercing. It's barely red there at all, and it doesn't hurt, not even a little.

Zayden is *good.*

"Not everyone's a good candidate for it." He spreads his fingers into a V shape in what I'm assuming is an imitation of a vagina. "You, you Brooke have the *anatomy* necessary. If you ever seriously consider it, check with me. I can give you a whole new orgasm with a properly placed piece of metal down there."

I'm blushing even though I have no clue why, but I don't acknowledge it, spinning to face Zayden with a smile as I point up at my eyebrow. It really does look great on me, the perfect little accent for an otherwise plain face.

"Based on how good this looks, if I ever do decide to bite the bullet and get my V pierced, I'll make sure to fly down to Vegas just for the privilege." Zayden smiles at me, clasping his hands together behind his neck as he looks me over. "Maybe you could show me around the city or something sometime?"

"I'd like that," Zay says as he looks me over carefully, smiling when his gaze comes to rest on my eyebrow. "I bet the boys in the shop would like to meet you, too. They're all smarter than me, too. The owner, Jude, has a degree in veterinary medicine. You'd probably get along great."

I laugh and pull my hair back into a ponytail at the base of my neck, brushing my bangs aside so I can see my new jewelry, turning this way and that as it winks in the light. I'm so focused on my reflection that I don't notice Zay moving up behind me, sliding his hands up my thighs and under my skirt.

The cool, waxy sensation of the gloves is so different that I gasp and fall forward, putting my hands against the sink to brace myself. When I look up, Zay's grinning mischievously at me in the mirror, sliding his fingers to my opening and using the slick wetness that's already there to tease me. Even though I can't see his hand, I can *feel* that glove, can imagine the darkness of it slicking over his hand as he plays with my folds.

I watch his face as he slips a pair of fingers inside of me, sending this erotic chill through my whole body that has my skin breaking out into goose bumps. The sensation amps up when he leans his muscular body over mine and uses his other hand to pull my shirt and bra away from my left breast, cupping the sensitive flesh in one black gloved hand.

My face fills with heat and my body rocks back into his hand, enjoying the subtle manipulation of his fingers against my core. When he introduces a third finger and slicks it across my ass, I tighten up a little.

"Relax," Zayden whispers as he massages my breast with one hand, my ass and pussy with the other. "I won't take it too far, I promise."

He teases and manipulates me, pinching my nipple and

alternating between finger fucking me and playing with my clit. When he finally slips that single, wet finger into my ass, I groan and shudder as new sensations ripple over me, a completely different sort of warmth filling my body.

It feels like there are strings from my nipples, my clit, my pussy, my ass, that all connect straight to the base of my spine, twisting energy together in an explosive orgasm.

"Do you like that, baby?" he asks me, but I can't answer. Can barely breathe.

Zayden's putting some gentle pressure against the wall between his fingers, that sensitive strip that connects my pussy and my ass. I almost come right then, but he stops me at the last second by pulling away and leaving me gasping.

"Turn around," he commands, moving his kit from the sink onto a shelf behind him. I do as he asks and let him use his left arm to take me by the waist, lifting me up onto the counter. My back leans against the mirror as Zayden steps between my legs and puts his right hand against my silken core. This time, I can look down and see the black fingers of his gloves slipping into me, teasing wetness onto the latex. That third finger slips back into my other opening and I have to bite my lip to keep from screaming. No way I'm letting that weird Shotgun Pot Guy hear me getting fingered.

Zayden leans in and captures my mouth, shifting his body as close as he can get it without interrupting the motion of his hand. We kiss sharp and fierce and hungry as his left hand finds my breast again and I look down to see all of that darkness obscuring the tattoos on his arm, kneading the pale round globe, pinching the pebbled pink of my nipple.

My hips arch up into his hand and Zayden chuckles.

"Fuck me," I say, wanting him to feel good, too, feeling self-conscious that I'm the only one writhing like an idiot.

"I am," he whispers against my ear, and then he picks up the pace, slamming his knuckles into me and sending sharp thrills into the base of my spine where all that energy's stored. I gasp and wrap my arms around his neck, trying to ride this out, to wait for him to undo his pants and push inside of me with his cock.

But he doesn't, watching me with half-lidded eyes as I find my pleasure with his hand.

I think his face in that moment is the hottest thing I've ever seen in my life.

When I come, I can't help it, I tilt my head back and let out the loudest, deepest, most embarrassing sound of my entire life, shuddering and bucking against Zayden as I come hard and fast around his fingers.

He waits there as I gasp and struggle for breath, his left arm circling my waist and holding me close, the sound of his beating heart thundering in my ears. Then Zay steps back and I watch with a heavy-lidded languorous expression as he strips off his gloves and tosses them in the trash can. His eyes look almost emerald when they take me in, sitting with my butt half in the sink and my legs spread wide. From the bulge in his jeans, I can tell he wants to keep going, but he holds back, reaching out his hand for mine and helping me up.

"Do you think your aunt's floundering under all those kids yet?" he asks me, and I smile, glancing over my shoulder one more time to look in the mirror. My piercing, it looks amazing—and so does the expression on my face. I have this womanly sense of satisfaction curling my lips that I've never seen before.

It looks nice. Really nice actually.

I turn back to Zayden and wrinkle my nose.

"I think she was floundering before she ever got started."

He laughs and then pauses when a fist slams into the wall next to us, gritting his teeth as he curls his hands into fists.

"That motherfucker better be out of there by the time my brother gets back, or I swear to God ..." I grin and reach up to take Zayden's face between my hands, pressing a quick kiss to his lips that shuts him up almost instantly before he grins back at me. Then I reach down and take his hand, leading him outside and over to his sister-in-law's minivan.

I don't look at his beat up old Geo because I really, *really* don't want to think about him driving back to Las Vegas in it.

Monica looks like she's halfway to the grave when we get home that night, already waiting on the porch with her coat on by the time we get out of the van. When she sees the piercing in my eyebrow, hers shoot up to her hairline.

"They're all asleep," she says and then breezes past us to get back to the sleek black sexiness of her car, zooming into the night without so much as a wave good-bye.

"Stupid bitch," I snap and Zay laughs, lifting up his hand for a high five. I smack him palm to palm and feel my toes curl when he wraps his fingers around mine and brings them to his lips for a kiss.

"Exactly. Fuck her," Zayden says, pulling me inside to the quiet, easy sounds of Sadie's breathing. The other kids must be upstairs because I don't see them. From my spot near the front door, I have a clear shot at the back and can see the dogs waiting eagerly at the glass.

I head over there to let them in, suddenly nervous about what's going to happen. Zayden and I just did it—twice. Are we going to go upstairs and do it again? Are we going to sleep in the same bed for the rest of his time here? Can I handle that?

I bend down and pick up Dodger, dislodging a few small twigs that are wrapped in the thin fluff of white hair around his head and neck. It's literally like, all of the hair he has and he manages to get stuff stuck in it. Figures.

"Want some leftover casserole?" Zayden asks as he spins his way into the kitchen and grabs a hold of his iPod. It's covered in a questionable sticky substance no doubt left by one of the children, but he doesn't care, just wipes it off on his shirt and picks a song, turning it to a low volume so he won't wake Sadie.

I groan.

BAD NANNY

"No," I say as I skip over and look for something that could be considered a compromise. "I hate Tove Lo," I say and Zayden drops his jaw like I've just insulted the Virgin Mary or something. "And I *really* hate that "Talking Body" song."

"Seriously? I think it's adorable," he says as he grooves to it in his too cute black and red Converse with the little skeletons on the sides. Yet another pair of knee-high wins in my book. Paired with the skinny jeans and the silly video game shirt, well, it's just precious. He's this naughty mixture of bad and nerdy with all those tats and piercings. I could stare at this guy for hours and not get bored.

Zayden ruffles the hair on the left side of his head as he pulls the casserole from the fridge and starts spooning it into a pair of white bowls.

I look through Spotify for a minute and decide that he might actually like "Game Over" by Falling in Reverse. I feel like it's pop-y enough that Zay could get into it.

"Check this out," I say as I start the music and Zayden starts bobbing his head, tossing the bowls into the microwave and pressing start. He dances his way over to me and puts his arm around my waist, dragging me into yet another impromptu dance session.

I go with it, letting him press our bodies together in a warm embrace that makes my thighs clench tight with need. It's a bouncy song, so our dance isn't exactly a romantic waltz, but it still makes me laugh when Zay twirls me in a circle and catches me again.

"This song's all about video game metaphors, I see?"

"Thought you might like it," I say as his grin gets huge.

"Tomorrow," he says, like that's super important for some reason. Zayden claps his hands together and I can't help but lock my eyes onto his tattoos, on the open book on one hand and the sword and shield on the other. The more I look, the more little things I see buried in there, like the cluster of balloons with skulls and crossbones on them, the smiling pit bull face, and the tiny hairless cat with a ... sweater?

I clamp a hand over my mouth to stifle a laugh.

"Tomorrow," I mumble as Zayden pulls the bowls from the microwave and curses at how hot they are. "What about tomorrow?"

"No school, no work. You want to stay up all night and play a game with me?" Zayden pauses and gives me a theatrical wink. "And not just a sex game, although we'll get to that eventually. You want to play something stupid and shitty and ridiculously fun?"

"Why the hell not?" I ask, hating the way my heart flutters and dances when Zayden does a fist pump and scoops up half of his casserole in one bite. I like the way he eats, with his bowl up close to his chin and his entire fist gripping the handle of the spoon. He scoops food into his mouth with a methodical sort of purpose. I don't know if I've ever actually noticed the way someone eats before. Is that a weird thing to notice?

"Come on," Zay says, tilting his head to the side and leading me into the living room. He's done with his food before we even sit down, putting himself up against the arm opposite the TV and dragging me into his lap. With Zayden's chin on my shoulder and his arms wrapped around me, I feel that shifting, sliding thing happen inside my chest and try to fight it back.

I'm not going to fall in love with a guy just because I lost my virginity to him.

No fucking way.

"Okay, here's your controller," he says, handing me a black remote from the coffee table. "Now, are you ready for me to beat your ass at this? I'm not holding back just because you've got a sexy mouth and a curvy little body."

"Hah." I set the food aside and take my controller in hand. "I'm ready for this. Bring it on, bitch."

"Oooh, gettin' all aggressive, I see. I like it." Zay licks the back of my ear and then turns on the TV as I shiver and fight back yet another rush of hormones and sex. *We'll get to that eventually, he says. Hmm. We'll see.* "Now pick a character and let's do this thing."

I smile and lean into Zay's warm body, loving the strength

of his arms around me and the patter of his heart. It's something I could get used to, if I were looking for love that is. But I have enough to worry about without adding one more thing to my plate.

No matter how much I don't want to, when it comes time to let Zayden go, I'll do it with grace and poise.

It's the best thing for both of us.

When I wake up on the couch, still wrapped in Zayden's arms, I almost have a panic attack.

We only have five days, four nights left. *Four.* And I just wasted one. I sit up suddenly and try to breathe through the irrational feeling in my chest. *This is so dumb,* I think as I look at his adorable sleeping face. He's sexy as hell, but like this, with his eyes closed and those full lips gently parted, he's kind of ... sweet, too. When I reach up and run my fingers across the shaved side of his head, Zayden stirs, yawning and lifting his arms in a stretch.

I don't remember when, but sometime during the night he took his shirt off. I didn't realize it until now, but the jewelry in his nipples, they're miniature swords. I reach out and tug on one, making him groan at the same time Sadie starts to fuss.

"I'll get her," I say as I stand up and Zayden yawns again, scratching loosely at his abs with those sexy fingers of his. The way his ink is done, it just draws the eye in an easy arc from fingertips to shoulder, across the chest, down the other side. I can never seem to just glance at it and then look away; I always have to stare.

I move over to the opposite side of the living room and pick Sadie up, setting her up on the carpet and changing her diaper. I haven't done this in, like, forever but I used to babysit in high school so I figure it out pretty quickly. Admittedly, it's kind of gross, but manageable. As I squeeze Sadie's chubby foot, I find that I can't stop myself from fantasizing about what Zayden's babies might look like.

And here we go again with the damn hormones.

I finish changing the kid, standing up and balancing her on my hip as Zayden lays on the couch with a satisfied, sleepy expression on his face.

"Since it's monsoon fucking pourin' out there," he says as he points toward the expanse of the bay window with his inked hand, "I was thinking: mall first. 'cause then we can get those big ass pretzels with the cinnamon and sugar on them and let the kids burn energy at the indoor play place. Then—and check this brilliance right here—we pick up hot wings and burgers and veg out right in front of the TV."

Zayden turns on his side to stare at me, propping his head up with his hand.

"What do you think?" he asks when I just get caught there staring at him. There's this surreal moment where it almost feels like the eight of us are a family or something ... and it feels kind of ... good?

"I—" I should probably tell Zay I have homework and use his free babysitting skills to get some studying done. But then I look into his eyes, into that pale color that burns so bright with playful energy that I can't say no. I just can't. Not going to happen. "Okay."

When he smiles at me, I feel almost dizzy.

How stupid is that?

"Here," I say, coming over to stand next to the couch. "You feed the baby, and I'll get the kids up." As I hand Sadie to Zayden, I feel his fingers slide across my skin, hot as coals, and pull away as quickly as I can. It's like, when our skin's touching, I don't think with a clear head.

"Don't make me give you another lecture about piercing hygiene," Zayden shouts as I start up the stairs and feel my lips break into a smile. "If you don't clean it properly, I'll know about it."

I grin and shake my head as I slip into Grace's room to wake her and Kinzie up.

BAD NANNY

I have a feeling that today, today is going to be a good day.

The play place at the mall isn't exactly the most exciting destination, but then, Eureka isn't the most exciting town in the world. The only things we have in spades here are outdoor beauty ... and rain. Sort of a frustrating dichotomy if you think about it.

Zayden buys the kids whatever treats they want from the food court and then sets 'em loose on the playground as we take a seat on one of the benches. I haven't been here since I got back in town and wow, it brings some old memories crashing to the forefront of my mind.

"The first boy I ever kissed, I kissed right here," I tell Zay, pointing at the hideous faux granite linoleum beneath our feet. It hasn't changed at all in the last ten years. The only thing that's different about this place are the stores. When I was younger, there used to be an interesting mix of local shops. Now, one whole wing of the mall is empty, advertising storefronts for rent, and the rest of it's been turned into outward facing big box stores like Petco and Kohl's.

Kind of depressing.

"For real?" Zayden says, turning to look at me with his pretzel clutched in one hand. His hair looks extra perfect today, spiked up on one side into a Mohawk, the other shaved with fresh stars. He's even put on the tiniest smidge of liner and changed out his piercings. They're all black today, all matching. His lip piercings are actual rings today instead of the studs he's been wearing since he got here. So hot. I want to grab 'em with my teeth and pull. *Kind of like I did with the piercings in his cock.*

I choke and glance away, back towards the kids, watching as Kinzie and Bella chase each other up the faux rock wall.

"Right on this very bench?" Zayden asks with a playful lilt

to his voice. I glance back at him just in time for Zay to lean forward and press his mouth to mine. His tongue flicks out hard and fast and I'm left sitting there with the faint taste of cinnamon on my lips. "I'm giving you new memories," he explains as I shake my head with a laugh.

"Not on this *exact* bench," I say with a roll of my eyes. "Just here, in the mall. Where'd you have your first kiss?"

"Mmm," Zayden leans his head back and stares up at the skylights in the ceiling. I use the term sky*lights* loosely because there's definitely not much light leaking through the glass; it's gray and dark and stormy as hell. "With my friend's older sister, in the bathroom of her church during a youth group meeting."

I raise my slightly sore brow as Zayden lifts his head back up and grins at me again.

"Youth group, huh?" I ask as he takes a massive bite of his pretzel and nods at me.

"Yep. That's me. Always challenging the institution." Zayden taps his green and black Dr. Martens on the floor with a steady rhythm. I am so in love with his fashion choices. Today, his shoes are this matte black color with a neon green skeleton foot on the side. Oh. And he's wearing black suspenders that aren't holding anything up. They're just hooked to his pants and then looped back around and reconnected to the waistband. "Did you know I was in a punk band in high school?"

"Does not surprise me," I say as I cross my arms over my own sad attempt at dressing up. I've got on a navy blue shirt with the world *Cal* scrawled across the front in gold that I got from UCB, a pair of dark skinny jeans and some fuzzy black velvet heels that I found in my sister's closet. I know, I know: I'm a total mess. I think I'm still trying to figure out exactly *who* it is that I am. I think all my clothes are doing is reflecting the confusion inside. Or something like that. "What instrument did you play?"

"Instrument? Please, Smarty-Pants, you give me too much credit. I just screamed shit into the microphone. That is pretty much it. I would hardly even call it music."

"Well maybe you could play some for me one day?" I say as Zayden finishes off his pretzel and wads the trash up, tossing it like a basketball into the nearest can.

"Yeah right. You already think I'm a nerd now. How much less cool would I be if I played the guttural garbage I used to spew as a kid? No, thank you."

"Being in a punk band totally makes you cool," I say as Zayden tucks one leg up on the bench and gives me a look.

"Being in a *good* punk band totally makes you cool. Being in a garage band with music recorded on some guy's phone back in the day. So not cool."

Zayden glances out toward the kids and I follow his stare, happening to catch some little kid rush up to Grace and grab hold of her pigtails as she runs. With a hard yank, my niece's head snaps back and she ends up slipping and falling to the foam floor with a scream. Before I can even react to the situation, Zayden is up on his feet and sprinting over to her.

I grab Sadie's stroller and chase after him as quickly as I can.

"Hey, hey," he says as he uses his thumbs to brush away her tears. "You're okay, baby."

"No, I'm not!" Grace screams, clinging to his leg and ignoring me completely when I try to comfort her by rubbing her back.

"Do you need surgery then?" Zayden asks, looking her in the eyes and getting completely serious. "Because we can go to the hospital right now."

Grace's eyes get huge and she shakes her head, reigning back the screaming sobs into gentle sniffles.

"Good. Then let's tough this out and get back up on that horse."

"There isn't a horse," Grace mumbles as she stands up and glares at the boy who pulled her hair. I have no idea how to handle this situation, but I'll be damned if I let some brat get away with that. I look around for an adult that could possibly be the kid's parent.

"Hey," Zayden says, walking right over to the boy and leaning down in front of him. "It's not okay to hurt people like that, dude. And don't ever touch a girl without her permission, buddy. So not cool."

The kid just stands there and glares at Zayden as a man in Levi's and a white t-shirt comes over and looms big behind the boy. His dad, maybe? I have no idea, but I decide to corral our brood before things get bad. I think our playdate here is over.

"Don't you talk to my boy like that," the man says as Zayden stands up straight and I'm pleased to find he's actually taller than the big man who's glaring at him. "You have a problem, you talk to me."

"Did you not see your kid pull my niece's hair? Knock her onto her back? That's some serious stuff, man. All I was saying was that I don't want your son to put his hands on her."

"Boys will be boys," the man says and I find myself gritting my teeth as I collect the twins and make them put their hands on the stroller. They're so slippery that Zay and I have almost lost them three times since we got here a half an hour ago. The only way I can keep watch on them is to play this game where they have to touch the stroller at all times.

"Boys will be boys? What kind of bullshit is that? So he has a right to act like a brat? Screw that. Tell your son to keep his fucking hands off my niece."

"My son has a right to be a boy," the man says and I watch in horror as Zayden's colored fists tighten, his knuckles turning into sharp points of bone beneath his marked skin. "Now back your faggot ass off and let's be done with this."

Zayden closes his eyes, takes a deep breath and then opens them back up to smile at the man.

"You might want to send your son away for this one," he says as the man starts to turn and then shakes his head at Zayden. Zay waits for a minute as the brat boy scrambles back into the playground and then reaches out and puts his hand on the father's shoulder.

"Fuck you," the man says as he turns back and scowls.

Without warning, Zay's fist explodes into the guy's face and

BAD NANNY

I kid you not, the man practically topples over, falling to the foam covered floor like a board. All around the playground, I hear the adults go silent.

Uh-oh.

"Want to play a game?" I whisper to the kids. "Let's all race to the car. If everyone plays fairly, you'll all get a prize."

I start pushing Sadie's stroller, grabbing Zayden by his muscular arm and dragging him away before anybody gets it together enough to stop him.

As soon as we hit the parking lot, we all start to run, and we don't stop until we're piling into the minivan and peeling the hell out of there.

Maybe I should be mad at Zayden or maybe I should be explaining to the kids that violence doesn't solve problems but … that guy was a serious asshole. Screw him. I feel like I've spent a good portion of my life trying not to rock the boat.

I glance over at Zayden as he shakes his head and smiles wryly, flexing the fingers of his right hand. Here's somebody who's definitely *not* afraid, who does his own thing when he wants and how he wants. Maybe he doesn't always make the right choice—punching some a-hole in the mall probably wasn't the right choice—but at least he stood up for himself, for Grace.

I smile.

"You are so goddamn stupid," I say as I look down at the hole in the knee of my jeans. When I glance back over at Zayden, he's looking at the road with his eyebrows raised and his lips pursed. "But also kind of cool."

His lips curl into a smirk as he reaches over and playfully taps me in the shoulder.

"Boys will be boys, right?" he jokes as I laugh my ass off, until there are tears streaming from the corners of my eyes.

"You're the best nanny ever," I say and he touches a hand to his chest.

"Aww, you flatter me," Zayden mocks, batting his lashes at me.

I smile back at him, but I hope he knows that I'm telling the

truth.
    I really am gonna miss this guy.

CHAPTER 23
ZAYDEN ROTH

I can see the change in Brooke as soon as the last of the kids falls asleep, the way she starts pacing and threading her fingers together, stretching them out in front of herself as she paces.

I cross my own arms over my chest and tilt my head to the side as I watch her. She looks so cute and fresh in her tight, little t-shirt and jeans, those crazy heels she's wearing. I'm inclined to grab her and toss her onto the couch for a quick fuck, but I think we need to use our last few nights wisely. I have yet to go down on her, and there is no way in *hell* I'm going home without showing her all of my tricks.

"You okay over there, Smarty-Pants?" I ask as she leans down to pick up Hubert in his stupid black and white striped sweater. Brooke cuddles him to her chest and he lifts that ugly pale pink head of his to rub against her chin. Friendliest I have ever seen the damn creature in my life, swear to God. "You look like you're about to shit a brick."

"I'm contemplating," she says with a lift of her chin, that long dark hair tucked in a braid. Hubs bats at it as she strokes her hand over his sweater.

I take a few steps closer and drop my hand to the cat's head; he hisses at me but doesn't bite me like he usually does. Score.

Even my asshole cat likes this chick.

"Contemplating ... fucking me?" I ask and laugh as Brooke rolls her eyes dramatically. "Because I have a very specific little game in mind for tonight. We've checked off a lot of boxes this week, Smarty-Pants, but we've missed one of the Big Four."

"Big Four?" Brooke asks, that perfect arched brow of hers accented by the piercing I gave her. It looks so goddamn good on her face. I wish I was going to be around to suck on it once it heals. Damn and double damn.

"Yep," I say, trying to be sexy as I lift up my right hand and splay it against the wall next to Brooke's head. I lean in all sultry and shit and then feel a rapid thumping against my boot, glancing down to find that stupid hairless rat going at it with my Docs. "Whoa. No means no, Dodger, you dick."

I shove him away with my foot as Brooke laughs and spins out of my embrace, moving to the opposite side of the coffee table as she continues to stroke and cuddle my cat. I turn and watch her with a smirk building on my lips.

"I'd so much rather you were stroking and cuddling *me*," I say as she nuzzles the stupid creature and he glares at me from his weird white-green eyes. I should take him down to the shelter and trade him in for a cute little orange tabby or something. But naw, I love the little fuck too much.

"What are the Big Four?" Brooke repeats as I sigh and tuck a hand into the back pocket of my pants, using the other to twirl my loose black suspender strap in a circle.

"Hand jobs, vaginal penetration, blow jobs, and VJs."

"What's a VJ?" Brooke asks as I shake my head and laugh.

"A vagina job. You know, like a BJ, only with a vagina? Come on, don't make me say *cunnilingus*. It sounds like a type of foot fungus."

"Oh my God! Add *that* to your list of things to never say again. It's getting kind of long, Zayden."

"Yeah, well, call it whatever you want, but we're still missing the last of the Big Four."

"You made that up, too, didn't you? Big Four and VJ are

BAD NANNY

not terms I heard on campus like, ever."

"Because young people while sexually rampant are woefully ignorant. How many of those douchers still think the pullout method is a hundred percent effective, hmm?"

Brooke sets Hubert down on the floor and the stupid cat immediately starts arching his back and rubbing against her legs. *Traitor.*

"Don't say young people either. You're not *that* old."

I put a hand to my chest as Brooke comes around the back of the sofa and pauses there like there's a shield between us, a magical barrier that can block sex hormones and pheromones. Hah. Fat chance. I can practically smell her sweet fruity vanilla scent from here. It'd take a fortress to keep me away.

"Not *that* old? That sounds like one of those compliments that's not really a compliment at all. I'm still in my twenties, okay Smarty-Pants."

"Maybe I should go upstairs and sleep alone tonight?" Brooke says as she challenges me with a look, running her tongue over her lower lip. "Not sure I want to hang out with some guy who decked a daddy at the playground."

"Oh? Come on. You told me I was a badass."

I start towards her and she ducks away, making me chase her around the couch.

"I never said badass," Brooke says, watching me as I go stone still and then hop the couch in one quick motion. She screams and starts for the stairs as I scoop her up into my arms, bride style.

Bride style.

Um.

Nope. I'm not carrying *anybody* over a threshold, let alone some twenty-two year old with the whole world ahead of her. Gross.

I set Brooke down again and drop my hands to her hips, yanking her close for a kiss as I fumble around with my right hand and jerk the curtains closed over the bay window.

"So, where do you want your first VJ? In the bed? On the couch? Sitting on the edge of the kitchen table?"

"Let's go upstairs," Brooke whispers against my mouth, dragging me up the steps and into her borrowed bedroom. Before I can even get the door closed, she's tearing her top off and kicking her heels aside.

I watch with hungry eyes as she shoves her jeans down her hips and climbs onto the bed with an eagerness that makes me grin.

Oh yes.

I reach back and tear my own tee over my head, leaving my boots and suspenders on as I move onto the edge of the bed and grab hold of Brooke's plain gray cotton panties. Yet another pair with kind of a saggy ass. Yet another thing that I shouldn't find sexy yet … surprisingly do.

"Turn the light off?" she pleads and I pause, rubbing a hand over the shaved side of my head.

"Why?" I ask as I take her knees and slowly push them apart. She offers a little resistance at first but finally gives in. "I want to see all of you, Brooke Overland. Every little bit."

"Some of my bits aren't so beautiful," she says with a slight shrug of her shoulders, but I'm already shaking my head.

"Every one of your bits is perfect."

"Says who?"

I raise an eyebrow at her.

"Says me."

Brooke groans and drops her head back into the pillows, putting her hands over her face as I slide my fingers down the soft white insides of her thighs. Her body is warm, breath already coming in harsh pants, even though we haven't gotten started yet. When I glance down, I see the shimmery dance of liquid on her pussy.

Oh yeah.

She's excited as hell for this.

I lift up one leg and start kissing at her knee, enjoying the way her body jerks and thrashes from even that small touch. I rub my stubbled cheek against her thigh and then drop down to press my lips to the bare expanse of space between Brooke's belly button and her clit.

BAD NANNY

My right hand traces down her left thigh as I kiss my way slowly from one hip to the other.

"You really do have a beautiful body, baby," I tell her as I trace a single finger down the wetness of her folds and watch as she bucks her hips in response. Brooke is definitely an animated lover. Might have to use some extra tricks to get her to sit still for this.

My finger slides up and plays lightly over her clit.

"The perfect anatomy for a VCH piercing, if you ever decide you want one." It turns me on to think about marking Brooke with my jewelry, stamping her with my art. Honestly, the piercing I'm talking about doesn't hurt at all—even less than your typical earlobe. A ring goes right through the thin tissue above the clit, and gently swings against it during sex. It's nothing short of amazing, or so I've heard from girls before. So I've *seen* with girls before.

I slip my fingers inside of Brooke and watch her bite her lower lip and grab the pillow on either side of her head. She is living for this, thrashing around and making those cute small sounds in the back of her throat. I fuck her swollen flesh with my fingers, loving the way the V and the E tattooed on my knuckles disappears inside of her with each movement.

When her moans devolve into a more guttural sound, I slide my fingers out and lean down, putting myself on my elbows and hooking my arms under her thighs, hands gripping tight to her hips. This way, when Brooke starts bucking, I'll be ready for it.

My tongue slicks down her bare flesh to the hot slit between her legs, dipping down to her opening and swirling a quick circle against all of that heat. She tastes as sweet as she smells, like flowers and vanilla, fresh and clean and aroused as fuck.

My lips trail hot kisses back up and around her clit, putting pressure against the hooded flesh before I try taking this any further. I want to rush, suck the hardened nub into my mouth and fuck her opening with my tongue, but I need this to be memorable. I want this moment ingrained into Brooke's history with a hammer and chisel. Normally, I don't give a shit if girls forget me later. I mean, I always aim to please, but if they leave our night together back in Vegas when they fly home to wherever-the-hell-they-came-from, I don't care.

With Brooke, I really, really do. I *need* her to remember this.

I tease and savor her with my mouth, using the sound of her breathing to plan my movements, keeping her locked in place with the strength of my arms.

When Brooke drops a hand to my hair and twists it around her fingers, shoving my face into her cunt, I grin and let myself go a little deeper, a little harder. She strains to thrust against me, ride my face as I finally give in and take her clit gently into my mouth, sucking on it and lightly grazing my teeth across it.

The sounds she makes are fucking *killer.*

I let go of Brooke's hip with my right hand and slip it inside her for a moment, getting myself nice and wet and slick. Then I shove it down to my jeans, tearing the button open and sliding my fingers down my shaft, using Brooke's lube to stroke my cock with smooth, slippery fingers.

I moan against her pussy as I bring us both to the edge of an orgasm, stopping myself short, so I can enjoy hers fully. My hand comes back up and locks that hip into place so that when Brooke starts to fight the orgasm, I can keep going, taking her over the edge as she slaps a hand on her mouth and screams against it.

I release her suddenly, sitting up and tearing one of my trusty condoms from the pocket of my jeans and slipping it on. While Brooke's still panting and shaking, I climb on top of her, put my lips to her throat and thrust hard and deep, the headboard slamming into the wall with each movement. I'll probably wake a damn kid again, but I can't stop.

I need this; we both do.

Brooke throws her arms around my neck and slides her fingers into my hair, squeezing me tight to her shoulder as I nuzzle against her throat, nibbling the smooth flesh with my teeth. Our voices draw into a crescendo, this loud, messy

BAD NANNY

sound that I've heard a million times before ... yet never like this.

I grab Brooke's hips and drive into her until she comes again, massaging my body with her own, encouraging me to finish inside her. I fight it for a few thrusts before I give in and let her drag me down into a groaning whimper, my face pressed close to hers, her body held up against mine, as close as I can get it.

"That was my favorite one of the Big Four," she whispers and then laughs, locking down on me hard. I groan and slide out, finding that I'm already half-hard again. Jesus Christ. This girl is so going to kill me. I toss my condom into the trash and get another from the box I stashed in her nightstand drawer. When I roll back over and she sees it, Brooke raises her eyebrows.

"Already?" she whispers and I shrug my shoulders, sweat pouring down my back, that weird male satisfaction creeping over me. I know Brooke's, like, her own person and totally independent and I'm a serious feminist and all that, but ... God, I so want her to be mine. Every fucking molecule in my body says that this is where I belong, here, with this chick and her ugly dog and her two inherited kids.

That fucking terrifies me. I know it's just because she gave me her virginity and all that, but I need it to stop. I need these feelings to go away because I have a *life* in Las Vegas. I have a condo that I spent my parents' life insurance money on, a condo that I have to make big payments on every month. I have a job and friends and a lifestyle that I love.

This girl, she can't take those kids to Vegas, and God knows if there's anywhere for her to study down here. And me, I could never move back to this shit hole in the middle of nowhere. I'd kill myself.

I start to panic and slick my fingers back over my hair.

"You're not down for another go?" I joke as Brooke blushes a little and turns toward me, reaching out to brush some hair off my sweaty forehead. The way she looks at me ... that's a little scary, too, like maybe I'm not the only person in this room with a crush.

I'd so totally ruin her life though; I know I would.

I look down at her, her pale green eyes somehow brilliant in the dim light, her chocolate braid thrown casually over one shoulder, her body pale and perfect and curvy.

That's the problem right there, I think, as I look her over. We just haven't fucked *enough.* I've been taking it slow and easy with this girl, but I need to do what I always do back home. I need to spend days in this bed with her, fucking her slow and fast and hard and easy. Just over and over and over again until this weird possession and contentment I'm feeling fades away into nothing.

"Please say yes," I croon, leaning forward and putting our heads together. If Brooke notices that I'm having a silent panic attack inside this crazy head of mine, she doesn't let on.

My right hand drops to Brooke's hip and squeezes the flesh, drawing a tiny moan from her throat.

"Okay," she whispers as I sit up and flip her over, drawing her ass up to my hips. I tear the condom package open with my teeth and slide the lubed latex over my shaft, surprised that I'm already this hard and needy.

I guide my dick to her opening and push inside the wet, swollen flesh, loving how tight she clamps around me, how she wiggles her ass back against me with each thrust. I let my head fall back and refuse to allow my thoughts to overwhelm me. Honestly, deep inside of her like this, they barely register. I let my body become a hot, messy twist of sex and need, taking Brooke hard and fast and … angry? Yeah, maybe I'm a little bit pissed, but it makes for good, hard sex, drawing this keening sound from her throat that drives me completely up the wall.

Two, three more rounds of this and I'll feel better.

Honestly, it takes like six before I can even dream of stopping.

BAD NANNY

Monday morning.

How fucking exciting.

It's like the most chaotic day I've had since I got here.

"Uncle Zay, Dodger's dogging the chihuahua again," Kinzie says as I struggle to get Sadie to take her bottle. She just flat-out refuses to eat this morning, screaming and wailing no matter what I do. It's not a diaper change she needs, not her fucking Binky, not a bowl of applesauce.

I even—and this is so fucking gross—took the kid's temperature with one of those butt thermometer things you're supposed to use. Nothing. No temp. The kid is fine.

"Okay, okay, I give up," I say, putting Sadie back in the crib so I can scramble around and get the rest of the pack ready for school. Brooke had some school thing and bailed early so it's just me, myself, and fucking cocksucking *I*. "Where's the dog?" I ask as I pause next to the mirror and find that my hair is sticking out every which way; I look like a crazy person right now. Fuck, I *feel* like a crazy person.

"In the front yard," Bella says, standing next to the door as Grace giggles and rushes down the sidewalk towards the road.

Holy. Goddamn. Hell.

I sprint outside and snatch the little monster under the arms right as a car zooms by and honks at me, flipping us off out the window as they jam down a residential street at fifty miles an hour. Fucker.

"Who let you out?" I ask the kid as she laughs and I drag her back to the front door, pausing to notice the distinct *lack* of dogging dogs. As gross as it is to see a Chinese crested mounting an ancient toothless chihuahua, I feel a wave of dread when I can't find the horrid sight anywhere in the yard. "Where are the dogs?" I ask Kinzie and Bella. "And who opened the front door?"

"They had to go to the bathroom," Bella explains as she tosses chocolate hair over her shoulder like her aunt. "So I let them out. Then they started dogging. I don't know where they are now."

I groan and slap my hands to my face.

"Okay. Get in there and find some clothes for school. We're already running late, okay?"

I usher the demons back into their lair and shut the door, jogging down the sidewalk to look for the stupid rats. *God, I hate little dogs.* As I'm running, my phone starts to buzz in my pocket.

It's Rob.

"Uh, yeah? Kind of busy right now."

"Well make some time. Are the kids in class?" I'm panting as I run, realizing as I catch the curious stares of neighbors that I'm not actually wearing a shirt. Oops. I took it off after one of the twins slapped a sucker onto my back and the damn thing wouldn't come off. Told ya: their spit is like *glue.*

"Not exactly," I say as stop at the corner and look around. No dogs in sight. Shit. I should've checked to see how many of the rats were missing. Aren't there like four chihuahuas or something? Or is it three? "We're running a bit late here. Look, Rob, I don't have a lot of time to chat. What do you want?"

"Wow. Just wow. Thanks for asking after Mercedes' parents, you asshole."

I start jogging back in the opposite direction, although I do cringe a little. He's kind of right. But then, he's also a complete dickhead.

"Last time I talked to you, you said they were stable. Did something happen?"

"They're doing great actually, thank you for *finally* asking. The doctors are saying we may actually be able to take them home tomorrow."

"Killer," I say as I move past the house ... and find the twins in the driveway with chalk, still wearing their *My Little Pony* pajamas. "Hey. Get your asses back in the house and get

BAD NANNY

dressed for school." The identical little devils screech and throw their chalk on the lawn, disappearing into the *open* front door of the house. I'm still standing there when the other two chihuahuas make a break for it. "Oh no you don't." I hook my broken cell phone between my ear and shoulder as I scoop the dogs up, one in each hand.

"Did you just curse at my children?" Rob roars over the phone as I struggle to get the dogs inside. "You better be talking to somebody else."

"Of course I'm not talking to the kids," I lie as I head back inside and toss the rat dogs onto the couch. Dodger and the old one will have to wait for later. I just can't deal with this shit right now. "Why? What do you want? I'm seriously swamped right now, Rob."

"I got a call from our tenant. He's moving out today. Normally I'd ask for a sixty day notice, but you know how long I've been trying to get rid of the guy."

"Yup, yup," I say as Sadie tosses her head back and lets out a banshee worthy wail. "What's that got to do with me?"

"I told him to leave the key with you, but he said you hadn't been staying at the house. Where the fuck are you? I need you to go over and check the place out, make sure it's clean, and then get it posted on Craigslist for me."

"Are you ... *kidding* me? When the hell am I going to have time to do that?"

"You're not at that girl's house still, are you? You're not a fucking nanny, Zayden. You don't know anything about children. And I don't want my kids exposed to your weird sex stuff."

"Weird sex stuff?" I echo and then notice the girls are standing on the stairs, eavesdropping. They giggle as I point a finger at them and mouth *go,* heading back to the crib to pick up the baby. "I'm not the one whose daughter saw him giving mommy a VJ in the shower, okay?"

"What? What the hell are you talking about? Zayden, get your ass back to the duplex. Don't make me call this girl myself and tell her you're a fraud."

"Look, she already knows I'm not actually a nanny, okay? You're a little late to the game. Besides, where the hell would you get her phone number?"

Sadie screeches and thrashes around as I struggle to get her into the high chair.

"What's going on?" I hear Mercedes on the other end of the line and groan, letting my head fall back. "Is Sadie okay? You know, if she keeps screaming like that, she probably needs to poop. The doctor said it seemed like she was getting constipated. When's the last time she went?"

"I ... have no idea," I concede as I feel a flutter of panic in my chest. Did I seriously almost consider staying in town? Like, even a little? I get that these aren't all my kids, that I get to give four of them back at the end of the week, but don't you think Rob and Mercedes would milk the shit out of me as a babysitter? No, you don't need to tell me. I know they would.

And then ... do I really want to seriously get with anybody? Dating people usually leads to kids at some point. It's practically inevitable.

"What do you want me to do?" I ask as I put a hand to my forehead and struggle to take a deep breath. A second later, there's an angry knock at the door.

"You might want to call up her pediatrician and see if you can get her in today," Mercedes says as I slog my way over to the door and find the neighbor standing on the porch with a dog in either hand.

"These are yours?" she asks, her wrinkly mouth pinched up, eyes flicking up and down my body with a level of distaste I haven't seen from a woman in a long time. "They knocked over my trash and pulled dirty diapers everywhere. Somebody's going to have to come over and clean that up."

I just stare at her as I take the dogs and drop them on the floor.

"I left the number in my notes. If you call her up now, I bet you could get Sadie in. She knows us. The co-pay is a little pricey, but you know how Rob's insurance is. Could you take care of that and we'll pay you as soon as we can? We've really blown every last cent on this trip."

"Yeah. Yep. Uh-huh." I stare at the neighbor for a moment and then tuck my hand over the phone so Mercedes won't hear. "My baby's super sick," I say, pausing for dramatic effect as Sadie lets out another scream. "I can't really get on that diaper thing like, right this second."

"Uncle Zay!" Bella screeches from the top of the stairs. "Kinzie stole my *Monster High* shirt and now she won't give it back!"

"She's a liar! This is *my Monster High* shirt. Hers is the one with Draculaura on it."

"Nuh uh!"

"If you can't come over here and clean up these diapers, get someone else to do it. Don't make me call animal control."

"Look lady, I don't know how a five pound rat could knock over your trash can. Maybe they took advantage of the diapers, but I doubt they knocked the damn thing over. Sorry, but if you want to call animal control then go for it, I just can't deal with this right now."

The woman huffs and spins on her heel as I slam the door and lean my back against it, sliding to the floor. We are so epically late at this point it doesn't even matter.

"Call the doctor. Got it. Check the duplex. Got it. Do I really have to post it on Craigslist?"

"We can't make the mortgage without a renter, Zay. I hate to ask, but if you could please get some pictures uploaded, that'd be great. You are such a doll. I love you, you know that, right?"

"Yup," I say as Dodger trots over to me and lifts his leg. Before my addled mind even really registers what's happening, he's pissed. All. The. Hell. Over. Me. "Can I go now, please?"

"Of course, honey. We'll see you in three short nights, okay?"

"Got it."

I hang up, struggling to get the end call button to work with my broken cell screen.

I thought I was getting the hang of all this, but I feel so off my game today it's not funny.

"Are we going to school now?" Bella asks as she appears in a pair of lime green fuzzy pajama pants, yellow rain boots, and a lacy tank top that I think she stole from Brooke. "I'm dressed now."

I lean over and put my forehead on my knees, trying to breathe.

Five days and it'll all be over. Just five short days.

I can so handle this.

I think.

When Brooke gets back from class, I'm just finishing up my dog piss/shit cleaning spree. I swear to Christ, if Rob doesn't start potty training these rats, I'm going to fly my ass up from Vegas for Thanksgiving and stuff the little fuckers for dinner.

"Hey," I say as I sit up and swipe an arm across my forehead.

"Hey," Brooke says as she comes in with another girl on her heels, a girl with electric blue hair.

A girl that I *recognize*.

"Holy shit," I say as I lean back on my heels and stare at Tinley Horton. She freezes when she spots me, raising a brow with four piercings stuffed through it.

"Holy shit yourself," she says as Brooke looks between the two of us with a confused expression flooding her face. "Zayden Roth. Wow. Never expected to see you here again—especially not on your knees cleaning ... is that dog poop?"

"Wow." I stand up and strip off the black latex gloves I put on for cleaning, looking my old flame over from head to toe. She looks damn good, exactly like the type of girl I usually go for, all tatted and pierced up and badass. "I thought you'd moved to New York?" I ask as Tinley shrugs her shoulders and

BAD NANNY

gives me an appraising once-over. If her expression is anything to go by, she likes what she sees.

"I did. But I moved back last year to take care of my mom." I nod as we scope each other out, shocked that the chick I took to senior prom is standing in Brooke's living room. I haven't seen her in like, eleven years.

"You two know each other?" Brooke asks, pointing between the two of us. Standing next to Tinley, she looks so ridiculously out of place in her big camel colored wool coat and neon red cocktail dress. It's so totally inappropriate for school—but in the best way possible. Paired with a set of white running shoes? Yeah. Total mess. Total adorable mess.

Tinley's got on these tight zebra patterned leggings and a neon pink tank that says *Fuck Men* on it. Huh. I like that, too, but not as much as Brooke's outfit.

"Brooke and I are actually in the same population sampling class, something I didn't realize until today since I hardly go." Tinley lifts her hand up and gestures at me. "I warned her about my ex last week, and that got us talking today. Didn't know I'd get to see you when she invited me over."

Tinley's lips curve in a very familiar shape, a shape that I've seen on a hundred other girls. It says *I so want to fuck you.*

Brooke notices and her face falls completely, crashing into this expression of dread that makes my heart hurt for her. Damn. Damn. Damn.

"I took Tinley to prom," I say, lifting up my palm in a useless gesture. I don't mention the fact that we fucked in the back of my Geo both before *and* after prom. Doubt Brooke wants to know about that.

"This is such a crazy coincidence," Tinley says as she moves over to me in her neon pink heels and gestures me in for a hug. She smells like this wild perfume, some hipster scent that smells like cloves and tobacco. Brooke watches our entire exchange with a a frown. "We were planning on studying, but now that I see you're here, maybe we could do something a little more exciting?"

"I have to pick up the kids pretty quick here," I say as I

reach up and scratch at the back of my head. "What did you have in mind?"

"The kids?" Tinley asks as she raises her brows at me, pink painted lips picking up at the corners as she takes me in again, much more slowly this time. It's not a mystery to anyone in here that she's checking me out. I feel bad for Brooke, like maybe I should say something. But we're not together, so what the hell am I going to do? Blurt out how I took her virginity last week? Naw. Not my style.

"Zayden's helping me with my sister's kids," Brooke says as she gestures at me and tries to explain our weird temporary situation. "She took off and left the country, so I'm taking care of them. I kind of hired Zayden as my nanny."

"That is so fucking cute," Tinley says as she runs her long rainbow colored nails through her hair and smiles wickedly in my direction. Either she's not picking up on the *leave my man the fuck alone* vibes that Brooke's giving off or she doesn't care. I'm not entirely sure what to think about the whole damn situation. I mean, it's cute that Brooke's looking at Tinley like she's the enemy, like I really am her guy. But it's also kind of terrifying, too. "Well, maybe when you get off work, the two of us could hang out?"

"I'm actually on my way back to Vegas in a few days," I say with a slight shrug, but that doesn't do much help Brooke's expression. "Kind of working nonstop until then. I've got my brother's kids to take care of, too, until he gets back into town."

"Vegas? Seriously? My best friend's getting married there next week. We're all flying out to hang for a weekend." Tinley gets her phone from her back pocket and passes it to me. "Plug your number in and maybe we could hang out then? What do you do there?"

"I work as a body piercer," I say as I toss the gloves onto the table next to Sadie's crib and start typing in my digits. Brooke watches me the entire time, but doesn't say a word, pushing her glasses gently up her nose. She's wearing the big, thick black ones again. No time for contacts since I made her late as fuck this morning.

BAD NANNY

A slight smile twitches my mouth that I think she misinterprets, glancing away towards the kitchen.

"We can study in here," Brooke says as Tinley curls her fingers around the edge of Sadie's crib and leans in to study her sleeping face.

"Awesome. I'll be right there," she says as she grins at the sleeping baby, and Brooke moves in a swirl of camel coat into the kitchen.

It's like so fucking awkward in here right now. Total bummer, too, since I was hoping Brooke and I would get a moment alone before the kids got out of school. Ugh.

"This is Rob's baby?" Tinley asks as I hand her phone back and tuck my fingers into the front pockets of my dark green skinny jeans. I nod my head as Tinley bites her lower lip and leans in again to run her fingers down one of the baby's chubby arms. "She is so goddamn cute." A quick, coy glance up from beneath long dark lashes. "Have any of your own yet?"

"Me? Oh, hell no. Not ready for kids yet."

Tinley nods slowly as she stands up straight, reaching up to adjust the dark sunglasses nestled in her electric blue hair.

"Me neither," she says as she smiles at me and I try to figure out what it is that I'm feeling right now. Off my game, that's for sure. No doubt about that. But ... I've got this hot as fuck chick staring at me like I'm tomorrow's breakfast sausage, and all I can do is stand here and stare. All I can do is stand here and feel *guilty*. Like, what the hell is that about?

Maybe it's because Brooke and I have an arrangement. I mean, we do, don't we? She was supposed to be mine while I was in town, so I guess that makes me hers, too, right? If anything's going to happen between Tinley and me, it'll have to be in Las Vegas after all this is over. Yep. That's the source of my guilt right there.

"Just trying to have a little fun in life, am I right?"

"Abso-fucking-lutely," I say as Tinley passes by and tickles her nails down my arm, leaning in to whisper in my ear.

"If I call you when I'm in Nevada, you'll answer, right? Because I'd love to see if you're as wild and crazy as you were in high school." She lets go of my arm and disappears into the kitchen as I cross my arms over my chest and lean my back against the wall, listening to the slight murmur of voices in the kitchen. Hard to hear 'em over the Bebe Rexha song that's playing.

I smile as it stops a moment later, and some raging metal trickles quietly out of the speakers.

When I swing around the corner, I find Brooke shrugging out of her coat, her shoulders smooth and pale and sexy, a stark contrast to the bright red of her silly little cocktail dress. She looks so goddamn young and innocent next to Tinley's tall, tatted form and confident swagger.

"You want me to make sandwiches or something?" I ask as I lean up against the counter and try to get a read on the situation. This is so not my scene, dealing with this kind of stuff. When your dating life consists of tourist chicks, it's easy to make sure they never run into each other. This is just ... a really weird coincidence.

"No thanks," Brooke says, giving me a tight-lipped smile that I can't even begin to interpret. "We're good here." She gestures between her and Tinley and then sits down, focusing on the open screen of her laptop like I'm not even there anymore.

I cross my arms over my chest as Tinley gives me one last, lingering look before she focuses on whatever advanced shit it is that they're studying. There's no way in hell I'll understand any of it, so I bail, heading out the back door and over to the tire swing to chill with my phone.

Jude won't stop sending me texts of all the vaginal piercings he's done in the last week. A set of inner labia piercings, an outer, another of those VCH piercings I was telling Brooke about. I wonder why the hell any of these girls would *let* him take a photo of their genitals, but hey, the man can be persuasive as fuck.

There's a group text about all the partying we're gonna do when I get back.

Strippers will rain from the sky, one of my friends texts and

BAD NANNY

I smile before I frown.

Hmm.

Damn. After seeing Brooke cry, after seeing the desperation in her eyes, I'm not sure if I'll ever be able to enjoy a strip club again. I mean, I get that not all girls feel the way she does about the job, but I'm not sure I'll ever be able to set foot in one of those places without wondering which ones are the Brookes, the sad virgin girls with no other choice.

I sigh and smack the cracked screen of the phone against my forehead.

There's another text from that girl, Kitty, on there, too, but I ignore that one. The little she and I had has run its course for sure.

I check my bank balance next and frown. Two weeks without working is really setting me back. I barely have enough for my next mortgage payment in there. Time to start using the credit card for a while I guess.

Tucking my phone into my pocket, I sigh and lean back on the swing, wrapping my hands around the chains as I swing slowly back and forth, my boots dragging across the grass as I sway in time to the creaking branch above my head.

Figure I'll wait it out here, either until Tinley leaves or the kids get home from school. Then we'll see how Brooke's feeling and work from there. If she's jealous, that's cool. So was I when she brought Dan the Douche home. I get it.

But give me five minutes alone with her and I'll make her forget *all* about it.

Tinley does not fucking leave, and my day gets even *better* when animal control shows up as I'm struggling to get something presentable ready for dinner. I tried making PB&Js but that shit did just not go down well. Kinzie feed hers to the dogs, and the twins flushed theirs down the toilet. I need to get some food in these brats and get them to bed early.

Sadie's doctor couldn't fit us in today, but we've got an appointment at nine in the morning. God only knows how I'm going to make that shit on time.

Oh.

And one of Rob's neighbors—I think it was actually that bible-thumper, Shiela (out of jail on a technicality)—called to tell him that the front door of the duplex was hanging wide open and that it was a "complete shit hole inside". Rob's words, not the neighbor's.

So now I've got to cook dinner, get the kids in bed, see if Brooke can take a break from her studying with Tinley to watch them, and then run over there to check on the place/clean it/take pictures for Craigslist.

I feel like I'm about to blow my damn brains out, kind of like the way I did when I first got here. And I thought I was getting the hang of all this shit? Please.

My phone is clutched in my hand when I answer the door, the answers on Google about how to make spaghetti waiting patiently for my attention.

"Yeah?" I ask when I find some guy in a brown uniform standing there. He smiles tightly at me.

"Hi there," he says as Dodger appears from out of nowhere and starts "dogging" the shit out of my leg. "My name is Christian Gross, and I'm from Humboldt County Animal Control. We received a complaint this morning about—"

Kinzie breaks into a violent scream behind me, shattering my eardrums into pieces as I struggle to remove the horny hairless dog from my leg. Things were going great. Awesome. Perfect, even. In fact, I was actually kind of starting to enjoy this whole thing.

Not so much anymore.

"One second."

I turn around and find Kinzie in a wild fistfight with one of the twins, pausing to scoop her up and deposit her on the fuzzy pink toilet seat cover.

"Seven minutes," I say as I step out and close the door,

grabbing the twin and parking him on the bottom step. "Four minutes. If you move, I'll know. Remember: I really do have eyes in the back of my head."

I step back up to the door and find that the animal control officer's already wrangled up two escapee chihuahuas. Dodger's still following me around and doing things to my leg that no human being ever has. Makes me a little uncomfortable, you know? I push the dog away with my foot and snatch the chihuahuas from the guy's arms.

"This is about that garbage can thing?" I ask and the man nods, giving me a really sympathetic look, especially when I grunt and stumble forward, turning around to find a football on the floor behind me. Bella is grinning and fist pumping across the living room while Sadie screams.

"I'm going to the first female quarterback in the NFL!"

"That's great, babe, but please don't throw footballs in the house, okay?" Bella nods vigorously and pounces over to grab her toy.

"Why did *I* get a time-out and she doesn't?" Kinzie yells, curled around the bathroom door, her butt cheeks still *technically* sitting on the toilet seat and therefore not violating the rules of her TO. I roll my eyes and lift my hands up.

"Because it was an accident. Stop talking or I'm adding time to your sentence, kid."

I turn back to Animal Control Dude as Brooke appears in the kitchen doorway looking concerned.

"You know what, just ... try not to lose your dogs again, okay?" The man starts to turn away, his eyes telling me that he'd rather be out rounding up strays than dealing with his nightmare. I don't blame 'im. Hell, where do I sign up for that shit?

"Everything okay in there, Zayden?" Brooke asks as she slings her coat back on and shrugs it over her shoulders. "Tinley and I were thinking of going out and grabbing a drink if that's okay?"

"Um." I ruffle my hair and bite my bottom lip as Brooke stares me down with those crazy beautiful eyes of hers. "Sure thing. What time do you think you'll be back? I need to run over to my brother's place and check on the empty duplex."

What I really want to say is *please, don't go out with this chick. Hang with me, and I'll show you a better time.* If I don't spend more time with Brooke, fuck these feelings out of my system, I'm going to be in serious trouble. Like, even now I'm looking at her in those big black glasses of hers like she's the cutest fucking thing since sliced bread.

Brooke and Tinley exchange a look before she turns back to me and shrugs her shoulders.

"How about ten?" she asks and I shrug back, stepping aside and holding my arm out towards the door.

I barely manage to get it closed before a football crashes against the wood and falls to the floor.

"Okay, squirts," I say as I suck in a deep breath and look at the big eyed faces staring up at me. "We are going to get our shit together right the fuck now."

"Curse jar!" Kinzie yells, still peering around the doorframe from her spot on the toilet.

I sigh and dig two dollar bills out of my pocket, depositing them inside the jar ... only to find out that the *other* twin stuck *his* sucker inside the glass. Now all the money I planned on pinching back is covered in sticky candy.

I narrow my eyes and take a deep breath, standing up straight and putting my shoulders back. They might be kids, but they'll get the message. No more shit. I was tough on them at first and they listened, but then this whole Brooke thing made me go soft.

Not anymore.

I'm done with the misbehaving ... and I'm done fantasizing about Brooke Overland.

Time to get this shit under control before Rob and Mercedes get back. Because once they do, Hubert and I are so gone.

CHAPTER 24
BROOKE OVERLAND

When I get back from drinks with Tinley, I'm even more pissed off than I was when I left. Not at her, not really. I mean, she saw a hot guy that she slept with back in the day and decided she'd go for him. He never gave her any indication that she *shouldn't*.

Even as I'm slamming my car door and heading up the front walk to the house, I'm fuming as I think about Tinley heading to Vegas with her girlfriends, stopping by Zayden's shop and throwing herself at him. He's made no secret of the fact that he's a pretty indiscriminate lover. Surely they'll sleep together. And then *I* will be the one that'll have to sit in class with her, maybe even listen to her stories. But I invited her over in the first place because I refuse to be friendless in this hellhole— even if it means being friends with a girl Zayden screwed in the backseat of that little Geo.

Yeah. I got the whole story in *excruciating* detail from Tinley.

I shove some hair over my shoulder and let myself in to find Zayden singing "Africa" to Sadie again. It's hard to keep the smile off my face, but I manage, closing the door softly behind me and leaning against it.

When he starts singing about wild dogs and Mount Kilimanjaro, that's when I start to chuckle.

"Hey, this song is a classic," Zayden says as he pauses and checks on the baby, making a squinched face of triumph. "Yep. See? Works every time."

Zayden bends down and lays Sadie on her back, covering her with a small pink blanket and stepping back with a sigh as he puts his hands on his hips and glances over at me.

"How was your drink date?" he asks as I move over to the couch and drop my purse onto it, shrugging myself out of the giant coat. "Meet any cute guys while you were out?"

I roll my eyes at him.

"Don't do that," I say and Zayden raises his eyebrows.

"Do what?" he asks, all perfect innocence in his face and voice.

"That. Act like ... this," I point between the two of us, "isn't happening. Do you really think I'd be checking men out tonight? With you waiting at home for me?"

"Listen," Zayden says, lifting a tattooed finger at me. "I'm not acting like anything. You're a single girl. If you want to check men out while hanging with a friend, who am I to stop you?"

"You're right. Just like you were flirting with Tinley, giving her your phone number, letting her hit on you right in front of me. A girl you took to *prom*. Don't you think that was a little awkward for me, Zayden?"

"Look, I'm sorry about that. How the hell was I supposed to know you were going to show up with Tinley Horton on your arm? That's just a freak coincidence right there. And if you'll take note, I did *not* flirt back, okay?"

"Are you going to take her call?" I ask as Zay raises his pierced brow at me. Mine seems to throb and hurt all of a sudden, but I think I'm just imagining it, pausing as I hear "Africa" start up on repeat. Who the hell does that? Puts "Africa" on repeat a hundred times and sings it off-key like that? "When she's in Vegas, are you going to fuck her?"

"I have no fucking clue," Zayden says and I feel my hands

BAD NANNY

curl into fists. The way he's looking at me, like my feelings aren't his problem, is heartbreaking. I get that this thing between us is temporary, that we were both using each other, but wow. If I needed a memo from him to remind me that he doesn't care, I'm getting it now. "What does it matter?"

"Don't you have to stop by your brother's place?" I ask as I move around the couch and grab the baby monitor off the coffee table. "I'll be asleep when you get back, so maybe you should stay on the couch?"

"Brooke," Zayden starts, but I'm already on my way up the stairs. When I hear him following me, I sprint faster, trying to lock myself into the bedroom before he can get there. He puts his boot in the way of the door anyway and pushes his way in.

Damn.

I was really only prepared for one dramatic exit.

"Hey, look, I don't want you to be upset," he says as I sit on the edge of the bed and hold the baby monitor in my lap like it's a shield. I didn't mean for my feelings to come out. Really, I didn't. I can't imagine that all of the twisty things I feel when he's around mean anything at all. This is the first guy I've ever slept with, so of course I'm going to feel some sort of attachment to him. I'd prepared myself for this.

What I hadn't prepared myself for was exactly how *much* I'd like him.

Zayden sits down on the edge of the bed next to me, our thighs pressed together in a warm line, one of his tattooed hands—the one with the open book—coming to rest on my knee. The tender way he touches me, and the softness in his voice when he speaks, they almost make things worse.

"Hey, if you want me to block Tinley's number, I will." There's a long pause there before he digs his phone out of his back pocket and shows it to me, scrolling through his texts and finding the one she sent over to give him her number. He blocks it as I watch. "There. Is that better?"

"It's not just that, Zayden," I say quietly, and something about the soft gentle darkness around us makes me feel brave. Moonlight slants across the carpet in front of my feet, silver-blue bars of pale light that just barely kiss the toes of my tennis shoes. "It's way more than that."

There's another long pause as Zayden exhales and sits up straight, streaking his fingers through his hair. I stare at him, but I don't much feel like looking him in the eyes, so I gaze at the black ring piercings on either side of his lip instead.

"You have a crush on me, too, huh?" he asks and it takes me a second to realize what he's talking about. *I've got such a huge crush on you, Brooke.* Oh. He did say that, didn't he?

I shrug my shoulders because I feel like I can't look at him right now, can't see disdain or rejection or even pity on his face.

"I like you, Brooke. A lot. More than most girls."

"Most girls?" I echo, because when you think about that statement, it's really not very flattering at all. Zayden shifts a little and reaches over to touch my chin, turning my face toward him. His brown eyes are soft in the darkness, his half-smile tilted to one side.

"Better than any girl," he says and a chill chases down my spine.

"Is that a line?" I ask, because I really don't want it to be. For once, I want something that's mine and mine alone. I want this. Obviously, I know I can't *actually* have Zayden, but … I want to be that one girl, just this one time.

"Nope. Just the truth. Plain and simple," he says, letting go of my chin and dropping his hand to the hem of my dress, chasing his finger underneath it and up my thigh. Each touch of his fingertips sends my heart skipping and bouncing, until it's beating an irregular rhythm just for him. "I really do like you, Brooke."

"Okay, so." I turn toward him, putting one knee up on the bed and tucking some hair over my shoulders. "What does that mean?"

"Mean?" he asks, hooking up an eyebrow. "Like I said before … it *means* something, but it doesn't *change* anything. You know that, right?"

"I just don't … I mean, I get it, but why?" When I look up at Zayden, I think I have tears in the corners of my eyes. Or maybe I just *feel* like I'm about to cry. "Why couldn't, you know, this," I gesture between us, "work? It's kind of awesome so far."

I make myself smile, but Zayden's expression has slipped into a gentle frown.

"I live in Las Vegas," he says, but that's not good enough for me.

"So?"

"So. You live here. You just up and moved, Brooke. And you have school, and the kids, and Jesus, you're only twenty-two. You can't put all your dollars in one slot."

"You're saying because I haven't slept with other guys that this can't work?"

"I'm saying you have no idea what you're feeling for me because you have nothing to compare it against. That's all."

"We could … do this long distance?" I say as Zay glances up at me and smiles. But it's not a good smile. It's kind of a sad smile, a why-are-you-so-pathetic sort of smile. It pisses me off. "What's so crazy about that? Not enough sex for you? Is that it?"

"You have enough to worry about without having me in the picture. And I have a mortgage and a job back at home. There's nothing here for me."

I purse my lips and glance away.

"Look, I know this seems really special now, but what about in two weeks? Or three? In my experience, relationships don't exactly work out. They're more trouble than they're worth. Let's leave this at a sweet spot and say good-bye when the time comes."

My eyes really do water then, and I stand up, moving away from Zayden as I take a deep breath. I feel like I'm in a prison of my own making. *I* got myself here. *I* invited him into my bed and into my life.

This sucks.

"We still have three nights left though," he purrs, his voice drawing my attention back to the bed. But then I look at him sitting there, looking so pretty in the moonlight, and I just feel sad. Maybe it's not even Zayden that I care about? Maybe I'm just lonely. I don't know. I feel really fucking lonely right now.

"You should go check on that duplex," I say as I squeeze the baby monitor in my hand. Zay stands up and starts to move toward me, but I back up and he takes that as a hint, holding up his palms in surrender.

"Okay. Alright. Look, if you change your mind while I'm gone," he pauses again and takes a few steps closer to me, leaning in to breathe hot words against my ear, "leave your bedroom door unlocked."

Zayden disappears out the door and down the steps. I wait until I hear it lock behind him before I move over to my own door and lock that, too.

The next morning, I dress all the way up for class, using a YouTube tutorial on my phone to apply my makeup, and picking out the most cohesive pieces of clothing that I own. I end up in skinny jeans, black boots that remind me of a pair I saw Zayden wearing, and a hot pink tank top.

I even get up an hour early to wash and dry my hair, combing it out until there's a sleek shiny chocolate wave tumbling down to my ass.

When I'm finished cleaning my piercing, I head into the hallway to the sound of … quiet? When I clomp down the stairs, I manage to catch a brief glimpse of five children seated around the dining table. As I pause to stare, one of the twins scrambles away and Zayden chases him down.

"Oh no you don't," he says as he swings the kid over his shoulder and then pauses to look at me.

There's a sudden moment of awkward where I wonder if I should say something. But why? Zayden made it perfectly clear last night that he didn't need to talk. *It* means *something, but it doesn't change anything.* Fine. If that's how he feels …

"Brooke," he says as I turn away and start for the door, reaching out a hand and resting it on the knob as I take a deep breath. "We cool?" he asks, his voice this soft breath that makes me shiver a little. "Because you know, it'd totally bum me out if you didn't come home after class."

I almost smile, but I can't quite force my lips to move. I keep thinking of that quiet dark and that slanted moonlight and Zayden's weirdly sad half-smile.

"I have plans with Tinley," I say, looking over my shoulder and shrugging loosely. "I'll stop in before work, okay?"

Zayden watches me for a moment and then nods, swinging his nephew back onto the ground and snapping his fingers.

"Back to the kitchen, kid. Let's do this. Military precision, remember?"

"Eat a dick!" the four year old screams before rushing up the stairs with screeching laughter. Both Zayden and I exchange a look over that one, the confusion about our weird non-relationship temporarily forgotten.

"Um," he says and then scratches at the back of his head. "I am so going to get it from Rob for that one, even though I don't actually remember saying it around him ..."

"Don't look at me," I say as I snag my bag off the coatrack and open the front door. "It definitely wasn't me. I already spent the last of my cash in the curse jar."

I smile tightly and slip out before things can get anymore awkward, moving quickly to my Subaru and climbing in before Zayden can think to come after me. I'm still trying to process what happened last night, push my emotions down and lock them away. Especially since I know I'm being ridiculous. I knew what to expect from Zayden Roth—and I definitely didn't expect his knight in shining armor meter to ping for long.

Guess I was right about that one.

After class, I head back to the house to change, finding a peaceful set of kids gathered around the TV with bowls of grapes in their hands, eyes glued to the flickering action of Zayden's video game. He's playing some wildly colorful platformer with his tongue sticking out the side of his mouth, his black hair spiked up into a wild crazy Mohawk, his shaved side impossible to see from where I'm standing.

As soon as I close the door behind me, he pauses the game and glances over, drawing groans of disappointment from everyone but Sadie.

"Aunt Brooke!" Bella says as she scrambles from her seat and comes over to give me a hug, presenting her daily report card to me. The kids get one at the end of each school day, and I'm supposed to sign them before sending her in the next morning. I don't remember doing it for the past week, and I wonder if Zayden's been picking up that slack? "I got a one hundred today."

She waves the paper around in front of me until I drop my bag and take it.

Zayden's cat immediately climbs up on the green canvas and starts scratching his nails while I roll my eyes at his rainbow sweater. It says *Go Gay!* on the back which is kind of funny, but ... a cat in a sweater? Come on. Never gets less ridiculous.

"This is my first one hundred *ever*," Brooke states proudly, copying me by flicking her dark hair over one shoulder. She gets the gesture down perfectly, the backhanded sweep that I've been perfecting since I was her age.

I smile and use my foot to detach Hubert from my bag.

"This is awesome, Brooke," I say, reaching my palm up to give her a high five. I bend down to give my niece a big hug, shoving Dodger away with my hand. If I couldn't literally see that the dog has no balls, I would never believe he was fixed. What's wrong with him? Why does he always hump everything?

I pull back with a smile and stand up, noticing that Zay's got a tortilla chip halfway hanging out of his mouth, a bowl of

BAD NANNY

grapes in his outstretched hand.

"You want some?" he mumbles around the chip, clearly trying to make peace. I give him a half-smile for whatever he did to encourage my niece to behave better in class, popping a purple orb into my mouth and chewing it slowly.

"I ate out with Tinley," I say, glad that today's hangout session had little to nothing to do with Zayden. There was one brief moment where Tinley started to bring him up, but I changed the subject. Doubt she even noticed I was doing it. "But thanks."

Zayden uses his tongue to pull the chip the rest of the way into his mouth and for whatever reason, I find that sexy as hell.

I glance away sharply which is dumb. There's no need for all of this drama, right? If I want to keep sleeping with him while he's here, he's made it perfectly clear that he's open to it.

"I'm going to start getting ready," I say as I move away and head up the stairs, taking them two at a time until I'm alone in my room. Part of me wishes Zayden would follow me up here, but then I know that's impossible. The kids are all here, and they're all awake, and I stayed out long enough that I don't *really* have time to do much before work.

Work.

Ugh.

Having a few days off was almost cruel. Faced with the reality of going back to the Top Hat, I feel nauseous. It's just not the place for me. I feel silly thinking that because, really, who *is* it the place for? But I know that each night I dance there, a little piece of me will crack and break.

And I've never been good at repairing fractures in my heart.

"Stop it, Brooke," I say as I slap my hands against my cheeks and shake myself out. This is ridiculous, sitting up here and fretting over a guy I've known for like, two weeks. So stupid.

I focus on picking out clothes for tonight, dropping the stack on the bed and heading into the bathroom to do my hair and makeup. Even though I leave my bedroom door unlocked, Zayden doesn't come up to see me like I secretly hoped he would.

I end up downstairs in my trench coat an hour early to find the kids wrapped around the table, elbows leaning against the wood as they watch Zayden play with one of those tornado-in-a-bottle things, with the two plastic soda liter bottles taped together. I vaguely remember making one in fifth grade, and it puts a smile on my face.

"Told ya I was a storm magician," Zayden says proudly as he stands up and lets the water swirl from one bottle into the other, a big grin stretched across his mouth as Kinzie narrows her eyes on him and then grudgingly leans in to watch the spectacle.

I smile and let myself slip out the front door before anyone can see me. I've had about enough questions about my "fancy waitressing job", thank you.

"Hey."

I pause with my hand on the car door, a little thrill licking down my spine as I listen to Zay's boots move up behind me. He gets close—too close, but what's new about that—and puts a hand on my shoulder.

"You sure you're alright? I wouldn't want you to go to work feeling ... I don't know, however it is that you feel." I glance back at him and *damn,* but he's pretty. I suck in a breath and pretend like his looks have no effect on me, like the love and care he puts into these kids has no effect.

"How I feel?" I ask, not entirely sure if even *I'm* aware of the answer to that question. "Maybe it's not me that has a problem, Zay? Maybe *you're* the one that needs to check into his feelings. You date girls you don't like, and you tell girls you do like that relationships don't make any sense. I mean, unless you're lying about the whole *liking me* part of that equation, then I think it's you that has the problem."

I open the car door before he can respond, listening to the long huff of breath he lets out as I get in and slam it behind me. Starting the engine up as Zay stands there and watches. He doesn't try to stop me though which kind of pisses me off. Guess that white knight meter isn't as loud as he thought it

BAD NANNY

was? Because I sort of feel like I'm drowning here.

"Stupid," I mutter under my breath as I start up some Nine Inch Nails and crank the volume.

At least the drive *to* the strip club is nice, rain drenched and shadowed by trees for the first half, fields where cows come out to graze in the mornings for the second half.

I head south past the community college and take in a deep breath as the round building comes into view, one entire wall of tinted windows facing the highway. On the roof, a cheesy fake top hat sits tilted to one side. Even though I'm early, the parking lot is already mostly full and I frown, feeling a tug and pull at my insides that makes me queasy.

Suck it up, Brooke, I tell myself as I pull into my usual spot near the top of the short windy driveway that leads to the cement lot. *Get yourself together.*

Since I have about an hour to kill, I tilt my chair back and close my eyes, letting the car rumble beneath me and the music play. There is no way in *hell* that I'm going in there early. Nope. Not a snowball's chance in hell.

After a couple songs from NIN, I switch over to old school Metallica and sit up, checking my phone for messages. There are a few new ones from my friends in Berkeley and a brief Facebook message from my mom with a few pictures of her and dad at the Edinburgh zoo.

I smile briefly as I respond, using a few of the ridiculous selfies Zayden took with my phone to show him off to my girlfriends. Even with the photos, they'll probably never believe that I finally took the plunge and did it with some random stranger from the park. It seemed like a bad idea from the start … seems like an even worse idea now.

I snort and shove my phone in my purse, climbing out onto the wet pavement in my heels and heading towards the back door. Inside, a few of the girls are changing costumes and they smile at me as I walk in, the gossip pausing for a brief few seconds before they readjust to my presence.

"He told me I had to get rid of the dog," Tiffany complains as she sweeps blond hair over one shoulder and fixes the booby tassels she's wearing. Yep. That's my world now. When I went to UCB, I was a part of the work-study program and got to work in the campus bookstore. Up here, there were no work-study positions available, so … it is what it is. And anyway, there's no way I could've paid rent and supported the girls on that kind of part time work anyway.

"Why?" one of the other women asks, her long dark hair in tiny braids, eyes watching me as I move over to the single bench in the center of the room. There are lockers on either side and a set of small steps leading up to the club. One of the big burly bouncer dudes stands right outside the curtain, arms crossed over his front like he works for the secret service or something.

"Because," Tiffany starts, standing up and adjusting the little black tutu she's wearing. "He knows I love that damn dog more than I love him."

Robyn laughs her ass off as I slip my trench down my shoulders and hang it up in one of the rusting teal lockers. The place is clean, but it could definitely use some repairs. Guess as long as it's raking in money, the owner doesn't much care.

"What's wrong with you?" Tiffany asks, coming over to press the back of her hand against my forehead. "You don't look all that great."

"I'm fine," I lie because I wish I were fine. Or that I was back in Berkeley. I suck in a deep breath and sling my purse into the locker. "Just tired is all."

"Sure, sure. Boy trouble, right?" I look at Tiffany with my brows raised.

"Not everything is about boys," I tell her and then it's *her* turn to raise her brows at me.

"Well, not everything is, but that face, that look of disappointment, that's got *man trouble* written all over it. Who else in this world do we depend on that could let us down so thoroughly?"

"I'm not depending on anyone," I say, more fiercely than I probably should. But I'm not. I always take care of my own business, always have. My parents were supportive, sure, but I

BAD NANNY

was always second place to Ingrid. I felt like the backup heir, the just-in-case kid. Even now, based on my mother's text message, she still hasn't grasped how hard this is for me.

Oh, and she said she had several voicemails from Monica that she hadn't wanted to listen to yet because, you know, *Monica always has* something *to say.* Can't wait to hear about my aunt's gossip this time.

"That's a girl," Tiffany says as she moves back and smiles at me. "And well you shouldn't. Now, if you'll excuse me ..." She takes a mock bow and disappears up the steps and into the club, the thumping bass beat teasing the soles of my feet through the floor.

Robyn watches me for a second and then goes back to her phone. The other girls are pretty close here, but I don't feel welcome yet. Maybe I never will? Maybe I don't care if I ever do? *I don't want to be here long enough to be part of their family,* I think meanly as I sit down at one of the mirrored vanity tables to my left and start to fix my makeup.

In a few days, when Zayden's gone and my sister's house is quiet and empty feeling with just me and the girls in it, what am I going to do? I really need to call Nelly up again and see if she'll reconsider watching the kids ... even if she is an endangered sea crustacean.

My mouth twitches as I stand up and head over to the curtain, letting myself into the main part of the club. Although California has a ban on smoking indoors—even in a strip club—the place still reeks of smoke and weed and the sound of clinking glasses and male laughter makes my skin ripple.

Tiffany is onstage, swinging around the pole and swishing her blond hair, her tutu discarded, wearing nothing but a tiny G-string. Technically since the club serves alcohol, full nudity isn't allowed, but everyone here knows if you pay the right price you can get a private nude dance in the back.

But not from me.

No fucking way.

I reach up to check my ponytail, slicking my hands over the shellacked hair as I move across the back of the room, my heels loud against the tiled floors. The rest of the building is carpeted in dark green with little gold circles on it, clean but old and smelling of smoke. This place is the *only* strip club within a four hour radius, so it doesn't have to be special; it just has to exist.

One of the bouncers, a guy whose name I can never remember, nods at me as I hit the two steps up to the second stage and put the most fake ass smile on my face known to man, breathing deep through my nose and trying to pretend that I don't notice the group of rowdy college guys near the end of the stage.

Only ... I actually do.

Crap. Crap. And fucking crap.

One of the dudes laughing and shaking dollar bills in the air is Dan the Douche, my study partner for survival analysis, and Tinley's ex-boyfriend. Great. Just great.

I think about retreating back behind the curtain, feigning a sudden illness or something, but our manager's standing across the room staring at me, his eyes narrowed and lips pursed. I'm on close watch after missing that first night apparently. Or maybe he just doesn't like me. I notice when he talks to the other girls, they look away, at the floors or the walls or the ceiling. I stare the man straight in the face, even that first night when I was crying.

Okay, I can do this. I can do this. This is about me supporting me, supporting the girls.

I step up onto the stage in black heels as a sensual rock song breaks into the room, and wrap my hands around the sleek black surface of the pole. I'm not the best dancer here, but I manage, swinging around in a slow circle as I warm up to the temp, my heels sliding against the floor.

My right leg lifts up slowly and I lay it against the pole, leaning forward like I'm stretching or something, like this is just a warm up for a workout. That's how I've been getting through this, pretending each dance is a different event. Keeps my mind off of the eyes below me.

I draw my leg back, knee up and swing my hair back, my

BAD NANNY

long ponytail flying dramatically as the men cheer and shout. Because we serve alcohol here, they're supposed to stay six feet away from the dancers at all times, but dollar bills rain down on the stage anyway. Anything to get me to come closer, I guess.

Oh, and did I mention the special around here is called *dollar titties*? Wave a buck around like the college boys at the end of my stage and get a girl to come and shake her boobs in your face. *I hate this. I hate it so much.*

My eyes close as I let go of the pole and bend down low, coming up slowly and flicking my ponytail over my shoulder, my red corset and skirt making me feel more secure. It's when those things come off that I feel the aching numbness start to take over.

When I turn and head to the front of the stage, reaching down to unhook my garters from the thigh highs, the boys go absolutely nuts—Dan especially. He cheers and yells something about knowing me, reaching out to grab one of the waitresses by the arm.

The bouncer is there in a second and Dan throws his arms up, ignoring the man as he heads back to his place near the booths. Some of the girls are giving lap dances in their bikini bottoms, but the bouncers have to be on it like crazy because the men (or the occasional woman) has to keep their hands firmly planted on the armrests.

When I strip the corset off next and turn around, I toss it aside and grab the pole, sliding down to my side and lifting my left leg up in a move the dancers here call the side pinup girl. It's a popular move, bringing more cash raining down in front, way more than I've seen before. These boys are *definitely* drunk as hell. Honestly, I'm surprised they're still here. Usually the manager likes to keep things low-key and kick out the rowdy patrons.

I slide back up into a sitting position and wrap my legs around the pole, swinging my ponytail back before I lean forward again and glide my way back up into a standing position. Next, I have to reach up and remove my bra, feeling the sweat pouring down my spine and chest.

I smell like the lilac perfume that Tiffany soaks herself in backstage, glitter sparkling all over my breasts as I toss the red bra aside and sway my way to the front, dropping low and sliding my fingers along my inner thighs, my thigh highs kept up with a little bit of well-placed body glue. It's a good trick for keeping them on after the garter belts come undone.

Dan and his friends are shouting for me to *flash some pussy* but that's not going to happen. Sorry. Thankfully that's illegal around here, giving me a slight reprieve and a small boost to my dignity.

I turn away and trace the stage again, pulling off the garter belt and spinning around the pole, dropping back and hooking my legs around the top so I can twist upside down and press my back to the metal, hair brushing against the stage. When I swing around and come back to my feet, I start one more round to the front, figuring that if Dan and his friends want to be crazy and throw money at me, I might as well take it.

I feel cheap as hell for even thinking that, like some dog chasing after bones.

Tears prick my eyes suddenly, but I blink them back, refusing to let myself go down that road again. I made my choice; I'm here; I'll make the best of it. For some reason, thoughts of Zayden pop up in my head: his smile, the warmth of his hands, his lips against my neck as he comes.

He's made this bearable so far, but I'm struggling to figure out how I'm going to do this once he's gone.

When I turn around at the end of the stage and use my shoulders for a little downward shimmy, things go from bad ... to fucking awful. Dan and his friends are still shouting, telling me to *show my shit,* their faces bathed in shadow and the awful edge of the spotlight above my head. As soon as I take my eyes off of them, I hear commotion and then suddenly there's just this hand in my hair, dragging me back so hard that I fall, heels slipping out from under me.

Just like Grace did at the playground.

I go down heavy on the stage, the breath exploding from

BAD NANNY

my lungs, and then I'm being dragged over the side. My body spins as I fall, knees and elbows connecting with the floor as the hand in my hair tightens and pulls. There's movement around me, probably the bouncers, but I'm still struggling to catch my breath and blink past the sudden tears in my eyes.

The rough old carpet digs into my knees and palms as I force myself to my feet and grab the edge of the stage to pull myself upright. As soon as I do, I see Dan in the arms of one of the bouncers, thrashing and cursing as he's dragged to the front doors. One of the other employees snaps a photo of him before he's thrown out; he won't be allowed back in here ever again.

"You fucking cunt!" he screams, right before he's dragged outside. I stand in stunned silence as the rest of Dan's friends are escorted out, crossing my arms tight over my bare chest as I struggle to keep my breathing slow, my eyes focused on the tinted doors at the front of the building.

God. I can't believe this is happening. And it's not just that my scalp hurts and my knees are bleeding, my elbows stinging. But I have to go to *class* with that a-hole. I have sit there during a lecture and wonder if his eyes are on me or what he's thinking about me. Not that I give a shit ... because I don't.

I swear, I don't.

Tiffany hustles over to me in a black robe and puts her arms around me. She smells like that floral perfume, flaking glitter all over my bare tits.

"Come on, honey," she says as she pulls me away from the main floor and the manager catches up to us, asking me if I'm alright, telling me to take a minute. At least he looks somewhat concerned, a nice change of pace considering his usual attitude towards me.

"I'm fine," I say, lifting up a hand as he pauses outside the curtain to the dressing room, and we go in. I slip on a t-shirt, let Tiffany set me up in one of the chairs next to the vanity and bring me a soda from the bar. The fizzy bubbles race over my tongue as I consider how the hell I'm going to deal with Dan come tomorrow.

"Are you okay?" she asks for the tenth time as she takes a

seat next to me. "Looks like you went down pretty hard." I cringe and reach up to rub at the back of my head, feeling a slight scabbing of blood on my scalp.

"I'm okay, really," I say as I stare at myself in the mirror. My eyes look huge and dark, and even though I've slathered on thick stage makeup, I look young. Too young. It's creeping me out a little to be honest. "Well, physically. I mean, it hurts, but that's not really the issue." I turn to look at Tiffany, and I wonder what *her* story is. She must have one, right? I bet all these girls do. Some—maybe all of them—might have stories worse than mine. "I go to school with that guy," I say and she nods, watching me with big, beautiful blue eyes. She has this mothering vibe about her that makes me think she's older than she really is. Looking at her now, she can't be any older than Zayden.

Zayden.

I sigh.

Too bad he wasn't here to punch Dan out for me. My mouth twitches a little.

"Well, remember, you're a stripper, not a slave. Don't let him treat you any different at school, okay? Make that boy behave." She slaps a hand on my knee and smiles, but I can't seem to make myself smile back.

"We're partnered together on a research project. Do I tell the professor that the guy assaulted me at a strip club?"

"If you have to. You shouldn't be ashamed of what you do to survive. Some people think this place is a last resort, that it's the worst thing possible. But what's really bad, what's really low, is when you start to believe all of that, when you let yourself doubt. Do what you have to do, but stand up for yourself, okay?"

"I will," I promise, and I know that's the truth. I might not be the bravest girl in the world, but I don't let people walk all over me either.

"I'm supposed to get off here in a minute, but why don't you sit for a spell and I'll take this set, alright?"

"Thanks, Tiffany," I say as she smiles at me and moves

away, leaving me alone with the sweet, faint smell of her perfume.

As soon as she leaves, this overwhelming sense of loneliness takes over me. Clearly, it's something that *I* need to work on, but ... it sure is nice to know that Zayden's going to be waiting for me when I get back.

Maybe he'll even be naked in my bed?

I almost smile again, but it just won't come. Still, I decide that even if we only have two nights left, I'm going to use them up for all that they're worth.

When I let myself in the front door, Sadie's crib is gone and I have a small moment of panic that Zayden's just up and left. But of course he wouldn't do that to the girls, not even to me I think. I really *do* smile when I hear the song that's playing from the kitchen: "Brown Eyed Girl" by Van Morrison.

I close the door quietly behind me and lock it, leaving my bag on the couch and trying to sneak my way over to the archway in the kitchen to see what he's doing. Doesn't work though because I end up tripping over Hubert and falling directly into Zayden's waiting arms.

"Whoa there, chickadee," he says as he grins and lifts me back up, his fingers hot against my skin as he rights me and we both look down at the stupid cat. He's yowling and flashing a new sweater, this one with a *South Park* character on the back of it.

It hits me suddenly that if Hubert wears a different sweater for everyday of the week then ...

"You packed, like, a dozen plus sweaters for your cat? *That's* what you thought to bring with you to Eureka?"

Zayden's still grinning at me, but as he steadies me and goes to release my arms, he sees the rug burns on my elbows and frowns.

When he tries to study the wounds, I pull away from him and cross my arms over the front of my coat, refusing to let my mind devolve into memories of Zayden pushing me against the wall next to the stairwell, coming all over my lacy teddy.

"Seriously. You packed cat sweaters, Zayden. Doesn't get any nerdier than that."

Zayden snaps tattooed fingers at me and leans in close, his expression softening into something a little goofier.

"If you're talking to me again, then I'm guessing I'm out of the doghouse?"

"You sure you don't *want* to be in the doghouse?" I joke as I move over to the couch and pull Dodger off the back of the old chihuahua. Seriously, what is wrong with this dog? Not only is he neutered, but of the three chihuahuas, the only one he seems to enjoy humping is the ancient old man with cataracts and a tongue hanging out the side of his mouth. Kind of weird. And gross. Super gross. "Dodger seems to get a *lot* of action, way more than you."

"Oh, snap," Zayden says, tilting his head to the side and snapping his fingers again. "You got me there, Smarty-Pants." A pause as I stroke the fat chihuahua and the hyper little one with the white spot on her head. I still have no idea what their names are. Kinzie calls them Little Bastard, A-Hole, and Poop Face. I am guessing those are *not* their actual monickers. "So what's up with the elbows? Did something happen?"

"I tripped on a transition strip," I say with a roll of my eyes, raising my brows as the song ends and starts up again, clearly on another of Zay's endless loops. "What's with the music? Are you trying to soften me up?"

"Um ... is it working?" he asks with his own brows raised. "You know, Brooke," he starts, but I can't take anymore of the weird sad half-smiles and the excuses. Clearly, Zayden is not ready for a relationship and you know what? Maybe I'm not either. I shouldn't cling to him when I can't even face the gaping yawn of loneliness inside of me. Besides, he's right: I'm only twenty-two. I have my whole life ahead of me. I don't need to get romantically involved with anyone for a while.

BAD NANNY

"Don't. Just," I pause as Dodger starts humping *my* leg, scooting him away with my heel. The little gray and white dog trots away and then ... tries to go at it with the cat. Fortunately he gets a nice curved claw in the nose. Serves him right. I look up at Zayden and shove some hair away from my face. "Don't make anymore excuses, okay? However you feel, whatever you feel, it's fine. I get it."

Zayden looks a little skeptical, but he purses his lips and then nods, the black metal balls on his lip rings spinning as he plays with them with his tongue.

"Gotcha," he says and then gestures for me to follow him. "C'mere. I want to show you something."

I follow him into the kitchen and over to the back door, watching in awe as he opens it to reveal a giant trampoline with netted sides.

"Holy crap," I say as we move outside and into the slight drizzle. "Where the frick did this come from?"

"Some guy on Craigslist," he says and then grins at me when I give him a look. "What? He just wanted to get rid of it. Only cost me fifty bucks. I wanted the girls to have something fun to remember me by."

A wave of sadness crashes over me at the thought, but I push it back. The night's too quiet, too pretty, for those kinds of thoughts. When I glance up, the porch lights turn the falling needles of the trees into white slices in the dark.

"Jump with me?" Zayden asks with a sharp grin. "I made sure to put Sadie upstairs, so we could hang out down here, watch a movie, or ... whatever else."

"I see," I say as I kick off my heels and move across the wet lawn to the edge of the trampoline. "You want me to jump on this thing in a trench coat and lingerie?"

"Nooooo," Zay says as he comes up next to me and spins around to lean his back against the trampoline, his green eyes sparkling. "I want you to jump on this thing in *just* lingerie. Lose the coat." He gestures with his thumb and then grabs the edge of the netting, pulling it back and climbing in. As soon as he's up there, he turns and reaches out a hand for me.

I stare at it for a long moment before I decide to take it. What the hell? I had a shitty night tonight, so I may as well go for it.

I climb up and shrug my coat off, noticing Zayden's appreciative smile as he takes my hands and pulls me into the center of the wet trampoline, my skin prickling under the cold air and the icy droplets.

"Wait," Zay says as he reaches back and grabs his shirt, tearing it up and over his head with a bright grin. "It's not fair if you're the only half-naked person out here."

"You just want to show off your chest, admit it," I say as Zayden wiggles his eyebrows at me and starts to jump, spinning in a circle as I laugh at his ridiculousness. "You are so *weird*," I say, but it doesn't faze him and it makes me forget all about Dan the Douche and the strip club and everything else.

"Bounce with me, Smarty-Pants," he says as pauses and reaches out to take my hands, droplets sliding across the firm, hard muscles in his chest and abdomen. It's hard for me to pull my eyes away and focus on his face.

"Do you know how bad my boobs are going to jiggle when I do that?"

"Um, yeah. Clearly that's the whole reason I asked," he jokes, sticking out his tongue and tilting his head to the side. I can see that the goofiness is amped up tonight, probably in some super secret genius way of his to make everything seem less heavy, less emotional. Zayden thinks he's stupid—or at least he pretends to think he's stupid—but I know he's a smart guy. "Bounce those boobs for me, baby."

"You're alliterating again," I tell him, but take a deep breath and start to jump anyway. It's so weird. I haven't been on a trampoline since I was fifteen, but holy crap it's fun. I try not to scream as Zayden bounces into my feet and propels me into the air, catching me on my way down and pulling me against his chest.

We fall to the surface of the trampoline and then in all that cold air and darkness, there's just suddenly this explosion of warmth as Zay's body slides against mine, as his mouth finds mine, his tongue slicking across my own.

I groan and lean into him, my body draped over his, those big tattooed hands of his gripping my ass, fingers caught in the lace of my red panties. My hair is already wet and heavy, sticking to the back of my neck, but it's easy to ignore with the hard press of Zay's erection through his jeans.

"You were bouncing around with a hard-on in your pants?" I ask and he smiles, this sexy, sultry impish little grin, right before he rolls me over and presses our bodies into the black mesh. Even with the porch light on, I can see a whole mess of stars behind his head as he blocks my face from the rain, his slicked up Mohawk drooping to one side.

I reach up and mess it up with my fingers as he drops his mouth to mine again, kissing me with all this heat and passion and need. When he does that, I can't understand *why* he doesn't want me, but I make it not matter. I'm going to enjoy this, no matter what.

"Should we move inside?" I ask as Zay drops his right hand to my breast, kneading the sensitive flesh through the lace of the red bra. His expression when he looks down at me is wry as hell.

"Hell no," he whispers as he puts his lips to my ear. "Why do you think I bought this damn thing? It wasn't *really* just for the kids. I think the bounce of the mesh should work out nicely."

"You're not freaking serious," I whisper, but I can't stop the trail of hot kisses down my throat, straight to the hard, pebbled point of my nipple. I gasp as Zayden's hot mouth slides over it, his tongue circling across the lace. When Zay sneaks his hands around my back to undo my bra, I lift my rib cage and encourage him to take it off, exposing my breasts to the wet cold night air.

He doesn't leave them bare for long, covering them with colorful hands, kneading them with inked fingers, sucking and kissing and biting. It feels like there's a string from my nipples straight down to my pussy, making me clench my thighs and bite my lip as I lift my hands up and tangle my fingers in the black netting behind my head.

"Did I ever mention to you how much I love your tits?" Zayden asks with another impish grin.

"I don't think you've said it outright, but I kind of got the gist," I whisper as I struggle to stay quiet. I know there's nobody around, but I'm afraid my voice will echo, that one of the neighbors will get it in their minds to come and investigate. "But mine are nothing special. They're pretty much just average C cups. I bet you've seen better."

Zayden looks up at me and runs his tongue across his lower lip, the motion driving me completely up the wall. Well, metaphorically speaking of course since I'm trapped beneath the hard warmth of his body, cradled in the bouncy mesh.

"Better?" He looks down at my boobs and I laugh, trying to cover them up with my hands. Zay pushes me away, grabbing my wrists and pinning them above my head as he leans it and teases my nipple just *barely* with the tip of his tongue. The sensation is hot and sharp enough to be almost painful. "Now, I don't know about that. They're not huge, but they suit your body." He squeezes my breast in his fingers, making a warm sounding purr in the back of his throat. "Full, ripe, soft as hell but lifted and perky. Nope. I can't say they get any better than this, and I like to consider myself a breast connoisseur."

Zayden winks at me and then dives back into teasing and licking and sucking my nipples and the soft skin around them, working me into a frenzy without touching anything else. My hips buck against his body, desperate for stimulation, hungry for release.

When Zay moves his mouth up to kiss and suck at my neck, I forget to care about hickeys or how about how cold I am and I even forget to be silly. I just succumb to his touch, his body, his presence. Because honestly, as hard and firm as his muscles are, as bright as his tattoos, as sharp as his piercings ... it's *him* that I find most attractive. I like his mannerisms and the way he smiles, how he takes such care to shave designs into

BAD NANNY

his hair in the morning. I like the way he holds the baby and plays with the kids and puts sweaters on his cat.

I pretty much like everything about him.

I breathe out suddenly and look up at the night sky, letting my thoughts drift away on the wind as Zayden starts kissing his way down between my breasts and pauses at the corset, reaching under me again to take it off. As soon as it's gone, he kisses my belly down to the panties. I left the garter belt and thigh highs off before I left the club, so it's nothing but smooth sailing from here on out.

Zay slides his tongue in an arc just above the waistband of the thong, grabbing the edge with his teeth and pulling it down. I think he sneaks his fingers under the fabric on the opposite side, too, but all I can see is him looking up at me with his brown eyes, his full sexy mouth curved into a smirk, the red fabric clenched between his teeth.

I sigh and drop my head back against the taut surface of the trampoline beneath my head. Zayden's weight pulls me in towards the center as he gets the panties off my leg and tosses them aside, reaching down to undo the crazy red and black striped belt he's wearing.

"Brooke," he says as he undoes his jeans and fishes a condom out of his back pocket. "Come here."

I sit up as Zayden reaches out for my hand, encouraging me to straddle him, a knee on either side of his thighs as he leans back into the mesh and looks up at me. His cock stands between us, thick and proud and ready.

Without a word, I climb up over him, aligning our hips as I reach down and take hold of his shaft, using instinct to guide him to the hot heat of my core. Zayden watches me with half-lidded eyes, his gaze heavy and direct, attention focused on my face, on the way the water sluices between my lips. My bangs stick to my forehead as I drop my head back and relax my muscles, sliding all the way down Zayden's cock until we're pressed together tight and my head is spinning from the rush of pleasure.

"I can't move," I whisper, because I feel trapped, frozen,

full. Zay reaches up and runs his thumb down my lower lip, taking hold of my hip with his other hand, the one tattooed with an empty, open book.

"Sure you can," he whispers, urging me to move with his hand as I drop my own to his chest, fingers splayed out across the wash of tattoos between his shoulders. I can barely seem to find my own breaths, each exhale getting caught in the night in a cloud of white. "That's it, right there. Work that cock, Smarty-Pants."

My first response is to laugh at that, but I can't get the breath for it. I feel tight and stretched and warm, leaning my body forward just enough that I can feel pressure on my clit. *Oh yes. Yes, I like that.*

"God yes," Zayden groans as I get into the movement, grinding our hips together, the bounce of the trampoline the perfect backdrop, letting our bodies rock into one another with each movement. "Faster, babe. Work me hard." I kind of want to tell Zayden to stuff it with the dirty talk, but then … I like it. A lot.

I work our bodies until the cold droplets of rain turn to hot drips of sweat, Zayden's hands sliding up and taking hold of my breasts as I drive him into me, actually enjoying doing the work more than I thought I would.

I feel powerful up here, in control. It's definitely fun both ways, but tonight, this is exactly what I need. Zayden is exactly *who* I need.

I move my body hard and fast until I feel his muscles clenching beneath me, his thumbs grazing across the tender points of my nipples as he comes with a deeply satisfying sound. My own body is thrumming and pulsing, desperate for a release of my own.

Zayden sucks in a deep breath and pushes me off, sliding down between my legs before I can even puzzle out what he's planning. Two fingers slide in deep as he presses that full mouth of his up against my clit, tongue flicking out and tasting me as Zay takes hold of my hip bone with his opposite hand, locking me in place.

BAD NANNY

The drizzle turns into a violent pour in an instant, the sharp salt scent of the bay drifting across my parted lips as I tangle my fingers in Zay's hair and pull his face against me. With the stars above and the warmth of him below, I don't want this to ever end. I want to stay here on this trampoline with Zayden forever, make love in the grass, on the tire swing, against the base of one of the massive redwood trees.

But my body's a traitor, grasping at me with the hot hands of pleasure and pulling me under, letting that bright white light of an orgasm crash over and consume me.

There's a single instant there where everything is clear, sharp, where it all makes sense. *I want Zayden to fall in love with me.* As quick as the clarity comes, it's gone, leaving me a tangled mess of cold and wet and shaking emotions.

"Oh, baby," Zayden says, sliding up over me and pressing his mouth to my throat. "Let's go inside."

I nod and let him help me up, the process complicated by the sway and bounce of the trampoline. Plus ... I'm sort of naked and wet—in more than one way. I let Zay jump off first and when he holds his arms up to me, I reach down and put my hands flat on his shoulders, jumping into him.

We stumble back a few inches in the wet grass and then pause, Zay's sea glass green eyes gazing down at me with a faint sort of wonder. I try to decipher it's meaning, but he blinks it away as fast as it came, pulling away and grabbing my hand to drag me inside.

The dogs burst out around our feet as soon as we open the sliding glass door, but Zay ignores them, grabbing a hoodie off the table and tossing it to me as he retreats into the bathroom for a pair of towels. He tosses one over as I sit my shaking ass in a chair, bare butt cheeks cold against the wood surface as I tousle my ponytail, trying to wick as much moisture out as I can before I yank the hoodie on.

"Is this ... does this have ... why do you have a sweatshirt with David Bowie on it?"

"Um," Zayden says, leaning over me with his sexy ass bare chest and nipple rings all up in my face. "This isn't just *David*

Bowie, okay? This is Jareth the Goblin King, duh."

I stare up at him and he sighs.

"Okay, you fucking millennial, this is from the *Labyrinth.*"

"I think we're both millennials actually," I say, but I don't really care about any of it. The *Labyrinth*—which I have seen, thank you very much—or millennials, but I'm all twisted up inside and I can't quite think clearly right now.

Zayden stands up and claps his hands together, using his foot to open the oven door. Inside, there's some sort of ... pie?

"What the hell is that?" I ask as he pulls it out and presents it to me. There's a shiny latticework crust on top and everything. Whoa. Fancy. "Did you ... *make* that?"

"Abso-fucking-lutely. Google, baby. Google will tell you *everything.* I could make a goddamn rocket ship with instructions off that damn search engine."

"So ... what is it?" I ask, crossing my arms over myself and letting my body sink into Zay's hoodie. It's soft and clean and smells just like him, that blackberry/cinnamon smell that I like so much. I'm painfully aware of my lower half though, of how naked I still am, how wet between the thighs. I tuck the fabric down as Zay raises an eyebrow and sets the pie on the counter.

"Chicken pot pie, Smarty-Pants. I'm making us plates and we're watching the fucking *Labyrinth.* If you can't recognize Jareth at first sight, you've got some serious issues, kid."

"Zayden," I start, but then I have no idea what to say, curling my fingers over my knees, pressing my fingertips into my skin until the flesh turns a pale white. I glance up to find him standing at the counter, slowly spooning food into a pair of bowls. His movements are awkward and weird, but when he glances over his shoulder, he's smiling again.

"A musical from the eighties with puppets. Doesn't get much better than that, right?"

I stand up from the chair, letting the hoodie fall over my ass; it's so big, I'm swimming in it.

My arms slide around Zayden's waist and I rest my cheek against his bare back. With a soft sigh, he drops the serving spoon back into the glass pie pan and turns around to look at me, his eyes suddenly dark, his expression taking me in with a slow careful intensity.

When Zay drops his hand to my face and lifts my chin, I close my eyes, savoring the feel of his mouth against mine. As soon as our lips connect, the atmosphere in the room amps up considerably. Zay turns us around and lifts me with an easy motion, setting my ass on the edge of the counter.

With a frantic flick of his hands, he opens his jeans and then digs another condom out of his pocket. *How many of those fucking things does he keep in there?* I don't have a lot of time to contemplate that because Zay's yanking me forward and guiding himself to my opening, shoving hard and fast inside.

My pulse skyrockets, and I find my breath escaping in small, harsh gasps as he drags me forward and pins my pelvis against the curved edge of the linoleum counter. Unlike the trampoline or the bed, there's absolutely no give when he thrusts forward, hitting me hard and deep with the thick solid length of his shaft.

My head spins, my hands thrown loosely around Zay's neck as I press our foreheads together and he makes a sharp sound in the back of his throat. It's a wild noise, harsh and desperate, kind of like his frantic motions, like the whimper that builds in the back of my own throat.

When the friction of his body against mine sends me over the edge, Zay bites down on that curved space between my neck and shoulder and empties himself with a deep, quivering growl that I can feel all the way in my bones.

I lean back away from him, noticing that the glitter from my breasts has rubbed off all over his face.

"Holy sweet baby Jesus," he whispers as he looks at me with some sort of awe in his face, blinking quickly and then sliding out of me, turning away while he removes the condom and fixes his pants. "You've got some sort of magic in you, Brooke Overland," he says with a glance over his shoulder.

I smile, but I don't have a response to that statement.

"Puppets?" I ask because I'm shaking and twisting and falling inside. *Falling for Zayden Roth.*

Zay nods and lets his mouth curve up into one of his signature smiles.

"You got it, doll," he says, helping me hop down from the counter.

We eat our food, watch the movie, and end up fucking through the last half of it.

It's seriously the best night of my entire life. Guess nothing can last forever though, can it?

CHAPTER 25
ZAYDEN ROTH

Aww, man.

I am like totally crazy, head over heels fucking obsessed with Brooke Overland.

I *never* smoke. Seriously. Never. Unleeeeeeess, I'm having a day as shitty as this one.

"Dude, what are you even going on about?" Jude asks as I exhale and ash my cigarette into the wood chip area in front of the bay window. I keep checking over my shoulder to make sure none of the kids catch me out here. Uncle Zay is so goddamn cool if they see me smoking, they'll probably take it up like tomorrow. "You're in love with some twenty-two year old *girl*? That's gross. Why are you even sleeping with somebody seven years younger than you. Isn't that illegal or something?"

"Shut your fat trap, Jude," I say as I take another drag on the cigarette and then cough. It feels really good to smoke once in a while, but also kind of gross. I feel this weird guilty pleasure as I savor the last cig I have left. I've kept it with me at all times for months, just in case of emergency.

This is so an emergency.

"I didn't say *in love,* did I?"

"Yeah, you didn't say the *exact* phrase 'in love', but you

listed pretty much every symptom and consequence of being in love."

"Like you'd know shit about that," I say, wondering what he's doing while he's talking to me. He might be my boss, but I don't trust this guy for crap. One time, I found out he was actually getting his cock sucked while we had a conversation about my dead parents. That's just plain nasty if you ask me ... *althooooough* I have been known to pick up my phone mid-coitus. Kind of like when Rob called me to ask about my driving up here. I should've let that shit roll to voicemail.

But then I never would've met Brooke.

"I've been in love seven times, you dick. How many for you? Oh, that's right: zero. Or if you count this Brenda girl, then it's one."

"Brooke, man. Her name is Brooke. Get it right, please."

"You need to get your *ass* back here before you ruin this girl's life. Leave her alone, man. You've got a chronic dating problem; don't inflict that on some poor woman with enough shit on her plate."

"Says the guy who supposedly fell in love 'seven times'," I make quotes with my fingers even though the only person around to see is the neighbor that called animal control on me. I smile tightly at her and she turns away with a huff. "And then *left* all seven of the girls he was in love with."

"Exactly. Because *I* am fully aware that I'm an asshole. I think part of you wants to believe you're some sort of nice guy or something. Face the facts, Zayden: you're a dick. You might smile and make a lot of jokes, but you're still just a single asshole from Las Vegas with no money and a condo you can't really afford."

I roll my eyes and take one last exhale, smoking my precious cigarette down to the filter. I drop it on the porch and crush it out, leaning down to pick up the butt. God knows if I leave it here, one of those dogs or hell, one of the little monsters, will probably eat it. That would be just my luck, wouldn't it?

"I called you for advice, bro, but ... that's kind of not what's happening right now. I feel like you're just taking advantage of the situation to insult me."

"You just don't like what I have to say," Jude tells me and I hear the jingle of the shop bell followed by the sweet chorus of giggling tourists. Makes me a little homesick. "Look, I gotta go. I'll see you on Thursday or what?"

"Friday probably. Takes me like a whole fucking day to drive."

"Say hi to your hairless pussy for me," Jude jokes with a laugh just before he flicks the switch on his charm and starts chatting to the women in the shop. "A clit piercing? I think what you mean is a VCH or HCH which I'd be happy to tell you all about. We do require a fifty dollar deposit for an anatomy consult—"

I roll my eyes and hang up on the idiot. He's been known to leave calls connected in pretty awkward situations, such as when he had his grandma on the line and started begging his then-girlfriend to deep throat his cock. Oh, Jude. If I'm a nerdy douche, then he's a dickhead douche. Nothing cute or charming about him at all.

"Uncle Zay?"

I jump and drop my cell phone ... watching as the screen cracks into spiderweb formation across the front.

Cool beans.

Guess I'll be replacing *that* when I get back to Las Vegas.

"What's up, honey?" I ask, grabbing my phone from the pavement and standing up, wishing that Brooke were here and wondering what she's up to. This morning was kind of weird, but I felt like we both understood each other, you know? Like all these feelings we're both having are just ... they wouldn't work out.

I run my fingers through my hair as I look down at Bella.

"Can you come jump with us on the trampoline again? It's only fun when you do it with us."

I smile and reach out to pinch her cheek. Bella wrinkles her face up and bats me away, turning around and sprinting towards the sliding glass doors with an adorable childish glee

—until she finds out they're closed and slams into them, ricocheting backwards into the kitchen.

Fuck.

Well, *that* can't be any good, now can it?

When Brooke gets back, she looks exhausted, her glasses sitting perched on the end of her nose as she hangs up that big ugly camel coat of hers and looks at the snot on my shirt with a raised brow. I can't help but admire that piercing gracing the sensual curve. Damn, I'm good.

"Don't ask," I say, pointing to the snot trails and the splatters of blood from Bella's nose. "We had a little incident with the sliding glass doors."

"Oh my God," she says, but I'm already holding up my hands.

"No worries. I got it under control." I point back at the glass and the three hundred plus stickers across it. "I asked Kinzie to help the twins put up one or two tasteful pieces as a warning while I cleaned up Bella's bloody nose, but ... we got this instead. If you want me to scrape them off before I leave on Thursday, I can definitely do that."

Brooke's face droops and she shakes her head, shoving back that long gorgeous fall of dark hair. The way she pushes and shoves it all the time, I get the feeling that she has no idea how pretty it really is, how curling up next to her and feeling the silken strands drape over my skin is like heaven.

"No. It's fine. It doesn't matter." A pause. "Will you be able to get the kids from school or ..."

"Yeah, of course," I say as Brooke takes in a deep breath and glances over at the couch. I think we both remember all the things we did there last night. Despite logging all that naughty time, I'm still not feeling my usual deflated interest, my need to move on. There's nothing here but want and need

BAD NANNY

in my chest, this super creepy man-hormone thing that makes me want to piss in a circle around Brooke.

Bet that would go over well, huh?

"I'll pick the kids up and bring Bella and Grace over here after. Then I'll have to book it to get to the airport on time to pick Rob and Mercedes up. Do you have someone to watch the girls that night?"

"Not really," Brooke whispers, her voice harsh and low. She does a good job of trying to hide her emotions, but her eyes ... that beautiful brown color is practically transparent. I can see right through her, straight down to her heart. I feel like it's beating for me, but then I wonder if that's just my crazy hormone shit turning fantasies for me.

Deep breath, Zay. Deep fucking breath.

"Well, you do now because I called your Aunt Monica up and got her to agree to watch the girls. I told her you had a waitressing job at the brewery. She didn't ask which one."

Brooke nods and then starts toward the stairs.

I stop her with a hand on the wrist, freezing her in the exact spot that we fucked, her back against the wall, her lingerie covered in my cum.

Jesus.

She doesn't know the plan I've cooked up for tonight, but maybe that would wipe the frown from her face? I wrap my fingers tight around Brooke's wrist and smile at her.

"It's gonna be okay," I tell her. "You'll get through this."

"Um," she starts, glancing down at my hand on her skin. When she looks back up at me, her face looks exactly like it did when we first met and she told me to get out and go home. "Can you let go of me now?"

I release her with a raised brow and watch as Brooke retreats up the stairs. She doesn't come out for some time, leaving me to bounce on the trampoline with the brats yet *again*. Doesn't even matter that it's raining. I can't seem to corral the little monsters.

When Brooke finally does make an appearance, the sky is dark and she's wearing her trench coat again.

"I'm off to work. I'll see you all in the morning," she says, giving the kids—and me—a bright smile. I smile back at her and give a little wave, sneaking over to the curtains and peeking outside to watch her pull down the driveway and zoom off down the street.

Brooke's aunt should be here any minute and then I am outtie, off to the Top Hat Club for a little show. I hope Brooke doesn't find it creepy, but I just really want to see her dance. Hell, I just really want to see *her.* No sense spending our last night apart, right?

I get the brats hooked up on the YouTube app and then—then I turn my ass right back around and activate those parental controls because *damn,* what were they just watching? Was that ... a porno?

"Those naked people were licking each other's privates," Kinzie announces as I groan and find some kitten videos for them to watch.

"Be good," I say as I bounce up the stairs and into Brooke's room to change. Can't go looking like a complete loser, right? Snot and blood all over my shirt is not exactly what I'd call *sexy.*

I put on black slacks and dark purple Docs, a white button-up, and a black suit jacket covered in pins. I brought it with me in case Rob wanted to go out to a family dinner or some shit. He likes to do that, have formal dinners out. Before he married Mercedes, he used to come down to Vegas and take me out. But I don't do suits, not like a normal person anyway.

I leave the top few buttons undone to show off my tattoos, and slick up the left side of my hair. The right gets a fresh shave and some spray on color to turn it purple. Yeah. It looks totally fucking *sick.*

I shove the arms of the suit jacket up and stack my arms with bracelets before heading down the stairs to find the children engrossed in a PewDiePie video. Gross.

The knock at the door doesn't even draw their attention—just a horde of barking chihuahuas and one ugly gray rat dog.

"You kids behave, okay?" I say as I open the door and use

BAD NANNY

my boot to sweep miniature dogs aside. "Come on in."

Monica squeezes past me, putting as much space between us as is humanly possible. Tonight she's wearing more reasonable looking clothes, like she learned her lesson last time. Jeans and a t-shirt will help with these kids a hell of a lot more than a designer dress or a *pantsuit*.

"Have no idea what time I'll be back," I say before the woman gets out a single word. This Monica chick, I know her type. You start letting a person like this talk and they won't stop. Best to just *smooth* my agenda right on through without any commentary. "Make sure the little shits are in bed by nine." I cup my hands around my mouth. "Love y'all! Later!"

I slip out the door and over to the minivan, climbing in and driving over to the nearest ATM to make a quick withdrawal before I head to the club.

When I get there, I park in front and head inside to a dimly lit interior with gold and green carpets and a faux wood paneled bar that's probably seen better days. It's not too seedy or gross, but I wouldn't exactly call it high-class either. In Las Vegas, a place like this would never make it. But up here, in the middle of the butt-fuck-nowhere-forest, this is the *only* strip club. I well remember my days of trying to sneak in here as a kid with a fake ID.

I make my way towards the stages, scanning them quickly for Brooke. Either I just missed her set, or she hasn't performed.

When I take a seat, a blond woman in nipple tassels and a short wisp of a skirt saunters over to me to take my order, letting me know about their *dollar titties* special. Huh. I look at her smiling at me, and I can't help but feel sick to my stomach.

I don't want my woman working here.

That that's the first thought that skitters through my brain in a sea of topless women grinding their G-strings against metal poles scares the *fuck* out of me.

My woman? How the hell is Brooke mine? First off, that's like so totally sexist. And anyway, I *can't* stay here. I hate

C.M. STUNICH

Eureka. Hate it. And I know from experience how quickly relationships devolve. One minute, you think you can't live without a person and the next, you sort of wish they would just up and die.

Why can't I let this thing with Brooke just stay beautiful?

I sigh and rake my fingers through my hair.

"Can I just get a beer?" I ask and the woman nods, moving away towards the bar. And when I say *towards,* I mean she has to stop three times for *dollar titties* and shake her shit in front of a bunch of drunk horny losers.

Fuck.

I start biting my lip, tapping my fingers on the armrests of the chair I'm sitting in, when my eyes wander over to the booths in the corner, to the women in shiny silver and gold heels, G-strings just barely covering up their cunts. Lap dances are going full force back there, three different ones at the same time.

As I stare at these women grinding their bodies on the clothed laps of their customers, I feel sick. And like a complete piece of shit. It's not like *I've* never had a lap dance before. But when I look at it like this, from an outside perspective, and imagine Brooke in those girls' places, I want to put my fist through a wall.

Maybe coming here wasn't such a great idea?

I tap my boot on the floor and consider leaving before Brooke sees me, but then the song changes and the woman onstage in front of me disappears into the shadows. I settle back as the waitress drops my beer on the table next to me and leans down to take my money between her tits. I loosely stuff a ten in and withdraw my hand, watching the darkness of the stage with a strange hopping sort of anticipation in my gut.

I'm starting to get the feeling that when I see Brooke onstage, I'm going to lose my shit.

The lights dim and then burst bright on Brooke's curvy form as she saunters down that stage like it's a catwalk in Paris, her heels tall and pink and the color of bubblegum. I want to fucking eat that shit all the way up.

BAD NANNY

I find myself leaning forward, my elbows on my knees as my cock solidifies into a substance that's a hundred times harder than diamond. Ouch, baby. Ouch.

Brooke's wearing this tiny lace nightie in pink, a pair of heart pasties visible on her nipples beneath the barely there fabric, a tiny thong the only piece standing between the crowd and the smooth, shaved expanse of her pussy.

I lick my lips and lean back, taking my beer in my hand so I have something other than my cock to grab onto. Two halves of me war: one part that wants to enjoy the show and the other part that wants to sweep her off that stage and out the door, promise her that she never has to work a night here again.

But, like, even if I wanted to, I don't have the money for that.

I suck back a huge gulp of beer and wrinkle my nose at the cheap bitter taste, setting it aside as Brooke approaches the pole, her gently tanned skin flashing with pink and silver glitter. It decorates her chest and belly and thighs, a nice compliment to the shimmery eyeshadow and lipstick she's wearing.

I feel my boot start to tap faster as her hands wrap around the pole and she swings in a half circle, that long hair of hers up in a tight ponytail, flicking across the stage like a banner. When she turns to look over her shoulder, her eyes gaze into the darkness with an expression halfway between resigned and angry. *She hates it here. Fucking hates it.* Jude once dated a chick who stripped, who *liked* to strip. She said it put her in control of her sexuality or whatever, and I believed her. I just don't think Brooke is that type of person; she *really* doesn't want to be here.

I lick my lips again and sit up straight, wondering if she can see me sitting out here, bathed in anonymous darkness as the men around me hoot and holler, tossing money onto the front of the stage. There's a curved portion that dips down in the front for them to toss bills, but the second any of the dudes gets within six feet of Brooke, the bouncers get antsy.

Me? I get fucking livid watching them stare at her like that.

My testosterone is blown all the hell up, wild and crazy and completely out of control. My hands squeeze into involuntary fists as Brooke slides her back down the pole, the firm round curves of her ass peeking out from beneath the tiny slip of the nightgown.

When she stands back up, she wraps her arm around the pole and leans back, lifting a leg up in a feat that's like, seriously Olympic gymnast level or whatever. The long, lean curve of her calf and thigh presses against the metal as she tilts her head back and sweeps the floor with her long beautiful hair.

Before I even realize what I'm doing, I rise to my feet and notice that one of the bouncers is inching toward me. Don't blame him. Hell, I probably look like a crazy person. If I saw a dude looking at Brooke the way I'm looking at her, I'd kick his ass, too.

I tuck my hands back in my pocket as Brooke sashays to the front of the stage and slides her palms down the front of her taut belly, curling her fingers around the hem of the lace, swinging her hips in a tantalizing circle as she lifts it up and off, tossing it to the end of the stage and tossing her hair around.

She marches back to the pole as sweat starts to drip down the sides of my face, down my spine, beads on my upper lip.

"Holy shit," I murmur under my breath, eyes glued to Brooke's form, to the sparkly pink hearts over her nipples, to the seductive way she moves her body to the music. My heart's fucking thundering at a million miles an hour, and it feels suddenly difficult to catch my breath. My ears start to ring as I take a small step forward and pause at the sound of the bouncer clearing his throat.

Well, fuck. Fuck him because that's not just some stripper up there; that's *my* girl.

I run both hands through my hair, over my shaved head, watching as Brooke does this crazy spin with her legs pointed out like a high heel wearing ballerina. She spins in a quick circle and ends up on the floor, doing this sexy crawl that has my balls tightening and my cock threatening to cream my

BAD NANNY

pants.

Fantastic.

I suddenly need to talk to her so bad I can't breathe.

My arms fold across my chest like a defense mechanism, locking back the surge of jealousy and desperation that I'm feeling. Doesn't work, but at least it feels like I'm trying something here—something other than coming in my damn slacks.

Brooke slides her hands up the sides of her body and rubs them across her breasts, the very same breasts I had my mouth all over last night. When she reaches the pasties, she slides her nails under the top edge and peels them away with a single motion, letting the discarded hearts float to the floor as she goes for one round on the pole and money drifts across the stage along with laughter and cheering.

It's only after she comes around in the spin and does one last trace of the stage, stomping like a supermodel, that she pauses and nearly falls over, squinting into the darkness at ... little old me.

Her face blanches and she slaps her arms over her breasts, effectively covering her nipples. As the song winds to a close, Brooke turns and flees the stage like a bat outta hell, men's laughter trailing behind her as her heels clack across the tiled floor and behind a curtain.

With a sigh, I grab my beer and pace in front of the chair until I notice people starting to look my way. I plop down to wait, my heart thumping and my dick throbbing and my brain all messed up and weird.

Tomorrow, I get to leave all of this behind, but I'm not quite sure how I feel about that.

"*Zayden Roth.*" A hiss comes from my right and I glance over quickly to find Brooke in a tight black midriff tee that says *Top Hat* across the front. Underneath it, she's got on a black mini and some leather boots. Without waiting for me to come to her, she storms across the carpet and snatches my arm, looking up at the bouncer and giving him a slight nod of her chin. "What the *fuck* are you doing here?" she growls as she drags me up and out of my chair, abandoning my beer as she tugs me towards a black curtain with a sign that says *Executive Lounge.*

Uh-oh.

We *all* know what happens back here.

"Who's watching the kids?" she asks when I find myself unable to answer. I can't talk right now, can't make any sounds move past my suddenly dry lips. Brooke's small hand on my arm is waking up all sorts of emotions that I wish I wasn't feeling.

Like love.

Like, I sort of feel like I'm in love with her.

Only I'm not though, right?

"Monica," I choke out as she passes several doors covered in black tufted leather, pauses at the last one and uses a key that's on a green plastic cord around her wrist. She unlocks it and shoves me inside. "What are we doing in here?" I ask as I examine the leather couches, the mirrors, the pole in the center of the small room.

"You watched me. Without asking, you came and watched me." Tears suddenly explode in her pale brown eyes and she dashes them away angrily as my jaw drops open and I feel a rush of crazy tenderness towards her. Damn it. My knight meter is pinging *hardcore* right now. "Why would you do that? Why would you come here?"

"You were fucking *beautiful* up there," I say, but she's not having any of it, pulling away when I try to touch her and pacing to the opposite side of the room. I stand there for a minute and drop my hands to my sides as I try to breathe. Sweet baby Jesus, what have I gotten myself into here? This girl is young and damaged and shit, I can see that she's attached to me now. She's emotional and way too smart for her own good and she's got two inherited kids, but ... damn it if I can't find fault with any of that. I like it all. All of it. Every single thing.

I lace my fingers together behind my neck.

"You were beautiful," I repeat as she sits down hard on one

of the sofas and looks up at me with weepy eyes. Those get me every goddamn time, those weepy eyes. I will do *anything* for a set of wet peepers. "I wanted to see you dance."

"This ... this isn't me dancing," she says as she gestures at herself, pink glitter flaking off onto the black fabric of the t-shirt. "This isn't *me* at all. I'm not *this*."

"Of course not," I start, but Brooke's already shaking her head at me.

"You shouldn't have come here. Seriously. You shouldn't have. And I don't *want* you here, okay?" Brooke rubs the heels of her hands against her eyes and smears all of that dark liner and pretty pink eyeshadow.

I move over next to her and kneel down, trying to take solace in the fact that this room smells like bleach. At least I know it's reasonably clean, right? I fold my arms across the bare tops of Brooke's thighs, resting my chin on my arms.

"I'm sorry," I say and I mean it. I had no idea she'd react to seeing me like this. I feel like I've cheated her somehow, stolen something that wasn't mine to take. "Do you want me to leave?"

Brooke sniffles and lifts her chin up in that defiant way of hers that I like so much.

"Why? You're already here? Why don't you just pay me for a lap dance and we can be done with all of this?" Brooke gestures loosely in my direction. "I didn't want you to see me like this," she adds in a whisper, before I can say anything else. "This isn't how I wanted you to think of me."

"And how's that?" I ask, my chin still propped on my arm as I stare up at those weepy eyes and try not to get all weirdly protective and shit. After all, who would I be protecting her from? Myself? "Because all I see is a tough ass chick who's willing to do whatever it takes to survive."

"You don't see a whore?" she asks, like she finds that hard to believe.

"You're not a whore," I say, and the words come out angrier than I intended. Whoa there, Zay, gettin' all deep and shit all of a sudden. This isn't me. I like to keep things light and fluffy and easy. This is all *so* fucking heavy. I'm finding it hard to breathe right now. "I didn't see anything up on that stage that was less than worthy, Brooke."

She closes her eyes and tilts her head back against the couch, the matte black of the ceiling painted with fake stars. It reminds me of last night, of having her arching above me as I gazed up at Brooke's beautiful face silhouetted against the night sky.

"They want me to start giving lap dances tonight," she says, and I feel a visible shiver go down her spine. "The manager told me I didn't have to at first, but now he's saying some of his best regulars are interested in me. He kind of insinuated I do it or get fired."

I sit back on my heels and try to breathe. Who the hell am I to tell Brooke what to do? What I want to say is *grab your shit and let's bail.* But then what? Does that make me responsible for whatever happens to her and the kids? What if she drops out of school or something because she can't find another gig?

"He can't do that," I tell her and she shrugs as she sits up. "It's fucking illegal as hell."

"So? He'll just deny he ever said it. California's an at-will state anyway. He can just fire me and pretend it had nothing to do with the lap dances." Brooke glances away as I stand up and reach down to touch her chin, encouraging her to look at me.

"Remember what I told you that first night? Don't do anything that compromises you, Brooke, that makes you feel like you're worth less than you are. I meant that. If you don't want to do this, don't."

"I feel like I don't have a choice," she whispers as she leans forward, and I realize this is about more than just the job or the lap dances, this is about me and the kids and her sister and this stupid fucking Podunk town. It's everything coming together in one angry mass. "I can't do this. I'm only twenty-two. Bella and I are only fifteen years apart. How am I supposed to parent her when I'm not even sure how to be an adult myself?"

Tears start to bead on Brooke's lashes as I flop my body

BAD NANNY

onto the sofa and pull her against me for an old fashioned Zayden Roth snuggle. From what I hear, I'm pretty good at these although I don't hand 'em out often.

"You're a good snuggler," Brooke sniffles out beneath my chin, her head tucked there like this is where she belongs. "This feels so good."

"Yeah, well, keep that shit to yourself, okay? Word gets out and all the women in this club will be paying *me* to take them back here."

Brooke laughs a little as I rub a hand in a smooth circle on her back, the smell of her hair and perfume invading my senses and finding their way straight down to my dick. I feel so goddamn guilty, but I can't help but be turned on with her sitting on my lap like this. The midriff shirt, the miniskirt, and the glitter don't exactly help.

I am *suuuuuch* a goddamn piece of shit.

"Zayden," she whispers as she sits up and looks me in the face, her makeup smeared and sitting on this dangerous edge between sexy and cute.

Awwwwww, man.

I am screwed.

Completely and utterly screwed.

I reach my hands up and place them on either side of Brooke's throat as she sighs and spreads her knees just a little wider, settling the warmth of her pussy right over the bulge in my slacks. I bring her face to mine for a kiss, dominating the action with my hungry mouth and drawing a whimper from her throat. She's vulnerable right now, and I shouldn't be doing this but ... Brooke rocks her hips against me and I feel a jolt of wild energy that's nearly impossible to control. Unless she tells me no, this is happening.

My hands hold Brooke's face in a firm but gentle grip, keeping her chin tilted up, her eyes focused on mine as she starts to move against me, giving me one of those lap dances she's so scared of. But guess what? *I* don't have to keep my hands on the damn armrests. Instead, I slide them down to Brooke's shoulders and then trail my fingertips over her arms.

She shivers and then lifts them up, putting her hands behind my neck as she works my body like she's been doing this for years. Must be instinct. Pure fucking instinct.

I kiss the glitter off Brooke's chest before my hands slide up her belly and under that ridiculously sexy half-shirt, finding her tits encased in a lacy bra. I pop one breast over the wire and shove the t-shirt out of my way to get access to the pebbled pink point of her nipple.

She tastes sweet, clean and soapy, but also a little bit like salt from the sweat of her performance. If I wasn't already about to blow my load ... eh, I'm actually pretty much there already.

"Holy shit, Brooke," I have to lean back and drop my hands to her hips, trying to slow her movements before I finish in my slacks. "If you don't stop that—" She cuts me off with a moan, putting her hand over my mouth as she arches her back and presses her breasts against my chest.

Watching her use me to get off like that?

Turns. Me. The. Fuck. *On.*

I flip Brooke over onto the tufted leather sofa, shoving her skirt up as I dig in the pocket of my suit jacket for a condom. They spill out and over the floor as I snatch one and put it on with record speed—record fucking speed, baby.

There's no time to take Brooke's thong off, so I just shove the piece of flimsy fabric aside and bury myself deep into her with a hard thrust. Her raw scream of pleasure drives me forward without mercy, burying myself all the way to the hilt with each movement. My piercings are hitting all the right places in this position, teasing her G-spot, turning that face of hers as pink as her eyeshadow.

"Oh yeah, Brooke, baby, take me over the edge."

"Zay ... den," she starts, her lids fluttering as her body relaxes and her cunt tightens, fingers digging into my scalp, head thrown back into a coil of chocolate dark hair. I cup Brooke's ass tight as I slide into her, watching her expression change from bliss to beautiful anguish. Her orgasm kicks my butt straight to the curb, and I can't hold on a second longer,

BAD NANNY

collapsing on top of her with a pretty ridiculous sounding grunt.

I sound like a fucking wildebeest or something.

But holy hell, it's hot. It's so hot. And I'm not done.

"Brooke," I start as we both freeze at the sound of a knock on the door. We exchange a look as she shoves me off of her and stands up, fixing her tits and stumbling over to the door to open it a crack.

"Nigel," she says as she leans out the crack. "What?"

The man outside yanks the door open and finds me stuffing my cock back into my slacks, a used condom tucked in my other hand. I know, it's gross, but what else am I gonna do with it? Leave it on the floor like some fucked up club customer? No thanks. I'll dispose of my own baby juice, alright?

"What the hell is going on back here?" *Like he doesn't already know.* I raise my eyebrow as I come up to the door and grab hold of it, pushing it open wider so I can stand there and give the short brunette dude a look. People seem to think because I smile and laugh all the time that I'm not really much of a threat. The thing is, I *really* am six three and I really do workout, sooooo ... I can kind of kick a lot of people's asses.

"You're the manager?" I start as the guy gives me a weird look, eyeing my outfit like he's not from Humboldt County and hasn't seen this shit before. "You're the one trying to force Brooke into doing lap dances?"

"Zayden," Brooke snaps at me, her brown eyes narrowed, but her breath still coming in panting flutters that mimic the movement of her muscles as she caressed and held my cock tight inside of her. I look at her for a minute and then turn back to the manager. "Don't," Brooke warns, but I can't help it. I'm so ... riled up right now.

"Brooke doesn't need this shitty fucking job or your bad fucking attitude." I take a step forward, but notice the bouncer waiting in the hall behind the small man. Shit. That guy's a little, um, huge? Anyway, I don't plan on actually touching the manager. Punching the asshole dad at the mall was bad enough; I'm just lucky he didn't sustain any permanent injuries or I'd have the cops looking for me.

"I see," the man says as he looks over at Brooke. "Is that the case? Are you done here? After I gave you a second chance?"

"I—" Brooke starts, but I'm reaching down and taking her wrist, pulling her into the hallway only to find the bouncer dude blocking us in.

"Uh," I reach up and scratch at the purple stars on the side of my head. "Can you, like, move maybe?"

"Brooke," the man asks as he peers around me. "Do you want to leave with this man?"

"I, uh," she start and then nods her head in a decisive motion. "Yeah, yeah, I do."

The bouncer gives her a long, studying look before he steps aside.

"If you leave right now, you're done here. You're fired," the manager says from behind us. I pause there and turn to look down at Brooke, my hands shaking with emotion. I stuff them in my pockets to still them. She stares back up at me for a long moment, searching my face for something. I guess whatever she's looking for, she sees, turning back to look at the manager of the Top Hat Gentlemen's Club with pursed lips.

"Okay. I understand," she says and then turns back to take my hand, dragging *me* down the hallway this time.

I have to go outside and come around the back to wait for her outside the dressing room, pacing in a tight line, raking my fingers through my hair as emotions war inside my chest.

I just took Brooke's job away. Because I'm a selfish dick.

"Ahhhh." I drag my hands down my face and drop them at my sides. What if she ... she might take this the wrong way or something. And it'll be all my fault. Why did I go charging in there like a bull in a china shop, messing up everything like I always do? "This is ... this is not good."

I kick a pebble with my purple Docs and suck in a deep breath, shoulders rising and falling with the motion.

"I'm ready," Brooke says as I turn around to face her. For a second there she's limned in gold light from inside the building, her silhouette a sexy, curvy shadow against the brightness. When the heavy metal door slams shut, and my eyes start to adjust to the darkness, I get a glimpse of her face. There's a quiet hopefulness there, a gentle smile, a smothering sense of relief. "We can take the van together, and you can drop me off here in the morning to get my car."

"Maybe we should just drive separately?" I say and then hate myself for it. "I've got to get over to the duplex in the morning and clean stuff up for Rob and Mercedes." I shrug my shoulders, but it's a seriously lame excuse. Like spending an extra twenty minutes to get over here in the morning would affect my schedule.

I want you.

That's what I should be saying.

Move to Vegas with me.

Too selfish. Brooke *just* changed schools midyear, and I want her to do it again? Provided there's any school around Las Vegas that actually has a biostatistics program. Heh. Doubtful.

"Are you ... upset with me?" Brooke asks, moving over to stand next to me in her half-shirt and her black mini. "Because ... you just stormed into my job, fucked me in the back room, and then told my manager to eat shit."

"It needed to be said. What kind of seedy motherfucker tries to force girls into giving lap dances?"

"I ... you ... don't you want to be with me?" Brooke asks, blinking long lashes. Even in her thick makeup, she looks fresh-faced and adorable and way too young for me. I shove my hands through my hair. "Isn't that why you came here tonight?"

"Brooke," I start, and I sound anguished when I say her name. The worst part about it all is that I know *I'm* the source of my own suffering. I fucking *know* that and yet I'm panicking here, acting exactly like my buddies back at the shop, the ones I make fun of all the time. "I've been trying to tell you that I like you, but that we can't work out. I've said it before. Why would it be different tonight?"

"This job was my lifeline, Zayden. What if I can't get another? What if I have to drop out of school?"

"You thought I came here tonight to say I was going to support you? I wish I could. If I had any money ... shit, things might be different. I'm living off my credit card now, Brooke. This two weeks has killed me. I have a *mortgage*, on a place I bought with the last gift my parents ever gave me. There are no jobs up here in this shit hole, you know that."

Her lips purse tight.

"Exactly," she says, and I realize what I've just said. "And no, I didn't think you were just going to sweep in and make everything better. I've seen your car, Zayden. I know you're not a rich man. I just thought ... I thought you were going to stick around for a while, help me find another job or something. I thought ... this was our romantic climax."

She lifts her hand up to indicate the round shape of the club's building and the neon pink lights that are staining the dark wet pavement with bright color.

"It felt like you were coming here to confess or something," she adds, and I feel my face fall. "I am such a *fucking* idiot." Her gaze snaps up to mine. "I knew I shouldn't let myself get involved with you, but ... you pushed and pushed and ... even tonight, why couldn't you just leave me alone? Now what am I supposed to do?" Brooke pauses and takes a deep breath. "You're really leaving tomorrow?"

I swallow hard and rake my fingers through my hair again.

I wish I was better with words, wish I could explain all the things I was feeling to her.

"I'll ruin your life, Brooke. I'm not the man of your dreams. I'm just some asshole from Vegas." I smile at her, but it doesn't feel real. Feels like bullshit to me. "I'm just the nanny, right?"

"Yeah, whatever." Brooke's voice sounds unstable, but when I take a step towards her, she moves away.

"Your aunt's got the kids covered for a while. We could go out and have some food? Try a little more exhibitionism. What do you say?" I make myself grin at her, but her face stays flat, her pale eyes dark and shadowed.

BAD NANNY

"Sorry, Zayden, but you can't goof your way out of this one. You know what? Why don't you go back to my place, pick up your kids, and go home. We're, uh," Brooke starts as she begins to back away towards her Subaru, "we're done here. Yeah, yeah. We're done." She stops after a few steps, a bag of clothes slung over one arm, and points a shaking finger at me. "I was okay with this being casual, but you pushed into my boundaries. *You* chased after me. And I hate being dicked around."

Brooke turns and climbs in her car as I pace in a tight circle and run my hand over my face. I have no clue what to do. In the back of my mind, I realize how goddamn easy this all is. I basically have two choices: go home tomorrow and forget about this, or ... stay.

Because I *could* stay if I really wanted to. Yeah, it'd be hard, but ... is Brooke Overland worth it?

The answer to that is easy. Sure she is. Of *course* she is.

I stand there on the wet pavement as her car zooms around me and splatters my slacks with dirty water. As I turn and watch her red taillights disappear into traffic, I decide it's time to head out and find somewhere to grab a drink.

Because I need to really think about this. Changing my whole life for a girl I've known for two weeks?

How is that any different from changing your whole life for two kids that aren't yours?

Whatever happens, I know this to be a fact: Brooke Overland is a hell of a lot stronger than I am.

CHAPTER 26
BROOKE OVERLAND

Even my angriest metal music can't help me. A cascading fall of guitar riffs and clattering drums can't take the shock of pain and anger away. I scream the lyrics along with the lead singer until my voice is gone and my throat hurts, but it makes no difference.

I am fucking *livid*. And sad. Really, really sad. I feel like this is the thing with Anthony all over again. Obviously, it's a very different scenario, but I see parallels here that bother me more than I care to admit. Anthony said he wanted me to be his perfect wife, but all he really wanted was a showpiece for his parents, somebody on his arm to play the good Christian with him.

Zayden … I invited Zayden into my bed and into my life, but he was the one that kept pushing my boundaries, weaseling his way into my heart. He said he was only up for a casual fling, but what he really did was charm the hell out of me.

So one guy says he wants me but doesn't and the other says he doesn't but clearly does.

"This is so shitty," I say as I pull up to a Dutch Bros and grab some coffee. Now that I don't have a job, I probably shouldn't spend the money, but screw it. I need this right now.

I pull over a few blocks away to take the lid off and blow

steam away from the dark liquid. Out of habit, I pick up my phone and check for messages. Several from my friends back in Berkeley, the sight of the familiar names in my contacts sending a pang of loneliness through me.

So how could I blame Zayden for not wanting to stay here with me? He hates this town as much as I do, and he's right: there are hardly any jobs here. His friends are back in Las Vegas. Hell, he *owns* his own place. And if I'm having this much trouble changing my whole existence for two girls that are my own flesh and blood, how can I expect some playboy dude to do the same?

I test my coffee and then put the lid back on, pausing for a moment as I take a sip. I want to go home and curl up on my bed, but at the same time, I *don't* want to go home. The thought of Zayden leaving turns my insides into this gaping, yawning hole. If I have to head back there and watch him pack his things ... I think I'll go crazy.

I put my coffee in the cup holder and start up my car, deciding to head over to my parents' place. I have the keys, and I'm supposed to water the houseplants anyway. I haven't done it once in the last two weeks, but oh well. I had more important things to worry about.

Like losing my virginity.

I cringe as I pull back onto the street and head towards Wildwood Community Park, a fancy name for the gated old folks neighborhood that my parents live in. They had me when my mother was forty-three, so even though it doesn't feel like they should live in a place like Wildwood, they do. Yet *another* reason why my parents couldn't take care of the kids; nobody under age eighteen is allowed to live on the premises.

I pull up to the front gate and key in my parents' code, heading over to their perfect oil spot free driveway and the manicured yard that the homeowners' association takes care of. When I get out and let myself inside, the quiet darkness settles over me and I take a deep breath, tossing my purse onto the counter and moving over to the couch to lie down.

Without realizing I'm doing it, I slide my phone from my

pocket and look at my texts for any messages from Zayden. Once it dawns on me that I'm doing it, I delete his number from my phone and put the damn thing away.

Hopefully he'll be gone when I get home tomorrow morning.

Hopefully he'll still be there when I get home tomorrow morning.

I sigh as the dueling thoughts fill my brain, turning onto my back and putting my forearms against my forehead as I listen to the almost disturbing silence of the neighborhood. When I close my eyes, the scene from the club replays over and over again on the screen of my eyelids.

As soon as I saw Zay in the darkness beyond the stage, I … I don't know what I felt, but it was powerful. And emotional. And so intense I could barely breathe.

"Crap." I put my hands over my face and try to think about all this in a logical way. It's best that Zayden goes home, really. I have a degree and two little girls and an ailing father to worry about. I don't need a man in my life. No way, no how.

But I want one. No, no, I want *this* one.

I take several deep breaths and let the pain of the evening wash over me. It's stifling, ten times as intense as the emotions I felt when I caught Anthony cheating on me. And I was with him for *three* years. Three years of hanging out and laughing and going to parties and restaurants, snuggling on the couch.

Two weeks with Zayden and it feels like his heart should beat in tune with mine. The sex part aside, I *love* hanging out with him. And I love the way he is with my nieces, with his own. He's the kind of guy that actually makes me want to have kids sooner, just so I can see him snuggle and kiss and play with them.

But if he doesn't want me, what can I do? I gave him a chance tonight and all he did was cost me my job. Now I'm back at square one.

Alone. Jobless. Screwed.

And in love.

BAD NANNY

I blink awake to bright sunshine, looking confusedly around at my parents' white and beige living room before I realize where I am.

Oh.

Strip club. Fight with Zayden. Last day. Last day and he's gone ...

My breath sucks in sharply and I surge to my feet, tearing my phone from my back pocket and checking for messages. There're about a hundred from him, asking me where I am, if I'm safe, threatening to call the cops.

I almost smile, but then the expression fades.

I slept through my class. Shit. Now I have *just* enough time to get back to my place before Zayden leaves to pick up the kids. After that, he'll drop them off with me and then ... drive away in his Geo and never come back.

Tears prickle the edges of my eyes, but I dash them away, heading outside and locking the door behind me as quick as I can. I feel so desperate to see him suddenly that it's like I'm choking on the emotion. I'm sure it won't change anything, but I just want to see his face, maybe give him one last kiss, feel his hands on my body for a brief second.

"Crap, crap, crap," I mumble as I sprint to the car and climb in, peeling out of there at a speed that'd probably give most of the old people living here heart attacks. In all reality, I should probably stay *away* from Zayden until he brings the girls home from school. He's due at the airport right after that, so he won't have any time to mess with my head, play around with my emotions, smile that goofy sexy smile at me.

I speed all the way home; it's a miracle I don't get a ticket.

When I get there, Zay's just finishing putting Sadie in her car seat, running his fingers through his hair. It's not styled at all today, the long side hanging messily over his forehead. He's wearing those knee-high Converse with the buckles, and a black shirt that says *Body Piercer, Baby* on it.

As soon as he sees me pull into the driveway, this rush of relief crowds his features and then he's just at my door, yanking it open wide and pulling me out and into his arms.

"Jesus fucking Christ, Brooke," Zay groans as he squeezes me hard enough to choke the life out of me. I don't want to admit how good it feels, how much I hate the things he said last night but still feel like forgiving him. "Where the hell were you?" he asks as he pushes me a step back and takes hold of my upper arms. "I called the police and everything. Fuckers said they couldn't do shit until you'd been missing some arbitrary fucking amount of fucking time."

"You're saying *fuck* a lot," I whisper, but the way his sea glass green eyes trace over my body makes me shiver. "I stayed at my parents' place last night. I just ... didn't want to be here with you." He lets go of me with a sigh and checks the time on his phone. He *really* needs to go or he'll be late to pick up Grace.

"Want to come with me? We can talk on the drive."

I shake my head and take a step away from him.

"Are you still planning on leaving today?" I ask as I look up at Zayden. He purses his lips so tight that the silver pointed studs he's wearing today poke out at me like swords. "I'll take that as a yes."

I try to move past him, but he reaches out again and gently grabs my elbow.

"I've been thinking about this all night ... and it ... I'll ruin your life, Brooke. I know I will. You have *so* much fucking potential. There's so much more for you out there than me."

"Whatever." I jerk my arm away from him and storm towards the front door. Part of me believes what he's saying, knows that this is the logical, smart choice to make. But it also sucks. And I hate it. And I want somebody that will choose *me* for me, that wants to be with me because I make them smile. If I'm not enough for Zayden to take a chance on, then that's okay. I can do this.

I feel tears dripping down my cheeks and move quicker when Zay's boots chase after me. I end up getting inside and slamming the front door before he can reach me, flicking the lock and turning to put my back against it.

"Come on, Brooke," he says as he tries the knob and then peers in the window at me. "Don't do this. Come with me. We should talk."

"Don't make Grace wait in the office with the principal; she hates that," I say and manage to keep the quiver out of my voice. When I look around the room, I see Dodger sitting on the couch, but all of the chihuahuas missing. Zayden's duffel bag is gone and so is Sadie's crib.

I bite my lower lip and close my eyes, leaning my head back against the door.

"Can we talk when I get back?" he asks, putting his hands against the glass and leaning his cheek against it.

I stand up suddenly and yank the door open, turning to face Zayden with my arms over my chest. My hair gets in my way and I shove it hard over my shoulder, blinking my salt soaked and sticky contact lenses at Zayden.

"Aw, Smarty-Pants," he says, and the soft sound of his voice and the adorable way he wears suspenders stuck to his tight jeans makes me crazy. I want to kiss him and punch him both at the same time. "Don't get all weepy again, or I won't be able to—"

"To leave?" I ask as he takes a few steps closer to me and then pauses as Sadie starts to cry from inside the open van. I gesture my hand at the car. "You can't just leave the baby in there," I say as he studies me with a careful expression and then rakes his fingers through his messy hair. "It's okay that you want to go back to Las Vegas," I lie, "I would, too, but you've got to just go. Leave me alone, alright. I'll be fine. I always take care of myself, and I always excel. What should make this any different?"

"You know, I'm just a phone call away if you need to talk. You have my number and—"

"I deleted it. Best to make a clean cut," I tell him as I dash the tears away and then cross my arms over my chest. I guess I'm being melodramatic here, but what else is there to do? I want him to want to stay *so fucking badly,* but I can't and won't beg for scraps.

"Brooke, I really … I do like you. A lot. I mean, I'm crushing hard here, Smarty-Pants. This isn't easy for me either."

"You can't or won't try anything with me, but you date girls that you hate. I understand. Zayden, you need to go. If you're not staying, then fucking *go.*"

I turn and head into the house, expecting him to follow.

When I hear the sound of the minivan starting, I feel the tears start to flow again.

Here I am, alone again. In my sister's house with my sister's kids.

Guess I better get used to it.

CHAPTER 27
ZAYDEN ROTH

Brooke's tears devastate me.

Like, break me into pieces and turn me raw all the way down to the core. *What are you doing, man?* I ask myself as I head to the airport with four screaming kids and a cluster of barking chihuahuas. I should probably intervene and try to do something about Kinzie and the twins, but I'm all up in my own head and I can't think straight.

When I dropped Grace and Bella off, Brooke wouldn't even come out of her room. As much as my heart wants me to stick around and badger her to come out, I have to leave now or I won't make it to the airport. No, no, hell if I didn't leave when I did, I'd probably never go. I'd move up here and let my condo go into foreclosure and I'd stick around and be Brooke's nanny forever.

"Jesus cocksucking ball fucker," I mumble, thinking the Daya song that's playing in the background will cover up my colorful expletives.

"Curse jar!" Kinzie screams, just full on belts out like a banshee. I reach up and turn the volume off on the stereo.

"Okay, that's it. I've had *enough*," I growl the word out loud enough that Kinzie stops screeching, the twins stop arguing, and even the chihuahuas go quiet. "Your mom and dad are gonna be tired after their trip, got it? I don't want to hear any nonsense or any fighting or crying or yelling. If you want to say something, think of something nice."

"You stole that from *Bambi*," Kinzie accuses, and I toss her a caustic glare in the rearview. A few seconds later, "I don't *really* think you're going to the H-place." I almost smile at that one. "And I don't hate you as much now."

"Good. Because I don't hate you either. Might even love you a little bit, kid. You cool with that?"

She nods at me and I turn the song back on, trying to drown thoughts of Brooke out by interacting with the kids. Even Sadie calms down and stops crying when I start singing about *looking pretty* with the pop star on my iPod.

The Arcata-Eureka airport is this dinky ass building in the middle of nowhere with *one* gate and a tiny café that serves as a restaurant. It has like, one flight a day in a shaky old puddle jumper that goes to San Francisco and comes back. That's basically it.

When we get there, it's easy as fuck to find parking because, well, there are like a hundred spaces and pretty much nobody in them. Calling this place an *airport* would be like calling a garage sale a mall.

Anyway, I'm grateful for it as I roll the van windows down a crack for the dogs and make the older kids put their hands on the stroller.

"On your best behavior or the time wizard will come and get you."

"What's a time wizard?" Kinzie asks scrunching up her face as we make our way to the front of the building.

"It's a monster made of toothpicks who eats kids that waste time. Now, put on some pretty smiles for your parents, okay? And try not to tell them about the torture chamber."

There's a laugh as Mercedes comes around the corner and then squeals, throwing her arms out and getting pummeled with a herd of children. Rob does his gruff, disinterested lumberjack stance in the background, but I see tears pooling in his gaze and

BAD NANNY

roll my eyes.

"I can't believe they're still alive," he tries to joke, but it comes out all stuffy and garbled as he picks Sadie up from the stroller and hugs her to his chest like he's been gone for years instead of weeks. As I watch my brother pull his wife and kids in for a hug, I get this ... weird feeling in my chest, this horrible pounding grind that takes my breath away.

I watch almost jealously as Mercedes and Rob snuggle their baby together.

Fuck, I want that. I want it so goddamn bad in that moment that it feels like I'm gonna puke.

My hands clench into fists, and I find it suddenly hard to breathe when I think of Brooke. *No, no, no.* She's twenty-two and she's going places and she has way too much shit in her life for me. Maybe this is just a sign that I'm ready to start a family? I should go home and start taking dating more seriously, look for a woman who's closer to my own age, have a baby or something.

"Jesus fuck," I murmur as I run my hand over my face and try not to freak out.

"Aunt Brooke got me this," Kinzie states proudly as she shows off a *Monster High* shirt that Brooke bought for her. She bought a matching one for Bella, too, to try and cut off their weird rivalry bullshit. It worked for about a day, but hey, better than nothing.

"Aunt ... Brooke?" Mercedes asks, looking up at me with a raised eyebrow. "Zayden ..."

Rob gives me this kind of creepy death glare, like he's convinced I had his kids hanging out with some hooker I picked up on Second Street.

"Brooke and Zayden lick each other's private parts in the shower," Kinzie tells them confidently, and I feel the blood drain out of my face.

"You son of a bitch," Rob snarls as Kinzie starts calling out *curse jar, curse jar.*

"Whoa, whoa, whoa," I say as I back up and put my palms out. "It wasn't us that she saw; it was you and Mercedes. She's just putting stories together. She thinks that's what couples do now, I guess."

Mercedes and Rob exchange a look before my brother turns back to glare at me, clutching Sadie to his side with a giant, muscular arm the size of a tree trunk.

"You have got a ton of explaining to do," he whispers as he walks by me and I roll my eyes. That fucker's thought he was my dad since he turned twelve. If he thinks I'm going to stick around and listen to his lectures, he's got another thing coming.

I feel stifled suddenly, desperate to get the hell out of here, like if I don't leave Eureka *now*, I'll never escape. I waited my whole life to leave this place and I finally did, finally found someplace where I could be happy.

If I stay for Brooke, we'll have a few blissful weeks and then everything will just fall to shit like it always does. I know that, *know* it and yet I'm finding it almost impossible to leave.

I push the empty stroller behind Mercedes as she lets the kids babble to her about all the things we've done while they were gone. You know, like how I filled the curse jar to the brim, punched a guy out at the mall, and had us permanently living with my new girlfriend.

Oh, and also how there's a banshee that lives at Brooke's house, one who sounds like a screaming woman in the middle of the night.

That's always fun.

Rob makes me drive the van to the house so he can sit in the backseat with his kids.

Mercedes sits in the front though and keeps looking at me with a raised eyebrow as we drive back to the duplex.

"This girl," she starts and I stick out my tongue at her.

"Nope. Nuh uh. Don't want to go there," I tell her as some god-awful kids' music plays in the background, keeping our conversation relatively private from my brother.

"Zayden," she begins, using this big sister voice on me that always makes me laugh since we're pretty much the exact same age. Maybe she picked it up from being a mother? "I know you, and I have *never* seen you like this before."

"You hardly ever *see* me," I joke as we head down the highway, past the ocean and the waving sea grasses. "Mostly we just talk on the mic during raids. Hey, did you know that expansion pack came out last week?"

"Don't do that," she tells me, shaking her head and reaching her hands up to brush back her wild curls. "Don't pretend that you're fine, try to cover up a wound with a bandage. It doesn't ever work, baby."

"When you call me that, it makes me feel like I'm ten. Can we please not? This conversation is pointless."

"Do you need somewhere to stay for a few days while you work things out? Is your girlfriend mad at you?"

"Brooke's not my girlfriend," I say, but it feels like she is. That same weird male possessive bullshit that I felt the other day comes raining over me like a tidal wave about to strike. "Basically, I'm dropping you guys off and Hubert and I," I reach down to pat the cat's kennel between the two front seats, "are going back to the desert. I don't know if you know it, but I like, haven't worked in two weeks and I'm pretty much down to zero in the money department."

"I know," she says, turning towards me and reaching out a hand for my knee. Mercedes gives it a little squeeze. "And I'm so thankful, Zay. Really, I am." Her eyes get all teary and I can't help but roll mine. Damn it. Such a sucker for pretty girls in distress. *Like Brooke.* I purse my lips and keep my eyes on the road. "It's nice to know there's somebody out there we can count on, you know?"

"Yup. Any time. Although hopefully not anytime soon because I'm dead broke."

Mercedes laughs and then turns to look at Kinzie as the kid starts in on a tale of "dogging" between Dodger and the chihuahuas. Yet another highlight of the past two weeks.

But I find myself smiling anyway because even though I thought this whole thing was going to be miserable and even though at times, it *was* kind of miserable, it was also kind of awesome, too, in it's own way.

Or maybe that was just Brooke?

Mercedes and Kinzie cry when I get in my shitty old Geo to leave, while Rob glares at me. Again, I don't take it personally because I can see tears shimmering in his eyes as I pull out of the driveway and Hubert starts to yowl. Believe it or not, this is actually our *second* time trying to get the fuck out of here but the first time, the damn cat took a dump before I got halfway down the block. I had to turn around and clean his kennel out, bathe him, and put on a fresh sweater that says *Total Feminist* on the back of it.

I crank up my pop music as I hit the highway going south, my heart thundering a million miles an hour in my chest as I start to put distance between Brooke and me, between her awesome girls and me, between a possibility of something I've never even glimpsed in my entire life and me.

"Shit, no way. No, no, no, Zayden," I growl as I shove hair off my forehead and try to keep my attention focused out the windshield. No matter how hard I try though, I seriously cannot stop thinking about Brooke.

I start laying my reasons for leaving out again in my head. *No money, no job, my condo, my friends, my lifestyle, Brooke's age, her inexperience, the two kids that she has.*

And then I start feeling like, um, I'm a goddamn fucking mental patient.

A hot young girl who's smart as shit, who's trying her goddamn hardest to make a shitty situation work, basically told me she has a thing for me, a thing that I think *I* actually feel ten times harder than she does and yet, I'm bailing?

BAD NANNY

Is this the kind of person that I am? Is this who I want to be?

I pull the car over to the side of the road and take a deep breath, climbing out and putting my hands on my lower back while I pace in a circle and try to stop the sudden wave of panic washing over me. It's dark now, but there's not much traffic on this part of the highway, so I get a nice, long, dark moment to think by myself.

"Holy sweet baby Jesus, Hubert," I say as I squat and look across the front seat into the passenger side of the car where my stupid hairless cat sits crouched in his kennel. He hisses at me, glaring with white-green eyes. "I'm such a *fucking* moron." I stand up straight and dig my phone out, pressing call on Brooke's number and waiting anxiously, bouncing up onto my toes as I curse under my breath.

When her voicemail pops up, I start chattering.

"Airbnb." That's the first thing I say which probably sounds dumb because come on, who opens up a … love confession? is this a love confession? … to somebody by mentioning a website where people rent out rooms and houses and shit. But to me, it makes perfect sense. I'll just put my condo on Airbnb, charge a ridiculous amount of rent to tourists who want to *live like locals* while they're in town. Of course, I'll probably get my shit stolen and the place burned down, but … hell. Hell, hell, hell. "That's what I'll do," I tell Brooke's voicemail, praying she actually listens to hers. I know Jude leaves his voicemail full on purpose so he doesn't have to get any new ones or bother listening to them. "I'll rent out my place and I'll … I'll just hang out here for a while, if that's okay with you. I can even stay with my brother if you don't want me at your place."

I pause and take a deep breath, realizing that I'm basically making zero sense right now.

"Okay, look, just call me back, alright? I'll send you a text."

I shoot a quick message to Brooke, telling her I'm on my way, and then I hop right back in my car and make a ridiculously illegal u-turn.

Aaaaaand yeah, I get a ticket—the cop looks at me like I'm crazy when I lay out my nutty romantic love story—but that's okay because Brooke's worth it. Totally fucking worth it.

Brooke's car is missing from the driveway when I pull up in my stuttering, janky ass Geo, climbing out and heading to the door to find Monica waiting with pursed lips.

"She's not here. She has work, remember? It was *you* that roped me into babysitting duties in the first place."

I stare at the woman and I ... kind of want to punch her in the face, but then, I don't hit chicks, even rich old ones who let their nieces drop out of a prestigious university program to come back to this shit hole town to take care of a pair of kids.

"Right, right. My bad," I say, not wanting to tell Monica that I got her niece fired from a strip club last night. "I'll, uh, try back later." I give the woman a flirty wink that makes her nose crinkle and turn on my heel, trying not to run back to my car as I go.

I don't know why, but I feel frantic, full to fucking bursting.

You're in love, bro.

I skid to a stop next to the Geo, opening the door and leaning my hand on the roof as the smell of fresh cat urine—thanks Hubert—wafts out and around me. It's not all that romantic standing there with the neighbor across the street glaring at me, and the cat hissing, and the old car's engine ticking, but it is what it is.

I'm in love.

Love.

Mother Mary help me out here.

I breathe out in a long, hard whoosh and climb in, not entirely sure where it is that I'm going. After all, Brooke's only been back in town as long as I have, and we've both been busy. It's not like either of us has had time to develop local haunts.

But then it just hits me, like a football thrown by the NFL's future first woman QB to the back of the head.

The park.

Brooke's got to be at the park.

CHAPTER 28
BROOKE OVERLAND

I'd completely forgotten about Zayden arranging a babysitting appointment with Monica, so when she showed up with pursed lips on my doorstep and glared at my drippy eyes and runny nose with complete and utter disinterest, I just grabbed my purse and left.

Of course, I barely have enough money to cover rent, utilities and food this month. If I still had my job, maybe I'd go out and treat myself to a burger or something, maybe even a beer. At least I'd grab a scoop at that ice cream place in old town where I went with Zayden.

As things stand, I don't have that luxury, so I head to the park where I first met the asshole.

Yeah, I'm a sucker for punishment, I guess.

It's dark when I get there, of course, but across the street at the park, there's a softball game, bright white lights illuminating the field and giving me something to look at as I swing slowly back and forth, my feet dragging in the wood chips.

I think I've just about cried myself out for today. For a few hours, I convinced myself that he'd come back, but he never showed. And then Monica was suddenly there and it became too real.

BAD NANNY

Zayden is gone. He left.

I know I shouldn't be surprised because seriously, we've only known each other for two weeks, but I felt something, and I know he did, too. *It means something, but it doesn't change anything.*

Guess he was right.

I'm crushing hard here, Smarty-Pants.

Gah. I can't think like that, can't let my mind keep repeating all of the things that he said. So what? Zayden will be a page in my history book and that's about it.

My hands squeeze tight around the chains of the swing as my body sways back and forth and I let my eyes slide closed, skin prickling at the memory of his warmth, his mouth pressed against my throat, his body pushing inside of mine.

"Fuck."

I open my eyes and make myself focus on the game, on the crack of the bat and the cheering of the small crowd. I think it's the local adult softball league over there, but the people watching must be dedicated if I can hear them shouting from all the way over here.

The rattle of a car pulling into one of the spaces behind me, draws my attention. This park has been known to have its fair share of weirdos and bums at night, and I'm not about to end a crappy day with an even crappier mugging.

The sound of a car door opening is followed by an inhuman scream, like some sort of dying animal in the safari, one that's being torn apart by a lion.

My head whips around to find Zayden climbing out of his Geo, leaning in to shush … someone. Hubert maybe?

My breath catches and my heart starts to thunder as I whip my head back around and stare into the darkness of the forest. *Oh shit, oh shit, oh shit.* What the hell is he doing here?

"Smarty-Pants," Zayden says, jogging up to me and coming around to the front of the swings to bend down. He's panting and he looks both excited and nervous as hell.

I feel like I'm about to throw up on his shoes.

Zayden puts his hands on his knees and tilts his head to the side, his hair a floppy mess. But even from here I can smell that blackberry and cinnamon scent of his.

My eyes open wide, wide, wide in an attempt not to cry again.

I try to play it cool.

"What do you want, Zayden?"

"Um, okay." He stands up straight and sucks in a deep breath, planting his hands on his hips. I hate how hot he looks all the time, those tattoos of his dancing down both arms in swirls of magnificent color. Even in the dark shadows of the park, I can see how goddamn pretty he is.

I watch with an aching heart as he slaps his palms together in a prayer position and puts his fingers to his lips, looking down at me with this weirdly tender expression.

"You're probably wondering what I'm doing here."

"Uh, yes. Yes, I am," I tell him as I continue to swing and fight back the sudden surges of emotion. I'm not sure if I should be happy or sad or pissed or all of the above. "Why aren't you on your way back to Vegas?"

"Well, see, that's a funny story." He sits down suddenly, crossing his legs and putting a hand on either knee as he settles into the wood chips. "I actually *was* on my way to Las Vegas, you see."

I cock an eyebrow and glance over my shoulder. I can still vaguely hear Hubert yowling.

"We got about, um, two hours out? And then we turned right back around. I tried to call and text you, but …"

"I blocked you," I say as I look back at him. "After you dropped the girls off. I don't think I can handle an occasional *hey, how are you,* Zayden. I'm sorry, but I don't want that."

"Yup, yup. I get it, Brooke. Oh God, I have so much to say. I just want to start babbling, but hell, I guess I better ask this first: can I stay at your place for a while?" He smiles as he asks this and I stop swinging, listening to another roaring scream from the crowd across the street. Next to the park, one of the town's water towers sits, the lot fenced off and filled with … goats. Yep. And that's one hundred percent truth right there

BAD NANNY

(come visit us in Eureka, CA and see for yourself). The goats make weird ... whatever you call goat noises as I stare down at Zayden.

"Stay at my place?" I echo as I try to figure out what's happening. He plays with his lip rings, using his tongue to slide them in and out of the holes. Aaaaand that was imagery I so did not need. "Why would you need to stay at my place?"

Zayden sucks in a deep breath.

"Airbnb," he says, and then I'm even more confused than I was before.

"Huh?" I reach up and start gathering the massive fall of my hair together, just to give my hands something to do. "Are you drunk or something?"

Zayden claps his hands over his face and makes a small sound of frustration, not at me though, at himself for sure.

"Okay, what I'm trying to say is, I'll rent my condo out on Airbnb."

"And ... why would you do that?"

"Brooke," he says, dropping his hands into his lap and looking up at me with an eager, open gaze. "At least for a little while, I'm staying here. In Eureka."

I blink at him.

"Did something happen with your brother?"

"No, silly Smarty-Pants, fuck." Zayden gets up on his knees and crawls toward me, pushing my own knees apart and getting in between them, grabbing onto the swing to keep me from swaying back. I should tell him not to touch me again, to leave me alone, but I just ... it feels really good to have him here. "I want to try this thing out between us. I got about two hours down the road before I realized what was wrong with me, why I was sweating and why my stomach hurt and why I had a god-fucking-awful headache."

"And why's that?" I have a hard time choking the words out as Zayden gives me one of his signature smirk-smiles.

"Because I'm suffering from a seriously nasty case of I.L."

"Um." I lean away from him and blink several times, some of my smarmy romantic swoon fading away. I was hoping maybe he was here to confess; instead he came to tell me he has an STD? "Is it contagious?"

Zayden tosses his head back and laughs, dropping his chin down and leaning in to press his face against the side of my neck. My body shivers without my permission as his hands curl around mine.

"I.L. stands for insta-love, you dope. I have no idea why because this has literally never happened to me before, but I'm, like, creepily obsessed with you."

I close my eyes and try to get a grip on my swirling thoughts.

"I don't understand," I whisper as Zayden leans back and lifts his hands up, cupping my face in that way of his that makes me crazy. I open my eyes and find him invading my personal space again, his own gaze way too close for comfort.

"What I'm trying to say, Brooke Overland, is that I want to be your nanny."

That's seriously the most romantic thing I've ever heard in my life.

"One second, 'kay," he says, standing up and jogging over to his car. I sit there in stunned silence as he opens the door and starts up some music.

It's Van Morrison's "Brown Eyed Girl" again.

I purse my lips together tight as Zayden appears in front of me.

"Please don't sing and dance," I whisper, but it's too late. He's snapping his fingers and doing this sexy groove to the music. It should look really stupid—and it kind of does—but with his tight abs and his tattoos and piercings, it's really just ... precious.

When he starts singing the words to me, I stand up suddenly and let the chains from the swing jangle behind me.

"You're ... in insta-love with me?" I repeat as Zayden pauses and nods, grinning nice and big as Hubert's yowls blend harmoniously into the music.

"Yep."

"And you're ... staying in Eureka ... for me?"

BAD NANNY

"Check and check, baby cakes," he says as he reaches out to touch me. I reach up to take his wrists, but all he does is twist my arms and grab me anyway, tugging me close. His grin turns a little softer, a little more tender as he rubs a thumb along the line of my jaw, leaving a trail of fire in his wake.

It's all so sexy and cute and romantic ... until the music changes to "In Da Club" by 50 Cent. Um. Yuck. *God, I hate this song.*

"Brooke, I'm ... sorry for the way I acted yesterday. It's not an excuse or nothin', but ..." Zayden pauses and looks into my eyes, his gaze searching deep. "I didn't expect to fall in love with you, and I sure as hell didn't expect it to scare me so much."

"You were awful yesterday," I tell him, and I mean that. "A mega dick."

"Godzilla sized dick," he agrees as he traces warm circles on my upper arms with his thumbs. He needs to hear how hurtful he was, how stupid he made me feel, what an ass he was. But later. Later because this is *my* romantic confession ... and I refuse to listen to rap or pop while it's happening.

"One second," I whisper, repeating his own words back at him as I dart to the car and use his iPod to start "The Air That I Breathe" by All That Remains. It's a nice, rough growling metal song that makes me feel all warm and fuzzy inside.

I jog back over to Zayden and pause in the wood chips facing him. He crinkles his nose up at my music, but he's still smiling.

"How long is a while?"

"Hmm?"

I put my hands on my hips and breathe deep.

"You said you were staying for a while. How long is that?"

"Well," he says as he saunters over next to me, hands tucked in his back pockets, and leans down next to my ear. "As long as it takes. Maybe a week. Maybe two. Maybe forever."

Zayden moves in suddenly and nips at my earlobe, drawing a sharp gasp from my throat.

"Come on, you know I'm not the only one crushing here,

right?"

"I'm still mad at you from yesterday," I tell him, but when he chuckles and pulls me into his arms, I'm putty.

"Did you know it's always been my fantasy to do a chick on a swing?"

"Did you know it's a federal offense to have sex on a playground?" I whisper back, but Zayden just laughs and tucks me against the hard, warm length of his body.

When he drops his mouth down to mine, my eyes slide shut of their own accord and I melt completely. My arms go around Zay's neck as his hands take hold of my hips, hot and hard. I can feel his erection through his tight jeans, so I wiggle closer, pushing myself against him until he moans against my lips.

I pull back and Zayden blinks sexy half-lidded eyes down at me.

"You're really staying?" I ask and he grins, reaching down and scooping me up in his arms.

I let out a small scream as I cling to Zay's neck and his grin gets even bigger.

"If you're still cool with letting a dick like me have a go at this whole love thing."

"You keep saying *love*," I tell him as I feel a slight flush color my cheeks. "Add that to your list of things not to say."

Zay raises his pierced brow at me.

"You're uncomfortable with the L-word?" I give him a look, but he just smirks at me. "Well how about you try this on for size, Brooke Overland: I'm in love with you."

"Insta-love," I whisper and Zay shrugs while still holding me. The fact that he can even hold me up like this is sexy as hell. "That's not the same thing."

"Sure it is. Whether it happens in an hour, a day, or a year, love is love. A Smarty-Pants like you should know that."

"I'll pretend that's not the second most romantic thing I've ever heard in my life," I whisper as my body starts to heat up from Zay's proximity. *Oh my God, my hormones are going crazy here.*

He crinkles his face up.

"Second most? What's the first?"

I smile at him.

"When you said you wanted to be my nanny. Now, take me somewhere and make love to me, Nanny Roth."

"Um, backseat of my car?" he asks hopefully, and I laugh.

Because I don't care if we're at the playground or in the car or at my sister's house, if Zayden's there, then that's exactly the place I want to be.

And that's the beginning of my story. His story. Our story.

That's the story of me, a couple of hairless pets, a cluster of kids, and a guy who's a bad boy ... and a nanny.

My nanny.

To Be Continued In...

Sign up for an exclusive first look at the hottest new releases, contests, and exclusives from bestselling author C.M. Stunich and get **three free** eBooks as a thank you!

Sign up here at
www.cmstunich.com.

DISCOVER YOUR NEXT FAVORITE BOOK HERE!

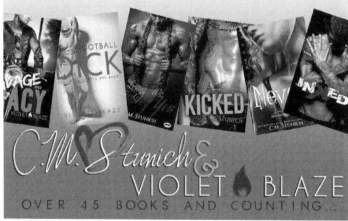

C.M. Stunich & Violet Blaze
OVER 45 BOOKS AND COUNTING...

KEEP UP WITH ALL THE FUN ... AND EARN SOME FREE BOOKS!

JOIN THE C.M. STUNICH NEWSLETTER – Get three free books just for signing up http://eepurl.com/DEsEf

TWEET ME ON TWITTER, BABE – Come sing the social media song with me https://twitter.com/CMStunich

LISTEN TO MY BOOK PLAYLISTS – Share your fave music with me and I'll give you my playlists (I'm super active on here!) https://open.spotify.com/user/CMStunich

FRIEND ME ON FACEBOOK – Okay, I'm actually at the 5,000 friend limit, but if you click the "follow" button on my profile page, you'll see way more of my killer posts https://facebook.com/cmstunich

CHECK OUT THE NEW SITE – TBA (under construction) but it looks kick-a$$ so far, right? You'll be able to order signed books here very soon http://www.cmstunich.com

READ VIOLET BLAZE – Read the books from my hot as hellfire pen name, Violet Blaze http://www.violetblazebooks.com

SUBSCRIBE TO MY RSS FEED – Press that little orange button in the corner and copy that RSS feed so you can get all the latest updates http://www.cmstunich.com/blog

AMAZON, BABY – If you click the follow button here, you'll get an email each time I put out a new book. Pretty sweet, huh?

http://amazon.com/author/cmstunich
&http://amazon.com/author/violetblaze

PINTEREST – Lots of hot half-naked men. Oh, and half-naked men. Plus, tattooed guys holding babies (who are half-naked) http://pinterest.com/cmstunich

INSTAGRAM – Cute cat pictures. And half-naked guys. Yep, that again. http://instagram.com/cmstunich

GRAB A SMOKIN' HOT READ – Check out my books, grab one or two or five. Fall in love over and over again. Satisfaction guaranteed, baby. ;)

AMAZONhttp://amazon.com/author/cmstunich
B&Nhttp://tinyurl.com/cmbarnes
iTUNEShttp://tinyurl.com/cmitunesbooks
GOOGLE PLAYhttp://tinyurl.com/cmgoogle
KOBOhttp://tinyurl.com/cmkobobooks
VIOLET BLAZEhttp://amazon.com/author/violetblaze

P.S. I heart the f*ck out of you! Thanks for reading! I love your faces.

<3 C.M. Stunich aka Violet Blaze

ABOUT THE AUTHOR

C.M. Stunich is a self-admitted bibliophile with a love for exotic teas and a whole host of characters who live full time inside the strange, swirling vortex of her thoughts. Some folks might call this crazy, but Caitlin Morgan doesn't mind – especially considering she has to write biographies in the third person. Oh, and half the host of characters in her head are searing hot bad boys with dirty mouths and skillful hands (among other things). If being crazy means hanging out with them everyday, C.M. has decided to have herself committed.

She hates tapioca pudding, loves to binge on cheesy horror movies, and is a slave to many cats. When she's not vacuuming fur off of her couch, C.M. can be found with her nose buried in a book or her eyes glued to a computer screen. She's the author of over thirty novels – romance, new adult, fantasy, and young adult included. Please, come and join her inside her crazy. There's a heck of a lot to do there.

Oh, and Caitlin loves to chat (incessantly), so feel free to e-mail her, send her a Facebook message, or put up smoke signals. She's already looking forward to it.

Made in the USA
Lexington, KY
17 January 2017